INTO THE BLUE AGAIN

Enjoy your
read!
XO
Marisa Billins

First Published in Great Britain 2022 by Mirador Publishing

Copyright © 2022 by Marisa Billions

All rights reserved. No part of this publication may be reproduced or transmitted, in any form or by any means, without permission of the publishers or author. Excepting brief quotes used in reviews.

First edition: 2022

Any reference to real names and places are purely fictional and are constructs of the author. Any offence the references produce is unintentional and in no way reflects the reality of any locations or people involved.

A copy of this work is available through the British Library.

ISBN: 978-1-914965-94-4

Mirador Publishing
10 Greenbrook Terrace
Taunton
Somerset
UK
TA1 1UT

INTO THE BLUE AGAIN

MARISA BILLIONS

Dedication

As always, for Stephanie. Your love is constantly my biggest inspiration.

This is for all the people who feel they are not worthy of love or healing. You are worth it.

Also, this is for Ryan French. Thank you for asking for this story to be told.

~ *Prologue* ~

R e p e n t

REPENT. IT'S AN ODD WORD. The dictionary has it defined as a verb, to feel or express sincere guilt or remorse for a wrongdoing or sin.

Emma Landry sat in the welcoming office of the prison psychologist and reflected on this word in silence, staring at the man she was mandated to meet with twice a week individually and once a week in a group setting for anger management.

Emma was supposed to be serving five out of ten years for manslaughter. Discovering her wife, Bailey, cheated on her with the man who raped her in college, sent her on an all-night bender of drinking and drowning in vacillating feelings of rage, pain and disbelief. Exhausted, emotionally and physically, Bailey came home from an all day and night fuck fest with the worst person in the world and then defended him to Emma. She snapped (although, if asked, she hated the word 'snapped' and would tell anyone who used *that* word to describe what had happened, though she had no plans, and was outside of herself at the time, she did *not* snap, but there really was no better word for it). After strangling Bailey, burying her body in the woods where her own father buried her mother (after he strangled her) and going on the run, she turned herself in. Her guilt and falling in love with a new woman broke her. She had been compelled to do the right thing.

She was now just over a year and a quarter into the five years she was supposed to be mandated to serve. The psychologist, Dr. Bennett, occupied one of the nicer offices in the prison complex. His walls, instead of the institutional white matte paint which surrounded everything in the prison complex, were a soft beige tone, and he put posters on his wall of art prints and other posters explaining the value of emotional health. His Ikea furniture was cheap, but it felt homey in his office. There were plants on the windowsill, which he took great pride in. They were well cared for and something about those well cared for plants made Emma happy and gave him some form of added credibility in his ability to help her make sense of the fact she was not just a killer like her dad.

His office always smelled like clean linen scented air freshener and eucalyptus, which added, in an odd sense, to the coziness factor in his office. The safe, quiet space was a vacation from the stark white walls, constant noise and buzzing, and scent of sweat and bodies which surrounded her most days.

Dr. Bennett was gentle in nature. His voice was always soft, and so were his dark brown eyes. His facial hair was well groomed, and he dressed in sweater vests and bow ties and loafers every day. Emma had very little hope she would ever get to the point of self-forgiveness, but if anyone could get her even close, it would be Dr. Bennett, she was sure.

"Tell me, Emma, about your relationship after you killed Bailey. You felt the need to get involved with this woman only to run away from her and turn yourself in."

Nearly six feet tall, long and lean, Emma stretched out across the cheap Ikea chair, draping her long arms across the back. Her sharp, self-described 'like sapphire blue' eyes and olive complexion were still striking at forty-six years of age. Even in prison, she took care of herself and did her best to maintain her vegetarian diet and consistent fitness. Her almost black hair still showed very little signs of gray, and though not in her typical well-groomed undercut, still gave most pause to notice her. Her vanity and the perception others had of her would constantly be considered one of her weaknesses. She cared about her image and worked hard to maintain it, until she killed Bailey.

"I didn't think I would find love again. I didn't want to find love. I was not worthy of it. Morgan just kind of happened. I thought, foolishly, that I could bury my past and move forward with her. But she eventually got curious. She looked me up and figured out what was going on. I felt the need to... I don't know... repent. I can't have a future without reconciling my past." It was an answer she knew would please Dr. Bennett, not one she necessarily believed in from her core.

"What does it mean to you, to repent?"

"Good question. I feel guilty. I'm here. I'm doing my time. I'm helping other prisoners who are less fortunate. But am I really repenting? I'm sitting on a massive amount of assets. When I get out, I really won't have to work except for the conditions of my parole. I don't know. I don't know if this is enough."

"What about Morgan? You said she wrote to you."

"Yeah. I think she's still wanting us to explore being together. She says she forgives me for not being up front from the beginning."

"Have you written her back?"

"No."

"Will you?"

"Should I?" She leaned forward, a chunk of her hair falling in her eyes.

"That's not for me to say."

Emma sat back into the chair, pushing her hair back with her hands, and exhaled.

The knock on the door indicating the end of her session seemed to come at the perfect time.

Emma hopped up from her seat and Dr. Bennett looked at her with his fingers steepled under his chin. "Emma, think about what you need to move forward in your life. To feel closure with what you did and your past, and what you want your future to look like. Remember, you won't be here forever, and your early release is pending."

Emma nodded and the door opened. Officer Williams, her favorite correctional officer, came in. "Landry, let's go." His large frame filled the doorway, and his deep, gruff voice reminded her of her basketball coach from college.

She nodded at him and let him guide her down the sterile-looking white corridors and back to the common room of her prison unit.

"You know Jacobs is getting out because of your help, right?" Williams informed her as they walked, rounding a corner. "I escorted her to the courthouse yesterday and sat in on the proceedings. This's the fifth inmate you helped get released."

Emma smiled satisfied. "She got a raw deal. A lot of these women have."

"Why are you so compelled to help them?" They rounded another corner passing the kitchen. The smell of canned green beans, and cooking chicken filtered out around them, as did the sounds of women talking loudly at each other across the kitchen and laughing in camaraderie as they made the best of their work detail together.

"Why not? I could have been them. I grew up poor. I got lucky because I was an athlete. I was talented. People saw more in me. Recognized my potential. I was able to climb up and out of that life. I made a lot of money. I invested well. I was a damn good attorney before I… before what I did. I have what it takes to help these women. Maybe by helping them they can go out and make changes in their own life."

"For what it's worth, Landry, I'm happy to see you doing it for them."

"Thanks, Williams. Honestly, it means a lot to hear it."

Prior to losing her shit (not snap) and killing her wife, Emma had been a successful attorney. A fierce litigator with a promising future. She and her best friend from high school had started their own firm after Emma rose through the ranks as a corporate litigator. Helping the women she felt were handed a raw deal kept her busy, kept her mind sharp, and gave her some semblance of the aspect of herself she was most proud of.

She entered the common room. Four large gray round tables, bolted to the floor, with half circle round benches also bolted to the floor took up the majority of the space. There was a large flat screen television bolted to a wall. A few of the long-term inmates nodded in deference to her. Her work in helping other inmates with appeals kept her in good graces and allowed for her to be left alone; it also protected her from any of the bullshit which tended to be inevitable in a prison situation.

She was a creature who thrived on habit and routine. Unsurprisingly, prison life suited her. She attended her twice weekly meetings with Dr. Bennett, and her assigned job of helping to teach GED classes, and then her self-created position where she volunteered with helping inmates review their cases and finding ways to help them win appeals. Any free time was spent in the gym when she was allowed. There were also regular visits from her best friend since high school, who was also her legal partner – Brandon. Bailey's mother, Mary Anne (who blamed herself for the situation – much to Emma's chagrin), also visited regularly as well as her friend Abby.

Repent. This does not feel like I'm repenting for any of it. This is not punishment for what I've done. This is a hiatus from my life. The only true punishment is being disbarred and I may not ever get readmitted. I didn't lose friends. I still have assets and they are now talking about releasing me early.

Her case was high profile, leading to her getting loads of mail from women (and a handful of men) who pledged their devotion. She threw those letters away without reading them. She only sorted through the stacks to see the return addresses. She found the different locations the mail came from fascinating.

She went back into her cell and opened a book on her shelf, flipping through the pages until she found the letter she kept safe amongst the pages.

Morgan Hale sent the letter almost three months ago. It sat in the pages of the book, where it would be saved from the occasional cell toss or just getting pushed aside in piles of files Emma kept in her cell to review. Emma would pull it out and re-read it every day.

She lay on her rack with the letter in her hands. *Okay, so maybe this rack is punishment. I miss my bed and my pillows.* She folded her pillow over to give it height and opened the letter again. She knew the letter by heart, but read it anyway, following Morgan's flowing and neat script.

Dear Emma,

I have started this letter and thrown it away so many times over the last few months. I didn't even know how to address it. Dear? Dearest? Anyway, here it all is. The words I feel need to be said. What you left behind in your wake.

I don't know what to say. You turned my life upside down. You woke me up and you made me love you. I fear that I will never love another like I loved you. I believe there was a reason us two broken people came together. I understand now what you said about two broken people trying to mash our broken pieces together, ignoring the cracks. I have so much that I never told you. So much I left out when I told you about my own past. But that is for another time. Another letter, maybe? I want to focus on you right now.

You said in your sentencing (I could not help but to watch every single bit of coverage), that the love you had with Bailey was electrifying and like a drug. I laughed out loud because that was how I described what loving you was like when they interviewed me. They didn't play that clip on the news. It must have been left on the cutting room floor.

I believe you. I believe, also, that you loved me. Maybe not in the way you loved Bailey. But no two loves are the same. But knowing you as I knew you, watching you go through what you went through, I know you have remorse, and you are a good and beautiful person. I know that you speak from the heart, and you feel things so very deeply. When you told me you loved me, you meant it.

I watched the documentaries about your case, and I read the articles. Everyone tries to figure you out. But I knew you. Even though you never talked about your past, so much of you makes so much sense now.

I have missed you so much in the days since you have been gone. I feel like I'm mourning a death again. I was harsh and judgmental when I sent you away. That was wrong. I should have listened to you and listened to my heart. Hurt people hurt people. You didn't mean to, plan to, or want to kill Bailey. It's evident. You were hurt. After a lifetime of hurt, the betrayal of the person who pledged to love you and protect you sent you outside of yourself.

I'm sorry for not listening to you. I'm sorry for not asking questions to clarify or seek to understand. I'm sorry for pushing you to turn yourself in. I understand why you did. I understand your need for penance.

You deserve love. When you get out, I will be here waiting for you, because I can never stop loving you.

Love Always,

Morgan.

PS. I know you are thinking you don't deserve my love. I've been there and felt I didn't deserve forgiveness or grace either. This quote has gotten me through the worst of times: 'Each of us is more than the worst thing we've ever done,' Bryan Stevenson.

Emma stared at the last line again. She committed it to memory. 'Each of us is more than the worst thing we've ever done.' *What on earth did you do that you chose this line to cling to?*

~ *I* ~

Love Can Mean A Lot of Things

The Present

Emma

EMMA SAT AT HER SMALL desk area in her cell with Morgan's letter open in front of her, a blank sheet of paper next to it and a pen in her hand. A copy of Bryan Stevenson's memoir *Just Mercy,* from where the infamous quote was taken, sat next to it. Emma read it through in one sleepless night. She had asked Brandon to send it to her after she read the letter the first time.

Repent. Forgiveness. Guilt. Self-love. Be open to love. The therapy, both group and individual – these tended to be the goals. She had been hearing those words like a mantra from day one of her incarceration. *Easier said than done. I cannot foresee a time where I won't feel shame for what I have done.*

She had Morgan's letter in possession for over three months. She read the letter daily. Sometimes multiple times a day. Each day, she sat at her desk with a blank sheet of paper and a pen and tried to think of the words she could say in response to Morgan. *There's nothing I can say. There's literally nothing left to say, and yet, so much I want to say. Need to say.*

Morgan was relegated to off limits in her mind for so long. She closed her eyes and could see Morgan's soft, full lips smiling, the wind blowing her hair into her face. She was a natural beauty, not one who used or needed to use a lot of makeup. Her hair, when they met, sandy blonde streaked with pink, but she dyed it the day they last saw each other, replacing the pink with sapphire blue, which sent her into a tailspin, taking it as a sign telling her she had to leave.

At one point, in the early days of their relationship, Emma wished she could have erased all her past and replace it only with Morgan. As far as she was concerned, Morgan was the definition of grace, warmth, and softness. *At the very least, you owe her a response to her letter.*

She exhaled and began to write.

Dear Morgan,

I am so sorry it has taken me so long to respond to your letter. Let me be frank, after I left the way I did, I felt unworthy to talk to you.

I've been spending a lot of time reflecting on what it is I deserve and whether or not I'm really being punished enough for what I did. Not just to Bailey, but to you. I owe you an apology. I am sorry for disrupting your life. I'm so sorry for hiding who I was and giving you a false sense of security in your ability to be with me and love me. But believe me when I say I was honest in my love for you. A fact which cannot be denied.

I re-read your letter over and over again and I stick on the last line. The quote from Bryan Stevenson. It makes me wonder if you are willing to tell me what it is you have done that you feel is so awful. We both left so much in the dark from one another. But you were such a ray of light in my life. You were this goodness. This peace. What weighs so heavy on your soul that you feel was unforgivable? Thanks to all the true crime channels and documentaries, you know my whole life story from beginning to where we left off. It is my turn to learn about you. Who are you, really?

I look forward to hearing from you again. I promise I won't wait months to write back.

Love,

Emma.

EMMA FOLDED IT AND STUCK it in an envelope and addressed it. *I have no idea what I hope to accomplish with this letter. Opening lines of communication with Morgan is probably not the best of ideas. But she started it.* Emma took a deep breath and exhaled loudly.

The sealed envelope sat on her desk in front of her. *Once it's in the mail, there's no getting it back. Once this line of communication is open, I am going to be forced to deal with the feelings that come with it.*

Hope. Love. Forgiveness. Guilt. She penned that she looked forward to hearing from Morgan again, and in a sense, she was, but she also feared the emotional floodgate this would open.

Emma picked up the envelope and walked it to the box where outgoing mail was collected and sent out. She paused and dropped it in the box before heading to her work detail in the classroom. *There's no going back, now. It's gone. Out of my hands.*

Morgan

SHE FELT MOSTLY UNSURE SINCE sending her first letter whether or not Emma would ever respond. She sent the letter to make peace with her own feelings as much as to let Emma know how she felt.

She certainly never intended to fall in love. She didn't think love or relationships were really her thing.

Morgan had been working at the RV campground which her father owned when Emma appeared out of the blue one day. She was carrying a ton of cash and wanted everything off the books. Morgan knew there must be some dark reason behind all of it. But something about this woman compelled her to let her stay. Whatever the particular compulsion was, also led her to strike up a friendship with Emma, the likes of which eventually became a full-blown love affair. And she fell hard for Emma. Based on all the documentaries about Emma's case, this was something most anyone who spent more than five minutes in Emma's presence was prone to do. Emma was irresistible.

But the reality of the situation was neither of them had been forthright in disclosing their pasts. And both of them held guilt and shame so deep that there was no realistic way a true foundation could be built for a lasting relationship. Not without addressing the past and facing the overwhelming trauma due to their histories.

She sat in a leather recliner facing the couch. She was sitting in this very chair the last night she saw Emma. She confronted her. After months of spending every night with Emma, loving her, living on every breath and moment shared with her, she finally caved in to the curiosity of the woman who captivated her heart.

Her search was set in motion when the night before, Emma cried out a name in her sleep. "Bailey." The tone in which the name was cried out, was a clue as to the relationship this Bailey experienced with Emma. It was a sorrowful sound. Pleading.

All that Morgan knew of Emma was that her wife cheated on her with a man who raped her when she was younger. She did not know where Emma was from. She knew Emma used to be an attorney, but she didn't even know where Emma lived prior to showing up in the campground or the name of her wife. She only knew she was this sexy, smooth being who wormed her way into Morgan's heart. She was handy, and she could cook, and she was the best lover to have laid in her bed. Methodical, skillful, attentive, responsive, patient, tender, and generous to be precise, and God how she missed those nights.

Both of them were able to sense they shared a common history one which was best left untouched. It was assumed by both of them that if they ignored their respective histories, they could push forward and make a future together. But curiosity had taken hold when she heard Bailey's name tumble out of Emma's lips in her sleep.

Emma had been strange the entire day after. Her eyes, normally so vibrant and full of life, were dim and lifeless. When she came over, she barely tumbled across the doorway and collapsed on the couch. She had gone dark in a way Morgan knew intimately. She was no stranger to such emotions herself.

Morgan sat in her recliner that night with her laptop aglow, and she searched for Emma and Bailey Landry. She found Bailey's (Bailey Frankson-Landry, PhD) social media pages. She saw pictures of the life Emma lived before showing up at her father's campground in South Lake Tahoe, with her

RV and her dog. She saw the affluence, the privilege, and the adoration Emma lived in. She saw the media coverage of Emma at trial through the years. Down, down, down the internet rabbit hole she went. Articles about her as a college athlete. She was dynamic, indeed.

Then she saw the recent articles. Both of them were considered missing. Emma was there on her couch. But where was Bailey? What happened to her? The pretty woman with the strawberry blonde hair and bright smile with the dimple in her cheek. Where was she? The woman who looked adoringly at Emma in the pictures. The classy, polished, elegant woman who cleaved to Emma's hand or arm in most pictures where they were together. Did she really cheat on Emma?

Emma finally awoke and when Morgan confronted her, she spilled the whole truth. She killed Bailey. Strangled her. Choked the life out of her. Buried her in the woods.

Morgan chilled by Emma's confession in the heat of the moment, sent Emma away. She tried to process this information that conflicted so greatly with who and what she had come to love.

After sending Emma away, Morgan went on a twelve-month quest to change her life. She cut her hair. She bought a small house near downtown with a view of the lake. She went to therapy. But she still missed Emma.

Now, Morgan sat in the chair, a glass of wine in her hand, a letter unopened on her lap. The ink, dark blue. The same color as Emma's eyes. Sapphire blue. Of course. And she missed those eyes, sharp and observant when dealing with the world around her, and how they would shift to soft and deep when she looked at her. The letters were neatly written across the envelope. What is Emma going to tell her? What can she possibly say? Will she tell her to fuck off and leave her alone? As she pondered the possibility of being met with total rejection, she pondered whether or not there may yet be a future with this woman.

Whatever may come, Morgan knew the answers would not come to her without opening the envelope. She held her breath and put the wine glass down on a small cherry wood end table and opened the envelope.

She stared at Emma's concise blue penmanship. She absorbed the words. She could not be mad at Emma for withholding her past. She had done the very same. Now it was time to come clean. She knew if she ever wanted a life with Emma, now that Emma's secrets had all been laid bare for the world to know (not by her choice, albeit), it was time for her own to come out.

She rose and poured another glass of wine and brought out her stationery, and a leather-bound journal she kept in a drawer in her bedside table.

She set the journal and the stationery on the table and sat down looking at it. She picked up the journal and thumbed through it looking at the pages she had filled as homework for the therapist she went to after Emma left. The therapist instructed her to write out her story so she herself could better make sense of her decisions and her life. She had filled the entire leather book in a matter of a week. It was not easy for her, and she found herself reopening wounds she hoped she could ignore.

Picking up her pen, she began to write.

Emma,

In the process of getting to know one another, we should have been honest with each other. We should have shared our histories. Would it have changed how we felt? I don't know. But we each owe it to each other to learn who we fell in love with.

I had the advantage of being able to watch all the documentaries about what happened to you and Bailey. I got to see all of it. I got to watch all the different analyses. And one day, maybe I can ask you questions about it, and you can tell me your story in your own words. I must say, it was so odd to see a television host explain the story of the doe to me. It was one of the few stories you told me. Explaining to me why you are a vegetarian after your dad took you hunting at the age of 8. I liked the way you told it better.

I'm sending you a journal I wrote as a therapy project. I want you to know me. I want you to know what I have done from my perspective. That way we are on equal footing with one another.

You asked what I did that caused me to feel like I needed forgiveness. This is all of it. This is my story in my words. Read it. Ask me questions. Or don't.

Maybe once you see all of me, you will decide you don't want me in your life. Maybe after all of this, we won't necessarily be in love, but we will understand each other. I don't really know how else to say it. Maybe I said too much. Maybe I've promised too much. I'm not sure what the future holds for "us", other than total truth and honesty from this point on. Friends or lovers. We owe it to each other.

Love,

Morgan.

THE NEXT MORNING, ON HER way to work, she stopped at the post office and put the envelope in the mail. No turning back now, Emma would have her whole history to consume and judge and whatever.

Emma

THE ENVELOPE FROM MORGAN SAT in her cell for two days before she summoned the gall to open it. She just kept it on her table in her cell. After opening it, the journal sat unopened for several more days.

Emma sat in her cell, holding the dark purple embossed leather journal. She thumbed through looking at the filled pages in Morgan's handwriting. Every page had been filled out. Different colors of ink had been used, and the penmanship varied from neat and flourished, to small and cramped, to frenetic scratching on different pages. Tears stained some of the pages. Some pages were scratched out and re-written later.

She read the letter multiple times and was scared to open the journal.

She was afraid that knowing the whole story behind the beautiful soul she had fallen in love with, would change everything. The first letter held the promise of love, but this second letter seemed to reflect a tone of uncertainty as to what the future would be. Perhaps, now Morgan bore regrets for reopening a certain line of communication between them.

She knew that no matter what they would have it would be love, whether it be platonic or romantic. She could not deny Morgan was someone she wanted in her life in some capacity.

After an exhale, she grabbed the journal and laid back on her rack with her pillow folded under head and she opened it and began to read.

Excerpt from Morgan's Memoir

IF IT'S GOING TO MAKE any sense, I need to start from the very beginning. I've been resisting this for a long time. It's embarrassing and it's painful and it's all true. I would rather it all had just been a bad dream, as it feels like it really was just a nightmare I was stuck inside of for a period of years.

So here it goes.

This all really starts with Jonathan, but I need to give a prelude to Jonathan. You have to understand Jonathan is a demarcation in my life. There was my life before him. And the utter mess left in his wake.

So, a quick introduction to who I was before Jonathan. My life was easy. Fun. Light hearted. There was a me who knew no pain or distress. As Jonathan would later describe me, I was a butterfly in the wind (I resented this description, because sometimes, the truth hurts). Careless and free.

Being an only child, and a girl at that, I was spoiled rotten. I was a daddy's girl on top of all of it. There was nothing my father would not give me or do for me. My parents were well to do. My father was in technology before the tech boom, and my mother was an interior designer with her own office in the affluent coastal town of La Jolla.

I grew up within walking distance of the Pacific Ocean, and a vacation home in Lake Tahoe. I was privileged and entitled, and I knew it, and I exploited it.

When I got into trouble at school for ditching or talking back to my teachers, I would run to my dad, and he would negotiate with the administration to get me out of it. But overall, I was a good student. I was in yearbook, drama, played volleyball, and was well liked by almost everyone. I was in the top twenty of my graduating class.

My mom was not exactly happy with how my dad would coddle me. I literally lived a life free of consequences. I can't recall a single time where I had to face accountability for my actions. Even when I was a total bitch to my friends, they easily forgave me.

I dated a bit in high school, but nothing ever got serious. I was too consumed with having fun, and when any relationship started to feel like work, I cut it off and moved on. Again, just further pushing aside any sort of consequence or liability.

My ease in life extended through college. I dated a lot. I still was not really into long-term relationships. I dated girls, boys, anyone who caught my interest. It didn't matter as long as you entertained me. But, as in high school, the moment anything turned into work, I severed ties. I just wanted to have fun. I just wanted to enjoy my life.

I loved my classes and my father paid for me to live in a nice apartment off campus. I excelled in college and was active in the campus community and around it. I liked to stay busy but keep it light. I got my Bachelor's degree and then went on to get my Master's in Education and a teaching credential to teach English. Partly because the summers off and long winter breaks fit in with traveling, which I loved. I would take trips with my friends, paramours, or on my own. It didn't matter, I just liked adventure and new experiences.

I managed to make it through all of this without ever getting serious with any one person.

I loved my life as a teacher. I thrived on my days in the classroom. My kids gave me life. I would stand in front of them and explain concepts to them and watch the lightbulbs go on over their heads as they understood and learned and expanded their minds. I advised the school newspaper and yearbook and taught eleventh and twelfth graders. I was satisfied with the way my life was going. I had zero complaints. I mean there were days where I felt no motivation, or I felt sad for whatever reason, but those days of dissatisfaction were few and far between.

Four years after I started my teaching career, with no signs of settling down and getting married, and no serious relationship to speak of, my father suggested I buy a home. I think his hope, and my mother's, was that if I began to nest, maybe I would want to get married and give them grandbabies. Dad told me if I found a place, he would give me the down payment. He said he would rather see me use my inheritance while he was alive and could see me enjoy it.

I found the perfect condo. It was near the bay in downtown San Diego, near the airport. It was spacious and had decent parking. The architecture was quintessential southern California, Spanish mission style. My mother decorated it for me to my specific style and taste. Cherry wood furniture, cozy and not overly girly.

Two years after I moved into my condo, I showed no signs of settling in. Mom and Dad gave up on me getting married and having babies and decided to buy the campground in Lake Tahoe and retire from corporate life. Mom sold her business to follow him. They came down to visit occasionally though, and once in a while I would go up and visit them, too. Every single visit I got the guilt trip, "Morgan when are you going to settle down?" I always answered, "When someone makes the work involved in a relationship worth my time."

I considered looking for someone to settle down with, but my life was easy and carefree. My life revolved around great friends, a great career, and a great condo. I mean, there were bad times, but they were so brief, and if anything I couldn't handle came up, my dad came in and fixed it for me. I never had to really worry or work hard on anything. I had an idyllic life and it's not an exaggeration and it's not just glossing over my life. It really is the god's honest truth of my existence.

I had just celebrated my 32nd birthday, and I was satisfied with my life. I was not lonely, and I was not longing for anything more than I had. I was in my classroom one day when one of my favorite students, Jordan, raised her hand and asked me if I was single.

The question took me off my guard. "Why?" The rest of the class got really quiet, really quickly.

"My Uncle Jonathan just relocated here from New York. He's living with my mom and me. And he's single. And he's a writer. Like a legit writer. He's won awards for journalism. He writes for a big magazine. You're an English teacher. He's good looking and you're pretty. It would be a good match. And he's home all the time. He needs to get out."

I laughed it off.

But Jordan persisted.

She brought up her uncle at least once a day. She offered to have him come in and talk to my school newspaper crew about journalism. I declined. She even invited me to go to her house and have dinner with them. I, of course, declined.

One day, it was a Wednesday to be specific, between classes, I was checking my emails and there was an email from this guy, Jonathan Staley. Jordan had given him my email and told him I was interested, and he asked me to meet him for lunch on Saturday. No pressure. He would be at the barbecue joint in Coronado, and he left his cell phone number.

Jordan came in with the biggest shit eating grin. "I gave my uncle your email address. I told him that you couldn't give me your number because of teacher student stuff, but that you said I could have him email you."

"Ohhhh, he emailed me."

"You're gonna make an amazing auntie," she giggled.

I waited until after school to text Jonathan. I asked him how I would know who he was if I was so inclined to meet him on Saturday. It never occurred to me, however, if Jordan was accurately telling me about him, I could have just *Googled* him.

"So inclined to meet me? You asked Jordan to give me your email address."

"I actually didn't. But what's done is done, right? Let's do this."

He sent a selfie, and it was captioned, 'your turn'. I scrutinized his picture. He was attractive enough. Brown hair, high cheekbones, dark brown eyes, and wire framed glasses. His lips were curled in a slight smile.

I pulled my hair from my ponytail and fluffed it up and took a selfie in response.

He didn't respond.

I waited twenty minutes for a response before getting in my car and driving home. I heated a frozen dinner and checked my phone again. Still no response.

What an asshole, right? Who does that?

Around 9:00 PM, I got a text back from him. "I'm so sorry. I got busy with work, and I meant to respond. All I can say is please don't be mad. I look forward even more to seeing you Saturday?"

I don't play games. Well, I didn't play games. Until then. Games went against my ethos of if it's work, it's not worth it regarding relationships.

I didn't respond until the next morning. I simply said,

7:45 AM

See you at noon at Little Piggy's.

Read 7:45 AM

7:46 AM

You're mad, aren't you?

7:48 AM

No.

Read 7:49 AM

7:49 AM

Yes you are.

7:50 AM

Why would I be mad?

Read 7:51 AM

7:53 AM

Because you put yourself out there, sent a
picture and then I didn't respond until late. That
was rude and I apologized. But I can tell you're mad.

7:55 AM

I'm not mad. We're still
meeting on Saturday. I will be mad if
you continue to insist that I am when I am in
fact, not.

Read 7:57

7:58 AM

Okay. I just want to make sure. I really am sorry.
Your picture is, as Jordan insisted you are, quite
beautiful.

> 8:01 AM
>
> What were you so busy with that you
> kept me questioning whether or not I was a
> troll?
>
> Read 8:02 AM

8:03 AM

I'm a writer. I work for *Hauteur,* and I freelance for
a few publications. I got a last-minute request for
a quick piece. I really am so sorry.

> 8:05 AM
>
> Apology accepted. I look forward to
> Saturday.
>
> Read 8:06 AM

I couldn't help but smile and it was a smile that lasted the rest of the day.

I SHOWED UP AT LITTLE Piggy's on time Saturday. I stood inside scanning the tables looking for him and he was nowhere to be seen. I was fairly sure he was going to stand me up when I felt a soft hand on my shoulder. "I'm so sorry, I couldn't find parking. I'm not off to a good start am I?" He smiled a sheepish grin.

I couldn't be mad. He seemed so genuine and so sweet. I was disarmed by him, honestly.

We sat at a picnic table in the restaurant and throughout our lunch he kept me laughing. Like really laughing. I don't remember having so much fun with anyone in so long. He was a political journalist and he kept me entertained with his tales of the different politicians and antics and behind-the-scenes gossip. And he was so intelligent. I was entirely captivated.

After lunch we walked around and found a spot with a view of downtown San Diego and just talked more. He asked me questions and I made him laugh with my stories about teaching and the unpredictable moments in the classroom and comparing our antics in college.

We wandered into a bar and got a drink, continuing to talk and laugh, and before we knew it, it was dark. I didn't want the day to end. I wanted more of him. I wanted him to come home with me. But I couldn't bring myself to ask him outright. He was different. Other men, I would have been frank, and thrown it right out there.

He walked me to my car, said good night, and did not even kiss me. He left me wondering. Were we just going to be friends? Was he just old fashioned? What was the deal? I thought there was chemistry. Maybe it was one sided.

On Monday, Jordan came into class anxious to tell me how much her uncle raved about what a great time he had. I just smiled. I was not going to put her in the middle of it. But what I wanted to scream was, "If he had so much fun, why hasn't he called or texted?" I just told her I enjoyed meeting him as well and thanked her for the connection.

I thought about texting him. I thought about calling him. I couldn't bring myself to do it. Here I was playing games. As I mentioned, I am not a game player, but for some reason, all of a sudden I was. Game playing was so much work, and I hated myself for putting in the effort instead of just texting or calling and being a complete adult about it and telling him thanks but no thanks. Or maybe this was the easiest let down ever. We would just ghost each other and nothing more would ever come of it. But I did not want him to ghost me. I wanted to see him again.

He kept me waiting until Thursday. I was sitting at home grading essays with CNN on in the background. It was close to seven and my phone rang.

I looked at the caller ID and saw it was Jonathan. I was tempted to let it go to voicemail, but I couldn't.

"Hello?"

"Hey. I'm sorry. I wanted to call you sooner, but I didn't want to seem clingy. I wanted to text, but that seemed too informal. To be honest, I don't know what I'm doing." He laughed a nervous laugh the likes of which completely melted me.

"Well… I have to say that makes two of us." I couldn't help but smile.

"I had a great time with you Saturday. I want to see you again."

"Again, that makes two of us." I was smiling despite trying to play it cool.

"Do you hike?"

"As a matter of fact, I do."

"How about I pick you up early Saturday morning? We can grab breakfast and go hike up to Potato Chip Rock?"

After yet another great day together, there was yet another goodbye without so much as a kiss. I normally, in the past, would have been the type to go for it if I wanted it, but something about him held me back, waiting for him to make all the moves. He was different. I found myself acting differently in response.

The men I dated in the past were not really intellectual, as a matter of fact, they were rather dumb. The kind of pretty boy jocks you keep around for a good time, not for their ability to talk to you on any level. I used to seek girls for depth. Men for fun. Jonathan was this strange hybrid of intellectualism, fun, and he was attractive in a refined sense. He was fit, but not a jock. Intellectual, but not boring. I was intrigued by him, and I didn't want to scare him off.

I learned a lot about him on the hike though. I learned that on top of writing for a major magazine and freelancing for other publications he was working on an anthology of short stories he planned to publish. He earned a double Master's degree in Journalism and Creative Writing from Northwestern. He traveled on assignments all over the world. But it was not all about him. He asked me questions about myself. The deep questions. Questions about my faith and what makes me happy. He made me laugh with more of his stories.

When he dropped me off, I invited him in for a drink or to order a pizza. He declined. "I promise though, I will not make you wait five days again. I will call you tomorrow."

I smiled inside.

He likes me. I know he does. But why take it so slow?

He didn't call me Sunday. Instead, he sent a bouquet of flowers. I had told him I loved the color pink and that peonies make me happy, and the bouquet was made up of large pink blooms. The card read, 'Thank you for making me happy yesterday. I hope this brightens your day.'

I called him. Fuck playing games.

"I got your flowers, thank you."

"Are you smiling?"

"I am."

"Good. I would love to talk more, but I'm on a deadline. Can I call you tomorrow night?"

"Yes. Thank you again."

I was sad he was not able to talk, but I understood. Deadlines are real, and he had this amazing career. Of which, I became somewhat of a fangirl of his work. After our hike, I *Googled* him and the publication he worked for. The stories and interviews revolved around huge names – *Hauteur* launched the careers of several well-known writers of our time. He was the next big thing. I ordered back issues of the magazines he wrote pieces for. I saved the online articles on my laptop. I read his pieces voraciously, enthralled in his words and how he laid out each detail. He was a genius. A second coming of Hunter S. Thompson, only without the drugs. Witty. Elaborate. Snarky at times. He possessed a distinct style which appealed to the masses.

We went on another three dates without so much as a kiss. Finally, on our fifth date, as we sat in his car in front of my condo, I turned to him and asked, "Where is this going? Are we just friends? Is there more?"

He looked at me for a long moment. I believe it would be called a pregnant pause. The light in his eyes went dark and he took off his glasses, looking down.

"Jonathan, what are we doing? I need to know. I like you. I really like you. I *want* you. But I don't know what you want or where we are heading. Am I in the friendzone or do you see more here?"

"Morgan, can I come inside, and we can talk?"

"Please. Yes. By all means, come inside for once." Bitterness I didn't intend dripped out in my words.

As he walked through the front door, he looked around at my cozy living room, passed the stairs leading to the bedroom (where I wished we were heading) and I led him to my dining room, where he sat at my cherry wood table. I could see him assess his surroundings, taking in the color of the wood and the dark blue paint on the wall, which gave the small space a more formal appeal. He laid his palms flat on the wood and took a deep breath.

"Do you want something to drink before you begin?" I asked him. I wasn't sure if I wanted to hear what he had to say with all of this build up. What could it possibly be? Is he married already? Is he a convicted sex offender? This build up must be leading up to something so damn awful. It was unbearable.

He nodded. I pulled a Stone Pale Ale out and popped the top off and grabbed one for myself and sat across from him at the round table.

He took a deep sip and reached for my hand. His hand was warm, and his fingers were gentle. There was an overwhelming chemistry – electricity ran like a current from his fingertips through my body. I couldn't help but imagine what his hands would feel like on my body. I wanted them on my body. I craved them. I hated how I craved them. Right now, I wanted to focus on what he had to say, not my desire for him.

"So tell me."

"Morgan, you are beautiful. You are bright. You are funny. You are, as my niece described. You are my type. I wasn't expecting it. I wasn't really looking. I didn't think Jordan could really peg it the way she did in finding me, literally, the perfect woman-"

"You have to know I'm totally into you, so what is the problem? If we are both into each other, why are we skirting around this?"

He sighed and looked down before bringing his eyes back to mine. "I am working remotely, as you know. My office is out of New York. But they are allowing me to work from here because I am healing. I have struggled my whole life. I have issues... I get dark... I have to take meds to control it. I know it's so very cliche being a writer and having mental health struggles, but it is what I've dealt with since I was teenager. I tried to kill myself when I was sixteen. My parents put me in a hospital. I have been on and off medications since then. I've been single now for two years because I've been trying to figure out how to be happy on my own. My last girlfriend couldn't handle it. I sucked the life out of her with my illness. I don't want to do that to anyone else. Now I'm here trying to figure out how to make myself fit into this world. I recently found myself in a dark place, mentally. I was unable to cope.

"I asked, finally, if I could come back home to California and work remotely. They agreed. Tiffany, my sister – Jordan's mother, said I could stay with them until I found a place of my own. Jordan, bless her heart, insisted I meet you. She thought – as teenage girls often do, that falling in love would fix everything for me.

"Which brings me to right here right now." He laced his fingers through mine and looked at me. "I find you, as I mentioned, to be the perfect woman. But I can't ask you to take me on as I am. I am broken inside. I'm not a fixer upper that you can just glue back together. I'm a mess. I can't ask that of you to deal with my lows. It's not fair to you at all."

"Don't you think that should be my decision, whether or not I want to deal with your issues? One I should make for myself? You don't find it unfair that you are making this decision for me?"

He took a sip of his beer followed by another inhale. "You don't know what you would be taking on."

He learned a lot about me in the last five dates and countless phone calls. I was not a person who dealt with any hardship in life. He knew I lived an easy, and for the most part, drama free life. What he was saying was not unfair or uncalled for.

"You don't think I can handle it?"

"I don't want to ask that of you. I will complicate your very uncomplicated life."

"How about we compromise? We take it one day at a time. Slowly. And if I can't handle it, I get to decide. I'm thirty-two years old. I think I can make up my own mind about what I am willing to do and the lengths I'm willing to go for someone."

He gave a wry smile. "I give you six months."

I untangled our fingers and made my way around the table and sat myself in his lap. I touched his face, and even his stubble was softer than other men. I brought his lips to mine and felt this incredible warmth. A warmth I was not expecting. It washed over me, and his kiss was soft and deep as his arms wrapped around me. I had never felt this way with any man. Usually, those kinds of feelings of being swept up and out of myself was something I felt with women. I was blown away by his kiss, by his warmth.

"Do you want to go upstairs?"

His lips found mine again. "Not tonight."

I nuzzled into his neck and found his earlobe. "Are you sure?" I could feel his heartbeat against my chest as his arms held me tight against him.

"I do *want* to. It is taking everything in me to say no to you. But after all we just talked about, let's just take this slow." He turned his head, so we were nose to nose.

I couldn't help but be slightly disappointed, but I also needed to respect what he was asking of me.

Reflecting back on it all, we got to know each other on a level of deeper affinity than I had ever gone with another human. He knew so much more about me than even many of my so-called friends knew.

I kissed him again softly. Not in an effort to persuade him, but to let him know I appreciated him.

I moved off his lap and stood against the wall facing him. "Thank you for telling me what you did."

"Thank you for not running away scared." He stood and came close to me and drew me back to him.

I felt like if he were to back away I would not be able to breathe. I was magnetized to him.

He kissed me once more. "I'm going to leave on this note. I look forward to seeing where we go from here." He was looking in my eyes, and I could see his wheels turning fast in his mind. After a pause he asked, "What are you doing tomorrow?" He still held me close, as if he didn't want to let me go either.

"Nothing. Grade some papers, plan for the week."

"My sister and mother and I are having brunch tomorrow for my mother's birthday. Jordan will be there, too, which might be weird for you. But I would like for you to come."

"You're asking me to meet your mom?"

"You're insisting on not running away, so it seems the natural progression." He was smiling impishly.

"I don't typically do the meeting of the family thing."

"So you've implied."

"For you, I'll do it."

And the next morning, there we were in his sister Tiffany's SUV driving up to Temecula Wine Country for brunch. Jonathan and I sat in the back, my hand in his, Jordan in the third row cracking jokes.

I loved Jonathan's mother Josephine – "Jo, for short, dear" she instructed me. She was delightful and I could see, in spending the time with her, Tiffany, and even Jordan where Jonathan got his amazing ability to captivate and tell stories. His sensitivity. Everything I found wonderful about him, came from these remarkable women in his world. And they loved him fiercely.

Toward the end of brunch in the winery, Jo asked me to go for a walk with her.

With her arm linked through mine, we wound our way through the vineyard amongst the rows of grapes. "Jonathan told me he told you about his struggles."

"He did. I know you are protective of him. But my intentions are good."

"Jonathan struggles more than he lets on. And he does so good with life and managing when he takes his medications, but he has tendencies to quit the medications. That's when life gets ugly. He gets so dark. He becomes a different person. I just want you to know that if he goes back into one of his dark phases and you are there – please call me. Let me be there to help. He came home from the East Coast because he couldn't fight alone any longer.

I'm here for him, and if you're planning to be here for the long haul, I know how to help when he goes dark. As does his sister."

"I promise you. If it gets to that, I'll make sure you are there for him."

With a haul of wine bottles and full bellies and happy hearts, we made our way back to San Diego. Tiffany dropped me off, and Jonathan walked me to my door, leaving me with a gentle kiss at the door and a promise to call me later that night.

After getting home and a few hours of scrolling social media in an effort to put off my grading and planning, I was sitting on the floor of my living room with stacks of essays around me, no makeup, sweats, and a ponytail, a streaming ambient music channel filtering through my speakers. There was a knock on my door. I hadn't been expecting anyone, so I was caught off guard as I got up to see who it was.

I looked out the peephole and saw Jonathan standing there.

"You can't get enough of me, can you?" I grinned as I opened the door.

"I just wanted to tell you how much Tiffany and my mother adored you."

"You could have called. Not that I'm not happy to see you." I moved aside so he could come in.

"I could have." He kept walking through the small entryway, past the living room, and to the stairs. He began to ascend the stairs as if he had made the trek a million times before.

I just followed. My heart was pounding hard.

"They said they could see why I was so captivated with you and continuously wax poetic about you."

"Wax poetic?"

"Talk about how beautiful you are, nonstop. Your smile. Your brilliance. Your wit. Your sense of grace and style. Your beautiful heart." He found his way to my bedroom and was standing in the doorway. He reached out and grabbed my hand and drew me into him.

He was slow and deliberate in the way he gathered me into him. I wanted to absorb every second of this. He was soft and tender and when I tried to pull him in with my eagerness he held me back.

Every time I tried to speed him up or push into him harder, he slowed me down. I was not used to this. Everything about how he interacted with me from our talks to our texts, and now to the way he made love to me was different. He was slow and gentle in how he touched me, making me want more of him, bringing me to an edge and keeping me there. There was no frantic rush for him. He was in charge of my body and my every reaction, and I willingly submitted to him. I was compelled to obey and let him lead.

This man blew my mind. Not just in his ability as a lover, but in all aspects of him. I didn't know I could feel this way for another human. He became like a drug for me. I longed for him and missed him when he was not with me.

The first six months we were together taught me so much about myself and life, and love.

He taught me independence from my father. When I had an issue, and I would go to call Dad, he would sit me down and ask me questions, leading me to find solutions on my own.

My parents adored him when I brought him up to Tahoe to meet them.

My dad shook Jonathan's hand firmly. "So, you are the reason Morgan hasn't called me to fix her life? As a matter of fact, she hardly ever even calls us now! Not even to say hello," he teased.

Jonathan laughed. "She has the capabilities on her own. She just needs a little push here or there."

"Well, we've never seen her this happy or independent," my mother gushed.

He was my anchor, my guide, my lover, my life. He taught me pain is part of life, when I witnessed his first down cycle. Days of him melting in self-doubt and loathing. Locking himself in a darkened bedroom at Tiffany's, Jo, Tiffany and I taking turns caring for him.

I let myself into the room and closed the door behind me. Feeling my way through the darkness, I laid myself down next to him. His head was warm, his face wet with tears against my chest. I was scared. Scared he would stay stuck in this darkness, and I would lose him. But we coaxed him out of it and back onto his medication, back into the light and the living.

I celebrated his successes as he was awarded time and again and lauded for his accomplishments. We lived this amazing rollercoaster life together. We had disagreements, as all couples do, but they were brief, and he taught me to apologize when I was wrong. He taught me to not quit on love and walk away. He taught me with work, we could build something together, and it was all worth it. He was worth it.

We were literally building this life together and it was beautiful, and it was ugly. It was fun, but it was hard. Despite his lows, the likes of which came from nowhere and lasted for days, being near him was what I craved. The highs were what I lived for.

He moved in with me after six months. Tiffany joked about being happy to get him out of her house. Jordan graduated and was getting ready to go to Notre Dame, in hopes of going to Northwestern after. Her father lived in the Midwest, and she would be closer to him. Jonathan and I took a road trip to drop her off on campus since Tiffany was unable to due to her work schedule.

Jonathan was good for me. But like all good things in my life, I threw it all away.

~ *II* ~

I Alone

The Present

Emma

BRANDON WAS SITTING ACROSS THE table from Emma. Despite the fact their entire friendship began because Brandon had a crush on her during their sophomore year of high school, asked her to Homecoming and then awkwardly tried to kiss her, he was her absolute best friend and closest ally in life. He was the first person she came out to, and she was his best (wo)man at his wedding, and then business partners in a thriving law firm. He represented her and stood by her with relentless loyalty. Aside from Bailey, he was the one person on Earth who knew her better than she knew herself. And unlike Bailey, he was unceasingly steadfast to her.

"How do you feel about being let out early? We are looking at sooner rather than later now."

Emma shrugged. "I don't know. I don't know that I've actually paid my debt for what I did. Look around, Brandon. There's a ton of women in here for the same thing as I am, many of them on lesser charges serving longer sentences. Why do you think I'm getting a break and they are not?"

"You are working to correct that where you can and when you can. What do you think you need to feel that you paid your debt? You've confessed. You were sentenced. You did your time. You're volunteering and helping other prisoners. You can't punish yourself forever. It was a mistake. An accident. I know you hate the word 'snapped', but you were outside of yourself at the time. You've even explained to me how you dissociated at the time. Emma, let yourself heal."

God bless you. You will never see me as anything other than good. I wish I could see me like you see me. Change the subject before you get all emotional. "Morgan reached out to me again."

"She did? For what? When?"

"Remember the quote she left at the bottom of the first letter? The one that says we are not the sum of the worst thing we have ever done? Well, I wrote her back and I asked her for clarification, so she sent me like a journal with her narrative."

"Are you going to read it?"

"I started it. She intrigues me. She always has."

"Let's go back to you getting out early. The tenants in your old house, Teta's house, their lease is going to be up in a few months. I told them we are not renewing. They understand and they will be out. So, the house will be vacant for a while pending your release from the halfway house. You can do some updates or whatever before you move back. Do you know what you want to do work wise? They will require you have a job. Are you coming back to the firm?"

Emma rolled her eyes. "Brandon, I don't know. I have been looking into starting a 501-C and continuing my work with convicts and wrongful convictions, over sentencing, and helping that way. I've done my research, I can reapply to the bar, and I most likely will be able to be reinstated. While I wait, I can consult on cases and work on getting the non-profit up and running..."

Brandon sighed heavily. "Your name is still on the firm. You are still a listed partner. You can use your space for whatever you need. Non-profit. Consulting. Whatever."

The guard called time before Emma could say anything else. She stood and looked at Brandon. "Thank you for coming. Thank you for standing with me."

"You know I love you, Emma."

A lump formed in her throat. "I know you do. I don't deserve it."

"Shut up. Re-read the quote from Morgan."

When she sat back in her cell, she pulled the pages from Morgan back out and re-read them. She could hear Morgan's voice in her head as she read the words. Then she re-read the first part of the journal again.

She knew Morgan's phone number by heart. She thought about calling her but changed her mind and instead pulled out her paper and pen.

Dear Morgan,

Thank you for being so candid in sharing your story with me. I thought about calling you, but honestly, I'm scared. I don't want to intrude on your life. But I miss the sound of your voice.

They are thinking about releasing me early, and I don't know that I'm ready to get out. I don't feel like I've paid my debts. I try to focus on the quote you sent me, but it has not fully sunk in, I guess.

I started reading your journal. I'm still looking for what it is you feel you did that was so awful. But I guess that's all relative. It's all ultimately how we feel as individuals about our actions.

Is calling you an option?

Love,

Emma.

EMMA PLACED MORGAN'S LETTERS IN the pages of the tome she kept the first one in. She laid back on her rack and contemplated what a future with Morgan would look like and whether or not it was even possible. *Friends or more, I feel like she is meant to be in my life. We met for a reason. But in what capacity does she belong? After leaving here, I still have to go to a halfway house for several months, and then parole which would require my staying in state. It's not like I can get up and move to Lake Tahoe to be with her. But I am grateful she's reaching out. Would she be willing to move here? Is that asking too much?*

The questions and uncertainties were frustrating her, so she changed her track of thought back to her house. She inherited the home when her grandmother, Teta, as she was called, passed away.

She moved in with Teta at the end of her Junior year of high school, and Teta died in the middle of Emma's second semester of undergrad, leaving her the house. She and Bailey started their lives together in that house, but as Emma rose through the ranks and her success grew, she moved them to a more upscale neighborhood. Unable to part with the home and astute in how holding property would build her wealth, she kept the home and rented it out.

She tried to think about renovations the house would need after the tenants moved out. *It's been since before I left that I have been through that house. Longer than that since it's been painted. So, definitely paint. Probably new floors, counters and fixtures. Savannah is good with all that decorating stuff. Maybe Brandon can ask her to pick that out for me and get it all ordered.*

To keep from having to focus on her own future, she sat back up on her rack and grabbed her notebook and pen. She began to make a list of renovations for Brandon to get estimates on. Flooring, paint (indoor and outdoor trim and garage door), furniture. She popped the list of requests with a note pleading to Savannah for her help in an envelope.

The thought of being back outside began to give her anxiety, so she moved on to thinking about her non-profit. She wrote out a to-do list for what she needed to be reinstated to the bar and starting a 503c. Her chest felt tight, and her vision became blurry. *I haven't even served two years. I haven't paid the price, have I?*

Bailey is never going to be back. That's my fault. Sure… I've turned myself in. I've gone to therapy. I've helped others along the way find justice in some sense. But Bailey, has she gotten justice? I'm re-evaluating my priorities and I will continue to make changes. She felt a heavy weight, and it seemed to her like this weight would be permanently taking up space in her chest.

Emma found herself focused on the uncertainties with Morgan, rather than the certainties of renovations for the home she would be returning to. She couldn't stop thinking about Morgan. Thinking about Morgan, even with the uncertainties, gave her a sense of peace.

She put the letter she wrote to Morgan in an envelope and walked both envelopes to the box for the outgoing inmate mail. She popped them in and made her way to the library. Working on a case would make her feel better. Work always made her feel better. Maybe she hadn't made changes after all.

Morgan

THE CLOUDS HUNG LOW OVERHEAD, there was no sugarcoating it, it was dreary, and Morgan just wanted to get home before it started to rain.

Right before closing she watched an RV pull in across the street to the ground and two women get out. She had one reservation left to check in, and this must be it.

The women were obviously a couple as they held hands and walked together across the street. Morgan missed Emma's hands. She sighed heavily as they came into the store and made their way to the counter.

She forced a smile, "Hi... You must be White? Rachel?"

The woman with a short-cropped haircut grinned. "Yes. That's me. Rae. Sorry, we made a pitstop at this barbecue joint off the 395 and it took a while. But it was worth it." Rae was personable and Morgan immediately liked her.

"It's all good. I have you down for one week-"

"Oh my god. I know why you are familiar now!" Rae's significant other chimed in, cutting Morgan off.

Morgan got this a lot. She braced herself and smiled but the smile didn't reach her eyes.

"Charlie, what is your deal?" Rae seemed slightly annoyed.

"No! Since we walked in I was trying to figure out why she looks familiar. She was on the one crime show. She dated Emma Landry. Remember that case we were glued to for weeks? The woman who killed her wife and went on the run? The lawyer?"

Morgan looked down and bit her lip. "Yeah. That's me. Yes. Emma stayed here. That's how we met."

"I'm sorry. I didn't mean to bring up anything bad."

"It's not. I mean… Emma and I are still in touch. We're friends. It's not bad."

Rae nudged Charlie with her elbow. "Sorry. My wife has no filter sometimes. Continue. You have us down for a week."

Morgan grabbed a site map and proceeded to tell them where they could park and ran Rae's credit card.

As they were getting ready to walk out, Charlie came back up to the counter. "I am really sorry. Look, my friend Sara is moving up here, which is why we are up here. That, and I wanted a getaway. But we are all going out to dinner tomorrow, it would be nice if you wanted to join us. Sara is going to need some friends up here."

"Thank you. I appreciate it. I think I can make it work. And again, don't apologize. It's really okay. I agreed to do the interview. I get it a lot. You were not the first to point it out and you certainly won't be the last." Morgan forced a smile.

"I appreciate that. I will be by tomorrow with all the details!" Charlie made her way out.

"MORGAN, ARE YOU STILL HUNG up on that Emma woman? It's been two years and you haven't been out with anyone. Aren't you lonely?" Her mother sat across the table in the booth of the small restaurant.

"I know you don't understand, Mom. I know you can't begin to understand. But I don't know. I've been writing to her. She's writing back. We are talking through what happened. And I'm going out to dinner tonight with some girls. So, I'm getting out." Morgan was gripping the brown ceramic coffee mug so hard her knuckles were white. The heat from the mug seeped into her palms.

"Morgan, she killed her wife." Her mother's green eyes narrowed. The red leather booth was against the window and looked out at the busy downtown area. Morgan looked at the tourists wandering the streets instead of at her mother's judgmental and harsh stare.

"Yes. I'm well aware. Are you ignoring the fact I'm going out tonight?"

"Julia, you know how Morgan is. She needs closure." Her father was still always quick to defend her.

A waitress came by and delivered the check which her father snatched up (neither her nor her mother would have tried to pay it anyhow), as the waitress took their empty plates away.

"It's not about closure. It's the fact that we don't know how we are supposed to fit into each other's lives. And we want to explore it. I think she still loves me. Neither one of us are really ready to let go. Even if we are not together as a couple, I believe she and I are meant to be in each other's lives. I can't make you understand it. And I'm going out tonight. Meeting new people."

"She killed her wife," her mother's voice was flat as she repeated the inconvenient fact.

"Aren't you supposed to be a Christian? Doesn't that mean you believe in forgiveness?"

"Murder is a deadly sin."

"I don't expect you to understand."

"I thought you worked all of this out in therapy. But here you go, falling back into old habits and poor decisions."

"Julia, please."

"Michael, you always defend her. This is why she went off the rails all those years ago. You allow her all the leniency in the world and then clean up after her. What are you going to do if that woman kills Morgan, too?"

Michael shot his wife a hard look.

"You guys, please, let's not argue. I'm a grown woman. I'm almost forty years old. Let me make my own decisions. Emma is not going to 'kill me too'. Emma... Just... One day, you will get to meet her, and you will understand."

"You are like those women on the television shows. Chasing after serial killers and people in prison. I just wish you had higher standards for yourself, that is all."

Morgan changed the subject to deflect from her mother's judgment and was able to escape shortly after. Her new house was within walking distance of the restaurant and the walk would do her good.

It was unseasonably cold out and her breath steamed around her as she walked. She dodged tourists who aimlessly were wandering the area. The trees were budding, and birds chirped around her. She should feel happy. She should feel invigorated, but instead, she felt a weight inside her chest. Her heart was heavy. She walked up the hill to her small two-bedroom house and let herself into her quiet oasis. When Emma was with her, she had something to look forward to. Their daily visits and times, and the wonderful endless nights were what she lived for.

In the last almost two years since Emma had been gone, she retreated further within herself. She kept a few friends she would randomly spend time with, but she seemed to find more excuses to avoid spending time with people and socializing.

She grew to love her solitude. She liked being alone with a book or a good movie more than dealing with others. She let herself into her quiet home and opened the sliding door to let the cool fresh air in. She tried to read a book and get her mind off Emma, but her focus kept sliding back to Emma's intent gaze. Those deep blue eyes and dark eyelashes – those eyes, sharp and observant, missed nothing.

Morgan rose and sat at her table with her stationery in front of her instead.

Emma,

I think it's great that you might be getting out early.

As for calling, I miss your voice, too. I miss you, to be honest. Please call me. It would not be an interruption. It would be welcomed.

I like that you are reading the journal. I want you to know the full story. Know all of me. I regret so much that we did not take that time when we had it. No matter how we proceed together, to have you know this story will do us both good.

I hope you call soon.

Love,

Morgan.

SHORT AND QUICK. BUT IF there was a likelihood Emma would call her, and she could hear her voice again, she wanted Emma to know she was open to it. She ran the letter to the mail box and went back to get ready for dinner with Charlie and Rae and their friend.

Emma

EMMA SAT IN THE QUIET of the prison library, her long legs kicked up on the chair across from her. Aside from Dr. Bennett's office, this was the place in the prison she loved most. Like Dr. Bennett's office, the library was quiet and devoid of the noise and buzzing of the halls and units housing the prisoners. Morgan's journal sat on the table in front of her. The purple embossed book sported a ribbon attached to its spine to use a place marker, and she toyed with the ends that stuck out.

Emma brought herself back to the present, and the young female inmate next to her. Emma was doing her best to write down notes and explain to the inmate how her most likely either overworked or under prepared public defender dropped the ball in her case and how to proceed with an appeal.

The girl was young – a high school dropout – barely eighteen, a single mother, and victim of domestic abuse. She was tiny and looked juvenile in her blue jumpsuit which was too big for her. Emma saw a lot of similarities in her fellow inmates. These women were more often victims of circumstance versus being of true criminal element. These women couldn't afford good legal representation and were often at the mercy of overworked and underpaid, under-resourced public defenders who could not contend with the government funded prosecution and the 'war on crime'.

Emma clearly wrote out points and questions for the inmate to take for her next meeting; writing them out in a way so the young inmate could understand and did her best to break down the difficult legal concepts. The young woman tearfully folded up the paper and looked at Emma across the table. "You really think this can help? I can go home to my babies? They are with my mom now, but she can't handle all that. She raised her babies. I need to go home and be their mom." She had two of them under the age of five. She had shown Emma their picture so that Emma could better understand what was at stake for her.

Emma smiled at her. "We can hope. See you in class later, okay? Keep your head up and take this time while we work on it to work on you. Finishing your GED while you wait will look good."

She nodded and hugged Emma hard before heading out of the library to her work detail. Emma cleared up the files, stacking them neatly on the corner of the table. She methodically put the books away before sitting back down.

There were files she could review and work on, but she was not in the mood, which was unlike her. She wanted to read more about Morgan.

Emma got up and walked down the row which shelved all of the heavy leather-bound law books. She selected the book she needed for the case law she wanted to cite and took it back to the table.

Opening the book, she looked at all the order and comfort of the written laws she knew so well. She added notes to the notepad to her right. She read over the notes and put the book back and selected another one.

She distracted herself with the order of working this case for as long as she could. She put the files away and picked up the journal as if it was calling to her instead.

Excerpt from Morgan's Memoir

IF I COULD GO BACK in time to a specific time when I was most happy it would be the beginning when Jonathan and I first moved in together. It was great in the beginning with Jonathan. He experienced far more good days than bad as he was careful about staying consistent with his medications. I would occasionally travel to New York with him when he attended meetings, and I was off from work. Or I would meet him if he was on assignment somewhere. He was at the height of his game. He was in high demand. He would be interviewed on the major news networks because of the articles he wrote. He was on an upward trend in his career and was far from his peak.

My little collection of his work grew and eventually took over its own shelf in my guest room, where he now kept his desk.

But as we came around to one year together and life began to settle in, so did routines. The days and nights of languishing in bed slowly dissolved into quickies and going to sleep. Though they were plenty satisfying. The routine was actually surprisingly agreeable.

When Jonathan would have his down cycles they were usually because he would quietly stop taking his medications. Those down days would come out of nowhere and he would stay in bed almost the entire day or sometimes days, with the room darkened. He would pick fights with me, but his mom had prepared me. She told me how to navigate the situations and not buy into his illness. Instead of fighting with him, I would walk away, or I would try to calm him by talking to him, sitting with him, and just holding him. I would persuade him to start taking his medications again. I got to where I didn't call Jo or Tiffany and handled these shifts on my own.

If anything, Jonathan really did teach me self-reliance in a sort of way. I refrained from calling my parents for a bail out, since before he moved in. I did not rely on Jo or Tiffany either. Jonathan was mine and I accepted the responsibility.

The worst of his downturns, as I called them, happened out of the blue. When I left for work, he seemed fine. He was sitting at his desk in the guest room typing away on a story. I brought him coffee and kissed the top of his head and he smiled at me. I came home from work to find him in bed with the curtains all drawn. This went on for so long I feared he would never come out of it. Days on end, extending over a week. I was terrified. I was scared for him, and I was scared for myself. He missed two deadlines during the prolonged dark time and lost one of his freelance contracts. Finally, after the second week began, I skipped work to level with him. I managed to get him back on track with his medication.

Once the medication kicked in, our life seemed to be fine again.

As I mentioned, my parents loved him, too. They were convinced I was finally a grown-up and I did not need them anymore. They did not come down as often, and Jonathan and I went up sporadically to visit. We reached the point where we had been together almost two years. I was proud of myself. I relentlessly refused to give up on him, or us. I would tease him about it, reminding him how he gave me six months.

Jonathan ended up with an assignment taking him to Cannes for the film festival and I scheduled for a sub and went with him. He normally did not do fluff pieces on entertainment or celebrities, but there was a controversial film based on a true story of a government cover-up set to win a bunch of awards, so Jonathan was there to talk to the writer and director and the lead actor about their research for their project and the process of making it.

Between interviews he was conducting with the various celebrities for his piece, we took a day trip to St. Paul de Vence, an artist colony built into a medieval town. We wandered the small town and shopped, buying unique pieces to bring home with us, and left to make our way back to Cannes, stopping at an old fortress overlooking the water. We explored the old crumbling ruins of the structure. I was standing on a small platform on the outside of the fortress looking out over the vibrant electric blue of the Mediterranean Sea when I caught him looking at me intently. The platform was small and uneven, and I could feel his heart beating against my back. He was holding me close.

"Thank you, Morgan." He spun me around, so I was facing him.

"For what?"

"For not giving up on me. For choosing to love me through it all. You could have been with anyone. Or stayed free. But you chose me. You continue to choose me every day. You choosing me through the ups and downs when you have always valued your freedom, makes me feel more loved than I ever thought was possible."

"Jonathan, of course. I love you and I love us. I'm not going to walk away. Your condition is not a choice. I understand that."

"It's funny, I never would have thought that my niece would fix me up with the woman who would be the love of my life." He was smiling his lopsided smile which always warmed my heart.

I moved my hand to touch his face, but he instead dropped to his knee. "Morgan, I don't want anyone other than you. You are my one. My person. The absolute love of my life. Will you marry me?" He pulled a beautiful princess cut diamond ring from his pocket.

Speechless. I was not expecting it. I think I may have choked out a yes or nodded. To be honest, I really don't remember, except somehow or another, I got a resounding yes across to him, I accepted this proposal. I remember crying happy tears and him holding me close and kissing me.

We celebrated the remainder of the trip, and I knew, without a doubt in those days, we were meant to be together.

Jonathan wanted a big wedding. I didn't care. I could do a big one or a small one. I suggested we just elope in Vegas, but Jonathan was a semi-devout Catholic. He wanted to be married in the eyes of his Church. I was just surprised, as were most of my friends that I made it this far with anyone, and above all, agreed to get married.

Upon returning from France, I was due for an update on my hair. I called Sabrina, the only person I trusted to do my hair for the last three years, to make an appointment. She was talented and easy to talk to.

As I excitedly chattered to her about my engagement and the proposal and how beautiful the ring was, she broke the news to me she was leaving. Her husband, who was on active duty in the Navy, had been given orders overseas and she was joining him. She gave me the number of a friend of hers, named Sunny, and apologized profusely and promised to stay in touch. But honestly, how could I be mad at such a thing?

I hung up with her and called Sunny and made an appointment.

When I showed up, I realized Sunny's name was completely ironic. Both of her arms were sleeved with vibrant tattooed flowers, her hair dyed inky black and a wardrobe fresh out of Hot Topic. But she was absolutely striking to look at. Her eyes were a strange light brown so light they looked almost golden yellow, and with her heavy black eyeliner, she looked almost feline. Her lips were full and painted a deep burgundy which set off her complexion against the silky black hair.

Her velvety voice gave me chills (the good kind, not the creepy kind) as she called me up to her chair.

I sat down and felt on edge and nervous. As her fingers started combing through my hair I felt an acceleration in my chest as an electric current ran through my body. She was sex personified in a human and it radiated from her. It was the first time since Jonathan had come into my life I found myself craving someone other than him.

"What are we doing today?"

"Um… I… I don't know. Highlights, trim, layer a bit?" I was barely able to choke out the words as my mouth was bone dry.

"What do you want to do with the highlights? Stay blonde? Go lighter? Maybe play with a bit of the color?"

"I'm a teacher, so I can't go too crazy." I found myself smiling at her.

"We can do some rose gold. It would give you a little pop but keep you soft."

"Yeah. Okay. That sounds fun."

"I will keep it blended underneath, peek-a-boo style, so it doesn't stand out too much." She winked at me in the mirror, and I think my heart stopped.

As she worked I found myself relaxing and talking to her easily. I told her about Jonathan and the engagement, and she told me about her girlfriend who was a fitness instructor for a swanky private club in La Jolla. I explained to her how I grew up in La Jolla and knew all about the club she worked at.

By the end of my service, she invited me to join her and a few of her friends at the bar later. I readily accepted.

I ran home after the appointment feeling upbeat, excited, and beautiful. I loved what Sunny did to my hair and I was on a high from our conversation and the idea of hanging out with new friends for the night. It had been too long since I was last social. Though I loved my evenings in with Jonathan, I was craving a girls' night out.

All of it came crashing down around me when I saw Jonathan was in a downward spiral. I looked at him and the disappointment came out faster than I could catch it. "Did you stop your meds?" My tone was hard.

"It's hard to write when I'm on the medications. It numbs me and I can't be as expressive as I would like." He was in bed with the room darkened.

"You can't just go off the meds, Jonathan. We've had this great go for the last – what? Year? You can't make this decision without talking to me."

"It's my body, my choice."

"No. That's not how that works."

"So what? You are going to leave me?" He was trying to pick a fight. I knew better than to fall for the bait. I was opening the plantation shutters and letting light into the darkened room.

I rolled my eyes. "No. I'm not leaving you. But we are not going to do this. You know what you need to do." I opened the window and let the breeze in. He pulled the blankets over his head and rolled over. I went into the bathroom and opened the medicine cabinet and grabbed his pill bottle and stormed back into the bedroom and tossed it on the bed.

He didn't move.

"Jonathan. Don't do this. Come on."

He didn't move. He didn't respond.

"Jonathan." I pulled the blanket down and laid next to him nose to nose. "I love you. I love you. I love you. This is not a game." I put my hand against his face.

He opened his eyes and looked at me. There were tears in his eyes. "I don't understand why you love me. I don't deserve you. Don't leave me. Don't stop loving me."

I kissed his forehead and let him cry as he held onto me. I reached across the bed and grabbed the pill bottle and opened it. I handed him the pill. He put it in his hand, and I slid out from his grip and went down the stairs to the kitchen and grabbed a glass and filled it with ice and water. I leaned against the counter and pulled my phone out of my pocket and texted Sunny. *There's been an emergency. I can't go tonight. Thank you for the invite. Next time for sure.* I sent the text.

She responded right away. *No problem. For sure next time. Are you okay?*

I will be, I responded.

I went back upstairs, and Jonathan was sitting up against the pillows with the pill still in his hand. He was looking at it intently, as if its presence in his hand mesmerized him.

"You're talented with or without the medications. I know it numbs you out, and that can suck. But what sucks worse?" I handed him the glass of water. "Take your meds."

It is hard to love someone who struggles like Jonathan did. Occasionally Jonathan experienced this impulse to occasionally just stop his medications, the impulses would often gather momentum and happen more frequently. The down days were epic and overwhelming. After a year without this happening, I thought we were in the clear. I began to worry again daily about what I would be coming home to each afternoon.

But Sunny and her group of friends were a new highlight. I started hanging out with them every Sunday as they brunched in Hillcrest. I would go regardless of whether or not Jonathan was on a down day or if he was home. And he was not invited to join us. This was my thing alone and I needed it. I slowly started spending more time with her and her group than with my own core group of friends. I truly just enjoyed being around Sunny. I was drawn to her presence.

The wedding plans were starting to come along. We set a date and found a venue. I bought a dress, and we picked a theme – Vintage Hollywood, since he proposed while we were in Cannes during the film festival.

We were six months out from the wedding, and Jonathan was away on assignment covering the upcoming election and he was booked for an exclusive with one of the candidates. He came home as I was getting home from work. He was irritable as he came through the door. His energy was rolling off him, intense and dark.

"Hey! Welcome home!" I wrapped my arms around him and kissed him.

He kissed me back, but it came across as obligatory, versus truly grateful to see me – a tense brush of his lips against mine before pushing away from me. "This is not going to go well. You know, I think this shit is rigged. We're going to be fucked as a country."

I moved back to him and placed my arms around his neck. "Jonathan, can we not? I really want to enjoy having you home right now. I am going to order dinner – stuffed chicken breasts, the ones you like-"

He placed his hands on my hips to move me aside. "Morgan, do you not understand how important this all is?"

"You stopped your meds again?"

"This is not about me. This is not about my meds. This is bigger than all of that."

"Jonathan, come on... Let's have a good night. You've been gone for almost two weeks."

"Morgan, if that guy wins, do you know what's at stake? He's evil. Pure. Evil. It was sickening to sit on the plane with him, to sit in a room with him. The avarice and the misogyny and... and... the dubiousness. It was maddening."

"Jonathan – I get it. You know I've volunteered for several campaigns in the past. But you've been gone. I've been missing you. Let's put it aside. Enjoy each other. It's been two weeks, and I've missed you!"

"For the record, I have been taking my meds. I just can't get this out of my head."

"Please? For tonight? For me?"

"You can be so selfish."

"Excuse me?"

"Think of something other than yourself for once. You live life like a butterfly in the wind. You flit away at the sign of anything that doesn't serve your interest or purpose."

I stared at him for a minute. I could come up with no response at all. I didn't know what else I could say or do. So, I grabbed my keys and I left. He was right. This argument did not suit my interest and I was gone. Like a butterfly in the wind. Fuck this. I don't need it.

I called Sunny as I was driving away. She agreed to meet me at a bar in the gas lamp district.

I sat at the bar and ordered a margarita while I waited for Sunny. The bar was dark and crowded. The bar itself was nicked and scuffed from years of glasses being slammed down, keys dragged across it, fights and other abuse. I sat on my high barstool running my finger over a deep scratch in the varnish, and watching the short bartender mix my margarita and rim the glass with salt. Her ample, very fake boobs strained over the top of her two sizes too small tank top. It was loud with chatter around me, and rock music was blaring from speakers mounted above.

The door opened and light poured in. Sunny had finally arrived. Per usual, as she came in, heads turned to watch her. A group of construction workers near the pool table nearly fell over themselves to chat her up and whistle at her. She was all curves and sensuality. She could have worn a potato sack and gotten the same attention. She was either used to the attention she got, or she was oblivious to it, either way she paid it no mind at all. She walked past all the watching eyes and came directly to me at the bar.

"What's going on?" she asked as she sat next to me on a high bar stool.

"I'm sorry. It's really stupid."

"Two tequila shots," she ordered as she sat down. "No, it's not. If it was, you wouldn't have called. But I'm glad you did. I need a friend right now, too."

"What's going on?" I asked as the bartender put two tequila shots, lime wedges and salt in front of us.

"Paloma, my girlfriend – she decided we are done. Over. No explanation. No second thoughts. She is just not satisfied, she said. So, she packed her shit and moved out today."

We each picked up a shot glass. My eyebrows raised. "Jonathan is being an absolute prick and I'm not sure I want to get married."

She clinked her shot glass to mine, "Fuck relationships."

"Fuck relationships," I echoed, and we did our shots.

She brought me up to speed on how in retrospect she could see Paloma was drifting away from her and not really happy, and I caught her up on Jonathan's infuriating behavior.

I did not realize my phone died as we did shots and ordered greasy bar nachos and lamented on how each of us were increasingly unhappy with our significant others.

We closed the bar down and as we stood outside, tipsy, I grabbed my phone to order a Lyft, and remembered my phone was dead. "Shit. I'm too drunk to drive and my phone is dead." I leaned against the building in the moonlight. "Fuck my life."

Sunny was facing me with a sly grin as she moved closer to me. "You are really beautiful right now."

I felt suddenly sober as my heart sped up. Before I could think twice, her lips were on mine. "I live two blocks from here. You are too drunk to drive, I think you should just come home with me." Her lips were on my neck and her voice was purring in my ear.

I could not come up with a reasonable excuse to just go home. The last two years of my life with Jonathan were not valid because I was completely shitfaced and as far as I was concerned, he was being an asshole, and Sunny lit my whole body on fire. All rational thought long since ceased, and decisions were no longer being made by my brain.

I followed her willingly. Her apartment was decorated with large black leather furniture, glass end tables and large canvases with brightly colored surrealist imagery.

I didn't have much time to absorb the setting as she was quickly removing my clothes. She was lips and hands and haste washing over me and drowning me in sensation. A nagging voice in my head was begging me to stop and think of the life I had worked so hard to build over the last two and half years with Jonathan. I was too drunk and too mad at him to stop.

She had me stripped and pushed me back onto the soft leather of the couch. I was lost in her touch and the feeling of her tongue and fingers. I was soaring in ecstasy. When I finally was able to get out from under her, I took my time making her wait as I slowly undressed her. Her body with its tattoos and pierced nipples was like its own form of art and I wanted to take it all in.

I enjoyed watching her body respond to my touch. I almost forgot how exquisite another woman could be.

We dozed off sometime around sunrise. I woke up a few hours later, racked with guilt. I jumped out of her bed as if it were on fire. Her eyes fluttered open. "Get back in bed! It's early!" I was completely mystified how given our activities of the prior night and couple of hours of sleep how her makeup still looked perfect.

Part of me was tempted to fall back into the soft deep violet colored cotton sheets with her.

"I can't. I want to. But I can't. I need to go home. Jonathan has got to be worried." I looked at my dead phone.

"Call me later?"

"I'll try."

She reached out and grabbed my hand and pulled me in and kissed me softly, sending fire back through my body. If it were not for Jonathan, I would have stayed. I wanted to stay despite him. To spite him? Part of me felt justified. Part of me felt guilty. There was an internal cacophony of arguments for and against my staying and leaving that I needed to beat back down to make my feet move and take me away from Sunny's bed and back to the home with the man I promised a future to.

I just backed away and all but ran back the two blocks to the bar and jumped into my car. What was I going to do with this now? How was I supposed to navigate this?

I was trembling as I drove home. Hung over, my tongue like sandpaper and my head throbbing, exhausted and guilt ridden as I navigated the streets back to the home I made with Jonathan.

I stopped for a coffee to buy time and get my head together. I had no clue what I was going to say when I walked through the door smelling like Sunny, and exhausted.

By the time I got through the drive through and sat on a side street downing half of the cup, I still had no clue and decided I just needed to go home and get it over with.

He was waiting for me when I walked in the door. He was sitting at the table with his coffee. He looked remorseful and tired. He wasn't angry. He wasn't in a down cycle. He was sullen. Dark circles were under his eyes. It appeared he didn't get any sleep. I almost wished he was still angry. But he wasn't. I could read it on his face. He was beating himself up, and not at all angry with me.

"Morgan, I am so sorry. I didn't mean to say the things I said. I didn't mean to be cruel to you. I just spent two weeks in this awful and toxic environment, and I think it just got to me. I am so sorry."

I was expecting anger, accusations and toxicity when I came through the door. It is what I felt I deserved. Tears welled up behind my eyes. I couldn't handle his softness.

He got up and made his way to me. "I'm sorry. I had too much to drink and I passed out at Sunny's." I was not lying. I did drink too much, and I did pass out at Sunny's. But I wasn't fully telling the truth either. Which made me feel like shit. "Let me take a shower and brush my teeth and we can talk."

I walked up the stairs and into the bathroom. Jonathan followed me close behind. I was scared he could smell her scent on my skin, he was so close.

"Morgan, are you not going to acknowledge what I said?"

"I heard you. But I have a splitting headache and I still don't know how I feel about yesterday." Again, not a lie. I didn't know how I felt. I had never been unfaithful to anyone before. If I got to a point where I was tempted, I just let them go. But I loved Jonathan, and I didn't want to let him go. I just didn't know how to navigate my poor decisions.

He sat on the edge of the tub behind me as I brushed my teeth, watching me in the mirror. "Morgan, I said awful things to you. Uncalled for things. And now I'm apologizing."

I popped a few Motrin and downed them with water from the sink before peeling off my clothes and starting the shower, stepping into the hot water, and washing the scent of Sunny's body off mine. There was nothing to say. I was afraid if I said anything it would be to the effect of not deserving his apology because I was a piece of shit who just cheated on him after one big argument.

I was hoping to feel my sins wash away in the stream of water. I stared at the drain as the water flowed down, but I didn't feel any cleaner.

Jonathan stripped and entered the water with me. "Morgan, I've given you so many reasons to not love me. To quit on me. You don't deserve that. I promise you, I have not gone off my meds. I was just caught up in the bullshit I had been immersed in. You know how that kind of toxicity can eat away at a person." His arms were around me, holding me against the firmness of his body, which was a harsh contrast to the soft velvet curves of Sunny.

I felt unsteady and like I was suddenly drowning. I felt trapped in the shower and in his embrace. The only response I could muster was to break down and cry.

"Morgan, my love." His hands were smoothing the wet hair back and away from my face. He kissed my forehead and my lips. "Baby, what's wrong?"

I struggled to regain control of myself. I didn't want to tell him I cheated on him with Sunny.

"I'm just overwhelmed. I am stressed with work and wedding planning and everything. And the way you came at me yesterday, I literally wanted to call it all off. And here you are, being everything I fell in love with in the beginning. I know that yesterday is not you. Not the you I know and love. And I was immature, and rash and I shouldn't have just walked away like I did. And my phone died so I didn't call you. And I'm sorry, too." He had to know on some level something deeper was on my mind. He had to suspect I was guilty of something more than just getting drunk and letting my phone die. But he didn't press the issue. He just took the time to take care of me like he did when our relationship was new. He washed my hair and conditioned it. Washing me slowly, letting his hands take their time as he moved the loofah over me, his hand trailing after.

He cut the water off and wrapped me in a towel and escorted me back to the bed where he made love to me slow and sweet.

We didn't leave the bedroom. We stayed in bed and talked and slept and made up for all we thought we had done wrong. I fell back in love with him that day.

The following day, I went for a walk along the bay, and found a bench and called Sunny while I watched the boats bobbing along their docks.

"Hey! I was wondering when I would hear from you again," she purred into the phone with the husky voice of hers making me crave her all over again.

"Hey! Yeah. I just wanted to apologize. I am so sorry."

"I've never had anyone run out of my bed so fast. I almost took it personally." I could tell she was smiling when she said it.

"Yeah. About that." I paused and took a deep breath. "I am sorry we went there. I mean you are my friend, and you are beautiful and sexy, and you are fantastic in bed… but I can't do it again. I hope we didn't kill our friendship?"

"By all means, no. We're still friends. We were drunk and emotions were high. You and Jonathan worked it all out then?"

"Yeah. I think so." I sounded a lot more confident in my answer than I actually was. In all honesty, I was so completely torn between the two of them. Hearing Sunny on the phone, with her sultry voice sent chills down my spine and made me thirst for her touch. "What about you and Paloma?"

"Oh no. She's gone. I'm done. We're done. She was really unhappy, and I am not one to beg."

I laughed uneasily and we chatted for a few more minutes before I went back home to Jonathan.

A few weeks later, Sunny called me to hang out. We drove up to La Jolla to go kayaking around the coves followed by lunch.

It was as if nothing happened between us, until we got back to my place. Jonathan was again gone on assignment. I don't remember how or why it happened, but we ended up back in bed together.

Soon, I found myself juggling between the two of them. I loved both of them for very different reasons, which made it hard for me to just end it with one.

And yes, I was so very selfish.

Sunny was easy and she made no demands of me to end it with Jonathan. Jonathan, however, was completely in the dark. He met Sunny on a few occasions, and he liked her. During a dinner, the two of them got into a very deep conversation about women's rights and inequality. I just sat back and watched the two of them go down the rabbit hole. I didn't even know until this conversation Sunny was so well educated, informed and passionate about politics. He never questioned me about my increased time spent with her, either.

She, on the other hand, liked to push the boundaries.

Jonathan threw a surprise party for my birthday and invited her. After the big surprise and several drinks had gone down, I was sitting on the kitchen counter next to the large set up of cupcakes. I was holding a heavily frosted pink cupcake in my hand and Sunny slid up beside me, leaning in seductively as she licked the frosting off its top. I could see Jonathan watching us from the doorway of the kitchen. I couldn't read his expression, and I'm sure it was because of my own guilt.

With a Cheshire Cat grin, Sunny looked around at him and winked at him. He just laughed, not assuming or suspecting a thing.

"You are going to get me in trouble," I whispered to her.

"I licked it. Therefore, it's mine." She grinned at me and stole the rest of my cupcake and sashayed off back into the mix of the party, passing Jonathan as she made her way back into the living room from the kitchen.

He just looked at me for a moment, again unreadable. "She's very different, isn't she?"

I just shrugged and made a point to look instead at the set up of cupcakes next to me on the counter, pretending to select a new one, even though they were all the same.

On the day we were to go meet the officiant for our ceremony, I was struggling. This was making my future with Jonathan more real. The officiant was a Catholic priest. Jonathan wanted someone more than a court officiant or who held a mail order certificate, and Jonathan was raised Catholic, as was I. But Jonathan put far more stock in his faith than I ever had. I found his faith to be a huge paradox in his being. Most people as liberal as he was tended to not put a lot of stock in organized religion. Not that he attended regular mass, but his rosary lived on the nightstand next to his side of the bed, and he sometimes went to church alone to pray, or even confession.

I was raised only to do the big events. Midnight mass at Christmas, baptism as a baby, and a first communion, and Easter mass. Other than those occasions and the occasional wedding and funeral, I never spent much time in church or contemplated matters of faith. It wasn't a priority to me. I certainly didn't pray.

We sat across from the priest in his office and he talked to us about love, honesty, and vows. Every second in his office made me burn inside. I couldn't breathe in there. I was choked by the smell of frankincense and my own feelings of guilt. I could feel the judgment of the Virgin Mary staring down at me from her pedestal in the corner of the office.

After we left, as Jonathan was driving us home I looked at him. He was so happy and had been doing so good. The sunroof of his SUV was open and in the golden hour of the setting sun and the outdoor scents of Southern California – salt of the ocean, eucalyptus, and jasmine -filtered in from outside. Light-hearted jazz music came pouring out of the speakers. His lips held a soft upturn as he cruised forward. He was so happy. He was so at peace.

I felt like shit.

I needed to be honest.

"Jonathan, I need to tell you something."

His hand reached over and gently took mine, bringing my fingers to his lips. "What's going on?" He side eyed me to keep his eyes on the road. His hand was warm and soft.

"I've been cheating on you. With Sunny." I just let it fly out. I could not dress it up and make it pretty, because it wasn't.

He let go of my hand like it scalded him.

The verbal vomit just continued to flow out of me. "I'm so sorry. I didn't mean to hurt you. It started that night I didn't come home four months ago. I didn't mean to keep it up. I wanted to stop, but I couldn't."

His hands gripped the steering wheel so tight, and I don't think he was breathing. His lips were a thin seam and his jaw pulsed as it clenched.

"You're joking, right?" His voice was terse, and he wouldn't look at me.

A giant lump formed in my throat. "No. I'm sorry. I'm being entirely honest right now, because I have to be. I understand if you want to break it off. I understand if you want to call off the wedding. I understand if you hate me." I choked out the words, wringing my hands. I didn't want him to break it off. I wanted him to forgive me. I wanted to take it all back. Rewind the clock. I should not have said anything.

He pulled off the road onto the shoulder and turned in his seat to face me. "It all makes sense now, how she was acting at your party. I get it now..." His voice trailed off as he reflected on the events of the past few months. "I don't hate you, Morgan. But are you ready for this? For marriage? For building a life? What is it that compels you to do this?" There was a perceptible shift in his being. His eyes were not the soft and sweet eyes he had when he looked at me normally. There was something cold and dark about them. The way his jaw set – everything was different. There was a hardness in him I never saw before.

I shook my head. "I don't know. There is something about her." The car shook as other vehicles sped past us.

"Are you in love with her?" He turned the radio off abruptly.

"I don't think so. I know I love you. I do. That I'm convinced of." I reached for his hands, and he pulled away from me.

"But you don't know if you love her, too?"

"It's not that simple."

"How can you love me and then do this with her?"

"I just... I have no answers."

We were both silent, and the golden hour was shifting to dark. Both of our eyes were wet with tears.

After an eternity of sitting in the dark and silence he asked, "Are you willing to cut off ties with her for me? To build this life we have planned?"

Looking at him, at the hurt on his face, I knew what I needed to do. "Yes. I will. I can. For you, for us. Yes."

"Cut off all ties with her then. No more. Delete her. Block her. Find a new salon to get your hair done at."

I nodded my head in compliance with him. We were less than two months away from our wedding. I knew I couldn't keep going with Sunny and getting married anyway. I also knew I couldn't have an honest marriage with Jonathan and not tell him the truth.

This was the first night he didn't kiss me goodnight. He did not hold me. He rolled over with his back to me in the bed. I barely slept feeling the weight and coldness between us.

The next morning, I called Sunny. This time, I called her on speaker, with Jonathan sitting across from me at the table.

"Good morning," her voice purred into the phone. Jonathan's eyes narrowed at the sound of her tone.

"Hey… hi. I need to cut right to the chase. Sunny, you are beautiful. Sexy. Phenomenal. But I have to make a choice. I can't keep doing this."

"Babe. I get it. It's been fun."

"I can't see you, talk to you, hang out. I have to let you go."

"That's a bit drastic."

"I know. But I have to."

"I understand."

There was nothing more to say. Nothing more I could say. I hung up and blocked her number and blocked her off all my social media in front of Jonathan. Temptation was done. Gone. Over.

~ *III* ~

True   Intentions

The Present

Emma

EMMA SAT LOOKING AT THE calendar. It was official. She would be released in a matter of weeks and off to the halfway house.

Intent. A word she was familiar with, even more so now as she worked with the cases of her fellow inmates. Intent was a word she meditated on over and over again. She did not have the intent to kill Bailey. She was absolutely certain. *Bear hadn't intended to kill my mother, either. He never went on to kill anyone else (that I know of). I will never again take another life. It's all intent. Mens rea. Basic law school 101 shit.*

So much of the decision in her case and the decision to release her was based on intent.

I've never been able to forgive Bear for killing my mother, regardless of his intent at the time. But he went on to keep that vital information from me. Letting me believe I was unwanted and unloved. He didn't tell me that truth until days before his death. This lack of information led me to have so many issues with who I was and how my world view was shaped. Where I differ from him is that I came clean. I ran for a year. But I came back and took accountability. I owned what I did. I'm not like him.

The judicial system considered her reformed. She will have paid her debt to society. A crime for which she lacked the mens rea, and prior to, considered to be a generally good person. Looking around her and at her fellow inmates she knew the generally good person category came from being wealthy, educated and white. Which is why she started helping her fellow inmates. Helping her fellow inmates added to her reputation as a good person and furthered the cause of her early release. An early release she did not ask for, nor anticipated.

Emma was in the visiting room, trying to focus on the visit with Abby.

The first person who really made an impact on Emma was Abby. She met Abby during her sophomore year of high school, after first meeting Abby's then girlfriend Simone at the mall. Abby and Simone became Emma's de facto big sisters and helped her truly come into her own and understand who she was and what she could be, as far as educated, out, and successful. And Abby was a staunch supporter of Emma, having her back through the sentencing.

Abby did not come as often as Brandon or Mary Anne for visits as she lived out of state, but she made it a point to come and visit at least once a month or every other month in the very least, and she wrote letters and sent books often when she could not make the trip up to visit.

She sat across from Emma. "So, this Morgan chick is trying to make it happen as a long-distance relationship of sorts?" she summarized after Emma brought her up to speed on the correspondence between her and Morgan.

"I don't know. I think possibly. But she also made it clear she's fine with friendship. And no, before you ask, I don't think she is one of those weird chicks that chases serial killers. We had something before I turned myself in. There was something intense and wonderful. Where we went wrong is neither of us wanted to face the demons of our past and we skipped over it and tried to move on together. We were both so damaged and so afraid of what we had done that we chose to ignore the demons and the damage only for them to come back to bite us."

"You're here now, dealing with yours. Did she ever deal with hers? Fully?"

"I think maybe. I don't know. I'm reading her journal of all that she dealt with. I'm getting her first-hand account. Where I'm at it is hard to say if she ever dealt with it."

"Do you think you still have feelings for her?"

"I know I do. I haven't sorted through all of it though. I know I want her in my life. I just don't know in what capacity. I don't know that I want to be romantically involved with anyone

again. But as a friend, for sure. And she feels the same. We are both trying to figure out where we fit in each other's worlds."

"Have you physically seen her since you left? Has she come to visit?"

"No."

"You were very attracted to her when you were with her. Do you think that just ends?"

Emma sighed. "I believe attraction can wane. But I don't know. You have a point. I need to be in front of her. I need the rest of the story."

"You don't see how these communications are actually building intimacy between the two of you?"

"I see your point. And yes, you are correct. This level of communication is deep and there is a level of intimacy in these exchanges and in her trusting me to read this journal of hers. But I think the true test will be if we ever get to be face to face again. There are also logistical challenges in having a future with her. We have thousands of miles of distance between us. One of us would eventually be required to move."

"What would be stopping you?"

"Parole."

"Which can be transferred."

"True. My practice. I can potentially be reinstated to the bar."

"Good point. What would be stopping her?"

"Her family. Her campground."

"That's all negotiable. Neither of you really have anything to stop you from being together. That is, if you really want it."

"Are you arguing for me to be with her? I'm so confused."

"No. I'm not arguing either way. I'm trying to help you figure it out for yourself."

A large female guard stood at the doorway, "Time, folks. Wrap it up."

Abby smiled a lopsided grin at Emma. "Til next time, my friend. The next time, you will be out of here."

"Yeah, I'm out of here in two weeks."

"I will see you soon." Abby reached in to give Emma a hug but a loud throat clear from the large guard discouraged the sentiment. Emma watched Abby leave and made her way to her cell.

She looked at Morgan's letter to her, sitting next to the journal.

Emma,

I know you don't understand my guilt. No one can. I can say that I've worked my way through a lot of it. Keep reading. I want you to understand what brought me to you, and why it took so long to fall in love again, and how it hit me when you left. It will also help you to understand why I have the feelings I do for you. Why I understand you as I do.

A lot of it could be the paradox of our situations. We've both been in a position where love has been a destructive force, but now we have this different situation. Maybe I'm just being a fool though. A hopeless romantic. Maybe we will only be friends from here on out. Who can say?

Call me soon. I miss you.

Love,

Morgan.

HER FINGERS TAPPED RHYTHMICALLY NEXT to the book.

She intended to spend the rest of her life doing good and making up for what she had done. She knew this without a doubt. Championing the cause for those who lacked the same opportunities she experienced would become her new obsession.

She wanted to feel good again. She wanted to be able to be proud of herself again. Getting out early was not helping her feel good about herself. It made her feel like she was cheating the process.

She also knew she wanted to hear Morgan's voice. More than anything else, she craved the sound of Morgan almost as much as she craved her touch.

She folded the letter and placed it in the same book she stored all of Morgan's letters in and made her way to the phone and typed in the code and the phone number.

Morgan

THE CLOUDS WERE UNABLE TO hold back, and it began to rain as she made her way home. She had enjoyed the dinner with Charlie and Rae, and their friend Sara was hot. She caught herself flirting with her and Sara eagerly flirted back.

Prior to the dinner, Charlie invited Morgan over to the campsite for a drink. Morgan knew it was so she could pry for information about her and Emma, but she went, and she answered all of Charlie's questions. How long were they together? Was Emma as hot in real life as in the pictures? What was she like? The standard fare Morgan would get asked. Usually, Morgan would brush it aside and say she would rather not discuss it, but she gave in to Charlie and spilled it all for her. Delighting her with the details.

Rae was busy bustling around and tidying the RV and tinkering with mechanics. She obviously couldn't care less about her connection to Emma. She gave Charlie the whole story – Reader's Digest version. Charlie was definitely curious as to what her deal was with Emma as well. Morgan played it off as they were just friends with no further plans of reuniting. She knew she was lying, but she didn't know how to define her feelings to herself much less anyone else.

She was grateful Charlie did not spill the information about Emma to Sara at dinner. It was something she would have to broach when and if it went anywhere further.

Charlie and Rae almost dissolved away from the table as she and Sara talked and teased each other. Charlie and Rae were an interesting couple. They had an odd dynamic she couldn't quite nail down. It seemed Rae was more often than not irritated by Charlie and vice versa. But who was she to judge? She had never experienced a long-term healthy relationship. Maybe this behavior was normal? She chose to just ignore them and focus on Sara.

Sara was taller than her, but not as tall as Emma. She had a platinum blonde, choppy, spikey pixie cut. Her eyes were blue, not the sapphire blue of Emma's eyes, but a crystal-clear blue. She was not Emma. But she was a lot like Emma. Not Emma was what echoed in her heart most of the night, though she persisted in her flirtations.

Before the end of the dinner, Sara grabbed Morgan's phone and put her number in it, then proceeded to text herself from Morgan's phone so she would have Morgan's number. Morgan just grinned at her as it went down. She was a sucker for a confident woman, after all.

Now that the connection was made, there were a few brief texts throughout the day which made her day a little bit brighter. Though she was not Emma, Sara was still someone that intrigued her.

Morgan linked her Bluetooth speaker and put on a streaming music platform. The music filled the empty and quiet space of her small home. She loved being alone most days, but sometimes the loneliness was cold and hollow. Today was one of those days.

The rain was coming down and tapping at her windows and a fog clung around the tips of the trees surrounding her neighborhood. Many of the houses on the winding streets around her were now used as Air BnB's for their close proximity to downtown and views of the lake. She didn't really have neighbors she bonded with and even if she did, she probably wouldn't have.

It was a day similar to this when she first kissed Emma. Cold and rainy outside. She had gone to Emma's RV to tell her how she felt. Emma had cooked dinner and served expensive, full-bodied wine. The electric fireplace was on. It was the perfect moment, and everything came together in a way that made it seem like it was right.

She was sitting on the couch with a book and an apple. A throw blanket was over her lap and her lamps were on to counterbalance the gray of the outside. She was so lonely that she began contemplating getting a cat, when her phone rang.

She didn't recognize the number when she answered. "Hello?"

"You are receiving a collect call from an inmate at the Midwest Correctional Facility for Women. Do you accept these charges?" an automated voice read out.

Having not spoken to Emma since the night of the confession, Morgan's heart was racing. "Yes. Yes, I accept." There was a click, and she could hear the background noises of women chatting and the hum of the line. "Emma?"

"Hi." She could hear the smile in Emma's voice. "You said to call, so I did."

"Yes. I did. I did say that." Suddenly Morgan was at a loss for words.

"How are you?"

"I'm good. I... I," Morgan gave a nervous laugh. "I really didn't realize how much I missed the sound of your voice."

"I missed yours, too. I need to start by telling you that I'm really sorry for how it all went down."

"You told me in your letter. But I understand. You want to know what's weird? Since you left I still don't let anyone in site 1170. It's still *your site*. That's weird isn't it?"

"No... I don't think so. I think it's sweet, actually."

"How are you?"

"I'm good. I keep busy."

"What's it like? Are you treated okay?"

"I mean, it's not the Ritz Carlton or The W." Emma was laughing. "And it's hard to be a vegetarian here. But I get by. People leave me alone because I stay to myself and work on helping other inmates with their legal issues and passing their GED's. But I've seen what happens when you are not in good with some of the inmates. It can be scary."

"You mentioned you may be getting out earlier than anticipated."

"Yeah, I have my date. I will be out in just under two weeks. Between Covid and my volunteer work I get to leave early."

"What are your plans when you leave?"

"I have to go to a halfway house for a little while and then parole for a few years. I will be moving back into the house that used to belong to my grandmother. Consult at my old firm. Maybe start a non-profit, work on getting reinstated to the bar."

"So, you are staying over there?" Morgan felt disappointed.

"I honestly don't know. I know I have to until my parole is done. I miss Tahoe though. And I do miss you. I honestly thought I would never hear from you again."

"How long do you get to talk for?"

"They love me around here. So, it doesn't matter. No one is going to rush me off."

Morgan was happy to hear this. It was an effortless conversation. Morgan lit a fire in her fireplace while they chatted and curled up under her favorite sherpa. She lost herself in the sound of Emma's voice. It could only have been made better by having Emma there with her. She missed Emma's tall, lean body, and how she would lay inside of Emma's embrace, letting those long limbs wrap around her.

After almost an hour on the phone, Morgan could hear a buzzer go off in the background. "I have to go, it's lights out soon."

"Thank you for calling me. I missed your voice."

"I miss you. And thank you for the journal, I've been reading it. I wish we made it a point to talk about these things when we were together."

"Would it have changed anything?"

"No. But I feel like it's unfair how you learned my story and now for you to tell yours in a journal."

"I mean, it is what it is. We can't change it now. I still care and I want to know you. I want you to know me. We will have to make it work how we make it work."

The buzzer sounded again. "Good night, Morgan."

"Good night." And the line was dead.

Morgan could not stop smiling. The loneliness and grayness she was feeling was replaced with a warmth lit inside.

Emma

AFTER HEARING MORGAN'S VOICE, EMMA was more determined than ever to read more of the journal. The conversation had not been extraordinarily deep, which Emma was grateful for since they had not spoken since she confessed. Both of them fell into old habits of keeping it light.

Emma explained to Morgan about how she helps the other inmates and Morgan told Emma about the book she was reading, and a movie she recently watched and loved, and her new friend Aaron – well, new since Emma left.

Emma strayed away from asking questions about the journal. She wanted to read it in its entirety before she asked questions. She looked at the journal on her desk. She added sticky notes to certain pages with questions which arose as she read. She wanted to know why and how. She wanted to know all of it.

Even after lights out, it was not entirely dark in the cells. It was something Emma struggled with when she first got there but adjusted to since, using the quiet time to read, or work in near silence.

As the lights dimmed and the block went mostly silent, she pulled the journal out and continued to read.

Excerpt from Morgan's Memoir

WE BURIED THE WHOLE SITUATION, Jonathan and I. The day after I blocked Sunny, we just went about life as if it never happened.

I missed Sunny though. I thought about her a lot. There was something particular about her which kept her on my mind. I missed the way she laughed. I missed how I could just talk to her about anything, and she was uncomplicated. In retrospect, it was the uncomplicated part I missed the most. I loved Jonathan, but he was complicated. He was deep. He had his issues and demons with his mental health. Those demons lurked in every corner, and you never knew when they would be unleashed.

The great paradox that was Sunny – the goth on the outside, rainbow on the inside bombshell – being with her was like a vacation… She hung out in the back of my mind. I hated myself for missing her.

Jonathan ended up going on another assignment which took him out of town. I became a recluse after the whole Sunny situation went down, so I called a few of my friends and asked them if they wanted to go out.

Shocked to hear from me after weeks of radio silence, they readily agreed.

It was three weeks prior to the wedding and though there was a bachelorette party scheduled for the week before, I felt the need to go out and tie one on. I needed to get out. My life was beginning to feel like work, and I was not enjoying it.

I met some girlfriends from work at an Irish pub in downtown. It was a place my friends and I used to frequent before Sunny came into my life and I began to hang out with her more than them. We were sitting at a high top and having drinks, it was a welcome reprieve to get out with them.

I was wholly unprepared when the door opened and in came Sunny with two of her friends. We made eye contact the moment she walked in, and the familiar stirrings of heat ran through me. It was not planned, and it was not a place I knew her to ever frequent.

I tried to not make eye contact with her, but it just happened. I couldn't *not* look at her. Our eyes met and she smiled with her cat that ate the bird grin, and I looked down and away. It was too late.

She and her friends came over to our table and I introduced them to my group of friends. We all moved around so there was more room for them. Sunny had met most of my group at my birthday party. None of my friends knew the true nature of my relationship with Sunny. I kept all of it quiet. Everyone just made room and it was more the merrier.

Sunny's chair was so close we were touching. The smell of her amber based perfume and occasional brushes of her hand or leg against mine threw me off kilter. After another drink, I got up to go outside to get air. I couldn't do it any longer. The darkness of the pub, the noise of the patrons, the loud music, and her so close to me. It was all absolutely claustrophobic.

Sunny followed me outside. "What is up?"

"I can't, Sunny. I can't be this close to you. I miss you."

She reached for my hand. "I miss you, too." I let her fingers interlace with mine. "Where's Jonathan?"

"On assignment in Washington, DC. He's gone for the next week."

"Do you need company?" Her low sultry voice was all it took, and I could feel the heat of her body as she moved closer to me.

There was absolutely no way I was going to say no. She knew it.

Every part of me knew what I was doing was fucked up. So fucked up. But I *couldn't* say no. I guess it would be more accurate to say I *didn't want to* versus I couldn't. But either way, I didn't.

I went back into the bar and excused myself to the bathroom. Sunny followed me close at my heels. She locked the door behind her and pushed me back against the wall. Her kiss was deep, and her body pressed against me. There was no escaping her. And to be honest I didn't want to escape her. "I've been missing you more than you know." One hand was undoing my jeans, the other, pinning my arm above my head, her body pressed against me. I could hear a line forming outside of the door.

"Sunny, not here." I was gasping as her hand slid down between my legs. I could feel the soft teasing of her fingers and I was torn between letting her continue and pushing her back to just take this back to my place.

She kissed me again and her touch got firmer, pushing fabric aside and finding me, urgent and demanding more from her. The light above us was flickering and buzzing, and bass from the music pulsated through the door. I could feel the cold cinderblock against my back as her fingers expertly worked me. Nothing else mattered except for the building heat within me and her eyes, locked on mine.

My hand slipped up under her skirt feeling and finding her. She moved against me and with me. Her soft moan in my ear and her flesh and her body were everything.

The knocking on the door was insistent and loud, but we didn't care. I cried out as she got me off. The feeling of her grinding against my fingers as she followed me with her own release, moaning into my ear as her body shook and trembled against me.

I kissed her and gathered her into my arms. She giggled at the knocking and impatient patrons outside the door. "Come home with me tonight," I demanded.

"You don't have to ask me twice."

We opened the bathroom door to the angry mob of waiting women and pushed our way back to the table. No one seemed any the wiser about what had been going on or that we were even gone. The conversations were going on around us. A mixture of work gossip and politics and pop culture swirling around us.

I waited a good twenty minutes, finishing another drink before excusing myself for the evening. As we had quickly arranged before exiting the bathroom, Sunny was going to wait and follow a few minutes later and meet me at my place.

I was shaking in anticipation. Waiting for Sunny at the door. It was so wrong.

Once she arrived, seconds melted into minutes which melted into hours. We were wrapped up in the blankets of the bed and I dozed off with her next to me. Here is where I always question, not only why did I so easily allow for this to even happen, but why did I take her back to my place? Why didn't we go to her place?

I thought I had heard the door open, but living in a small condo, you often heard the neighbors, and it was easy to write off sounds and noises.

It wasn't until Jonathan was standing in the doorway of the bedroom, with his arms across his chest, that I was able to put together that it was in fact my door that I heard open. I sat up and sucked in my breath.

"Did I wake you?" His voice was dripping with acid. I could see his jaw was clenched. Sunny stirred and opened her eyes. She took a moment to register what was going on before she put her hands over her face in realization exhaling a quiet, "Oooohhhh ffffuuuuuccckkk."

"Jonathan–"

"Save it, Morgan. I don't want to hear it." He turned to walk out. I could hear his footsteps on the stairs. I untangled myself from the sheets and threw on my bathrobe and ran after him down the stairs. "Seriously, Morgan. Don't bother," he called out to me as I gained ground at the bottom of the stairs.

"Jonathan, stop!" I chased him through the living room. We were standing in the dark kitchen. Everything was coated in blue from the moonlight.

"What is it about me that I am not enough for you?" he asked, still not facing me. His voice was not filled with anger, but with sorrow.

"That's not even it, Jonathan. You are enough. You really are. I just-" I reached up to grab his shoulder and pull him to me, but he swatted me off him.

"You just what? You are thirty-four years old, Morgan. You just don't know if you want to be gay or straight? You just don't know what you want? What is it?" Now the frustration was creeping in.

"It is not that simple." I was crying. I still don't know what exactly I was crying for, though. Was I crying at the thought of losing him? Was I crying at my own lack of self? Maybe all the above.

"I came home early because I missed you. I wanted to surprise you and spend the weekend with you. Fuck. Morgan, why?" He turned and faced me. I could see his pain in the blue of the moonlight. His eyes were red rimmed, and he was fighting the tears in his eyes.

I went to reach for him again and he batted my hand away. "Jonathan, please."

"I'm going to go to Tiffany's for the night. Or get a hotel. Or something. I don't want to be here. I don't want to see you. I can't bear to look at you right now."

My heart broke to hear him say those words.

I watched him walk out and I was stuck to the floor. I could hear Sunny's footsteps on the stairs behind me shortly after Jonathan left. "Do you want me to leave?" she asked.

I just nodded my head, yes.

She made her way past me and out the door. After she left I went back upstairs and lay in the bed. I couldn't sleep so I just stared at the ceiling, watching the ceiling fan move lazily around. The bed smelled like Sunny.

I took the pillows she had been laying on and threw them on the floor. I grabbed my phone and texted Jonathan. *I know you are mad at me. I know you don't understand. I don't understand myself. But I love you. I want us to figure this out.* I clicked send.

I could see he read it. But he didn't respond.

The next morning, I peeled myself out of the bed. I finally dozed off for a bit, but really I got no sleep. It seemed my sins were made uglier by the light of day. I was disgusted with myself. I needed to make this right. I knew with all certainty I must atone for what I did to Jonathan, and I could not bear the thought of a life without him.

I made my way to Tiffany's. I could see Jonathan's car parked in the driveway. I pulled in behind him and texted him again. *I'm out front. Can you come out and talk to me?*

He read it but didn't respond.

I waited a few minutes and nothing. Sitting in my car, leaving it running to keep the air flowing. The sun was beating down through my windshield. I couldn't eat anything, and my stomach felt empty. But the pain in my chest was worse. I just sat and stared at the door and checked my phone periodically. No response and he didn't come outside. The read receipt came through. He saw my message. I thought I saw movement in the upstairs window. But he never came down or out.

After several more minutes, I got out and knocked on the door. Tiffany pulled open the door and glared at me. "Less than a month before you are set to marry my brother? Really? You had to cheat on him? You know how fragile he can be, and you do this to him?"

"Tiffany, please. Let me talk to him. I need to know he's okay."

"No. Morgan, you don't get to just waltz in here and see him. He's devastated. He's a wreck. If you cared so much, you should have thought twice before spreading your legs for some gothy hairdresser."

"You have every right to be angry with me. I hurt Jonathan. I did. But I need to know he's okay. I need to tell him how sorry I am. I need him to know I love him. I'm done with Sunny. I only want him. I do only want him. I do." The tears flowing from my eyes were uncontrollable as I pled my case to her. I was not lying. I knew what I said was true. I only wanted him. I wanted the life we planned. I wanted to marry him and have babies with him and grow old with him. I was sobbing. "Tiffany, please. Please. Just let me see him."

"You have three minutes to walk yourself back to your car and get the fuck off of my property." Tiffany was cold as she turned her back and slammed the door.

I sent Jonathan several more texts throughout the day.

11:34AM
I'm so sorry.
Read 11:36AM

12:07PM
Please. We need to talk.
Read 12:12PM

12:53PM
I love you. I love you. I love you.
Read 1:02PM

2:14PM
Forgive me.
Read 2:32PM

2:45PM
Please just talk to me.
Read 3:06PM

3:18PM

Please tell me you're okay.
Read 3:42PM

4:15PM
I'm so sorry. So. Sorry.
Read 5:15PM

6:02PM
Jonathan, I love you. I want us to work this out.
Read 6:49PM

8:13PM
I hate myself for what I've done to you. To us. Please, give me something.
Read 9:27PM

9:34PM
I'm sorry.
Read 9:41PM

10:07
Please. Say something.
Read 10:12PM

He read all of them and responded to none.

THE NEXT DAY, I WAS at work. I was unfocused and a mess. I had not planned any lessons for the day. I told the students it was a study hall day. Get caught up on your missing assignments. I stayed behind my desk, tired and haggard. I could see and hear some of the students whispering. I was not that teacher, typically. A few of them asked me if I was okay. I forced a smile and told them I would be. It was nothing they needed to concern themselves with.

Sitting at my desk, I sent texts to Jonathan throughout the day.

9:26AM

Jonathan, I love you. I'm sorry. Come home.

Read 10:07AM

11:11AM

I get it. I fucked up. Stop ignoring me so we can talk.

Read 11:15AM

1:34PM

Maybe I need to get therapy. I will. So I can understand why I did what I did. But I love you.

Read 2:45PM

3:31PM

You have to forgive me. I know what I did was wrong. We've been through so much together. Don't walk away now.

Read 3:57PM

5:12PM

I want you. I want only you. I miss you. Come home.

Read 6:36PM

6:45PM

Please. Jonathan. Just say something.

Read 6:46PM

6:46PM

I'm sorry. I'm so sorry. I'm begging you.

Read 7:58PM

8:47PM

Forgive me.
Read 9:24PM

10:38PM
Please come home. I love you. I miss you. I need you.
Read 10:42PM

All left on read.

On the third day, I went to work trying to look more together, deciding I needed to at least step it up for my kids. I sent him one text.
1:45PM
I love you. That is all.
Read 1:45PM

1:46 PM
I'm coming to the house to get some of my things.

1:48PM
Don't leave. Wait for me so we can talk.
Read 1:52 PM

IT WAS HARD TO WAIT through the last two hours of work. I just wanted him to be home when I got home. Be angry. Be hurt. Be whatever. Just be home. If he was home, we could work through whatever. If I could love him through his down cycles, he could love me through this. If he's home. Just be home when I get there. It was a plea and a prayer on a loop in my head as I watched the clock tick down until I could bolt to my car in the parking lot and speed home.

I came home and his car was parked in its spot in front of the condo. There was hope. So much hope. I ran in through the front door and called his name. I was met with silence. Something didn't feel right. The quietness, maybe? It was too quiet. I stood in the kitchen, and I remember the sound of the faucet dripping so clearly. I remember listening for his voice. A certainty inside of me knew something was not right. The very energy around me was off. The silence and stillness was suffocating and thick. I made my way up the stairs and called for him again. Still no response.

I opened the bedroom door, and he was there, on his knees, the chair I sat on at the vanity turned on its side next to him. There was a belt around his neck, fixed to the door of the closet. He was slumped forward, eyes bulging, and glasses askew. His tongue was out, and his face was purple. His arms dangled in front of him, slack. I stood there for what seemed like forever. My brain couldn't make sense of what I was seeing. This wasn't my Jonathan. Not the handsome, smooth, deep thinking, beautifully broken man I loved. No. This isn't him. But those are his glasses. That's his hair. Those are his eloquent hands with the long fingers that danced over his keyboard as he wrote.

I began to cry. I remember because I could feel the tears falling. But my brain still didn't know what it was I was seeing. It was fragments. Purple. Glasses. Swollen. Jonathan. Knees. Chair. Belt. Dead. Hands. I finally registered what it all was. Jonathan took his own life. And he did it in a place where it would be me who found him. It was his final statement. His final word. I was what broke him beyond salvation or repair. No pill would fix this. He gave me six months in the beginning. I hung in there for over two years, only to destroy him. He didn't break me. I broke him.

I screamed. And once I started, I couldn't stop. A neighbor came rushing over. I say rushing, but I really don't know how long I was screaming before she was next to me. I just know she was just there. My concept of time from the moment I got home is a blur.

She was not someone I knew well, but God bless her for being brave enough to come over while I was screaming. She wrapped her arms around me after she saw Jonathan's body and I continued to scream. She steered me out of the room and down the stairs. I remember her holding me and rocking me back and forth while she called 911. I knew she was a neighbor. I had seen her periodically here and there before, but I never saw her again after. It's almost like she was sent to help me.

The rest of this night only exists in my memory as flashes. Vivid moments in time amongst a blackness devoid of any real information.

I vaguely remember police officers came. And so did the coroner. Jonathan was wheeled out in a black vinyl bag on a stretcher. I tried to claw my way through the officers to get to his body as it was being wheeled past me. The officers were holding me back.

I don't remember how I ended up there, but I was seated in the back of an ambulance. I had stopped screaming. Only because my voice went hoarse. I was shaking uncontrollably. There was nothing I could do. I was completely helpless. Every time I closed my eyes – even if it was just to blink – I saw him, dead, slumped, purple, disfigured.

Sitting in the back I could see my condo grow smaller and the flashing lights against the road. I remember the feeling of rocking back and forth as we made our way. There was a blanket around my shoulders, but I still felt cold. I was shivering and my teeth chattered loudly, and I was so exhausted. An officer was in the back with me and the paramedic. I was taken to the hospital, and put into a room, a doctor was there and the officer who rode with me was standing near the foot of the bed. "Miss Hale, can I ask you some questions?" he asked. His voice was gentle, and I remember his expression was kind. His name tag said Jiminez. I don't remember answering anything. Just looking at him. I couldn't understand what questions he could possibly have for me.

I don't remember anything else. I know I was sedated. I woke up the next morning in a hospital room. A psychiatrist came in and asked me questions about wanting to hurt myself and how I felt about what happened the day before, and Jonathan taking his own life. Did I want to hurt myself or anyone else? Jonathan was really dead. He had really taken his own life. I found his body. It was real. It was really real. The doctor gave me a prescription for anti-anxiety medications and a sedative so I could sleep.

Not a threat to myself or anyone else, they sent me home. I didn't want to call anyone and opted for a Lyft.

When I got to my condo, I stood in front of the door. Jonathan's car was still parked in front. I knew when I opened the door I would be faced with the reality of what happened.

The only thought in my mind was how I knew I needed to notify the district of my absence. There were several missed calls from my school admin team. I was supposed to be at work today. I sat on the step of the porch. I vaguely remember calling HR. I got a note from the psychiatrist I would have to give them. I handled it while sitting on my porch step. I did not want to go inside. I couldn't go inside.

I stood. Paralyzed on the porch for a long time. I sat back down on the step for a while longer. I was not ready. I don't know how long I sat outside. I called my parents. They were wrapping up a European vacation. My dad answered, sounding happy and relaxed. I sat back down again on the steps of the porch. I couldn't find my words. "Morgan? Are you there? Are you okay?"

"Daddy… Daddy… Jonathan killed himself. He's dead. I cheated on him, and he killed himself." My voice was barely a whisper into the phone.

"Oh… Oh. Morgan. We can come home."

"No. I don't want you to come home. But I needed to tell you. I needed to say it out loud. He's dead. He killed himself. It's my fault. I cheated on him. I broke him."

"Morgan, you are not okay."

"I will be, Daddy. Don't leave your trip. Stay. I will be fine. I shouldn't have called you."

"No, Morgan. You should have. If you feel you can't handle it, call me back and we will be on the first plane home. I promise."

"I love you, Daddy." I hung up and sat in the sun on the porch for a while longer.

The doctors wrote me a prescription for anti-anxiety medications before I left. I had them on board and several bottles in a bag. I just sat, numb and afraid. Cars drove past and the sun moved across the sky, and I couldn't move.

Finally, after what seemed like forever, I stood back up and forced the key in the lock and willed myself into the entryway.

I vaguely remembered the officers asking me if there was a note. I hadn't looked – I didn't want to look. To see it would have solidified the reality of it. I don't think I gave them an answer when they asked me. I walked through the condo looking across surfaces for a paper or note.

I made my way up to the bedroom and sitting on my bedside table was a piece of paper folded with my name scrawled across the top of it in Jonathan's neat handwriting.

I picked it up and held it. I looked over and could see the closet door from which he hung himself just the day before. The carpet still bore the impression of his body weight. The chair was on its side, in the same place. The closet door cracked open so they could release him and the belt that had held him there.

The room felt cold, and it was starting to get dark. A plane coming in to land flew over, and a cadre of military members were running in formation outside with a call and response cadence. I focused on the sounds around me and the feeling of the paper in my fingers.

I sat on the edge of the bed and traced my name in his writing with my finger. I was scared to open it. Scared of what he might say. Scared of how I hurt him.

I laid myself down on the bed and finally opened it. I was not sure what I was expecting. Maybe a long and detailed description of how he felt about what I had done to him. But instead, it just said, 'I'm sorry. I love you – Always – Jonathan.' Maybe I was expecting more words to magically appear. A real explanation. An accusation. Something more. But I just stared.

I didn't know what to do next. I didn't know what to do with this note. I didn't know if Tiffany or his mother were notified. His cell phone was in his pocket. His mother was still his in case of emergency contact. Was I supposed to notify the officers of this note? I didn't know. I didn't care. I couldn't deal with it, so I took two of the Xanax and let it carry me off to sleep.

I woke up in the late evening with my phone ringing and vibrating against my body. My eyes blurry, I looked at the screen. A picture of Tiffany and Jordan, Tiffany's name scrolling across the screen. "Hello?" I could barely speak with my tongue thick and dry and my head fuzzy.

"Morgan, when were you going to call us and tell us?" She was crying.

"Tiffany? I don't know. I didn't know if they called you. I didn't know if you knew what he had planned. And frankly, I couldn't deal with it. I found him. He did it here so I would find him. I was made to see him. I was forced to see him like that."

"'This is on you." She was sobbing. "You did this to him."

"Tiffany, I don't need this right now."

"You are so selfish. You only thought of yourself from the start. Never considering him. Never considering what he dealt with. I told him to be careful."

I hung up. I didn't say anything else. I mean, what was there to say anyway? I looked at the time, it was 10:30.

I took another Xanax and slept. It was after eleven in the morning when I woke up again. It was a police officer pounding on my door that woke me. I was still holding Jonathan's note in my hand.

I made my way down the stairs and opened the door to let him in. It was the same officer who rode to the hospital in the ambulance and sat with me in the room. Jiminez.

"Ms. Hale, I'm sorry, but I need to ask you a few follow up questions. Did Mr. Staley leave a note?"

"Actually, yes. He did." I handed it to him and walked away into the kitchen.

He followed me.

I proceeded to pop a k-pod into the Keurig and stick a mug in the machine. "Coffee?" I asked him as he sat at my table and opened the note.

"No, thank you." He was staring at the note. "This is all he said?"

I stood with my back to him watching the cup fill with coffee. I nodded. There was a lump in my throat making it hard for me to answer verbally.

"Do you know why he would do it?"

I grabbed my full mug, added a touch of cream into the steaming mug, and sat across from him. "I cheated on him. He found me. He struggled with mental health issues. I was careless. Thoughtless."

"I've been doing this for a few years now. This isn't my first suicide call. I've learned a lot. I can tell you, Ms. Hale, this isn't your fault. You can't blame yourself for the actions of others." No matter what he said, I couldn't bring myself to buy into it.

"In this case, I can." I sipped my coffee and stared at the note in his hand. Jonathan, the prolific writer of beautiful award-winning prose, his last words. Scant. Bare. Without detail or explanation. This in and of itself spoke volumes. He made his life making an impact with his words. These few words were louder than all the rest. But you had to really know him to see it. His choice to use so few words spoke so many more volumes. He left it unsaid but known. It was the biggest "fuck you for what you have done" he could give. I wasn't worthy of his words.

Jiminez looked at me across the table and I could feel his pity.

"This is going to be ruled a suicide. Everything now is just a formality. It will be a few days and the body will be released and you can proceed with making arrangements."

"His sister and mother I'm sure will be claiming him. I don't think I'm going to be welcome for that."

"I encourage you to still get your closure. Whether or not you are welcomed by his family."

"I think I had enough closure."

Jiminez got up. I stood also. "It's okay. I can see myself out. If you need anything," he handed me a card from his pocket, "call me."

I took the card and set it in front of me on the table and watched him walk out. He left the note. It was useless.

~ *IV* ~

Pills, Prayers, and Forgiveness

The Present

Emma

"IS IT WRONG THAT I fell in love after what I did?" Emma asked Dr. Bennett. Instead of sitting in her normal seat she was standing by the window feeling the waxy emerald-green leaves of a plant, looking out at the gray and raining weather outside. *I miss the feeling of rain. The smell of rain. Hard to believe in less than twenty-four hours I will be able to be outside. Back in the world.*

"Why would it be wrong?" It was their last meeting before she was to be released and he was still not giving her any answers.

I'm not going to say it. Outside of her elocution, she did not speak it out loud again. "You know why."

"You still haven't forgiven yourself. Everyone else in the world seems to have forgiven you. Why have you not forgiven yourself?"

"I went across the country in an effort to make sense of what I did. Instead of making sense of it, I fell in love with Morgan. I tried to bury my past only to confront it. And now Morgan has reinserted herself back into my life. I feel guilty. Not worthy of her love and affection. I called her a few nights ago. It was nice to actually hear her voice. She also sent me this journal where she chronicled her story about her fiance's suicide and how she felt or actually still feels responsible. I think she feels that her role in his death is equivalent to my role in Bailey's death."

"Is it?"

"No. He was a broken man when they started their relationship. I think he was on that path to take his own life regardless of what she did to him. She just gave him the excuse."

"How do you feel about the comparison?"

Emma made her way back to the chair. "I feel it's unfair for her to think that it's the same."

"Do you think you get to own being the worst person in the room?"

"No."

"Is she entitled to feel her guilt?"

"I mean I guess so. But she bears no real responsibility in Jonathan's suicide. None. She was made to feel that way by his family. By him. Things happen. She shouldn't have cheated on him. Repeatedly. But cheating on someone shouldn't result in a lifetime of guilt. Or death, for that matter, either." *She cheated and it resulted in Jonathan's death. Bailey cheated and it resulted in her death.*

"But you said she knowingly cheated on him, knowing that he was fragile mentally. Do you think you might be idealizing her somewhat?"

"You are never going to get me to agree on this."

"Emma, you were an attorney. Think about both sides." The word 'were' made her bristle.

"Easier said than done on certain things."

The blessed knock on the door for the session to end and Emma to be returned to her cell. "Saved by the bell."

Emma stood up and looked at Dr. Bennett. "I get what you're saying. I get your philosophy."

"Emma Landry, it has been a pleasure. Best of luck back in the real world. Keep doing the work. And think about what I said. Consider both sides with Morgan. She's not a saint."

Emma closed her eyes and exhaled. *Don't make me do this. I am not going to participate in this activity.* She had been willing to do all the work given to her. She wanted to do it. A willing participant in anything that would help her make sense of her life and what she had done. But this was something she felt no right to do. Allowing Morgan to lower herself to the guilt and shame of being responsible for the death of another was not going to be something she was willing to do. She knew Morgan. She knew the light, witty, sweet woman with beautiful energy and a softness and vulnerability she'd never before witnessed.

She walked back to her cell, silent. Her mind was reeling.

She sat at her small desk and pulled out her paper and began to write.

My Beautiful Morgan,

I know I don't write or call as often as you want me to. I've also been taking my dear sweet time with your journal. I need to absorb it. I need to understand your words and your story and process it the way it deserves to be processed.

You are not responsible for Jonathan's death. You are not a killer. It's not in your nature. Were you capricious and careless? Perhaps. But you did not intend or set out to harm or hurt Jonathan.

I know, though, how guilt can eat away at your sanity and the nightmares invade your thoughts and days when you bear the brunt of that guilt. You have alluded to the spiral you went down after you found him. It breaks my heart to think you carried that, and to this day continue to carry such guilt.

I know nothing I say will absolve you of these feelings. I wish only for you to know that in my eyes, given what I know and having read your story, I can never see you as the cause of Jonathan's demise.

Don't write back to the prison. I'm moving to the halfway house. I will call or write from there. Not sure yet what the rules will be.

With Love,

Emma.

EMMA FOLDED THE PAPER AND put it in an envelope. By the time the letter reached Morgan she would be almost technically free.

Morgan

MORGAN WAS EXHAUSTED AS SHE got into her car. The night before she stayed out way too late with Sara.

Sara was definitely her type though, and she caught herself flirting a lot more than she intended to. Sara was definitely flirting back. She was conflicted on whether or not she should feel guilty about this.

After kissing her goodnight, Sara promised to reach out to Morgan in a few days after learning Morgan was taking a trip to San Diego for a few days. Morgan looked longingly at Sara and contemplated asking her to come inside, but guilt held her at bay.

She was obsessed by Emma's last letter. And Emma. Always on her mind. Emma. What was the deal with her and Emma anyway? The possessive use of 'My' in the salutation of the letter both touched her and scared her. 'My Beautiful Morgan.'

Morgan had gotten an early start on the road despite the lack of sleep. She spent almost the entirety of the day in the car. When Morgan arrived in Tahoe from San Diego she had been strung out and the long hours of sitting in the car hadn't bothered her. Now she was making her way south-west back to San Diego, for the first time in years. She barely stopped to refuel and get something to drink. Her eyes were tired and her back stiff from the hours of sitting.

The air was dryer and warmer and the sun was setting. The traffic was definitely something she didn't miss at all. She couldn't remember how much time had passed since she fled this town. It was a period in her life she chose not to dwell on. It was her rock bottom and filled with shame at her ineptitude in handling life as a functioning adult, and destructive love affairs which ruined and ended lives.

Morgan found a hotel near downtown and parked in the self-parking structure. She winced at the price of parking, she didn't remember parking being so exorbitant when she lived here. Or maybe it was, and she was just used to it. The hotel lobby boasted high ceilings and black and white tiled floor, faux crystal chandeliers and a replica art deco ceiling above, giving the place a swankier and trendier feel than it probably rated. Morgan could see the boats tethered to the marina across the street. A deep part of her missed living here. San Diego is technically a big city, but it is a small, big city, and the overall vibe being relaxed, it was a good mix of city and suburbia. Bars were filled with regulars mixed with tourists and most people were pleasant, unlike when you drove up to LA.

Just being here made her miss the life she threw away. Blurry vision from tears overcame her as she looked out the window at the marina and tried to control her emotions.

Once she got into her room, she opened the curtains and looked out, seeing the last of the sun sink below the horizon. She let out a sigh and moved back to the bed and flopped on her back, reaching for the phone. She passed up food stops all day and was starving.

She picked up the receiver and ordered an Impossible Burger from room service. Even though it had been over two years since Emma left, she was still trying her best to abide by a vegetarian diet.

For a brief moment, she scrolled through the contacts in her phone and considered calling some of her old friends to get together. But that was not what this trip was about so she thought better of it and turned on the television instead. Besides, most of them hadn't even heard from her since Jonathan died. It would just be weird and awkward, and she was definitely no longer the person they remembered her to be.

Room service came and she picked at the burger and tried to follow along with a true crime documentary on the television. Her mind was on whether or not she was doing the right thing by reopening the possibility of a life with Emma. Literally every relationship she started ended badly. Why try again? And then Sara. But so far, Sara was casual. She didn't see anything really escalating right now. But that kiss held promise.

After a restless night's sleep, Emma's most recent letter playing in her mind ('My Beautiful Morgan'), she woke up early and showered and dressed. She made her way past the lobby and retrieved her car. As the sun was rising and the sky was streaked with pink and gold, she drove to the cemetery and found her way amongst the generic and flat tombstones until she found Jonathan's stone. The grass was recently mowed, and no one else was around. In a nearby tree, she could hear crows cawing to one another to greet the day.

Cross-legged she sat at the foot of Jonathan's grave after placing a few long-stemmed white roses at the head of the stone. "It's been years since you died. I still think about you all the time. But I think you know that. I loved you. But I think you know that, now, too. Maybe you didn't know it when you made the choice to end your life. But I think you know it now. I think you gain a certain wisdom when you cross over. You see things more as they should have been seen. Maybe I'm lying to myself in an attempt to feel better for my part in your not being here.

"I wonder so often what our life would have been like. Our kids. Our home. Whether or not we would have stayed here in San Diego. I picture you publishing your books and becoming a best-selling author. You had so much talent.

"But you made the choice you made. Despite my part in it. *You* made that choice. It was *not* the choice I would have made for you.

"I moved up to Tahoe. It's a quiet life. Not the life I planned. Nothing I planned seemed to come to be. How does the saying go? Life is what happens when you are busy making other plans.

"I thought you were the great love of my life. The only person I would ever really love, but I met someone. She's unfortunately in prison right now. She killed her wife. And I know it sounds crazy that I would fall in love with her, but she's actually not a bad person. She was driven to what she did after her wife betrayed her. You took your own life after I betrayed you. It's a weird parallel. I know. But it works.

"Anyway, I think you would like her. She's very deep. Thoughtful. Mercurial, like you. She reminds me of you in a lot of ways. But I don't know if we are really supposed to be together. It's a whole thing. I have another new person, too. But it's just casual. But really, I'm okay. I am.

"I came here to make peace. To let my ghosts of you go. To let go of my guilt. I have to. I can't keep carrying it with me. I need to let it go and live my life. I want to let it go and live. But honestly, I'm so stuck right now. I am afraid. Scared. I destroyed you. I hurt everyone I touched after you. Maybe I'm better off alone?

"I love you. I'm sorry. I'm forever sorry."

She sat in the stillness for a long time. Not sure what she was expecting to see or feel, or if there would be any real change.

Morgan finally stood and made her way back to her car and went to a coffee shop for breakfast.

Emma

EMMA'S LAST NIGHT IN PRISON, she couldn't sleep. Not because she was so excited to be getting out, but because she still struggled with her guilt.

Emma went through her belongings she had been allowed to keep in her cell. She slowly separated the items she was taking with her. Some of the books. Letters. Files. The rest she put in another box she would take to the fellow inmates in the morning and disperse to them.

She wrote a thank you note to Williams for being there for her. She wrote a thank you note to Dr. Bennett for helping her gain insight.

She still couldn't sleep.

She tossed on her thin rack and wondered what the bed in the halfway house would be like. It had to be better than this.

She grew excited about going back to the office. Brandon had kept her long-time secretary in place even while she was on the lam. She would have to buy a gift for her. Morgan may not be a saint, as Dr. Bennett put it. But Greta... Greta was definitely a saint.

Emma finally gave up on sleeping and grabbed Morgan's journal from the box.

Excerpt from Morgan's Memoir

I NEED TO EXPLAIN WHY I can't just let the ghosts of my guilt die so easily. It's not like I dealt with any of it in the most healthy of manners.

I ate the Xanax I was prescribed like candy. It was a month's prescription, and I tore through them in a matter of days. I didn't want to be seen as crazy. I wasn't crazy. Yet. I just wanted to be numb. I wanted to sleep. I wanted to wake up and this was all a bad dream. So that's what I did for days. Xanax and sleep. Sleep deep. Don't answer the phone. Don't talk to anyone. Just sleep.

Mom called me once their plane landed in Reno after returning from their vacation. I had avoided their calls since I first called them after Jonathan died. I just wanted to sleep, you know? I couldn't handle talking to them. "Morgan, when is the funeral?"

"The wake is the day before we were supposed to get married. I swear it's just Tiffany being passive aggressive. The funeral itself is at the church we were supposed to be getting married at. On our wedding day."

"Oh, baby. I'm so sorry. Dad and I are coming down tomorrow."

"Please don't, Mom. I can't deal with it. I'm not even going. I can't go. I can't face them." I had another Xanax in my hand. I just wanted to go back to sleep.

"Morgan, honey, you need to get closure. We will come and we will be there to back you up." Odd, coming from my mother. She was not one to offer to help or be there.

"No. Uh uh. I'm good, Mom. Just stay up in Tahoe. There's no need for you to come down here. I'm really not going. And I am not up for company."

"Do you know what funeral home? Dad and I should at least send flowers."

I gave her the name of the funeral home and made a hasty excuse to end the call.

Making the call took every bit of strength I possessed and required two more Xanis afterward.

Tiffany went out of her way to make it clear to me she was the one who would claim Jonathan's body and I had no more rights to him. She called me the night before the wake. "I don't want you there. You don't belong there." Who the fuck was she to say that to me? I loved him, too.

I didn't argue. But I didn't respect her wishes either. I let her have her say, and I hung up without any true acknowledgment of the call.

I was not lying when I told my parents I didn't want to go. But her telling me I was not wanted there made me want to go.

The morning of the wake, I had to find one of my black dresses. It required me to move the overturned chair away from the door, nudging it with my foot. I didn't want to upright it or move it too far and open the door to the closet. I refused to touch it since his body was removed. It stayed where it was left. How many days had passed since he took his life, I couldn't tell you. They all just blurred into one another.

Once I moved the chair – nudging it just a foot or two to the side – I just stared at the closet door. The door which held the belt in place so he could choke the life out of himself. So he could show me his pain. I could see his clothes neatly hung on one side of the closet and my own on the opposite side. His smell still lingered in the small space. I held one of his sweaters to my nose inhaling him. Smelling him made this more unreal. He couldn't be gone. His smell said this is unreal. That he is still here. He's just gone temporarily. I shook my head to bring reality back. Jonathan is dead. He was hanging from this closet door. He's not coming back. I hastily grabbed a black dress. Any black dress. It just so happened to be one Jonathan loved on me, once.

It was sexy, and tight, low cut. Probably inappropriate for the occasion, but I couldn't bear to go back into the closet with his smell so present in there and look for another dress. I looked in the mirror and I remembered the only other time I wore it. We were going to head up to LA to see *Wicked* at The Pantages. I could hear his voice in my head, "I don't know how I am going to make it the whole night looking at you in that dress without wanting to peel it off of you." His hands were all over me, lips against my neck. I dragged him out of the house by his tie like a leash to keep him from undressing me.

God, what did I do to the man? I slicked my hair back into a tight bun at the back of my neck to hide the fact I hadn't actually washed it in days, and put on my makeup, trying to keep it from smudging as I fought tears.

As I finished getting ready, I could hear my door open, "Morgan?" It was my mother's voice calling from the doorway.

I rushed down the stairs and into the arms of my mom and dad. They looked exhausted from traveling, but they were there and dressed in their funeral attire.

I took the last of my Xanax sitting in my car, before heading to the funeral home. I tried to be stealthy about it so as not to draw attention from my parents. We walked in, my parents flanked on each side of me, holding me up, and people saw me and whispered. I could hear them. "The audacity." "How dare she?" "Who does she think she is?" The whispers came from all around as I made my way to the casket. Tiffany apparently made all our business known amongst the mourners. Or maybe it was because my black dress was inappropriate. Jordan was standing near Tiffany. She narrowed her eyes at me and made it clear she was not okay with any of this. My mother kept her head held high and if she heard the whispers, she pretended not to hear them. My dad squeezed my hand tight.

I broke free from them. "Go sit down. I need to pay my respects." I could barely speak beyond the knot in my throat.

Looking around, I recognized a few of Jonathan's colleagues from New York. Some of his family members that lived out of state. It was a large crowd. Many of them were set to be in town for our wedding anyway. Today would have been our rehearsal luncheon, followed by a large dinner for the out of towners.

There were a few of our mutual friends there as well, but I made no effort to speak with them. I was focused on getting to the metal box with the remains of the man I loved. The man I destroyed.

They picked a sleek black casket with white satin lining. White flowers and plants and wreaths surrounded the coffin. It was tasteful, and I think he would have approved.

I made my way up the aisle ignoring the gossip and whispers. I kneeled at the side, with my hands on the rim. I studied his face. The funeral home did a beautiful job of making him look natural. He looked as he did in my bed so many times before. Asleep and peaceful. His lips were curled into a slight smile. My fingers brushed over his lips. They were cold and unresponsive. He was dressed in a black suit, with a silver tie. I put my hand on his chest, and it was empty. The warmth and steady beating gone. My throat was tight, and tears flowed uncontrolled.

I removed my hand and reached into my bag and pulled out the box with what would have been his wedding band and laid it in the casket with him. I don't know why I did it. I was compelled for him to still have it. I felt like it should have been with him. Hindsight, maybe it was tacky of me to assume it should be there. Or that I should be there.

I placed my hand on his, it was stiff and cold. A river of tears continued to pour. I wanted nothing more than to feel the warmth of his touch and his eyes to open and for him to tell me this was all a bad dream.

I don't know where she came from, but Jo was suddenly next to me. She approached slowly and silently and took me by surprise. "Who do you think you are? What gives you the right to be here? He's in that box because of you. You killed him. You! Killed! Him! Destroyed him!" She was shouting at me.

Like an abused dog, I cringed away from her. I moved from the bench where I was kneeling and backed away hoping not to bump into anyone, but not taking my eyes off of Jo. I wanted to apologize to her. I wanted to wrap my arms around her and tell her I never meant to hurt anyone. Words were failing me, and my brain refused to come up with a logical way of explaining any of it to her.

She reached into the casket where I left the ring box, and she pulled it out. Flinging it hard, aiming for my head, it whipped past me – I could feel the breeze of it graze my cheek as it flew past me – and hit the wall behind me with a thud, popping open. The platinum band with the row of inlaid diamonds sparkling garish in the overhead lighting. "Get out of here! Go! You disgusting bitch!" Her fists were clenched as she screamed at me and stomped her feet. Her brown eyes – Jonathan's brown eyes – red rimmed and tears streaked down her cheeks.

I looked over at Jordan and she glanced away. She blamed me, too.

The funeral director came in and took my arm. "Miss, I think it's best you go."

My parents were out of their seat, and Mom went to approach Jo, who shook her head at my mother; if looks could kill, my mother would have dropped dead on sight. "Don't you dare say a word to me," Jo spat in her direction.

Tiffany was standing near the door. She opened it for me to exit. "I hope to never see you again," she hissed as I exited the building.

Part of me wished my parents would have respected my wishes and not come. But instead, they were here and forced to witness my humiliation.

I went home, peeled off the black dress crawling into one of Jonathan's Northwestern sweatshirts and a pair of pajama bottoms. I poured a glass of wine for myself and my parents.

"They were all so angry with me. I put Jonathan's ring in the casket with him, and Jo pulled it out and threw it at me while she screamed. I'm so embarrassed." I spoke it aloud as if they hadn't just witnessed it for themselves.

Dad put his arm around me. "I'm sorry. They are hurting, too. They can't see past their own pain right now."

I sniffled and wiped my tears. "I lost him, too. And our whole future. I know what I did was wrong. I know I fucked up. But I lost him. I loved him."

"Are you going to the actual funeral after that shit show?"

"I don't know. I don't know anything right now. I just want to sleep. I want to sleep and wake up and this was all a dream."

"Alright. Alright." Mom was rubbing slow circles on my back while I cried.

"Why don't you try to get some rest and we will clean up here and go back to our hotel room. We will see you in the morning."

Later, as I tried to sleep, I saw Jonathan. It was the first time I 'saw' him after he died. He was not the handsome and sweet man I loved, nor was he the handsome man in the casket. He was the purple, bloated and disfigured thing I had seen hanging from the closet door.

And he was hanging there. On the closet door. But he was struggling and banging against the door. Choking and gasping and gagging. And banging again and again. I was crying and couldn't look away.

"Jonathan, please… I'm sorry. I'm so sorry."

He just struggled harder, bulging eyes looking through me.

"I know you don't believe me! But I am sorry! I love you! I love you! I never meant to hurt you." I was shaking and I couldn't move away, and I couldn't look away.

I watched him struggle and choke all night. Listening to the banging and gasping and choking.

As the daylight finally broke through the window, the vision or ghost or hallucination or whatever it was, dissipated. It took me a long while, sitting in my bed, still staring at the closet door, choking sounds echoing in my mind before I could peel myself up and out of the bed and down to make coffee.

I needed closure. The all-night taunting of his spirit told me this. That's what I convinced myself anyway, while sipping my coffee at the table.

I resolved to go have my peace with Jonathan and go to the church for the funeral. I didn't care about how Tiffany and Jo ordered me away from the wake. I had the right to be there, too.

Again, I moved around the overturned chair and stood in the place where he gasped his last breath, forcing myself to open the door. I held my breath before stepping in. I pulled another black dress from my closet and re-did the tight bun at the back of my head. On his bedside table, his rosary sat with its ruby red glass beads coiled next to the lamp and the book he had been reading. I grabbed it as I moved out of the room.

My parents showed up and we went to a small breakfast joint before going to the church. I just sat in the booth and stared at my toast and pushed my eggs around my plate. I wasn't hungry. I was out of Xanax to help me through this.

We made our way into the church and sat in the back pew. Light filtered through the stained glass, and ceiling fans spun in slow circles above. This was the church we were supposed to be married in. This was supposed to be our wedding day. I listened as the priest talked about forgiveness and sins being washed away. He was asking us to forgive Jonathan's spirit for leaving us. Jonathan's casket lay open behind the priest, under the crucifix. The colors of the stained glass made him look like he was alive – just sleeping. An elaborate prank. But I knew despite the tricks the lights played, he was dead. The sound of his choking and gasping echoed in my head.

His rosary was clenched in my hands. The smooth glass beads were hot in my hands from my desperate clutching of them. I could feel the points of the metal crucifix dig into the flesh of my palm. Being what I called a Casual Catholic, I didn't even know how to recite the rosary, and never went to confession. I was capable of reciting a few standard prayers, but I never prayed for forgiveness nor really ever bought into any of it. But here I was – holding this rosary and begging for God to forgive me. Forgive Jonathan. Give us both peace. Just give us peace.

I was sitting on the end, my mother to my left and my father next to her. I really wished they weren't there and yet was grateful they were there at the same time.

My eyes were tear filled as I looked at the suspended figure of Christ hanging on his cross over the podium, looking down at all of us. I felt small and pathetic.

The priest brought Tiffany up to speak. She stood in front of the church and her eyes found me in the back. I looked at her pleadingly, hoping the words of the father had sunk in.

"Today, we were supposed to be gathered here to witness my brother get married. I never thought he would get married. He was such a nerd. Always studying. Always with his nose in a book. Always busy looking at life from the analytical standpoint. He had to break everything down. All the time. Always seeking answers. He was sensitive. He hurt easily. He couldn't stand to see suffering or unkindness. And then – he met someone. When he got home from their very first date, he told me she was the one. He was in love. He was going to spend the rest of his life with her. I was happy for him. Cautiously optimistic." Tiffany's eyes did not break from mine. She stared me down as she spoke. Her words were not written down but came extemporaneously from her lips. She paused, still not breaking eye contact with me.

She took a deep breath and continued, "Jonathan was younger than me by four years. He was my baby brother, and I took a solemn oath to always protect him and love him. To be there for him, no matter what. I was there for him when he was diagnosed as a teenager after he tried to take his life. I was there when he graduated from college and from graduate school. Through break ups and make ups. I had seen him through fits of fancy and ups and downs. He was a hopeless romantic. He believed in love. He wanted to be loved. He wanted to give of his heart. He wanted a forever. And he thought he found it.

"When he proposed to this woman, I thought I was handing off my duty as protector to her. I had no idea she would be the cause of his destruction. She would be the reason we are here, not for a wedding, but for a funeral. She took advantage of his love and his goodness, and she put out the flame that lived within his heart and soul. And here she sits in this church, playing the victim and preying upon the sadness of my family."

Slowly all the heads turned and looked at me, and the whispering and gasping and faux outrage bubbled up from the pews in whispers and murmurs in front of me as accusing eyes narrowed at me.

Finding a steely composure from deep within myself, I stood up – my mom hissed for me to sit down and I ignored her and walked up the aisle – not in the white dress I never picked up from the tailor, in a slow wedding march as it was supposed to be on this day, with my father at my side – but a deliberate walk, alone in my black dress, not breaking eye contact with Tiffany, until I was next to her. I spoke loud enough for the entire church to hear me, "I loved him. Despite what you think you know. I loved him." I held out my hand with his rosary coiled in my palm. "Take it. It was his. He would want it." When she didn't take it from me, I spilled it onto the open pages of the Bible on the pulpit, the beads rattling as they spilled out of my palm.

I went to the casket and kneeled before it one last time. I placed a final kiss on Jonathan's cold, dead, unmoving lips and walked back down the aisle. My parents stood as I reached their aisle and got in line behind me as I continued to walk.

I stopped at the door and turned and looked at Tiffany standing cold. "It's a shame the beautiful words of forgiveness have been lost on your ears. Jonathan believed in forgiveness. Jonathan would be ashamed of how you acted yesterday and today." I retained no right to speak for him, but I believed it to be true.

My parents drove me home and I convinced them to leave me alone after much fussing about. I convinced them to head back to Tahoe and I would call them tomorrow. I watched them leave from my bedroom window.

I left my house and made my way to where I knew he was to be buried later in the day. I sat in my car several rows away. The mound of dirt that would soon be covering his casket loomed near the open grave he would be placed in. It seemed like forever before the hearse pulled in followed by the caravan of mourners. I hung back and away, unseen as I watched him lowered into the ground. Flowers were dropped on the shiny black metal, one by one by the mourners. Tiffany and Jordan held Jo up as she dropped hers in. As she released the white rose, a cry escaped her lips. Her cry, primal and undignified, ripped through my chest as it echoed across the cemetery.

Holy water from the priest followed.

I waited, watching from my car, until the last person left, and the tractor dumped the last pile of dirt on the casket. The sound of the engine grinding and the dirt hitting the metal box echoed in my ears. I thought about putting the radio on, but instead just listened to the engine and watched the dirt fall on quite possibly the only person I'd ever been in real love with.

Once the cemetery was empty, everyone had gone, and the sky had gone dark, I emerged from my car and made my way to his grave. I laid myself out on the cold dirt covering the casket and filling the hole. The exhaustion of not having slept in over twenty-four hours was hitting me hard. The sky grew darker, and the temperature grew colder. I didn't have a sweatshirt or blanket. But I didn't really register being cold, I was too tired. Drained and emotionally exhausted, I just laid there in the dirt, willing him to come back to me somehow. I cried and begged him to come back.

There is no telling how long I laid there in the dark, crying alone before I dozed off. Peaceful and content, curled into a fetal position as I slept, I was awoken by a flashlight glaring into my face. "Ma'am. Excuse me, ma'am. You can't sleep here. Do you have a home?"

I sat up, shielding my eyes. "Yes. I'm sorry. This is my fiancé. We were supposed to be married today. Instead, we buried him." I was crying despite myself.

"I understand. You need to go home now, though." He offered a hand to help me up, which I took. "Are you okay to drive?"

"I am. I haven't been drinking."

He helped escort me to my car, and his car stayed behind mine for several miles as I drove back home.

When I got home, Jonathan's car was gone from the street in front of my condo. Tiffany or Jo must have come and retrieved it.

I let myself in, trailing dirt from the grave in my wake and stripped off my dress, covered in earth, which left a small pile on the floor of my bathroom, and took a shower.

I watched as the soil stuck to my bare flesh from his grave melted down the drain.

I managed to get myself into the bed and collapsed into my pillows and looked forward to the nothingness of sleep. I willed for a night of sleep so maybe in the morning I could figure out what I needed to do to regroup and get my life back on track. Begin to make sense of what happened.

As I drifted off, I could hear the banging on the closet door again. I could hear the gasping and choking. I put the pillow over my head and tried to drown it out. I looked over and there he was again. Distorted. Eyes bulging, purple faced, swollen. Banging and choking.

I got up and took my pillows and blanket to the living room and laid on the couch. But I could still hear him. The sound echoed from the bedroom down to the living room, reverberating off the walls and into my ears.

This went on all night. No matter what I did or where in the house I went, I could hear him.

Only while I was not in the room, I could hear him choke out my name. "Morgan! Morgan! Come see what you made me do!" It was strained and anguished and garbled. But it was repeated over and over with the loud banging against the door.

I was exhausted. I was distraught. I was guilt ridden. I was angry. I was hurt. I was a mess.

Again, it all faded when daylight came. I found the card the psychiatrist gave me and called to see if I could get in on an urgent appointment. The kind-hearted secretary squeezed me in, and I drove to the office.

I tearfully confessed to the psychiatrist how I felt I might need to be admitted because I was losing my mind, or maybe I had already lost it. I was shaking and my eyes were red. My hope and prayer was how the doctor would likely admit me and sedate me back into a comatose state until I felt better.

He looked at me devoid of expression as I spoke and scribbled on a prescription pad and handed it to me. It was a refill of Xanax and a prescription for Klonopin.

I left his office and went down the hall and down the elevator to the pharmacy and filled them. The pharmacist explained to me how to take them and the interactions. I didn't bother to listen. How hard is it? Take a pill and swallow it. Feel better.

Exhausted and drained of emotion, I went home and popped both pills and downed them with a glass of wine, curling up on the couch with the news on to drown out any potential noise from the bedroom. I slept for almost twenty-four hours.

When I woke up, there were several missed call alerts. Friends were checking on me. Family. People who tried to be there for Jonathan's funeral who were not there because I never bothered to share the information. Posts had been made and gossip made its way around. People knew how Tiffany and Jo treated me at the wake and the funeral. Screenshots of the gossip were texted.

Voicemails of, "That's so fucked up. I'm sorry. Girl, if you need me, call me." Text messages, 'I heard about the funeral drama. I hope you are okay. Let me know. I'm here.'

A message from Sunny: "I'm so sorry. I heard through the grapevine what happened after I left. I should have left well enough alone. I hope you are okay. I'm still here if you need me."

I turned my phone off and tossed it on the table. I couldn't deal with any of it.

I dropped off my letter stating I was not able to work right now from the psychiatrist to my district. The letter gave me thirty days to sort through my trauma and get my life together. Those thirty days would carry me through to the end of the school year. I would burn through my sub time, but I didn't care. Dock my pay, I have bigger things to deal with.

I went to the cemetery and sat at Jonathan's grave. "I'm sorry. I know you don't believe me, but I am. Please forgive me. Stop coming to the house. Let me heal, now."

I just sat there, again waiting for the sun to fall. I cried and I stared numb at the mound of dirt on top of his coffin. I stared dumbly at his name on the stone. It was surreal. It was like I was in some fucked up nightmare dreamscape.

Jonathan had brought up that as little girls we are raised to believe love fixes everything. That was Jordan's hope when she went above and beyond to put us together. I wondered if she was blaming herself right now. But she believed in love as so many of us were taught to. To love someone and for them to love you in return is all it takes to make everything right in the world. What a fucking lie. What an absolute fucking lie. My love destroyed a human. My love left a wake of destruction. It destroyed Jonathan. Jonathan's destruction left me broken and psychotic.

I went home, numb and exhausted. I took the pills prescribed to me and attempted to sleep in the bed. I laid down and pulled the blankets up and around me. I put the television on low in the background to lull me into a sleep state. I put on CNN as Jonathan used to and listened to the voice of the anchor as he dissected a breaking news story. I had never been one to sleep with it on until Jonathan came into my life. He liked to fall asleep with the news on low. It was like the information would seep into his mind and he would wake up with inspiration.

I don't know if I fell into a dream state or if Jonathan's spirit was truly there. But his disfigured body, instead of hanging from the closet, was now next to me in the bed. It smelled putrid. The bulging eyes stared at me accusing me of all I had done to hurt him. I was stuck. I tried to wake up, but I couldn't, which led me to believe I wasn't really dreaming, but I was awake.

His cold hands reached out for me. I could feel his fingers touch my face. He was choking out words I couldn't understand. His voice was hoarse from the crushed windpipe and his words muddled by the swollen tongue. I was stuck in this suspended state between dream and reality, unable to move. Letting his cold, dead fingers touch my face, listening to his choked words, smelling his rotting flesh.

I couldn't move. I couldn't wake. I couldn't scream. I was frozen and helpless.

When daylight broke, my eyes flew open. I was alone, but the pillows next to me, I swore bore the indentation of a head having lain there. I threw them across the room. Shaking, feeling unrested and sick I fled from my bed. My head was swimming and I barely made it to the toilet as the acid rose from my gut to my throat to my mouth.

I didn't know who to talk to about this. Absolutely positive I was going crazy, I was afraid to talk to anyone I knew. Feeling a need to get out of my house, I drove around aimlessly for a while. After swinging through a *Starbucks* and picking up a coffee I drove some more, without destination or purpose.

At a loss of where to turn, I found myself at the church, and asked to see the priest who presided over Jonathan's funeral. I was ushered to a small office.

"What can I do for you?" the priest asked as I sat across from him. He possessed a gentle smile and soft voice.

"What does suicide do to a soul?" I asked him.

He leaned forward over the desk, looking me in my eyes, his smile fading. "Are you thinking about hurting yourself?"

"No. You presided over the funeral for Jonathan Staley. He was my fiancé. He killed himself."

"Ah, yes. I remember. I remember you. You brought his rosary. I was able to get it into the casket with him. Are you a Catholic?"

I felt a small sense of relief knowing the rosary made its way into the casket. I wondered briefly if Tiffany knew. I tried to switch gears back to his question as he looked patiently at me waiting for my answer while I was busy thinking about the rosary. "Kind of. I was raised Catholic. Baptized. We were going to be married by the other Father at this church. I was never confirmed, though." My leg was vibrating up and down fast, and my head felt foggy with the lack of rest. I fidgeted with my *Starbucks* cup.

"Have you ever studied the Bible or theology?"

"No. Not really. It's never been my thing. I know suicide is a sin akin to murder though."

"There are a lot of ways to think about it and consider it. I believe, from what I heard from the family, Jonathan was a tortured soul. He was seeking relief from that suffering. He was a good person otherwise. Kind, and charitable. I believe God doesn't just dole out punishments based on one bad deed but looks at the overall content of the person who has passed on. One sin cannot wash away a life of goodness, no matter how grave."

"Can souls be stuck? Like ghosts?"

"What exactly are you trying to ask, child?"

"I think Jonathan's soul is stuck in our home." I explained how Jonathan took his life in our home, and what I witnessed over the past few nights.

"Would you like me to come bless the home?"

"Is that something you can do? Will it help? Will it help his soul get rest if it's stuck?"

"It can't hurt." His gentle smile returned.

"Am I crazy? Or is this really happening? Is he stuck? Or is it me? Father, I need help." I was crying.

"I can't answer that."

"When can you come over and do this?"

"I can come after the services are concluded on Sunday," he said after consulting a large calendar on the desk.

It was a Thursday. "Is there anything I can do meanwhile?"

He grabbed a small empty glass jar and led me to the baptismal font, brimming with holy water. He dipped the jar in, filled it, sealed it with a silver lid, and handed it to me. "This should help. Sprinkle it in the areas you are experiencing his spirit. Say a Hail Mary and an Our Father. Ask the Holy Father to have mercy on his soul."

I gave my address and confirmed the meeting for Sunday and left with the bottle of holy water clutched in my fist.

Not ever having been a person of faith, this all felt like some superstitious bullshit and I doubted it would work, but I was willing to try anything. I was desperate.

I walked in my front door and stood still. I used to love my home. I looked forward to being there and it felt good and cozy. But now, I was dreading each moment there, waiting to see or hear Jonathan torment me for driving him to suicide. I went through the rooms of the condo and sprinkled the water on the closet door and the bed. I said the prayers as instructed. "Please God, have mercy on his soul. Have mercy on me. I'm so sorry for all that I've done." I felt the apology from the depths of my being. I was truly repentant. I wanted His forgiveness for both Jonathan and myself.

I did not feel any different for having done what the priest asked of me. I just sat on the couch with the television on to drown out my thoughts. I was not really processing anything on the screen. I drank a glass of wine, and picked at the dinner that was delivered, stomaching only a few small bites.

When the sun went down, I took my pills and passed out in the bed hoping for a good night's sleep.

I could hear choking and laughing. I could almost make out the words, though I refused to look, laying on my side so I was facing away from Jonathan's side of the bed. "You don't even believe in that bullshit. You have to believe for it to work," is what it sounded like he choked out. I could feel his icy fingers pull down the blanket and touch my waist like he was spooning me. Ice down my back, up against my body. Icy breath breathing on my neck.

I was crying, begging God to forgive him, and for him to forgive me.

Again, I was paralyzed in this state. I couldn't wake. I couldn't move. I was stuck.

Cold and putrid, he was up against me, holding me close. Breathing and choking into my neck as his fingers pressed into my hip and his face burrowed into my neck. I just cried, frozen and incapable of moving away or waking. "Morgan, why don't you love me anymore?" He choked out the words, the cold spit hitting my neck.

As daylight finally broke through the windows, when I finally could wake and move, I looked over at his side of the bed. I didn't have any recollection of ever putting the pillows I had thrown back on the bed, but they were there, and the indentation of his head was apparent. Acid in my stomach was beginning to rise and my head was swimming.

I threw them again. This time I got up, the room was spinning, and a clammy sweat covered my body, and opened the closet and threw them in, before running to the bathroom to vomit.

Later in the day, instead of returning home, I got a hotel room. I thought perhaps if I was not home, he couldn't follow me elsewhere. If he was stuck, wouldn't he be stuck at the house where he took his life?

I was wrong.

I took my pills with two small bottles of wine from the mini bar, expecting to sleep deep and relaxed. I nuzzled deep into the marshmallow like comforter and pillows.

Without opening my eyes, I could smell him. He was there. Sitting in the chair by the bed, choking and laughing at me all night. He laughed mercilessly while I cried, prayed, and was forced to stare at him. Unable to wake (was I dreaming though?) and move.

There was no avoiding him. And these pills were not helping me. I would wake feeling exhausted and terrified and sick.

After yet another sleepless night, and morning spent bent over the toilet expelling what little I had been able to eat the night before, I took the remainder of the holy water and went to the grave site and dumped the bottle on his grave asking for forgiveness and asking God to forgive him and let him rest in peace. I sat there all day and through the sunset, praying, begging, and crying. The sprouts of grass starting to pop up, vibrant green in the brown dirt, made me nauseous all over again. I swallowed the acid and buried my head between my knees.

The sun sank below the horizon. Feeling the epitome of exhaustion, I again fell asleep at his grave site, and I was again awoken by the same kind police officer who previously shooed me off the grave.

With a flashlight shining in my face, his gentle voice, "You again. You know you can't sleep here." His voice was gentle.

I burst into tears. "I can't sleep at home. I can't sleep anywhere but here. He comes to me and it's not good."

His hand extended and he helped me up to my feet. "I'm not sure what that means, but I can't let you stay here."

"He haunts me. His ghost. He killed himself and he is not at rest. He comes to me no matter where I sleep, except here. I get to rest peacefully when I'm here with him." I tried to explain. But the second part being the only correlation I could come up with, was how Jonathan was keeping me close, I was scared to say out loud. I truly felt like I was hovering on the brink of insanity.

I made my way home, dreading each moment I would be forced to face Jonathan and my guilt.

I threw my keys in the bowl next to the door and made a pot of coffee. I didn't want to go back to sleep. I resolved myself to stay awake until the priest came to exorcise the spirit who was plaguing me.

By the time the priest came, I had been up for over twenty-four hours. "Do you think this will work?" My head was fuzzy, and I was exhausted.

He took my hands in his. "If you have faith, it will work."

I reached into the depths of my soul and tried to find some shred of faith left in me.

He said prayers and sprinkled more holy water. I followed him, holding onto his words and trying to breathe in faith from him. But how do you suddenly have faith when it's never been a thing for you? I was searching in my soul for it, but came up with nothing. My hope was riding on Jonathan's faith. If his soul was trapped, maybe this would speak to him and release him.

When he left, I took my pills and hoped for a restful night. Dozing off as the sun set, I clung to a feeling of peace and respite, but there he was again.

He had gone nowhere despite the pills and the prayers.

There was only a slight improvement. Jonathan was not bloated and rotting. He was as I fell in love with him. He was cleaned up and handsome as ever. Instead of the putrid smell of rotting flesh, he smelled of his freshly showered skin and cologne. A scent so specific and unique to him, it used to make me smile, even if he was not in the room. A reminder he was mine. Now, it struck a pit in my gut, and caused a lump in my throat.

He was sitting on the edge of the bed. I could feel the weight of him sinking into the mattress.

"Don't think to ask me to forgive you. There will be none of that."

"Jonathan, please."

"No, Morgan. You will learn you just don't get to do whatever you want, whenever you want. There are consequences in life."

"I never thought there wouldn't be any consequences." I was sitting up now. A vast improvement to the paralysis I previously experienced.

"That's such bullshit, Morgan. You tumble through your life not thinking of anyone but yourself. It's evident in how you treated me." He was nose to nose with me. I could feel the coldness of his body. His breath on my face was reminiscent of sitting in front of an AC vent on full blast. I could feel goosebumps spring up over my flesh.

"I promise you will never go another night where you get to rest and escape the consequences of what you did to me. To us. You don't get to rest as long as I don't."

I came up with no response for him. I just sat there staring into his dark brown eyes with tears flowing from my own.

"Do you know what today is? I've been in the ground ten days now. We should be coming home from our honeymoon right now. We were supposed to be living it up. A final night on a cruise through the Greek Isles. But I'm rotting, six feet under while you sit and play the victim. You are not the victim, Morgan."

"I never said-"

"Stop it! Stop your crying!" he roared and the wind from his breath blew me back, foul, sour, and cold.

It was a standoff. I sat holding back my tears while he just glared at me.

When the dawn broke through and the room lightened, I woke and he was gone. I was sitting up and stiff from hours of holding the position. I resigned myself to never sleeping again.

My head was spinning, and I was nauseous again. I got up and flushed the pills down the toilet, after throwing up whatever little food I managed to eat over the last day.

I wasn't escaping my own guilt. I felt plenty guilty for my role in Jonathan's death. I just could not deal with what I was seeing.

Maybe I was crazy? Maybe he really was haunting me. I really don't know. I know how it must sound though.

~ *V* ~

A Brand-New Life

The Present

Emma

THE DAY SHE CHECKED OUT of the prison, she gave Officer Williams her thank you letter she had written him. She gave away whatever possessions she wouldn't need or want to inmates with plenty of time left on their sentences. Williams followed her talking to her as her possessions were handed off. "It was an honor knowing you, Landry."

"I'm gonna miss you, Williams."

"Keep doing the good work on the outside, Landry. And stop beating yourself up, okay? Go get that girl of yours in Tahoe, too."

She smiled, bittersweet as he escorted her to collect her things. Emma was given her suit, her Rolex which once belonged to the grandfather she never met, her wallet, and paperwork instructing her to go check in at the halfway house. She carried a stack of files and books she collected and chose to take with her.

She put herself together in her bespoke suit with her watch and looked at herself in the mirror. *I look like myself. But I'm not the same. I will never, ever be the same person I was.*

Emma fought back her tears as Williams walked her to the gate where Brandon was waiting.

"How much time before I have to take you to the house?" Brandon asked after she put her box in the trunk and sat beside him in the passenger seat.

"I have to be there by 5pm for check in."

"Are you hungry?"

"What do you think? I need a decent meal." Emma grinned at him.

He reached into the glove compartment and handed her a new cell phone. "New number, new phone. New life." He smiled.

"Thank you, for everything." Emma looked at him earnestly, taking the phone and sliding it into the pocket of her jacket.

"Of course. Emma, stop thanking me. You would do the same for me. You are family to me."

Emma knew it was true. After thirty years of friendship, they were family.

Brandon navigated them to a restaurant they used to frequent on double dates with their wives. Emma was struck by a brief memory of Bailey and her walking together up to the door their last time here. Bailey glowing in the gas lamps lining the walkway. Fat snowflakes glittered in the moonlight and caught in Bailey's strawberry blonde hair. She shook her head to release the image.

Seated at the table Emma ordered a glass of wine and picked at the bread.

"How does it feel to be out in society?"

"I'm okay. It's weird. I know this doesn't make sense, but I kind of liked being inside. The world in there made sense to me. I was suited to it. It was all about routine and being on my own."

"You still are not sure you belong in the world or to be forgiven?"

"Kind of."

"Are you ready to get started back to work? I had Greta get the paperwork together to file for your non-profit. The application for you to reapply for the bar is waiting for you as well. I also filed for some interns to help you with the non-profit and getting going."

"I'm excited about that. I think it will help a lot. Just getting back into my career and doing something worthwhile with my life."

"Have you heard any more from Morgan?"

"Yeah. We've been writing and talking on the phone a bit. I need to find out what the policies are about contact when I get to the house. I think I want her to come visit. I need to see her. I need to be face to face with her so I can see what it is we really feel for each other after all of this. Now we know all our ugly histories, I wonder if it will still be the same for us."

After lunch he escorted her to the door of the halfway house where they were greeted by a manager. She was an older, stern woman with a large crucifix around her neck. "House rules, no sex, no drugs. You must give me your schedule for each week before Sunday evening. Unless you have an approved work schedule that requires you to work past 8pm, you need to be in the house before that time. No guests. Your cell phone will be turned in by 9pm each night and you can retrieve it by 6am each morning, unless you have to be at work with an approved schedule. After two months, you may have weekend passes to go home. You will be drug tested at random. Keep your space clean and clean up after yourself in any common area."

She looked at Brandon and hugged him hard. "Thank you. I will see you in the morning at the office."

The manager showed her to her room, which had two twin beds set up. "You have a roommate. Your bed is the one by the door. That's your dresser, and there is a shared desk. Share the closet accordingly."

Emma set her belongings on the foot of her bed. "Thanks," she said quietly. The manager walked out, and Emma sat at the desk and opened the screen of her phone. Brandon had loaded all her contacts in it for her. She scrolled through and found Morgan's number. Bailey absent from the contacts. *Indeed. A new life.*

She looked at it and considered hitting call but turned the screen off and decided to unpack instead.

Morgan

THE CAMPGROUND WAS FULL (EXCEPT for site 1170) and business was good. The bar was lively and filled with patrons and the paddle wheeler came in from another full tour of the lake.

She enjoyed her routine, and her life was settled into a simple checklist of daily duties. She kept the campground running along with its adjoining businesses. She maintained the schedules and daily operations of it, and it was not so bad. Her father rarely handled any of it any longer, allowing Morgan to make all decisions. He was ready to retire and hand it all off to her, and she had proved over the last three years to be more than capable. He barely asked questions any longer.

She had been texting and talking to Sara sporadically.

Sara was busy trying to get her life together up in Tahoe after relocating from the Inland Empire. And honestly, she was still conflicted as to how Sara and Emma each fit into her life.

She liked talking to Sara. A lot. She was a welcome distraction. She was sexy in an effortless kind of way (like Emma). She was smart and quick-witted (also like Emma). She bordered on over confidence at times (very much also like Emma). Morgan pondered if she was just trying to fill the hole Emma left with a knock-off version of her.

Morgan closed out her register and shut the shop down for the day and forwarded calls to her cell.

She stopped at the grocery store on her way home and picked up a bottle of wine and fresh spinach to make a salad for her dinner. She was a shitty cook, but she could manage a salad easily.

After making small talk with the cashier, Morgan drove home with a nagging loneliness eating away at her. At least Aaron and her parents will be happy she had plans to actually go out tomorrow.

She got back to her house and looked around at the cozy space and thought maybe she should get a cat, but laughed at the thought, as it would be cliche, the lonely cat lady. She missed Emma's little dog Charlemagne. In the time they spent together, often Charlemagne would be under her feet at the apartment, in Emma's RV, or often even at the store as she worked.

She unloaded her groceries and opened the bottle of wine and poured a glass as she began chopping the spinach and other toppings to throw into a bowl when her phone rang with an unlisted number. She sent it to voicemail.

The number called back, and she sent it again to voicemail. "Get the hint," Morgan mumbled.

A text message came across.

"Answer your phone. It's me. Emma."

The phone rang again and this time she answered. "I was just wondering if I was going to hear from you." Morgan smiled. She hated that Emma's voice still had that effect on her.

"It's been a big transition. I'm back in the real world. It's amazing how overwhelming it is after only a few years. I can't imagine those people who serve decades, what they have to deal with."

"What's it like?"

"The halfway house? Work? Being on the outside? Which part?"

"All of it. How's work going?"

"I can't actually be a lawyer until I'm readmitted to the bar because, well, I'm a felon. And honestly, it's not even guaranteed, but I can consult while I'm waiting for approval. So, I'm working with my best friend, former partner on setting up a non-profit to work with underprivileged people who are stuck with public defenders and assist in their defense and appeals. The house, well, it's like living with someone's strict church mom. That's whatever. So, I guess I'm getting by. How are you?" It all came out in an effortless, breathless rush.

"I'm good. Just happy to hear from you." Morgan had set aside her food prep to focus on Emma.

"What are you doing now?"

"I just got off work. I'm home now."

"Should we plan a reunion at some point? I will have weekends free in two more months."

"I mean, we can talk about it." Morgan, suddenly gun shy, couldn't explain her response. "I mean, I guess what I'm saying is, I would like more than a weekend."

"I would too. But I also really just want to see you. I think we need to see each other."

"I will think about it."

Emma was quiet on the other end. After a moment she changed the subject. "What are you doing now?"

"I'm making dinner and drinking a glass of wine."

"What kind of wine?"

"A red blend. I think you would like it."

Emma exhaled. "I miss wine. What are you making for dinner?"

"Spinach salad with strawberries, feta, chickpeas and vinaigrette."

"Now you are teasing me. Although, I don't think the wine pairs properly. I would have paired it with a rosé. Or a white Bordeaux. But I don't care for whites, so yeah, rosé."

"Not everyone is fancy like you. You're over there missing wine, and I am here missing you."

"I do miss you as well."

"Do you?"

Another sigh. This one defeated in sound. "Yeah. I do. Which is why I think we need to talk about a reunion. I don't want to. I wish I didn't."

"Wait. Why do you wish you don't?"

"I need to figure it out still, honestly. But I think mostly I just don't want to be responsible for someone else. But I need to explore the feelings more. You can't tell me you are feeling 100% all in right now either. I think we both have a lot of thinking and deciding to do."

"I understand. And you're right... I'm not 100% all in, as you say. Right now, it's easy because you're not here. It's a weird predicament we're in, isn't it?"

"Completely. I feel guilty for loving you. Wanting you. I feel like I'm holding you back from living your life."

"You're so not holding me back." Morgan paused thinking about Sara. She quickly deflected. "Have you been reading the journal?"

"Yes, actually. I have been. Why?"

"Where in it are you?"

"You are seeing Jonathan's ghost. Ten days after his funeral."

"Keep reading. You'll understand, eventually that us talking and exploring how we feel now that the truth is coming out, that you are not holding me back. Scary enough, it's the healthiest relationship I've ever had. And actually, it may be me holding you back."

"I don't know if that is sad, or not." Emma laughed softly.

"It might be a bit sad." Morgan was laughing, too.

After a bit of silence, Emma asked Morgan about her day to change the subject. After an hour longer on the phone, Morgan could hear a knock on a door in the background.

"I have to go. I have to turn my phone in to the house manager," Emma said, her voice carrying a note of sadness.

"For what it's worth, no matter how this all comes out in the end, I love you. Friend. Lover. Whatever we end as. I love you."

"Perfectly stated. Good night, Morgan. I love you, as well. No matter what."

Morgan hung up and poured another glass of wine and sat on the couch with her salad. She sat it on the coffee table and grabbed the remote. She streamed *Schitt's Creek* to break up the silence creeping in around her after hanging up the phone.

After a bite of salad and a sip of wine, she flinched. Emma was absolutely right. The salad paired miserably with the wine. She texted Sara and asked if she wanted to meet for a bite to eat and a drink.

A winky face and yes came across her screen in no time.

Emma

AFTER HANGING UP WITH MORGAN, and turning her phone over to the manager, she came back up to her room. Her roommate was a tweaker with questionable habits and hygiene.

Even though the salad Morgan described and the wine she picked up would pair poorly, Emma wished she was sitting with her at the round cherry wood table in her small apartment enjoying it with her. Even though she knew Morgan moved to a house since she left she missed the apartment. She knew if she was there, such a faux pas would not be an issue. She would have handled the meal and wine selection.

She missed cooking meals for Morgan in the small kitchen of her apartment or in her RV. She made the mistake of letting Morgan cook for her only once and decided it would never happen again.

Emma made a point to not keep anything of value at the house, not even her suits. She kept those hung in a closet at the office and chose to change there. She even locked her watch in her desk at the end of each day.

She found it hard to even be in the same room with the woman who fidgeted, and side eyed non-stop.

Emma grabbed Morgan's journal from the top of her dresser and sat on her bed and began to flip the pages looking for where she left off. She was careful not to dogear the pages, finding it disrespectful, choosing to use the silk bookmark ribbon attached to the spine instead.

She also flagged several sections with sticky notes and wrote out questions she had for Morgan when they were again face to face.

"What's that book?" her roommate asked.

"A journal from a friend."

"Why do you have it?"

"She wants me to read it, so I understand her situation better."

"Is she like your girlfriend?"

"She was."

"But she's not now?"

"Not exactly."

"So why are you reading her journal then?"

"Why do you care?"

"I'm bored."

"So read a book. Draw a picture. Something. I'm trying to read."

"Anyone tell you that you are kind of a bitch?"

"A few people, yes." Emma was not ruffled.

"Why are you like that?"

"Like what?"

"A bitch. Think you are better than me?"

"Nope. Not at all. But I am trying to read. So maybe now is a good time to shhhhh."

"I hope they give me a new roommate soon."

"Me too." Emma sighed and did her best to ignore the tweaker so she could focus on Morgan's words.

Excerpt from Morgan's Memoir

I DON'T KNOW WHAT IT was. I don't know if it was really Jonathan's spirit or manifestations of my feelings of guilt. I would like to say it was the latter, but I really just don't know. There were a lot of coincidences, like the pillows. But I could have been out of my mind in grief and not realized I put them back on the bed. I don't really know. I just know I didn't want to deal with it anymore. I couldn't.

After I flushed the pills, I called the first person since Jonathan's funeral. I had avoided everyone since he died. I didn't call a soul. I didn't return texts. I called my friend Lori and asked her if I could come over.

I met her in our high school sophomore history class, and we have stayed friends ever since. She married young and spawned two kids. We didn't see much of each other because she was always busy being PTA and soccer mom, and we didn't really relate to each other any longer. But she was stable and no matter how much time always passed, she cared and was easy to be around.

"Morgan, come on over. Please! I know things have to be tough for you right now," she gushed into the phone.

I tried to stomach some breakfast, but just ended up throwing it back up. I managed somehow to shower and made my way over there. Both of her kids were at school. Her husband made good money and their home was neat and well organized. She lived inland and north of San Diego, but they owned land and horses. It was always like a vacation going over there to visit. I was in need of distraction and needed to be around someone who would take my mind off of my increasing insanity and isolation.

I sat in her plush living room, and she brought in two glasses of wine and a cheese and meat board.

"What happened? Do you even want to talk about it? You and Jonathan seemed so happy together. I seriously thought this was it. You were finally going to settle down!"

I shook my head no. I didn't want to talk about it. What could I say? She was conservative. She had been with the same guy since we graduated high school. She wouldn't understand. She never did get my revulsion to relationships or domestic life. Plus, how do I explain how I was being terrorized by his vengeful ghost? She would have me committed. I just wanted to be around someone who could distract me from my Hell and entertain me with their lives. But I gave in after a moment of silence. "I thought this was it, too. I really did. But then, I don't know. I was stupid. Careless. Whatever. I cheated on him, and he found out. He was already a fragile man. He had issues, you know? And he... he couldn't handle it. He killed himself in our bedroom. I found him when I got off work..." My eyes welled up and my throat constricted.

She got up from her seat and put her arms around me. "We don't have to talk about it if it's too hard." She was rubbing my back like a child. But honestly, I think once she was faced with the true ugliness of the truth of the situation, she didn't really want to talk about it, either.

I nodded and moved back away from her.

I let her change the subject and made small talk and listened to her update me on her husband's work, the kids. She was updating me on how her oldest son was struggling in school with his grades and behavior and how she took him to the pediatrician and got him diagnosed with ADHD. A story I witnessed many times in my classroom. Now he was on Adderall. Then she went on to tell me how different her boys were and how amazing her youngest does in school and how successful her husband is and how difficult it can be to be a stay-at-home mom. I smiled when it was appropriate, I asked the questions that would come across as interested and polite. I thought it would feel good to be around someone else, but it was physically and emotionally draining. I just wanted to go back to my haunted condo and be alone, with or without Jonathan's ghost. At least there I wouldn't have to pretend to be a normal, functioning human.

I excused myself to the bathroom after the first glass of wine. Her powder room was undergoing renovations and she asked me to use the bathroom her boys used. I took my time behind the closed door. I didn't really need to go. I just needed to be alone.

I opened the medicine cabinet and saw the white plastic pill bottle of Adderall. I poured a few peach-colored pills out of the bottle and stuffed them in my pocket. I had never taken it before, but I knew a lot of people in college who did. I knew I could expect to stay awake and not feel tired. I watched my friends crush and snort them over the years either for clubbing or just to get through deadlines for term papers and projects. The immediate rush it provided was well documented from their experiences. The long-lasting alertness and ability to stay alert.

I flushed the toilet and washed my hands and sat back in the living room. The pills seemed to be burning in my pocket. I knew what I just did was unconscionable. I just stole drugs from a kid who may or may not really need them. I was shaking and I could barely look at Lori while I tried to make small talk.

After about thirty minutes of fidgeting and not being able to add anything valuable to the conversation, I made an excuse to leave.

I drove home shaking and sick to my stomach. I couldn't believe I stole medication from my friend's child. I tried to justify it with the thought he probably didn't need it and Lori just wanted an excuse for his poor grades and behavior.

When I got home, I pulled the pills out and lined them up on the counter and walked away from them. I was not fully resolved on the decision to even take them. I was not above smoking pot occasionally, or having experimented briefly with X in college, or a hit of acid or mushrooms at a festival. But I tended to stay away from anything noted to be highly addictive. I witnessed quite a few of my classmates develop dependence on stimulants and historically they scared me. But now, my guilt and the ghost of the man I once loved scared me more.

By nightfall, I decided I was not going to take them. I didn't feel good about it, and I didn't want to.

As I dozed off on the couch with the television on, Jonathan was with me again. He again, was not the bloated and disfigured ugly thing. He was handsome and well groomed. And the clean crisp smell of his skin overwhelmed me. My heart ached. He sat down at the foot of the couch, careful not to crush my feet. He adjusted the blanket and cleared his throat so I would pay attention to him.

He was smiling at me, amicable and mischievous. I couldn't breathe.

"You took yourself to a new low today. All to avoid me."

I pulled the blankets tighter. I was suddenly cold.

"Yeah, I'm cold, too." He moved the blanket to get under it with me. It was like a blast from the freezer once he moved under the blanket. His cold arms were wrapped around me, pinning me in my place.

"I would do anything to join you. I don't understand why you did what you did or why you insist on doing this to me night after night."

"Who says it's me? What if it's you?"

"You think I am doing this to myself?"

"Maybe you are. I mean, I'm dead." He laughed. "You broke my heart so hard I couldn't bear to face life. You were never, ever going to love me enough to make me whole. You played with my heart. Cheated on me. To see you in bed with that woman. I mean, it's the fantasy most men would give their left nut for, until they realize they have the full potential to lose their woman to another woman."

"You were not going to lose me." I was shivering and my nose was runny from the cold.

His hand moved to my thigh, and it felt like icicles. "I already had lost you. If you loved me, respected me truly, you would have never gone to bed with Sunny."

"I was stupid. I've apologized. I apologized before you even took your life.

I don't understand why you insist on this." I was reduced, again, to tears. "Please just leave me alone."

"I can't. I simply can't. I want you to feel the same despair and pain that I felt. I want you to understand the feeling of helplessness that you reduced me to."

"You win. You absolutely win. I don't even know what's real anymore. I don't know if you are real, or if I am conjuring you. I can't deal with this."

He was laughing. And it was an awful laugh. Distorted, tinny, and it echoed off the walls and in my ears.

"I loved you. I loved you so much. I was stupid and immature and greedy. I get it. I begged for your forgiveness."

"Maybe you should just join me."

"Maybe I should." My tears felt hot against the cold emanating from him. My teeth chattered loudly.

"It's the ultimate way to show me you are sorry. Join me. Be with me forever over here." His nose against mine, lips so close to mine. It was such a familiar position for us to be in. It was how we ended most days together. Laying entwined nose to nose while we spoke quietly about whatever. He didn't smell like the foulness of death as he had before. He smelled like his crisp and clean cologne. But the cold was unbearable. It was an inviting possibility. To be again with him. For this torment to end.

I closed my eyes to keep from seeing him, so close to me. His hands were on my face, and I could feel his weight next to me, almost on top of me. I wanted to be able to just make the choice to join him. I missed him. I longed for us to be as we were before.

"I can't do it. I can't do this." I sprung up from the couch and Jonathan was gone.

I looked at the clock. It was almost three in the morning. I took a hot shower. Cranking the hot water, scalding my skin. I still could feel his cold hands on my body. I was chilled to the bone and needed warmth. I couldn't get the feeling of his cold hands off my body.

After I got out of the shower I went into the kitchen and took one of the

Adderall, crushed it with the side of a coffee mug, rolled a twenty-dollar bill into a straw, lined the crushed pill up with my credit card and snorted it. I chased it with a cup of coffee.

Almost immediately, my heart began to race, and my mind seemed stunningly clear. Everything was in sharp focus. It was like the world around me was suddenly in HD.

As dawn began to lighten the windows, I was restless. I needed to be somewhere. Anywhere. I got in my car and drove to Jonathan's grave.

I sat at the foot of the grave as the sun was coming up. Wind rustled through the palm trees and California Oaks lining the walkways. The sun streaked pink through the sparse clouds as it crested. The flowers placed there from his burial were wilted and dead. I prayed for forgiveness, and I prayed he would find peace. After what seemed like a long time, I rose back up and cleared the dead flowers and threw them away. I came back standing, looking down at the stone with his name on it. I knelt back down and kissed the stone before leaving.

I went home and cleaned my condo. I cleaned my car.

As the pill wore down, I crushed and snorted the second one. I felt euphoric and positive. There were three pills left. Therein lay the problem. I had to figure out how I would get a lasting supply, and I did not intend to continue to steal them from my friend's son.

I took the third pill, I had been up for over twenty-four hours. I felt good though. I didn't feel the weight of exhaustion or guilt. I was alert. I was happy. My house was clean. I began to go through and pull Jonathan's possessions from the closets and drawers. I made a big pile of his possessions.

I then organized all his possessions from the one pile into neat piles. His clothes, his toiletries, anything associated with Jonathan was piled into the guest room and out of my bedroom. I still couldn't upright the chair he sat in with the belt around his neck. It stayed on its side next to the closet. I then organized the piles into items I wanted to keep, items to donate, and items to potentially give back to Tiffany and Jo.

I sat amongst his clothes and put on his favorite sweater. Well, it was my favorite on him. I put on his cologne and sat amongst his things. I didn't feel sorrow. I felt accomplished. I sat at his desk and thumbed through his notebooks. I read his neat handwriting. Notes for upcoming pieces. Notes to himself. I loved his handwriting. I flipped through every page and let my fingers trace the shapes of his letters as I lingered on his thoughts.

I flipped through the pages of one of the notebooks and found a receipt with a note to pick up the item stuck in the back. It was a receipt for an antique store in Old Town, it was supposed to be picked up a few days before our wedding.

It was late morning, and according to the hours printed on the receipt the store would be open. I drove into Old Town, still wearing Jonathan's sweater, and parked and walked in the bright sun past the old mission and historical courthouse and one room schoolhouse, and past the restaurants and bars, and found the store. Everything was vivid and sharp, and the sunshine felt good on my face after being indoors amongst a dead man's possessions for endless hours.

Double checking the business name on the receipt and the name on the sign to verify I was at the correct location, I walked in and looked among the clean cases full of estate jewelry and other polished and shining antiques.

A salesman in a white button-down shirt and tweed vest came up and asked if he could help me.

"I have a receipt for an item to be picked up. My fiancé... died... and I found it in his notebook." I handed him the slip, sliding it across a clean glass showcase.

He looked at it and smiled, gentle as he looked back at me. "I was wondering if this item would ever be picked up. It was supposed to be a wedding gift." He disappeared into the back.

I looked at the glittering and polished jewels sparkling and mesmerizing me as they reflected the glare of the sun and overhead display lights, as I paced awaiting the clerk to return.

He came back with a black velvet box and handed it to me. "Do I need to sign anything or is there a balance?" I asked.

"No. It's paid in full. I'm sorry for your loss, dear." He took the slip, and I took the box and walked out.

There was a courtyard with a large California Oak across from the store. I sat in the grass under the tree. Kids were running around, and the shade offered relief from the overbearing sun. I held the black velvet between my palms and felt the warm softness of the fabric. The box itself was heavy. I sat in the soft grass and stared at it. I needed to get the resolve to open it.

I was sitting cross-legged and finally decided to set the box in the grass in front of my calves. After an inhale, I opened the black box. I looked in at a beautiful, heavy antique silver heart-shaped locket.

The memory flooded me. An inconsequential day at the time. I took an impromptu day off as Jonathan would be traveling out of town the next day. We had brunch in Old Town and wandered into the shop and I was enamored with the antique lockets, specifically a heart-shaped one. This one. I didn't even think Jonathan was paying attention as the clerk handed it to me. He was on the other side of the shop, looking at the antique nautical tools in another case.

I gently flipped it over and looked at the other side. The backside was engraved with what was supposed to be our wedding date. Inside, photos were inserted. A childhood picture of Jonathan and a childhood picture of myself on the opposing side. I closed it and pulled it from the box and fastened it around my neck. It hung heavy, like a collar chaining me to what I lost. This was the gift he intended to give me for our wedding day.

I had purchased Tiffany cuff links for him. They were stashed in a drawer in my dresser, waiting for our wedding day. He would never have them, see them, or wear them. I held the heavy locket in my hand as I walked to alleviate the weight on my neck as I walked away from the tree, away from the store and back to my car.

I made my way from there to the nearby college campus. I remembered where on campus my friends would score pills or other sundry at the dive bar across from the quad.

I walked in and sat at the bar. It was a stereotypical hole in the wall bar.

Outdated posters of women scantily clad holding cans of cheap beer on the walls (as if any of them actually would drink those cheap beers). Dim lighting, the smell of stale beer and greasy food. The sanitation of the place left one wondering how they were allowed to remain open. A jukebox lit up against the wall, a handful of booths lined the walls, with their red leather well worn in and sagging in the middle. Classic rock from the 1970's was playing over the speakers. I sat up at the bar and ordered an Irish coffee.

The bar was mostly empty. I made small talk with the bartender, a tall, reed thin man with stringy long hair in a thin ponytail, who went by Jace, before asking him if he knew who could provide pills or other uppers.

"Are you a cop?" he asked.

"No. I'm just in need," I assured him. I considered telling him why I didn't want to sleep, but I didn't want to end up committed to the hospital.

He went to the landline and dialed a number. He spoke softly into the receiver, and I couldn't make out what was said.

"My boy will be here in twenty minutes," he told me after he hung up.

I pushed a $20 across the counter to cover my drink and a hefty tip for his assistance.

He rang me up for my drink and handed me the change which I left on the bar for him to take.

His friend showed up, as promised twenty minutes later. He was scraggly in worn out jeans and faded black t-shirt. He was too thin, with a shaved head and beady eyes and missing teeth. His stubble was coming in salt and pepper. He smelled like hair grease and smoke. I wondered how he could smell like hair grease with a shaved head. He sized me up and shook his head.

"Whatcha lookin' for, Cupcake?" he asked me as he sat next to me.

"Adderall? Ritalin?" I asked.

"How much?"

"I have $400 on me. What will that get me?"

"Twenty Adderall."

I pulled the cash out of my bag and handed it to him. He counted it in front of me. "I will be right back."

He exited the bar, and I ordered another drink. Jace made another Irish coffee for me and set it on a small white napkin in front of me.

The wiry bald man came back in and sat down next to me, sliding a small clear plastic bag across the bar at me. Inside were 20 peach-colored pills, looking exactly like what I smuggled out of Lori's house.

"If I want to get in touch with you again, how do I reach you?" I asked.

His hand quickly darted in front of me on the bar and slid my phone across to him and asked me to unlock it. I did as I was instructed. He typed and handed it back to me. I looked at the screen, Donny and his number entered into my contacts.

"I'm Morgan," I told him. "I will be in touch."

"Nice to meet you, Cupcake."

I put another twenty on the bar and headed home with my little baggie of peach-colored salvation.

The sun was setting, and I had been up for forty-eight hours. I decided to let myself sleep. I needed to. My body was weak. I had not eaten. I made scrambled eggs and forced them down and my body collapsed into my bed.

I vaguely remember Jonathan being there. But I couldn't interact. My brain finally decided it couldn't. The absolute overload led my body and mind to allow itself to shut down.

It was my new key. Thirty-six – forty-eight hours of no sleep staying distracted, manic, and alert. I woke up nauseous. I threw up the scrambled eggs I had choked down, and made a cup of coffee, crushed and snorted a pill.

I called Tiffany and told her she had twenty-four hours to let me know if she wanted Jonathan's things.

After no return call, I sorted through the piles keeping a few more favorite shirts and his cologne. I also kept the notebooks, and his laptop, and of course the heavy silver locket permanently hung around my neck. My collar. My link. My sadness and guilt personified, heavy around my neck.

I hauled everything else to the dumpster. I attempted to move the desk, but I couldn't get it past the door of the room and moved it back to its spot, placing the items I kept neatly on the top as a shrine.

I pored through his laptop. His files. Saved pictures of us. Happy. In love. Drafts of his articles. Short stories.

After almost forty hours awake, I blissfully allowed myself to collapse.

The school year ended without my return. HR reached out, but I never bothered to reconnect. My days and nights became indistinguishable as I kept myself medicated. Medicated, I could avoid my feelings. I could avoid dealing with reality. I could avoid sleeping and seeing him.

I met with Donny for a 'refill'. Weeks rolled by. I didn't check my phone. I didn't talk to anyone. I cleaned my condo obsessively. I re-read the stories and files on Jonathan's computer. Stared at pictures.

I was met with shock one morning, after already having been awake for days and looking forward to a blissful rest, when there was loud knocking on my door. I made my way down the stairs and opened the door to my parents standing on my doorstep.

"Morgan Elizabeth Hale, you better have a good reason for not answering your phone or returning calls. It's been three weeks; we have been trying to reach you. Your voicemail is full. You don't check in on social media. The only reason we even know you are okay is we can still access your bank activity, and you are still sharing your location with us. What is going on?" My mother pushed past me with my father in tow, through the entryway.

"I'm sorry. I've been having a tough time since Jonathan."

"You look like hell, Morgan. You look so thin. Are you eating?"

"Yes, Mom." I sat on the couch and pulled the blanket over me.

"Get dressed. Take a shower. We are going to get breakfast."

"Mom, I haven't slept. I need sleep."

"Why aren't you sleeping?" Dad asked.

"Because I'm grieving. I mean, I only found my fiancé hanging by a belt from my closet door."

"Michael, this is why I begged you not to baby her too much. She can't handle any stress or any real-life situations," my mother chided. She always nit-picked my father and bore some petty jealousy for how he treated me. My being pampered rubbed against the grain of her practical Midwest upbringing.

Her philosophy was always pull yourself up by the bootstraps and power through. Keep trying!

In retrospect though, she was absolutely right. I didn't know how to be an adult or deal with anything really on my own. Maybe if I had taken more from her practicality and less of my father's babying, I would not be the mess crumbling on the couch before their very eyes.

"How long are you here for?" I asked them.

"Three days," Mom was looking around the living room trying to find something else to criticize me for. But my home was immaculate. In my hyper-focused delirium, and lack of anything else productive to spend my energy on, I cleaned relentlessly. Not a speck of dust, or item out of place. Even my vacuum marks were perfectly aligned, like Van Gogh's 'Starry Night' brush strokes – perfectly measured and even and all matching.

"Sweetheart, what are you doing to cope with this situation?" Dad asked.

I pulled the blanket up higher, shaking my head. "I don't want to talk about it."

"Are you doing anything? Getting counseling? Going to church?" Mom asked.

"Can you leave? I was just going to take a nap. When I wake up we can go get something to eat or something. But I can't talk about this right now." I was exhausted. Nauseous.

"Morgan, it's been well over a month since he died. You need to pull yourself together. Have you been seeing anyone for help?"

"Mom, do you expect me to just snap out of it and be okay? I cheated on Jonathan. Repeatedly. With a girl. He found out. He was already broken when I got him. This broke him further. He killed himself to get back at me. He did it in our bedroom where he saw me cheat on him. He did it so I would find him and be hurt. I'm hurting. I can't sleep. I need you to go now. I can't take any more guilt trips from you. I suck at adulting. I get it. Fucking go now, please." I didn't move from the couch. I didn't have the energy.

"Morgan, you need help. Your hair is dirty and stringy. Your eyes are dead and sunk in. Your complexion... You're so skinny."

"Yes. I look like shit. Because my appearance is the number one concern here." I decided to just put them on ignore. I closed my eyes. "If you want to stay, fine. But I'm taking a nap now."

I heard them leave after a few failed attempts to talk to me further.

Six hours later, my mother was standing over me again. "Morgan, wake up and take a shower. We are going to dinner."

I couldn't put her off any longer, and based on her tone, if I did not obey, she would physically force me. I complied and I showered and dressed. I was shaking, my jaw was clenched. I crushed one of my peach saviors and inhaled it as I drank a strong cup of coffee standing in my bathroom staring at my reflection. I tried to see myself as my mother was seeing me now. I was skinny. I had barely been able to eat. I was constantly sick or nauseated. My eyes were sunken in, and I had lost a considerable amount of weight. I wasn't cute, that's for sure.

I met my waiting parents in the living room. My mother was sitting on the couch flipping through one of the last magazines to carry an article by Jonathan in it. I couldn't bear to throw it away. Or any of the other hard copies purchased during our time together – including back orders. Most of them, except this newest one, were neatly organized on the bookshelf against the wall in the guest room. Jonathan found it charming I collected all his work. My heart hurt to see it being handled. His story was one of the cover stories on the glossy overlay with a scantily clad actress in the center. "Please don't touch that," I said as I descended the stairs. My mother looked at me and put it down gingerly on the coffee table.

"He really was talented…" her tone-deaf reply trailed off. I love my mother. I do. But generally, I don't like her much.

As we were seated outdoors at a Mexican restaurant under the market lights of the patio and the warm salty San Diego breeze, my father stared at me across the table. I could feel the weight of his disappointment. "Morgan, we are worried about you. Why don't you come back to Tahoe with us? Just for the summer. Work on grieving. Work on feeling better. We know a fabulous therapist that will do you a world of good."

"I'm fine. I will be fine." I stared at the menu in front of me, not really reading it, clenching the locket around my neck.

My father was never really one to get upset or make demands of me. He let it drop. My mother was not so inclined. "Morgan, honey, you look like shit. Even after a nap and a shower. You look terrible. You're shaking. Your eyes don't look right."

The waitress came and I ordered a margarita and a quesadilla. I wasn't really hungry, but at least I could pick at it and give some semblance of normal behavior.

"That's because I'm kind of going through hell right now. Would you like to continue to make me feel worse or can we please enjoy our dinner together?"

Surprisingly, my mother complied and kept the conversation light for the remainder of dinner. She endured her share of challenges in her life, but nothing as heavy as what I was facing currently. She had no leg to stand on with her criticism.

My parents tried one more time before leaving to go back to Tahoe to persuade me to come with them. I declined and continued on my path of self-destruction.

The school year ended without my return. I was able to get the psychologist to extend my leave. He was so overworked he didn't notice my shift in appearance or behavior. He scribbled my note out and handed me another prescription for Xanax and Klonopin.

It was at the psychologist's office when I realized, however, that almost two months had gone since Jonathan died.

I scanned my memory for whether or not my cycle came during this time and realized it had not. My consistent nausea I had written off to stress and side effects of the pills. But now I was second guessing everything.

On my way home I stopped and bought two pregnancy tests. It could have been my malnourishment and weight loss. I hoped that was what it was. I prayed that was what it was. We decided I was going to come off birth control a few months prior, given my age and the fact we wanted at least one kid. We were not going to outright try, but we wouldn't prevent it either.

I sat on the bathroom floor and waited for the results. The first one came up positive, so I took the second. False positive. It has to be a false positive. Please let it be a false positive. I sat and cried as I waited only to see the word 'positive' appear on the screen of the second one, too.

I succeeded in reaching a new low in my emotional state. I sat on the bathroom floor, staring at the closet door where Jonathan hung himself, the overturned chair untouched still after two months, and continued to cry, clutching the locket.

I had destroyed my body over the last several weeks with my chronic abuse and lack of nutrition. There was no way this child was going to come out and be able to thrive, much less survive the wreckage my body had become. Or survive the wreckage I myself had become. There was also no way I could change course and provide for it. I knew it. There was no way I could be a mother. Not now. Not without him. Even if I changed course and cleaned up, I would destroy this tiny being as I destroyed its father because let's face it – I'm toxic.

I needed a clear head for this decision and to fully understand the sentiments I carried in regards to this development. I let myself grow tired, avoiding my stash and the compulsion to crush up a peach pill. Not being medicated was strangely odd now. But I needed to see Jonathan. I needed his presence. I needed to rectify what was done, and the choice I was about to make.

As the sun set and night drew in I laid in the bed, snuggled in his sweater, hands on my belly and I drifted off. I was awoken by the feeling of ice-cold hands on top of mine, on my belly. The crisp clean scent of his cologne made my heart ache with longing. Jonathan was next to me.

"Don't kill our baby, Morgan."

"I've already destroyed it. There's no way this baby can be okay."

"You killed me. You are going to kill the baby, too? How much blood can you handle on your hands?"

"You can't keep doing this to me. I tried to apologize, and I tried to make it right. This one… This one is on you. I would never have started this path had you left me alone."

He was next to me all night, crying and begging with his icy hands on my belly. Pleading with me to reconsider. I just stared at the ceiling fan spinning in a lazy circle overhead. I was resolute in my decision and there was no changing my mind.

I called the women's health clinic and was able to schedule the procedure a few days later. I stayed awake in the days leading up to it. Being medicated did not help, though. I was hyper-focused on the situation, and I had completely alienated myself from anyone I knew. I had no one to talk to, no one to unload this emotional burden on. I went through the hard copies of Jonathan's articles and organized them by date of publication.

On the day of the appointment, I sat in my car for a long time before going in. I almost backed out and left.

There were picketers in front of the clinic and my jaw was clenched. As I got out of my car, a woman yelled at me. A gory picture of a dead baby on a picket sign in her hand. Pamphlets were shoved at me. The signs were pushed in front of me. I put my hands over my ears and ducked my head as I walked in. I could still hear the slurs and names tossed at me. "Baby killer. Sinner. Whore. Monster." It was all true, but I still didn't need to hear it.

I sat in the waiting room, teary-eyed and alone.

I was called in and as I lay on the table, a nurse explained to me what to expect. She sounded like Charlie Brown's teacher to me. I understood nothing. I just stared at the fluorescent lights flickering and buzzing over me. I nodded to show her I understood.

After the appointment, I couldn't reconcile my emotions and my thoughts, either. It is so hard to explain my feelings when I left the clinic. It was a sense of emptiness unlike anything I experienced ever before. I felt empty inside my body, my heart, my head. It was all just… empty.

Jonathan's death, as I had thought it was, turned out to not be my rock bottom. This was rock bottom. I was distraught, and I just wanted to feel good. To feel better.

I called Donny and he asked me to meet him at his home instead of the bar. It was a run-down box of a cinder block house near the border. It was in various states of disrepair throughout. What was supposed to be a lawn was a dusty brown patch of dirt with sporadic green patches of weeds. A cracked sidewalk led to a sagging wooden porch. Several kittens and a stray cat lazed below the wooden porch.

A woman who may have been at one point beautiful, but now looked worn down, too thin, dark hair dirty and stringy, streaked with gray, and dark shadows under her dull brown eyes opened the door as I knocked. "Que?" she asked. Her sagging breasts nearly fell out of a too thin, worn out, white tank top.

"Donde Donny?" I asked in my very limited Spanish.

She ushered me inside and motioned for me to sit on the musty and threadbare beige couch. It was facing an old wood burning fireplace. I didn't even know any houses in California were built with actual wood burning fireplaces, ever. Mismatched blankets and sheets hung on curtain rods to cover the dirty windows in lieu of actual curtains. On top of the mantle of the fireplace a statue of a saint looked down at me. His inscription below said his name was St. Jesus Malverde. Behind him was a large ominous looking skeletal figure with arms outstretched. I just stared at it while I waited for Donny. The candles flickering on either side of it made it look more foreboding.

Donny came out. "Hey, Cupcake. I'm out of Adderall. I tried, but my guy won't be back from south of the border until tomorrow. Can you wait? Come back?"

I started crying. I couldn't control it, and the harder I tried to stifle it, the harder I cried. My hands covered my mouth to stifle my sobbing. I wasn't really crying for the lack of peach pills. I was crying because I was here. I was crying because I needed something. I was crying because I didn't have anyone or anything else to cling to. I was crying because I hated what my life was.

"Tears are not going to fix the situation."

"I know," I sobbed.

The woman who let me in sat next to me and offered me a tissue and patted my knee.

I just looked at her helplessly wiping tears.

She said something in Spanish to Donny, who answered her back in fluent Spanish.

"I have something else you can try, if you want it?"

"Anything. I just need something. I can't bear to sleep. I can't close my eyes," I sobbed.

He was not even fazed by my insanity. In retrospect, I'm sure he had seen and heard much worse.

He left the small dark room and came back quickly.

He sat next to me on the couch, the woman on the other side. He handed me a clear glass pipe.

I held it mystified. I didn't know what to do with it, or how. He saw my confusion and so did the woman. He nodded at the woman who took the pipe from me and lit it expertly drawing the smoke into her lungs. She exhaled and handed it back to me. I realized right then, it was meth.

I didn't care. I just needed to feel better. Why the fuck not, right? I killed Jonathan. I killed our baby. Why not continue a descent into the lowest depths of what I could be? I took the pipe from her, and I followed her lead, inhaling the harsh smoke down into my lungs.

The high that hit me that afternoon was unlike anything I had previously ever experienced. I was beyond the euphoric feeling I got when I took the Adderall. It was an exaltation unlike anything I knew or felt. I understood why people were so addicted to it. I was invincible. I was happy. I was everything and nothing.

I was laughing with the woman, who I figured out was named Mariella, even though I understood nothing she said as she spoke to me in rapid fire Spanish. She reached over and touched my locket, clutching it in her small bony hand. I batted it away, and she laughed maniacally.

I laughed at Donny as I watched him reorganize his vinyl records looking for something to play. Time stopped. My body vibrated and tingled. I walked around in the yard under the hot sun with his three pit bulls in the barren yard. I ran in the yard with them, letting them chase me in the dirt, tackle me and slobber on me. Time flew and stood still at the same time.

Coming down, hours later (or was it days? I don't know). I was laying on their dirty, dilapidated couch, facing the old wood burning fireplace. The flames on the candles next to the saint were long burnt out. The glass gate was dirty. I stared at the smudges on it. I could see what appeared to be a handprint on the backside of the glass. A small, tiny handprint. A baby's handprint. I knew enough about medical waste to know most of it is incinerated. The tiny fetus that once resided inside of me was most likely incinerated. Tossed in a fire.

I stared at the handprint. I heard a baby screaming from somewhere. I sat up and listened, tuning my ears to the direction of the sound before I saw it. I saw a baby in the fireplace. I heard it crying and saw it burning.

Jonathan was kneeling next to the fireplace. He reached in and pulled out a beautiful baby. It wasn't burnt or deformed. Just a beautiful, precious baby with deep and soulful eyes like his own.

"Look at our daughter, Morgan. Look at her. She's beautiful."

I sat up and wiped my face down. My heart was beating so hard, my head throbbed with each beat. I couldn't breathe. I needed out of this small dark room. Away from this house. I was crying, sobbing uncontrollably, shaking as I ran out the door. I could hear Mariella and Donny fucking hard and loud down the hallway.

I vowed, though the meth high was the best I ever felt, I could never do it again, feeling lucky I could make that decision, as I scrambled to make sure I had all the possessions I had when I arrived as I collected myself. Though I could feel the weight of the locket around my neck, I still clutched it to make sure it was there, remembering how Mariella touched it longingly. I kept looking back at the tiny handprint on the glass of the fireplace. I could still hear the baby crying.

I let myself out and made my way back to my car. I didn't know how much time had elapsed, but I figured out I could go to Mexico on my own. Donny clearly said his guy was in Mexico getting the pills. Mexico was only a little more than a half hour from my front door. I had a passport, and I had money. It would be nothing for me to go into Tijuana or all the way down to

Cabo or any other town along the way and hit a few farmacias and buy my own supply. I was surprised the thought never occurred to me sooner.

I made my way home to pack and retrieve my passport.

~ *VI* ~

The State of (In)dependence

The Present

Emma

ONE OF EMMA'S GOING AWAY presents was a painting done in the art therapy room by one of her fellow inmates. She repeated the Bryan Stevenson quote Morgan sent to her, to this inmate who asked her to repeat it three more times as she wrote it down. She painted a beautiful sunrise scene of a melting winter and budding spring with the quote delicately written in script over the top of it. 'Each of us is more than the worst thing we've ever done,' Bryan Stevenson.

Emma hung the painting in her office in a space where she could see it from where she sat. The inmate who painted it had no chance at appeal after Emma went over her case. She was convicted for murder, but she had gone to trial and pled not guilty in self-defense. The jury didn't find her sympathetic and she was sentenced to life in prison. There was no misconduct, and her defense was adequate.

The quote resonated with her as it did with Emma and pretty much all of those who were wasting away in the correctional facility.

It felt good to return to the office. Her office especially. Her large oak desk, shelves of leather-bound law books, the small round table with wood to match the desk where she would sit with clients as it seemed more personal than from across her desk, and the leather chairs and lush green plants, and the sunlight pouring through the window. Her secretary, Greta, outside her office. Brandon had not touched her office, and it was as she left it.

To sit in her office again made her feel like her old self again. Except, as the ankle tether reminded her annoyingly, she was not the same person anymore.

She looked at the painting and thought of Morgan. She took a picture of it and sent it to her.

"It's beautiful. Did you paint it?" she responded.

"No. I've never been a great artist." *That was Bailey. Bailey was the artist.* Emma felt the lump in her throat and twinge of guilt.

"Thank you for sharing the painting with me."

"Thank you for sharing the quote. It's helped me a lot."

"Can I look forward to your call again tonight?"

"No promises. I'm busy with getting this non-profit up and running and have a lot on my plate. Soon for sure though."

Brandon was standing in the doorway. "It's good to see you here in the office again."

"It's good to be back." Emma stretched over the back of the chair with her fingers laced behind her head. It felt good even after being gone over three years – almost one year on the run and two served in prison.

Brandon came in and sat across from Emma. "What are you working on?"

"I need to finish filling out the forms for the non-profit and get them to Greta and have her mail them off. I have some files I brought with me when I was released. I need to take some time to go through them, and I need to go buy a car. Though I appreciate your fine taxi services, I need to have my own car."

"I'll go with you to the dealership. My schedule's pretty clear until later this afternoon."

"Wanna go now? Get that out of the way?"

Brandon grinned at her across the desk. "Then lunch?"

"Yes, sir. Let's do it."

It was good to be back with Brandon. Though both of them were dedicated to the business, they also learned an appreciation for work life balance (it took Emma much longer to catch on to this lesson, though). Whenever one was down to blow off duties the other was sure to follow since going into business together. Work always found a way of getting completed, for sure, but occasionally there was an easy excuse to attend to it later.

Emma was decisive in what she liked and what she wanted. She was in and out of the dealership and drove off the lot with a new SUV. It was the easiest close the salesman ever experienced. She walked up to the salesman, asked for a test drive, signed the papers and left.

She sat across from Brandon at a deli they loved to go to near the courthouse. The coffee was strong, and the sandwiches were huge and flavorful. The colorful crowd, mostly local regulars and courthouse folk they knew well came in and out. Many came up to shake Emma's hand and welcome her back. She was unsure how to feel about the attention but was grateful for the seemingly genuine greetings.

After a group of clerks walked away from greeting Emma, Brandon looked at her with an impish grin. "I saw Lizbeth Newsom is on your calendar for a consult."

Emma racked her memory for Lizbeth Newsom. She was a public defender whose wife didn't care for Emma. They had met briefly at a fundraiser before the March 2020 shut down. It was to raise money for a political candidate. A silent auction. Emma and Lizbeth were up at the bar and struck up a conversation. Bailey was sitting at the table staring at her stupid phone. So, Emma was in no rush to finish the conversation. Lizbeth's wife glared at Emma from her spot. When the conversation didn't seem to wrap up anytime soon, her wife came up and slid her arm around Lizbeth possessively. Emma had tried not to roll her eyes. She forced a smile, shook Lizbeth's hand and went back to her table to be ignored by Bailey, wishing Bailey had shown an ounce of that possessiveness for her.

"Oh. Yeah," Emma shook herself from her memory. "I remember her."

"You know she's divorced now…" Brandon was still grinning at her.

Emma just shook her head at him. "Not interested." She was only half honest in that reply.

DAYS STARTED TO BLEND AND blur. Each day led her to feel a deeper sense of normalcy. Lunches out. Her office. Being outside on a whim.

Her only real dilemma now seemed to be how to fit Morgan back into this life she was rebuilding. Or if Morgan was supposed to even fit in it. The last thing she really wanted was to go back in the dating world and confuse things more. She half-heartedly Googled Lizbeth Newsom. She dug back through Lizbeth's social media accounts. Her now ex-wife owned a popular restaurant that hosted drag brunches on Sundays. It appeared their divorce was amicable. Lizbeth still shared posts advertising events at the restaurant.

Emma sighed and clicked out of pages. It's not like Lizbeth would even be slightly interested in her. She was single because she killed her wife. Lizbeth would not want to get mixed up with that. She knew that. Morgan understood her. She knew that too.

She knew she was ready to be a functioning member of society. She knew she hated having roommates in the halfway house.

The tweaker popped positive on a drug test and was sent back to prison. Her new roommate was a slob, and loud, and abrasive. She knew she didn't really fit in with the crowd she was living amongst and did her best to keep her head down and make it through until she could be released back to her own house, reminding herself she was not better than anyone else who was there.

To keep her away from the halfway house, Brandon agreed to make her schedule for seven days a week, so even on the weekend, Emma was allowed in the office and her days were scheduled twelve plus hours at a time. Emma was fine with being in her office all the listed times in case her parole officer popped in on her. She loved her office. And seven days a week, that's exactly where she could be found.

Morgan

MORGAN LIKED GETTING THE ALMOST daily texts and sometimes short phone calls from Emma. She liked the idea that Emma thought about her throughout the day.

After Emma left, she did start seeing another therapist. She felt like she needed to explore what in fact was wrong with her, seeing how she was so hung up on a woman who killed her wife. In Morgan's viewpoint, they were both responsible for the deaths of the ones they promised to love in some way, shape or form. In and of itself this was a bond they shared on top of the incredible chemistry. No one else could ever understand what it felt like to carry guilt so heavy as this.

She felt like, despite her parents' judgment, she was making a healthy decision in her feelings and pursuing and attempting to reconcile them. She knew she would be judged for this decision, but she didn't care. She never really cared much about what others thought of her choices.

Since moving up to Lake Tahoe, Morgan had pretty much kept a solitary life, making only a few friends she managed to socialize with occasionally. Her closest friend being Aaron, a shop owner on the main drag who also came up to Tahoe to escape his own reckless past.

Since re-establishing his life, he met and married his now husband, a ski instructor named Kevin, and seemed to have established a, for all intents and purposes, provincial life. Morgan met him as she wandered into his shop one day, bored. He sold crystals, rocks, metaphysical sundries, and books. The shop was decorated with repurposed wood shelves and neatly organized. Aaron sat at the front of the shop behind a counter with his register and often made small talk with many of his visitors.

Morgan wandered into his shop and sat herself behind the counter with Aaron on a stool.

"Hey, stranger." He gave her a peck on each cheek.

"Hey yourself."

"You seem agitated. Has this anything to do with Emma?"

"It does. I don't know what I want, and I don't know what she wants. We don't know what to expect with each other or how we are supposed to be with each other."

"She hasn't seen you in over two years. Maybe you need to go to her. It's hard to say how either of you will even feel about each other when you have not been face to face in forever."

"She's getting out next week. They are making her go to a halfway house for like six months."

"Maybe you should plan to go visit her?"

"I'm scared to just show up. I don't want to scare her."

"Maybe you are scared?"

"That too, for sure."

"She's safe. Your relationship and your dynamic, it's all safe while you are thousands of miles apart and she is tucked away behind bars. You get face to face again, and all your skeletons have been laid bare, it's different. What you had before she left was surface. You didn't really know each other. You didn't really know all the pieces of each other. It was just hot sex and chemistry, and planning for a future that never could be."

Morgan looked away and fidgeted with a bundle of sage on the counter.

"You know I'm right. You have created this ideal of who she was, and who she is."

"I think it was real when we were together. What we had was absolutely real. You have no idea."

"I know what lust is about. Believe me. And I've seen all the documentaries and seen the pictures. Like everyone else, I was obsessed with the case, too. She's absolutely hot. I would totally do her, and I don't even like women."

"No. I mean we had an… I don't know… A spiritual connection. We were meant to be together. I know it. I can't shake it. I can't even think of another person in that way. My thoughts always go back to Emma. And I've tried. I signed up for the dating sites and after two days, I delete the accounts because no one holds my interest like she does. I am talking to Sara though. She's been a fun distraction."

"Whatever with Sara. You know that's never going to go anywhere. You know it's Emma you want. Go to Emma. Once you have been face to face, come back to me with this."

Morgan exhaled and stood up. "I'm taking this with me," she said indicating the sage bundle. "I need to go figure some things out."

"Yes, you certainly do."

Morgan went back home and texted Sara to meet her for dinner.

Emma

EMMA COULD SENSE THERE WAS something Morgan was holding back from her in the past few text exchanges and calls. But she didn't want to push.

Lizbeth Newsom had indeed come in for her consultation. Emma did her best to keep it related to the case and turn off her charm.

She was what Emma would consider to have been, her type. Aggressive, ambitious, smart and beautiful. Her caramel-colored hair was slicked up and back in a French twist, and her suit, if not customized, was at least tailored to fit as such. Her perfectly arched eyebrows and golden colored eyes were accentuated by dark framed Tiffany glasses.

Suddenly, Emma realized she was lonely. Her eyes locked with Lizbeth's and she had to force herself to remain professional. Her initial thought was to ask her to forget the appointment and just go somewhere else. *Morgan who?*

As they talked about the case, they found themselves going back and forth from case facts to personal information. She learned first-hand, not through a random Google search, Lizbeth was recently divorced. Her ex-wife owned a popular restaurant in town, and it was a friendly divorce. They just wanted other things.

The meeting carried over and went long past their scheduled time. Emma considered asking her if she could call her sometime, but she choked. Lizbeth was familiar with her case, and that knowledge made Emma hesitant. *There's no way she knows about me and would want to get mixed up with me now.*

She could feel Lizbeth's eyes lingering on her, and she appreciated her wit and candor, so it was a bit of a struggle during their meeting.

When Emma looked at her watch and excused herself for a conference call with a national non-profit she was modeling her own after, Lizbeth looked disappointed. She had opened her mouth to say something but stopped herself.

Emma smiled at her and shook her hand and thanked her for coming in. "You can see Greta on the way out. She will schedule you for a follow-up if you need it. Or you can shoot me an email or text directly." She didn't mean to come across as flirty in telling Lizbeth she could text her directly, but she caught her own tone.

Lizbeth smiled, a hint of deviousness underlying her expression. "Thanks, I will be in touch."

Later that evening, as she was getting ready to head back to the dreaded halfway house, she got a text message on her screen from Lizbeth. 'I know your life is complicated right now, and I would hate to add to it, but I would love to see you again. Not work related.'

Emma froze staring at the message. She didn't know how to respond. She typed and then deleted four different responses. She knew if Lizbeth were looking at her phone she would see the dots start and disappear. That added to the agony of suddenly not knowing what to do.

She finally responded with, 'Yes, my life is fairly complicated now. I appreciate your acknowledgment of that inconvenient fact. But I would love lunch sometime. Let me know when you are free, and we can work something out.'

A response came quickly. "Friday, at Terry's by the lake, 12:30?'

Emma knew the restaurant well. It was a small local seafood restaurant with a nice quiet atmosphere. She bit her lip and exhaled. 'See you there.'

She went back to the halfway house and felt guilty about making what could potentially be a date with someone that wasn't Morgan. She texted a quick good night to Morgan before turning her phone in and retiring up to her room with the journal.

Excerpt from Morgan's Memoir

MY FIRST TRIP TO MEXICO, I had no idea how long this road would be or how hard. I held no desire to explore healing. I just wanted to avoid all of it.

I drove across the border and found my way into the first farmacia I could find in Tijuana.

It's amazing how easy it is to simply wander into a farmacia and get whatever medication you want without prescription (I could easily get on a soapbox about American for-profit medical systems and drug companies, but that is a tangent not suited for this healing process). I was also highly peeved to figure out the mark up I was paying Donny on the pills. I was scoring at them at under a dollar a pill at the farmacias and paying Donny $20 per pill.

I bought two bottles at the first farmacia in Tijuana, then drove down to Rosarito and bought two more bottles. All for less than I was paying Donny for a handful of pills.

I was not prepared for the line to get back across the border. My GPS said it was only a mile, but the traffic was at a standstill. As I sat in my car, merchants and beggars filed past me on foot selling blankets, food, jewelry, pottery, you name it. Elderly people and the young with children and nothing to sell walked with hands out, or empty garbage bags to collect recyclables.

I kept my eyes forward and windows up. My air conditioner struggled to keep up with the sun beating through my windshield.

I saw a young woman with an infant swaddled to her chest with a blanket tied in a knot over her shoulder walking between the rows of cars. She couldn't have been more than twenty. The infant was barely weeks old by its size. She was carrying a long rod with sparkling bracelets and rosaries hanging from it. The various colored beads glittered in the sun, and I stared at her as she walked toward me. The small peach fuzz head of the baby and the glittering stones. I felt an emptiness in my belly. Hollowness through my entire center.

I rolled my window down and flagged her to my car. She tried to talk to me in Spanish, but I shook my head and handed her a $100 bill, pressing it into her palm. She pulled her hand back and looked at it. I began to roll my window back up and she shot her hand back in, "No, no! Un momento," she pleaded.

I rolled my window back down, as she fiddled with the stick. She pulled a bracelet with glittering beads off it and tapped her wrist to indicate that she wanted mine.

I stuck my hand out and she placed a sparkling beaded bracelet on my wrist. In the center, was a large blue bead to symbolize protection from the evil eye. She then handed me a red beaded rosary, identical to the one Jonathan kept at his bedside. The one I returned to Tiffany at the funeral. She pressed it into my palm. "Bless you, always." She bent close to my window and her eyes were level with mine. I could smell the newborn smell of the baby. My tears were flowing without will or want.

Forcing myself to break eye contact with her, I rolled up the window and she moved on.

I stared at the rosary in my hand and bracelet on my wrist.

Other vendors were approaching my car after seeing how I patronized another. They knocked on my windows as they passed. Clean your windshield? Churros? Bottled water? Pottery? More jewelry? I ignored them, inching closer to the border, staring at the rosary and bracelet.

The songs shifted on the radio and the sun got lower. The line was still slow. I eventually slid out of my stupor and hung the rosary from my rearview mirror. I couldn't see him, but I could hear Jonathan snort sarcastically from the passenger side. "Whatever," I whispered. I took the bracelet off and hung it on the mirror with the rosary.

Once I got to the border, it was evening, and I was able to clear the border check – no issue. Border Patrol did not even look twice at me or my documents or ask to search my bag or car. This was all too easy. I asked the border agent the best days and times to cross the border without a wait or how long it would take to get Global Entry to expedite the process. I made mental note of the days and times, and to start the process for Global Entry.

After getting home, I parceled off some of the pills for myself and set aside a stash I would sell myself. I would sell them for half the cost of Donny and still turn a profit.

Back to the bar near campus, inside its darkened room, sitting at the well-worn bar full of nicks and scratches, with the jukebox playing eighties' rock ballads, I sat and smiled at Jace.

"You here for Donny?"

"No. I think I am done doing business with him."

"What can I get you? Irish coffee last time, right?"

"Sure, that sounds good. Jace, I want to offer you a deal. How much does Donny cut you in?"

He shrugged. "He doesn't. I just hook him up. I've known him since we were kids."

"Next time you have someone looking for Adderall or uppers, let me know. I'll give you a cut. And I'm cheaper than Donny."

"How much?"

"Donny is selling for $20 a pill. I will sell for $15. You get $5."

"Deal." He shook my hand.

I gave him my cell number. We chatted while I finished my drink.

My justification in this new arrangement was Donny had a steady business. He didn't need the leads from the bar. There was room enough for both of us.

The calls started rolling in the next day. This was the easiest money I had ever made. The first day I made almost the same amount of money as a day's worth of teaching. No politics, no grading, no planning. However, my stash was already running low. I was shocked at the volume in which people bought these pills, and their reasons for needing them. College kids finishing papers. Housewives trying to hold it all down. You name it. The users and abusers and new clients filled every category of person across the socioeconomic, racial, and ethnic divides.

I MADE ANOTHER TRIP TO Mexico. I was scared to hit the same two farmacias, so I hit two different ones, and bought twice as much, and added Xanax and a few other high demand pills.

This stash went almost just as fast. College kids and grad students were my primary customer base.

I made a longer trip, going from Tijuana, to Rosarito and to Ensenada. I hit as many farmacias as I could in three days' time. I was getting nervous I would be flagged for going over the border as often as I was, but it never happened. Just a lone, middle-class white lady in a nice SUV.

I was also using more and sleeping less. I was trying to manage my newfound business and needed to be able to show up when Jace called or texted with a buyer or a refill.

The school year began without my return. I didn't think twice. The district tried to call me more than a few times. I never answered. I never returned the calls.

One evening, as I was at the bar delivering a packet of pills, the group of college boys who were buying, invited me to go back to their frat house to party with them.

Not having anything better to do, I followed them.

It was September, five months since Jonathan killed himself, and the night was hot. I had no real inclination of the time of year, or what day it was. Looking back, I can tell you when it was, but at that time, I don't think I could. There were hundreds of people pouring out of the house and onto the lawn. Girls were dressed provocatively, and the boys all around were trying to play it cool. Loud bass music reverberated around the house and pulsated through my chest. Honestly, I was way too old to be there, and I knew it. But being as how I had nowhere else to go, I said fuck it and kept moving into the mix of people.

There were people everywhere. It was the most socializing I had done since before Jonathan died. I successfully alienated myself from my friends and was avoiding my parents' pervasive calls to check on me. I also carried a hefty stash on me, just in case.

Someone handed me a plastic cup full of beer with too much head as I walked around. I took it even though I had no intention of drinking it. Thick white foam spilled over the top and down my hand. I smiled a thank you at the poor underage kid who poured it and handed it to me.

As I walked a few of the young frat boys smiled and checked me out. I'm sure they were wondering who the fuck invited me or why I was there. I was dressed in a tank top with a baggy flannel (one of Jonathan's that I couldn't throw away) and distressed jeans with a pair of Chucks. I was not in the crop tops and short shorts of the young girls that were everywhere. My face was worn and haggard. My hair was limp and in a messy bun, and I think my makeup was three days' old.

I found my way to the back of the house. There was a group of girls and a guy sitting around a coffee table with lines of cocaine in fat, neat rows.

The guy in the center nodded at me after I made eye contact with him. I recognized him as a past student of mine but could not remember his name. He called out to me, "Miss Hale! What are you doing here? Have a seat. Join us!"

Two of the girls moved aside and I sat in between them. Why not, right? A matter of weeks ago I was doing meth in my dealer's shitty living room. Why not coke with a gaggle of college girls and one of my former students?

The conversation was moving fast around me. They were discussing some course they were all taking, and I couldn't keep up, and I didn't care to.

They were doing the lines one after another and I was nudged indicating that it was my turn and was handed a straw.

The burn and the after taste down my throat were immediate. My pulse began to race, and my mind went into an overdrive I never knew possible. It was a stronger surge than the mild buzz of my Adderall high.

I was moved quickly into a state of paranoia and panic. I was sweating. Sitting between Former Student and Probably Underage Girl, I felt claustrophobic and suddenly everything was just too much. "Thanks. I got to go," I mumbled as I got up and wandered back out pushing my way through the crowd and through the pulsating music. I didn't understand how not only anyone could enjoy this sensation but enjoy it enough to do it repeatedly. I just needed to get out of the mix of people. I just wanted my heart to stop pounding so hard and fast.

I walked down the street away from the frat house, passing the bars and coffee houses near the campus. Everything was super sharp and bright. I couldn't come back to myself. I couldn't get my heart to slow down. I was clammy all over. All my sensations were in overdrive.

I found an outdoor table belonging to a busy taco shop. I sat down and put my head between my knees. Maybe it was interacting with the Adderall. I don't know. I couldn't remember the last time I used any. I just knew I was not enjoying the feeling I was experiencing.

I had no control over my thoughts as they were racing. I was hyper-focusing on what I had done and hoping I wasn't going to die. Or maybe I did want to die? Death would be welcome at this point. Just make this feeling stop.

Someone tapped me on the shoulder and put a taco and a soda in front of me, with a $5 bill. Oh my god, they thought I was homeless. That's how I looked to someone on the outside of my head. Like an insane street person. They smiled kindly and walked away. I was mortified.

I couldn't understand how this drug was considered addictive. Who liked to feel this way?

Blissfully, it didn't last long, and as the world slowed down around me, I got back up and I found my car and made my way home and took a hot shower. Hoping it would soothe my nerves and help me come back to myself. As the hot water poured over me, I leaned against the cool tiles and tried to ground myself.

The hot water went cold before I got out and stood dripping in the middle of the bathroom. Standing and dripping and cold for several minutes staring at the foggy mirrors before I dried off and popped a few Xanax. Looking in the mirror, as the fog dissipated, I decided I did not like who I was anymore. I did not like my life. I did not like who I had become. I didn't even recognize myself as I looked at the shell of a human in the glass. Dark shadows and heavy bags under my eyes. My hair was limp and thin, and I could count my ribs effortlessly. My lips were dry, and my cheeks were gaunt. My insides matched my outside. I was the walking dead.

I called Jace and asked him to meet me at my house. I counted out what was left and told him to use his discretion and I would expect my fair payment when I returned. I needed to get away.

I didn't know where else to go, so I went south back into Mexico. It was an eight-hour drive to get to Cabo San Lucas. It was where Jonathan and I went for a romantic get-away – our first vacation together. I found the resort we booked for that stay and managed to get a suite for five days.

I could see how the other guests looked at me as I walked through the lobby. My clothes barely fit me and hung from my body. I was going days without eating. My hair flat and lifeless hung in my face as I made my way through the swanky lobby with its high ceilings and crystal chandeliers, and large bright flower arrangements. The scent of lavender vanilla pumped through the vents.

I put my head down and made my way to the building, riding in a golf cart with the bellman who was responsible for my luggage. The sun was setting, and I could see the view over the ocean. I could hear the waves crashing against the shore and I sat on the balcony and took it all in.

I hadn't taken anything since I got on the road, and I was getting drowsy.

Jonathan was sitting next to me in the golden light.

He didn't speak to me. He just looked at me, soft and tender with a slight smile on his lips. I wanted to take his hand. I wanted to feel his arms around me. Everything in my body hurt. My jaw ached from clenching it. I didn't even realize I was doing it. I looked at him watching me and I relaxed.

When the last of the sun sank below the horizon, I went inside and collapsed into the bed and slept deep and long. It was dreamless and deep.

My room was dark from the blackout curtains when I woke up and I was disoriented. I looked to the side of the bed expecting to see Jonathan there. My hand reached toward where he should be, thinking he was supposed to be there, but it was smooth and person free. I got out of bed and looked at my pill bottles and chose to not take anything. I was shaky and weak. I showered, dressed, and made myself look as presentable as I could. Maybe it was time to detox and get my shit together?

I went down to one of the restaurants in the resort to have breakfast. Sitting alone at my table, a plate of chilaquiles and an espresso in front of me, not really hungry. Maybe food would make me feel better?

I watched as couples sat together and families gathered around the tables. Happy, rested, peaceful. Love and peace. Smiles and suntans. Laughter and brightness. Everything I had seemingly forsaken. I decided I would try to wean myself off my pills and try to get back to normal. I needed to get my life together. I knew I was a train wreck and the rate I was going was completely unsustainable. For fuck's sake, I'm in my thirties out here living like a twenty something. My mother was so right.

At one table over from me, a couple caught my eye. He was handsome and charismatic. His haircut was fresh, black hair, perfectly in place. A sharp aquiline nose and piercing dark eyes. His clothes were perfect, pressed and crisp as the rest of him. He flashed a perfect smile as he looked adoringly at the woman across from him. Her chestnut hair was in a thick braid, her skin tanned and golden and large golden-brown eyes. Her lips were pouty and full, and her eyebrows were perfectly arched. Her short sundress flared perfectly over her crossed legs.

I caught myself staring at them and pulled my focus back to myself. I was wearing distressed jeans now too baggy, and one of Jonathan's white t-shirts. I threw a straw fedora style sun hat over my flat, dull hair. I at least managed to put on some makeup before coming down, but my complexion was getting noticeably worse. I looked like an addict. There was no disguising it.

I was starting to feel groggy and irritable, and what little of my breakfast I managed to get down sat in my gut like lead. I signed my bill to the room and went back upstairs. I inhaled half of a little peach pill and enjoyed the sensation of watching the world go from fuzzy to ultra-high def. My resolve to get my life together went out the window as fast as it came in. I had somehow reached a point where I felt some strange normalcy in being high.

Deciding the pool was a good place to spend the morning, I grabbed my bathing suit out of the suitcase. I looked at myself in the mirror after getting it on my malnourished form. My hipbones jutted out, my ribs were showing. Gross. I looked like an extra from *The Walking Dead.* To spare the other guests, I threw a cover over my swimsuit and went down to the pool area with a book in my hand.

All five of the resort pools were bustling with people, music and noise. With all of them busy and crowded I just settled on one closest to my room. Couples sat in chairs sipping frozen drinks and holding hands, kids ran about playing and giggling. I adjusted my hat and sat in an empty lounge chair. I decided to keep my cover on to keep from scaring any of the other people with my skeletal appearance.

I laid back and tried to lose myself in the book I had been trying to read for weeks. A waiter came by, and I ordered a pina colada and continued to read. Out of the corner of my eye, I saw the striking couple from breakfast show up. Directly across from me were two empty chairs and they took them, standing out again as if they had been ripped from the pages of *Vogue*.

I watched as he delicately spread sunscreen on her back. She gave him a peck on the cheek and laid on her belly to sunbathe. I found it hard to not watch her – well both of them, really. She was beautiful as was he, and he doted on her.

He saw me watching them and smiled politely at me. I smiled back and pretended to go back to my book and sip my cocktail. The bass from the music the DJ was playing reverberated around us, and I tried to remember to unclench my jaw.

After a few moments he got into the water and swam across. He crossed his arms over the edge of the pool. I must have been staring more intently than I thought I was. He was probably coming over to chastise me for being a creeper.

"Hi," he said.

"Good morning."

"I'm Eli. That's my wife Sophia."

"Nice to meet you. I'm Morgan" I smiled trying to be polite but feeling uneasy under all of it.

"We saw you at breakfast and now here at the pool. Are you by yourself?"

I put my bookmark in its place to buy time in my response. I didn't know how to respond, or why this beautiful human was speaking to me.

Sensing my insecurity he said, "I'm not trying to be weird or creepy. I just want you to know, if you see us and you are alone and you don't want to be alone, you can join us. It wouldn't be a problem."

"I appreciate it, Eli. More than you know." My voice cracked, touched by the sentiment.

He pulled himself out of the pool and sat on the edge. "Are you okay?"

"My fiancé killed himself. We came here once together for this wonderful trip. I'm just trying to make sense of life again. I wanted to come and be somewhere where I remembered what it felt like to be happy."

"I'm so sorry. That has to be so difficult?"

"It is. It was my fault." I had no idea how he had me vomiting so much personal information.

"You can't accept responsibility for someone else's choices."

"In this situation, I can. Anyway, wow. I don't know why I feel so compelled to tell you this stuff. You are here on vacation with your extremely beautiful wife. I do not want to burden either of you with this drama."

"It's not a burden. I promise. But I can see you don't really want to share right now. How about joining us for dinner tonight though? We have reservations at the steak house tonight. We can add one more."

The steakhouse at the resort was legendary and always booked. "Sure. Yeah. Thank you. What time?"

"Eight tonight."

"Okay. I will be there. I promise. Thank you."

"See you then!" Sliding back into the pool, he swam back to Sophia. I watched as he pulled himself out of the pool and filled her in. She peered over her shoulder back at me and smiled.

I smiled back at her, suddenly nervous.

I waited a few more minutes, pretending to read before heading back to my room.

I didn't want to come down completely before dinner, but I didn't want to be entirely strung out either. I inhaled the remaining half of what I took in after breakfast.

I pulled a sundress out of my suitcase and blow dried my hair and did my best to make myself presentable before dinner. My complexion, something I used to be extremely proud of, was now sallow and uneven from neglect. I tried to cover it the best I could and went above and beyond with my eyes so no one would notice my skin.

Still having an hour to kill after getting ready, I wandered down to the bar and picked up a cocktail and took it to the beach.

I walked along the shore and tried to gather a sense of calm and peace before joining Eli and Sophia. My heart was racing and heavy at the same time. Jonathan and I once walked this beach hand in hand planning our future together. We decided on this very beach we were meant to be. We would be forever.

I missed him. I hated myself for what I did. I hated myself for missing him. I hated being there alone.

No matter the setting I would find myself in, I could not escape the overwhelming feeling of pain, sadness, guilt and discord. It followed me everywhere, and there never seemed to be an end to it.

I made my way back up to the resort from the beach and to the steakhouse. The patio we were seated on boasted a view of El Archo in the distance as the sun was sinking lower. As I approached their table, Eli and Sophia both stood. They waited until I got to my seat before sitting back down.

Sophia smiled warmly at me. "Thank you for joining us." Her voice was silky and smooth, holding a slight accent I couldn't place.

"I appreciate the invite." My nerves were amped. "I feel like I'm crashing your otherwise very romantic trip."

"Not at all. We come down here a lot. It's kind of our place," Eli tried to reassure me.

"What do you guys do? For a living?"

"We own a foundation. It's a kind of spiritual retreat. Non-denominational. We take the best of all the major religions and incorporate their teachings to raise the overall positive vibrations of the world to make it a better place. We hold personal development workshops, yoga classes and meditations. Our workshops are both business and personal. We've had quite a year, actually."

I thought he was joking, and I laughed until I saw how both of them were very serious. "I'm sorry. I'm very sorry. I thought you were joking."

"No, it's okay. We get that a lot." Sophia continued to smile. She was disarming in the way she spoke and made direct eye contact like she was looking into my soul.

I took a breath and a heavy sip of my cocktail. "Where is your church?"

"We don't like to call it a church. Church denotes Christianity, which we do incorporate in a way, but not in its entirety," Eli explained. He was not being condescending or superior in his explanation, but rather patient and soft in his manner. "We have taken the basic tenets of a simplified Christianity, the be kind to others, do not judge, and then taken out the basic misogyny and God will be angry if you sin. We added in the nature and peace of the Pagan Wiccan religions, and the joy and meditation of Hindu and Buddhism. Our Society is in the North County San Diego area."

"I live in San Diego! No kidding!"

"What do you do?" Sophia asked me.

"I am a high school English teacher."

"Bless you for what you do!" Sophia laughed.

"Actually, I'm not really teaching right now – long story. Anyway, where in San Diego is your, as you called it, Society?" I asked.

"We just bought a building in the North County area, near Fallbrook," Eli said proudly.

"That's actually very interesting."

"You should come by when you get back to town," Sophia invited me.

"When are you going to be heading back?"

"We are here for another two days." Eli reached into his wallet and pulled out a card to hand me.

It was shiny and black. 'The Society' was written in silver script. The address, website, and phone number were imprinted.

"But this is not why we invited you out. Eli really did just notice that you were all alone. We are not trying to recruit you or anything nefarious like that." Sophia's hand touched mine. The warmth of her fingers traveled from the top of my hand through the core of my body. I had not been touched by another human being in so long. Even such a small intimacy set my heart racing, followed by a deep current of guilt.

"Oh, no. That never even crossed my mind." I slid my hand back to my lap.

I ended up having a wonderful evening with Eli and Sophia. I was captivated by them. I learned they had been married almost ten years. Sophia was born in France and lived there until she was twelve before coming to The States. The conversation flowed easily and by the end of the night I felt almost human.

I said my goodbyes to them with a promise to stay in touch and watched them walk hand in hand back to their building. I waited until they disappeared before making my own way back to my room.

I felt like having met them was a gift from the universe. They gave me a sense of normalcy after months of chaos.

I went back to my room and slept peacefully and dreamless. The next morning, though, I awoke to an email from the district human resources. I had failed to notify them of my intent to return in time, nor had I bothered to even return for the first few weeks of the school year, and my contract was in effect now terminated.

I was spun back out into a feeling of chaos and despair. Being a teacher was all I knew how to be. It was a part of my identity. Losing what I considered to be such an integral part of my identity was the last piece of what tethered me to who I had been.

So, I went to the farmacias in town and purchased as many pills as I could get my hands on. Adderall. Vicodin. Xanax. I bought it all.

I spent the rest of my time in the resort in my suite and wandering the beach, back in my rhythm of using and collapsing.

I was not ready to heal yet. I was not ready to forgive myself. I wasn't ready to face reality.

~ *VII* ~

Saints and Sinners

The Present

Emma

EMMA UNDERESTIMATED HOW BUSY SHE would be with consulting on cases and getting her non-profit up and running and reapplying for the bar.

She found it hard to spend much time on the phone with Morgan. A three-hour time difference made matters worse. When she woke up at five in the morning to get a workout in before work, it was only two in California.

Emma was back in her old pattern of working all waking hours. She would send a quick text or a quick phone call or FaceTime when she could, but she was lucky if they spent more than five minutes.

Working made the time go by faster and she was able to avoid the general misery that was the halfway house and the revolving door of tweakers, addicts and thieves who were assigned to be her roommate. Two months flew by, and she was awarded her first weekend pass and was able to go home, whatever home meant now.

After rescheduling a handful of times for a variety of reasons (including generally having cold feet and a number of other scheduling conflicts on both sides), she finally met Lizbeth for lunch. Her caramel-colored hair, which Emma had only seen in tight French twists or buns was down and flowing around her shoulders. Her hazel eyes were not shielded by her typical Tiffany frames. Emma felt her heart skip a beat. This was definitely being considered a date.

After a few awkward moments at the table overlooking the large lake, Emma cut to the chase. "I'm sorry. I don't know how to act right now."

Lizbeth smiled. "You've been through some shit. I get it. There's no pressure. I mean, I'm obviously interested, which is why I asked you here."

Emma smiled back. "I appreciate that. I appreciate how forward you are, also. But I'm not sure I'm ready to date or anything. I mean, it's not like I can invite you back to the halfway house for a nightcap."

Lizbeth rested her chin on her hand and smiled. "I'm interested, I'm not easy." She was grinning at Emma.

Emma grinned back. She knew if her circumstances were different, Lizbeth would be easy. "I mean, I do have weekend passes starting tonight though." She met Lizbeth's gaze directly. A hint of her old cockiness coming back through.

Lizbeth blushed and looked away.

Throughout the rest of the lunch, though the flirtation was heavy and almost bordering on direct innuendo for parts, Emma enjoyed her time with Lizbeth. The chemistry was right, and Lizbeth was her type. Beautiful, witty, thoughtful, and sensual.

She walked Lizbeth to her car in the parking lot as both of them had afternoon appointments to make. Emma leaned in instinctively and let her lips brush over Lizbeth's lightly. "Can I call you this weekend?" she asked.

Lizbeth pulled Emma back to her and kissed her with more fervor. "I hope you do."

AFTER HER SENTENCING, SHE ASKED Brandon, who was her power of attorney over her assets, to take Mary Anne through the home she had with Bailey. Mary Anne was to take any and all possessions she wanted. Brandon then packed up Emma's clothing, shoes, accessories, and books and put them into storage. Everything else in the house was sold, donated, or dumped before the house was put on the market to be sold.

She kept the house she inherited from her grandmother, having used it as an income source as a rental property. She had not set foot in the house in several years, so to call it 'home' was a loose translation of the word. Teta, the name she called her grandmother – never knew Emma even existed until Emma showed up on her door at sixteen years old. Emma only found her after she demanded the information from her father, Bear, about her family. Teta took her in after she was nearly expelled for continuously fighting with Rhys Mills – Bailey's ex-boyfriend. Teta died of an unexpected brain aneurysm when Emma was in college, leaving her everything, including this house.

Emma moved back into the house when she went to law school. She loved the energy of the house and the neighborhood it was in. It was the house her mother grew up in, though she never knew her mother. Teta made her feel welcome and loved in this house.

Returning to this home now she felt misplaced. It had been years since she occupied this space. The last time she occupied the space, she was climbing the ladder of success with Bailey by her side. It was a rental property for the last several years, and Emma paid for renovations and updates along the way. Aside from the bones of the house, it was different now. Brandon dropped her dog, a brown and white Cavalier King Charles Spaniel, Charlemagne, off that afternoon as the delivery men were leaving. His tail wagged excitedly as he was reunited with her.

She bought new furniture for it and had been able to schedule the delivery for the Friday afternoon of her first pass. She directed the delivery men around and when they cleared, and she was done settling in it was almost 8pm. She almost went to look for the house manager before realizing she was home without supervision all weekend.

She found the box with the wine glasses she ordered and opened it, setting the glass next to a bottle of red she opened to let breathe.

Emma walked up the stairs to the bungalow area, where she had the workers bring her desk. Boxes of books were stacked along the walls near the shelves Bailey installed the summer she herself was busy interning. Something that had not changed. Emma touched the shelves and sighed heavily.

Sitting at the desk, looking out over the darkened street through the window, Emma closed her eyes and pondered the rebuilding of her life in this home and wondered if it was a mistake.

She was surrounded by the quiet. No buzzers. No people talking. No one else moving or breathing around her. She had craved the quiet for the last several years, often staying awake after lights out to enjoy it, though even then, it was never entirely silent.

Down the stairs and into the bedroom, she moved past her boxes of clothes along the walls and found the box with the sheets and bedding she ordered. She made the bed and went back to the kitchen and grabbed a wine glass and poured herself a healthy glass, Charlemagne tagging along behind her as she went from room to room.

Morgan

LOOKING AT THE CALENDAR, SHE knew Emma was now allowed her weekend passes. Allowed to come and go and hang out with anyone and be herself.

She had so many questions. She didn't know Emma in real life. She knew Emma first as a woman on the run, and then as an inmate.

Sara was still hanging around in the background of her life. She knew Sara was into her. And if she could bring herself to let Emma go, maybe she could be into Sara, too.

Sara knew Morgan was still in contact with Emma, but she was not clued into the level or depth of the lingering feelings Morgan still bore for Emma, and until Morgan had clarity, she planned to keep it as such.

Aaron was encouraging Morgan to just go visit Emma. Get in front of her. So now Morgan was avoiding Aaron.

Now, however, she was no longer a captive audience and faced with the distractions of life, would Emma even want to maintain contact? She started questioning all of it. Emma was striking, even in her mid-forties, she drew looks and attention. She knew a few years behind bars wouldn't change how she would be perceived by others. It would be a matter of time before someone took interest in her. She tried to abate her sudden onset of jealousy.

She held no viable claims on Emma. She was the one who sent Emma away and was now waffling on where they stood. In their last few letters and calls, Emma made it very apparent she was open to re-trying to have a future with Morgan with no secrets left to hide.

It was a Friday, and she knew this was Emma's first weekend pass. Her first weekend at home. True freedom. She picked up the phone and called her.

It rang several times before Emma picked up. "Hey. Sorry. I was just wrapping with a box."

"Oh! I'm sorry. I can call you back?"

"No. I'm good now. Hold on. Let me open a bottle of wine. Actually, yes. Let me call you back in a few minutes."

Morgan acquiesced and waited by the phone.

When Emma called her back, it wasn't via phone. It was FaceTime. It was Morgan's turn to freeze. They hadn't laid eyes on each other since the night Emma had confessed.

Morgan fluffed her hair and answered the video call. She felt her heart stop as she looked at Emma on the screen. She was sitting on her couch surrounded by boxes, the soft light of lamps illuminating her features. She saw Emma's expression soften as well as she was taking her in. "It's been too long," Emma said. "I know that's not your fault. That's mine. But it's been too long."

Morgan felt overcome with emotion and wiped a tear. "I know. I know it has been. My god. I forgot how I feel when I look at you."

Emma smiled and looked away. "I haven't forgotten you. When can I get you out here for a visit?"

Morgan was tongue-tied for what felt like an eternity. Unable to take the silence, Morgan began again. "Emma, I want to see you. I do. But I am scared of jumping back into things. I don't think being around each other we can take it slow. We have history and chemistry. I think if we are together we will just rush back in." She didn't want to have this conversation. Not like this and not now. But it had to happen. So, she pushed it right out there.

Emma sighed. "I'm not wanting to rush things, either. But I can't stand having this unanswered, unresolved whatever this is." Morgan sensed there was something deeper to it. But she was too scared to dig deeper for that. Not now.

"How do you think we are supposed to navigate this? Where do you think we belong or fit with each other?"

"We are definitely meant to be in each other's lives. Think about it. Think about how our lives intersect. How we fit into each other's lives, that's another story. I believe that's what we've been trying to figure out. It would be easier to figure out if we were face to face."

"That's all fair." Morgan pondered it for a second.

After another loaded pause, "Maybe now isn't the time for us to be talking about this. Maybe it's too soon." It was Emma's deflection this time.

Relieved, Morgan moved on with lighter topics. She stayed on the phone with Emma until her phone nearly died. Emma told her about a few of the cases she was working on, and she filled Emma in on the various characters she encountered at the campground. She left out any information on Sara though.

After saying good night to her, Morgan sat out on her patio and watched as the sun set. As the sky darkened, streaked with golds and pinks through the deepening blue, it got colder, Morgan thought back to the feeling of Emma's arms wrapped around her. She missed Emma's affection and warmth. She missed warmth in general.

Morgan picked her phone back up and texted Sara. 'Wanna come over and have a glass of wine?'

It wasn't long before she got the response. 'On my way,' with a winky face emoji.

Ten minutes later, Morgan was letting Sara in the front door. She put a fire on in the fireplace and down tempo ambient music played in the background.

She looked at Sara's deep brown eyes as she handed her a glass of red. There was definitely a hint of chemistry there, and there could be more if she let her walls down.

Sara took the glass from Morgan and leaned in closer to her. Morgan allowed herself to push away thoughts of Emma as Sara kissed her, kissing her back.

Emma became thousands of miles away as she let herself be present in the moment with Sara.

Emma

EMMA WAS TOO WIRED TO go to bed. She unpacked her sheets and bedding and made her bed. Excited for pillows that were not flat and high thread count sheets and a king-sized bed she could sprawl out in, she put her bed together.

She pored over the events of her day. Lunch with Lizbeth. The taste of Lizbeth's lips. Morgan on the screen looking at her with that look.

She was not anticipating the Lizbeth situation. But she also decided she wasn't going to fight it either. Life is too short for that.

If anything was making her feel like her old self again, it was feeling wanted by two very incredible women. Women who were very different from each other. But nonetheless remarkable women.

Her bed put together, Charlemagne didn't miss a beat and jumped up onto the foot of it, circling several times before settling in. Emma undid some boxes to clear her mind of her burgeoning post prison love life.

After an hour of unpacking and organizing, her mind clear as her space was coming together, Emma curled herself up with Morgan's journal in an effort to wind down.

Excerpt from Morgan's Memoir

COMING BACK FROM CABO IS when everything got worse. I thought I had hit bottom, but I still had lower to go.

After getting back, I increased how much I was using. I was getting careless. I was sleeping less. Eating less. But I was making money hand over fist and my trips to Mexico were planned out well.

I would go down every few weeks, just spread out enough to not raise red flags at the border. I hit the farmacias in a particular order.

My former identity melted away. It was now two months since my Cabo trip, six months since Jonathan's death. I was able to piece the timeframe together based on the date of my termination email. Aside from that, days melted into one another. Nights were few and far between.

I was no longer any shred of who I had been before he died. I did not talk to any of my friends. I stopped using social media. I did not speak to my parents.

I was no longer a teacher.

I was anonymous. I was ugly. I was a loner. My insides matched my outside as far as I knew or understood.

I was a full-blown drug addict and dealer. I was skinny. I was haggard. I was mean. I hated myself and I hated what I had become. I felt like I deserved the unhappiness though.

Jace was proving to be an efficient business partner. I could trust him with a stash and to take his appropriate cut. He never asked for more and he never let me down.

Eventually, Jace's nephew who was a student on the campus began taking on some of the business. I took a smaller cut giving more to Jace to allow his nephew to earn as well. It was our own little MLM pyramid.

We had a good thing going. We were running our little operation easily and drama free, expanding from Adderall and Ritalin into Xanax and other party favor pharmaceuticals I could procure on my trips. It got to when I would show up at the various farmacias, the workers knew me and knew what I was there for. No questions asked, though. Time continued to fly.

Before I knew it, I was coming up close to the one-year anniversary of Jonathan's death. Looking back, I can say it was ten months after Jonathan died. At the time, I think I only comprehended it was close to one year.

I managed to stay so strung out, when I would allow myself sleep, he didn't come to me. Or if he did, it was brief, and I barely had the cognition to acknowledge him.

I was on one of my allotted nights of rest, passed out when I was awoken by the sound of glass breaking. I sat up, groggy and exhausted, and I could hear footsteps moving up the stairs.

"Morgan! Morgan! Get your skinny ass down here!" It was Donny's voice. I had not spoken to him, nor seen him since the day he got me high on meth in his shit box little house near the border.

I could hear his woman ask him a question in Spanish and he responded.

I didn't know what to do or where to go or what to say. I just pulled the blanket over my head and hoped he would think I wasn't home and leave.

The bedroom light popped on and the blanket was pulled off me.

Donny's hands gripped my hair and pulled my head back. "Wake up, Cupcake." His breath was rank, and based on his pupils, he was strung out.

"I'm awake! I'm awake."

He pulled my hair harder, my neck was bent back as far as it could go, making it hard to breathe, and he slapped my face hard. The pain burst through my cheekbone and eye into my head.

"Donny! What are you doing? Why?" I pleaded.

His woman was going through my closet and dresser drawers pulling stuff out. She was bantering loudly to herself in Spanish as she dumped drawer after drawer onto the floor and pulled items out of the closet, tossing them haphazardly around.

"You think it's okay you steal from me?" His fist made contact with my gut. My breath left my body on impact.

"I'm not stealing from you. I've never stolen from you," I managed to gasp.

"You and Jace are not doing business? Taking money and food out of my mouth? Out of Mariella's mouth?" He back-handed me on the other cheek. As my lip busted open the warm copper taste of blood dripped into my mouth.

Mariella found one of my cash stashes in a drawer and took it. I watched her flipping through it. Donny was on top of me pinning me down. His knees dug into my forearms, pinning me to my mattress. He pummeled into my ribs with the discovery. My body was one large explosion of pain and ache. I could hear a snapping sound and felt light-headed as my breath was ever harder to catch.

Mariella was in the bathroom pilfering cabinets and drawers. I was not a very astute drug dealer. I kept my pills in the obvious place: neatly organized in the medicine cabinet over what used to be Jonathan's sink in the bathroom. She found my stash and I could hear the pill bottles being shaken as she collected and shouted out with rapid fire Spanish.

Donny landed blow after blow into my face and body, a barrage of names as each blow landed. Bitch. Cunt. Slut. Mother fucker. I became the target of all his rage. There was no choice but to take it. I couldn't move under him. I couldn't breathe. The world became fuzzy, and the pain was suddenly gone. I could no longer feel anything. I thought I was going to die. I hoped I was going to die. I did not resist. I welcomed death.

The beating seemed to last forever. I must have been crying out, though I have no memory of it, because I could hear sirens making their way down the street. Donny suddenly stopped pummeling me and yelling at me. Donny and Mariella bolted fast down the stairs – I could hear their footsteps pounding down and away from me, and back out the window they burst through. I could vaguely hear more glass tinker to the floor as they went out, presumably the way they came in.

A flood of cops were in my room and radios were crackling and I could only catch one word here or there. I couldn't follow anything as darkness came in and went out in waves. A paramedic was sitting next to me with a flashlight in my eyes.

I was moved to a stretcher and pain exploded through my body as I was moved, bringing me back from the fading darkness. I cried out in distress. I remember that cry, and I remember the world going black.

I must have gone unconscious. Jonathan was next to me on the stretcher. I was so cold. His arms were around me and his eyes were sad. His cold hands stroked my face and hair. "Morgan, are you trying to join me? Do you think you are ready?"

I couldn't answer. I wanted to answer, but my mind could not form words or thoughts.

He let go of me and faded away.

He was there again, holding a baby – our baby. She was reaching for me with her fat little baby fingers. My fingers reached out and touched her hand. Ice cold. They were gone. I wanted to tell them I loved them. I wanted to be with them. All of us. Together. A family at last.

Jonathan was yelling at me, "Morgan, let me go. Let me be. Just let me be. I'm not yours any longer."

But you will always be mine. I will always be yours. Nobody really understands this except for you and I. The words were there, but I couldn't say them.

The next thing I remember was being awoken in the hospital room. My parents were standing over my bed and the same kind officer who was there when Jonathan died, the one who showed up the next day and looked at the note, was also standing by my bed. What was his name again? Jiminez I remembered.

"Morgan?" My mother's voice came shrill through my ears.

"Hi, Mom," I whispered.

"Ms. Hale, do you remember what happened?" Officer Jiminez asked me.

I lied. I knew to say what actually happened would land yet another target, a much larger one on my head. "No. I don't know what happened. I woke up and there was a strange man in my house, and I was being beaten. And I heard a woman's voice. There was a woman there. But I didn't see her. Just heard her voice."

"You didn't recognize him?" Officer Jiminez asked.

"No."

"If you saw a picture of him, would you recognize him?"

"Maybe?" I lied.

"You didn't see the woman?"

"No." Such a liar I am.

"But you heard her. Did she say anything that would indicate why they were there?"

"She spoke Spanish only. I don't really speak any Spanish."

"We were able to pull several prints, so maybe in a few days I will follow up with you."

He nodded to me and left after giving me a minute to absorb this information. I'm certain he was waiting for me to cave and tell him the truth.

I wanted him to stay, because as long as he was there, my mother would not berate me. Everything in my body ached. I wanted to close my eyes and disappear and see Jonathan. I wanted to join him. I knew I wanted to just die. I did not want to be there. I was tired. I reached for my locket and my neck was bare. My hands desperately searched around my neck frantic.

My father grabbed my hand gently. "All of your stuff is in a bag in the closet, including a necklace. Is that what you are looking for?"

I nodded, relieved they didn't take my locket, remembering how Mariella admired it.

"Morgan, what is going on? You have no job. You don't call us. You don't return our calls or answer the phone. What in the hell have you been into?" My dad, normally never angry or frustrated with me, was furious. It was him, not my mother laying into me for once.

"Nothing. Don't worry about it," I barely managed.

"You've been unconscious for days. Days! The doctors told us based on your tox screen you had heavy levels of Xanax and Adderall. You are dangerously underweight. You were beaten within an inch of your life. Broken ribs, punctured lung, broken eye socket, broken teeth. We went to the condo, and it was trashed. I'm not entirely sure it was all from the break-in. Morgan, I think it's time you come back up to Tahoe with us."

"No. I don't want to go up there. I don't want to live up there."

"You don't have to live there forever. Just come up and recover. Get your life together." My mom was pleading with me. My stoic, demanding mother was actually crying. Her lip trembling and mascara running down her cheek. "Morgan, you are not okay. I'm scared."

"No. I will do it down here. I promise. I can do it down here. Who even called you?"

"You still have us listed as your in case of emergency in your cell phone, Morgan." My father's voice was terse. This role reversal between them was too much for me to handle.

"I need to go back to sleep. I'm so tired. Can you guys just go? I promise; I will be in touch, I will do better. I will even come up for a weekend soon. But I can't go there. I don't want to. Please, just let me be."

After some protesting and me reassuring the both of them I would call them, they left me to rest and contemplate my life. They came back to check on me a few more times before heading back to their respective home.

During my first week in the hospital, I had been fed, and began to heal (physically, at least) and detoxed. The dreams of Jonathan were rampant though again. Some were peaceful and healing, and many were violent and angry again.

The peaceful dreams of him were what I craved. I wanted to live in them. He would lay with me, wrap himself around me like he did when he was alive. He would caress my face and hair and hold me. Sometimes he would be holding the baby, too. Not always, though. They made me want to die and be with him again. I wanted death. It was evident in how I had been living. I didn't care about my life or continuing it. If I wanted to live, I would have worked toward healing and becoming a better person. I looked it all up after I got out of the hospital. It's called the death urge. It is real, and it was stronger than I was.

In the violent dreams Jonathan would yell at me and tell me I was a fool. Telling me I couldn't join him. My penance was to learn to live with the guilt of what I had done. It was time to learn to become a better person. I was stuck here until I figured it out.

Psych was having a field day with me, but I was resistant to their help. I would wake up screaming at night or crying. A technician or nurse would come running in, delivering a higher dose of sedatives to knock me back out.

After another week in the hospital, my bruises began to heal, and the swelling was gone. I was fully detoxed and attended several meetings with the therapists in psych and gained some of my weight back. I was sleeping, regardless of Jonathan's visits or what they entailed. I was finally discharged and went back to my place.

Kind and wonderful Officer Jiminez, who seemed to always be there when my life was upended, called me as I was being driven home by an Uber. He was waiting for me on my porch when I arrived.

I opened the door and Jiminez followed me into my trashed and destroyed condo. I had only just now been able to see the extent of the damage caused by Donny and Mariella. It looked like a hurricane blew its way through. Furniture was upended, drawers emptied. Knick knacks from my various travels and adventures (mementos from when my life was easy and fun) were smashed.

Officer Jiminez with his kind eyes and gentle nature, looked at me as I assessed the damage with tears in my eyes. I picked up the smashed frame with Jonathan and my engagement photo. This was no longer the home I wanted. This was now the site of everything I hated in my life. My lowest points were in this home. This was the center of rock bottom.

He reached out and touched my shoulder, "Ms. Hale, are you okay?"

I nodded silently.

"After pulling the prints, we have some photos and compiled a line up. If you look at the pictures, do you think you will recognize who did this?"

"I can try." My voice was quiet. I went and pulled the table upright with his help and two chairs.

He sat across from me (where Jonathan sat the first night, and sat every night after, whenever we sat at the table, I swallowed hard the lump in my throat) and handed me a photo sheet with the pictures of six men, all with shaved heads. I could see Donny clear and easy. I shook my head no. "I can't tell which one was him. I was sleeping when the attack began, and I couldn't be sure. They all look the same to me."

He sighed heavily. "How about her?" He handed me the photo sheet with six women, with long black hair and dark eyes.

I could see Mariella plain as day. But I shook my head. "I didn't see her. Only heard her. And she spoke only Spanish." I was sticking to my story.

"It's okay, even if you don't recognize them in the photos. It just would have made this much easier. We have their prints. They say their prints are here because you're friends. We don't think that's likely. And since you are telling me you don't recognize them, there is no way you would have invited them to your home..." His voice trailed off and he looked at me. I think he knew I was lying.

"Thank you."

"For?"

"For being the one who has responded to the two worst days of my life. You seem to always be here. It's like I'm stuck in a dream, and you are a symbol of something. I know it doesn't make sense. But it's like there is a reason you are the one who always responds."

"This is my beat."

"I get that. Like I said. I know it doesn't make sense. But it does to me. And thank you."

He got up and I walked him back to the door.

I spent days cleaning, organizing, sanitizing. I put my home back in order. I also slept a lot. Willing Jonathan to come back. He didn't.

I got someone out to re-fit the window. I slept more. No Jonathan. Everything was empty and quiet and alone.

I went to the dentist and had an implant put in where my tooth had been knocked out by one of Donny's blows. I continued to clean and organize and sleep. No Jonathan. Just a void.

I considered using again. It would be easy to go back to Mexico. But how would I fund such an endeavor? Considering what Donny did to me, I was scared to know what was done to Jace.

As I was cleaning, I found the shiny black business card belonging to Eli and Sophia. I flipped it over and over in my hand, watching the light reflect off its shiny surface. I could go back to Mexico, or I could go see what this place was all about. I met them for a reason. I found this card for a reason.

I got dressed in one of my nicer sun dresses, and I did my hair and makeup. I was finally looking somewhat like I used to. I was definitely fuller than when they met me in Cabo, and my skin, though pale, was clearer and my eyes less sunken.

I made my way to North County to the address on the card. Sitting in the car in front of the building once I found it I contemplated just turning around and going back home. Maybe I should have called first?

Their building was not what I thought it would be. It was not an office building. It was a midrise apartment complex, shaped like a blocked off figure eight – having two wings on each side each with their own courtyard, 6 stories high. It was terracotta colored, and each unit had a spacious balcony. The name suddenly made sense to me. The Society. They all lived together. This was a commune.

I walked into the center doors where a receptionist sat. She was wearing cotton leggings and a tank top with a lotus flower and 'namaste' scrawled across the front. Her hair was pulled up in a high ponytail and she smiled at me graciously. "Can I help you?"

"I'm looking for Eli or Sophia."

"May I ask who is looking for them?"

"Morgan Hale. They met me in Cabo a while back."

"Certainly. Have a seat. Would you like some water while you wait? It's alkaline."

"Yes, please."

She went into a small room off her desk and came back with a glass filled with ice cold water.

I sipped it patiently while I waited. Not sure what the difference was between 'alkaline water' and regular water, it didn't taste any different, and I didn't feel any different drinking it. I contemplated just leaving, but something held me there. There was a certain peace emanating from just the waiting area. It was airy, and light streamed in. New Age music came softly from the speakers.

I got up and walked around the lobby area. It was clean, and the floors were polished to a shine. Potted plants flanked all the windows. There were doors to each of the courtyards off the lobby area. A pool and spa and barbecue area were in one courtyard. In the second, there was a neat grass area with a garden and several stone statues depicting various gods, goddesses, and animals from various world religions. Suddenly, I caught myself wishing I lived amongst this peace and tranquility.

Eli and Sophia came out holding hands, both of them smiling politely. "Morgan! It is great to see you!" Eli exclaimed. "We were wondering if we would ever cross paths with you again."

"Hi! Yeah. I meant to come by a long time ago. But I just... I don't know. I just never have been good at this kind of thing."

"You were not ready," Sophia said in her soft voice.

I nodded, fighting the urge to cry. She nailed it. I was not ready then. But I was ready now. Something about just being in the lobby made me feel like I wanted to stay in this space.

"Come back to our office." Eli motioned for me to follow. "Sola, will you order us delivery from that new Indian restaurant? Some Saag Paneer, butter chicken, naan, Samosas."

My stomach growled. I had rediscovered my appetite since I quit using.

"Yes, sir." She went back to her desk to call in the order and I followed them into a spacious room with two desks on opposing angles facing each other and a couch and loveseat in the middle. There was a sliding door leading out to the courtyard with the garden. The door was open allowing for a gentle breeze. I could smell the star jasmine that was crawling up the lattice on the side of the building.

"Have a seat," Sophia motioned to the couch.

I sat on the loveseat and looked at them as they sat next to each other on the couch. Her hand rested on his lap.

"I'm going to be honest, Morgan. When I first saw you in Cabo, alone, you looked haunted. I knew we crossed paths for a reason. Tell us why you are really here." Eli's dark eyes looked not just at me, but through me. There was going to be no bullshitting him.

"What you said about building a community of faith. I need faith again. I need peace." From there I launched into an abridged version of everything. Jonathan, my infidelity with Sunny, his suicide, the hauntings, the drugs, the dealing, the assault. I ended with, "I need peace. I need to heal. I don't like where I've been or where I was heading. I feel like where I'm at right now, I just don't even want to live. I need to find myself again. Joy. Peace. Things I've lost. I didn't just lose my love, my mate. I lost myself."

"You said you were a teacher, is that correct?" Sophia asked.

"Yes. I was."

"This is so kismet you would come find us today of all days. Honestly, I had a dream you would be coming back to us. You were going to find us. Join us." Sophia looked away and blushed. She took a breath before continuing. "It just so happens a large portion of our residents here have children and several of them are wanting to homeschool. Would you be interested in maybe moving here and working with our children?" Sophia asked eagerly.

"I... Um..." I was hung up on her stating she dreamt of me. And how fast this offer spilled out of her lips.

"Sophia jumped the gun. I'm sorry. I hope she didn't scare you off. Let me explain. The Society is growing. We have eight centers in three states: California, Arizona, and Oregon. This is our first center that also houses members for a full-time experience. We are planning more eventually. Our job is the care of the members of The Society. Sophia takes it very seriously and very personally when they have a need. At our last group meeting last night, several of the members told us they felt their children were exposed to too much toxicity at school. I told you about our system of beliefs in Cabo. We are all about the best parts of the spiritualities that make this world go 'round. We have daily meditation twice a day. All members are required, if they are in the building, to attend. Several who don't live on site also join. We do daily yoga practices, as a healthy body leads to a healthy mind. Alcohol only in moderation. Processed foods in moderation. Fasting occasionally. The majority of the members do live on site, right now. Several members provide services for the community as their career. We do charge a small rent considering the premises to help with upkeep and payment of the services. We take rent directly out of the paycheck. Would you like to look around? I'm not saying you would even need to live here, if you want to work with us."

I nodded. Why not? Considering where I had been going this was an upgrade. The condo was a constant reminder to me of all that was wrong with my life.

The main floor held two conference rooms where they held workshops. Those workshops were aimed at corporations and businesses, though Eli also went to them to teach. He was the one who did the motivational speaking and taught those workshops. He also boasted several books he published on everything from mindset, to the law of attraction, faith, marriage, and more. There was a small shop with yoga mats, t-shirts, Eli's books, and other sundries fitting the lifestyle they encouraged.

They had several rooms that were booked out for retreats that they hosted as well. They were minimalistic and geared toward the austerity of meditation and cleansing.

There was a room which could be used as a classroom on the courtyard side of the building. On the poolside, there was a full gym and a meditation room and a yoga studio.

We took an elevator to the sixth floor and went down a hall. Midway down, Eli used a key and unlocked the door. "This would be your space. It's just under 800 square feet. Look around."

There was a large master suite with a bathroom and a walk-in. A smaller second room like an office or den with a powder room off the main area. A spacious living room with a balcony overlooking the courtyard which faced another balcony across the way. The kitchen was open and supplied with stainless steel appliances.

"What would the financials look like?" I asked.

"We researched the salary scales for local teachers. We unfortunately can't compete with the years of service promotions. We know a teacher of your caliber would make significantly more in a school setting. But we can talk specifics downstairs. Water, electricity, cable, Wi-Fi are included in the rent."

I did not even need to think on it. "I'm in. Like all in. I need a fresh start. I believe you are absolutely right, we met for a reason. Kismet, or whatever. This sounds like the life I need right now." I was not going to wait to consider it. Looking at the space and thinking about going back to my condo where I was supposed to build a life with Jonathan, where Jonathan took his life, where Donny beat me within an inch of my life, I wanted to start fresh. This was starting fresh.

"Let's go downstairs and fill out some paperwork. Legalities. You know, that kind of stuff." Sophia smiled as she took my arm to lead me back to the elevator. Her warm arm linked through mine, and the smell of her amber perfume and the undeniable promise of a fresh start made me giddy.

I didn't read any of the paperwork. I just allowed Sophia to summarize everything with her lilting voice and subtle accent. A morality clause, clean eating, no credit cards, commitment to live by the principles of The Society, rent and payment agreements.

I set my move in date for the following week, allowing me time to get my affairs in order and list my condo for sale. The lunch was delivered while I was signing the papers and we ate as Eli clarified my expectations.

"Your schedule will be regimented. You will need to be at morning meditation followed by yoga practice by 7:30 each morning. Daily habits help keep the mind focused. For your groceries and other needs, there is an approved list of items you can select. Put your order in by 7pm the night before and one of our assistants will do the shopping and deliver it to you. These items will be deducted from your pay, as is rent. We want to ensure all items are earth friendly and not processed. What we take into our bodies affects our minds and what we put out."

"I'm not trying to be obtuse, but we are eating food from a restaurant. I met you at a resort, eating prepared food."

"Obviously, it's not possible to control 100% of the time. But we limit ourselves when and where possible." Eli was patient and not at all patronizing in his response.

I nodded in understanding.

"Morgan, it's not that we want to control all things at all times. We just want to control what we can. We are working on a micro level to start by creating a better society in our little pocket. Hopefully, it spreads and gets bigger and bigger. We control what we can where we can and let the rest fall as it may. It's about intentions, possibilities, and positivity. You will notice how your life and your mindset will change as you live and grow with us, as will the world around you. Around us."

I hugged Sophia and Eli and thanked them before I left. I felt hope for the first time since Jonathan died.

I went home and called my realtor friend to list my condo and began to pack my belongings. I called a moving company and scheduled my move to The Society.

The San Diego real estate community is extremely competitive, and my condo was in a desirable location and went fast and above market value. I had an accepted offer within 3 days of listing. Even with the mandatory disclosure of how Jonathan had taken his life on the closet door almost one year ago.

The night I went into escrow on the condo, was the first night in a long time I had a visit from Jonathan. He didn't say anything to me. He just looked at me quietly and sad. I didn't say anything either. What more was there to say?

When moving day came, and the condo was vacated I did not feel even the slightest bit of regret or remorse. I gladly handed the keys to my realtor and made my way to my new life.

~ *VIII* ~

Options

The Present

Emma

ANOTHER WEEKEND PASS FOLLOWED BY another. Emma lived for her weekends in her own space.

Time was flying. She was busy.

Lizbeth was becoming a fixture in her schedule. She would pop in and bring Emma coffee and pastries on certain mornings. They would sit at Emma's table and take in a few moments to debrief on what their day entailed.

Brandon made it very clear it was a match he approved of.

Emma had made it clear to Lizbeth that she did not want to rush into anything. At least not until she was out of the halfway house.

Lizbeth made it clear that Emma's past was a non-issue to her. It was her past. Part of the journey in making her who she was, and adding to her already fascinating persona, but a non-issue, nonetheless.

Emma looked forward to the impromptu coffee visits, usually preceded by a quick 'Can I come by for a minute?' text.

Luckily for Emma though, both of them were extremely busy and these coffee flirtations and lunches had clear timeframes and helped her keep her boundaries in check.

Their Saturday dates that they were able to squeeze in around trial preps and visiting with Mary Anne and Brandon and just in general getting her home in order were a more difficult matter for Emma and her boundaries.

Lizbeth was doing her best to maintain respect for those boundaries as well.

On a Saturday morning, Emma woke up to a text from Lizbeth. 'Brunch?'

'Only if I can bring my dog.'

Lizbeth sent her the link to a restaurant with an outdoor patio that was dog friendly.

'Meet you there,' Emma sent with a heart.

Her house was finally in order. Her clothes organized. Books on shelves in the upstairs office. All her projects and renovations complete. Either by her own hand on her weekends or by contractors she or Brandon hired.

She showered and got dressed, appraised herself in the mirror. *Not bad, Landry.*

It was unseasonably warm for spring. Lizbeth's hair was in a thick braid over her shoulder, and her thin sweater clung nicely to her curves. Her distressed jeans and Converse tennis shoes made Emma smile. She thought Lizbeth was incredible in her suits, but she loved the more relaxed Lizbeth even more. Her carefree style outside of work reminded her a lot of Morgan. An effortless kind of beauty.

Emma let herself onto the restaurant patio with Charlemagne. Lizbeth squealed at the sight of the elderly brown and white Cavalier King Charles. She had yet to meet him. Boundaries.

"I pictured you having a big aggressive dog. Something that would match your personality more."

"Big and aggressive? You don't know me that well yet, do you?" Emma teased. "This is Charlemagne." She picked him up so Lizbeth could pet him.

After brunch and mimosas, Emma's resolve was ever more weakened. "Would you like to come back to my place? I don't want to call it a day yet."

Lizbeth nodded. "I have nothing else today."

She followed Emma to her house, taking in the neighborhood. Emma gave her a brief run through of the history of the home, leaving out Bailey's hand in its history.

She took Lizbeth through the rooms showing her the renovations.

When Emma got to the bedroom, Lizbeth snaked her arm around Emma's waist. "I have nowhere to be until tomorrow afternoon."

Emma let her walls down and gave in, giving up on her boundaries.

Lizbeth's hands on her body, her lips against hers, and the warm breeze coming through the windows carrying the scent of spring lilacs that covered the fence in the backyard carried Emma away. She lost herself in the moment as she pulled the lightweight sweater over Lizbeth's head and watched the tiny goosebumps appear as her fingers brushed over her silky skin.

She pushed Lizbeth back onto the bed and lost herself in the feeling of Lizbeth's touch, her lips, her whimpers and breaths. The way her body moved and the feeling of being touched and giving herself over after so long.

When the sun began to set and they finally emerged from the bedroom, mostly because Charlemagne was whimpering to be let outside, Emma glanced at her phone and saw a missed text from Morgan. 'I miss you. Maybe call me if you can this weekend?'

Emma typed back a quick, 'Call you tomorrow. Swamped with a client.' She hated that she was lying. But in all technicality, Lizbeth was a client first. At least that is how she started out. And Emma was still technically consulting on one of Lizbeth's more complicated cases.

She let Charlemagne back in and pulled out a bottle of wine and two glasses. "I don't have any food right now. I can DoorDash some dinner if you want?"

It was a sense of normalcy Emma hadn't felt in years. And for the first time in a long time, there was no shadow of guilt lingering. She was just content.

Morgan

IT HAD BEEN OVER A week since Emma called her last. They texted each other every day. She usually got a 'good morning' text every morning and she always sent a 'good evening' text. She loved waking up knowing Emma thought of her. Though it was a small gesture, it meant the world to her.

There were check-ins throughout the day asking how the day was going. Morgan didn't want to push. She knew Emma was busy with putting together her non-profit and she was consulting on cases and trying to readjust to a life of freedom. Morgan did find herself filling in the gaps of time with Sara. She was concerned though, as Sara was getting more serious than she was.

After work on Saturday, she met Sara for a night out. The restaurant had a fireplace toward the back and looked out over Lake Tahoe. Sara was seated at the table next to the fireplace. Her short cropped tousled platinum blonde hair appeared to glow orange in the firelight. Morgan looked at her and appraised her from where she stood. She was stunning. Her brown eyes were sharp and observant, and she looked like she was smiling almost all the time. Even when she wasn't, which Morgan found charming. She was wicked smart, and the sex was good. But she still felt like she was not in it all the way.

Sara looked over and caught Morgan watching her. She smiled and motioned for Morgan to come sit down. As Morgan approached, Sara stood, leaned in and kissed Morgan lightly.

"Hey, how was your day?" Sara asked.

"Good. Busy. You?" Morgan sat across the table from Sara.

Sara reached for Morgan's hand across the table and laced her fingers through hers. "Do you want to take a trip with me?"

"Where?"

"The Pacific Northwest. My friend Riley moved up there after her wife was killed, north-east of Seattle."

"Um. Maybe? When?"

"Next week. A long weekend. Fly up Thursday evening and come back Monday evening."

Morgan was unsure if she wanted to go. She felt like it would make things between them too official. "I need to make sure Dad can cover the campground, or Patti. Can I let you know in a day or two?"

Sara appeared to sense the hesitation. "Is that really all there is behind it?"

Morgan looked down at the table as the waiter came. "Can I get you both a drink while you look over the menu?"

"Titos with soda and lime," Morgan ordered. It was Emma's favorite cocktail, and she grew to love them in their short time together as well.

"I'll have the Justin Cab." Sara didn't break her gaze from Morgan as she ordered.

The waiter turned and left as Morgan sighed. His leaving meant it was time to talk.

"Sara, I think the world of you. I do. I was standing at the front of the restaurant watching you in the fire light. I was thinking just how amazing you are." Sara smiled and looked down. Where Emma was cocky, Sara was humble. Emma expected it because she got it all the time. Morgan appreciated each of them for very different reasons. "Things for me are very complicated. I haven't told you a lot of it, and I guess it's time I do tell you some of it."

"I want to know you. We've been increasingly spending a lot of time together. I think it's fair we either drop the pretenses and take the next step, or maybe we walk away?"

"I knew it was heading here. I guess it had to, huh?"

"What do you want?"

The waiter returned with the drinks. "Are you ladies ready to order?"

They both put their orders in, and Morgan waited for him to walk away before answering the question hovering in the air.

"I honestly don't know what I want. I need to be fair to both of us and be honest about that. Things for me are complicated. They've been complicated for a few years now."

"Life is complicated, Babe. It's never going to be not complicated."

"I don't buy it. I used to be a very non-complicated person. Now shit's a mess." Morgan forced a smile. "Let me give you a run down. You can decide if you still want me around after."

Throughout dinner, Morgan explained Jonathan to Sara. After dinner, Sara followed Morgan to her house, where Morgan brought her up to speed through Emma, leaving out how she and Emma were still navigating what they meant to each other. She wasn't ready to go there.

Sara spent the night, but for the first time, they didn't make love. It was just a peaceful night.

When they woke up, Sara made them breakfast before kissing her gently before leaving. "Your story doesn't change how I feel about you. Talk to your dad and Patti. See if you can come with me. If you want to. Let me know so I can buy tickets."

Morgan nodded and smiled as Sara made her way out the door.

It was Saturday and she had the day off. She texted Aaron and invited him to come over, but he was busy at his shop (and probably mad at her for blowing him off lately).

Tired of the status quo in her small house, she took herself into the animal shelter and asked for the cats. She finally gave in. She would be the crazy cat lady.

She wandered down the hall and looked at all the cages and wanted to take them all home with her, but she did the responsible thing and selected only one. She took her lack of impulsivity as growth, for sure.

It was a cat with grayish almost blue looking fur and vibrant green eyes which seemed to know things she selected. As she walked past the cages, those vibrant green eyes looked at her in a way that told her this was her cat. She was wise looking and expressive. Definitely the cat she needed. She could talk to this cat, and this cat would listen.

She took the carrier with the new cat and went to the pet supply store to buy bowls and a litter box, food and toys. She took her home and within an hour, it made itself right at home, finding a seat on the back of the couch, nuzzling in Morgan's hair purring softly. She already felt less lonely, taking comfort in the soft rumbling purring and warm, soft fur against her skin.

Morgan took a selfie of herself with the cat snuggling her and sent it to Emma (and to be fair, one to Sara as well).

'Who's your friend?' Emma replied almost immediately.

'Meet Ophelia. I just adopted her today.'

'She's beautiful like her mama.'

Morgan blushed. She wondered when she would ever not react to Emma.

'Thank you,' with a heart emoji was all she could think to send, when her phone rang with the distinctive 'FaceTime' ring. Her heart began to race as she realized Emma was FaceTiming her. She held her breath as she answered. "Hello, stranger." Her voice cracked as she smiled.

She was met with Emma's disarming deep blue eyes and sultry half smile. "Gotta love technology, right?" Her head cocked to the side as she examined Morgan in the screen.

Morgan was looking at the background trying to figure out Emma's setting. "Where are you?"

"My office."

"It's Sunday."

"I know. I've always been kind of a workaholic. I'm consulting on a big case that's being heard this week. I was going to work from the house, but I concentrate better here."

"Let me see your office. Show me around."

Emma turned the screen around and gave Morgan the tour of her space and then the rest of the suite belonging to Fitzgerald and Landry.

"It is so weird to see you in that context," Morgan stated. "I knew you in a different way. A different life."

"You did."

"I mean, your name is on the wall. You have an office and a secretary and a partner. You have a whole life you are returning to."

"This is all true."

"How do I fit into this life?"

"I think we are both trying to figure that out now." Emma had the phone propped against something on her desk. She was sitting with her feet kicked up on her desk. Morgan's heart continued pounding hard. If she could crawl through the phone and into Emma's lap, she would have.

Emma was grinning at her again. "Why are you looking at me like that?"

Morgan knew she could sense her desire. Emma had always been very aware of her effect on others. Emma's confidence was one of the attributes Morgan was a sucker for. She licked her lips and exhaled, defeated. "I think I forgot, well tried to forget how you make me feel. I mean talking and writing was one thing… and now I'm rambling." She hated how she was so flustered. She wanted to play it cool.

It took her a few more minutes before she was able to ease back into herself and have a normal conversation. She was able to tell Emma was actually charmed by her being flustered.

She was able to see the sun set in the window behind Emma as they talked endlessly. It was like there had been no separation as they chatted. Emma's wit and sarcasm still thrilled her. Emma sat and watched and listened as Morgan read her a passage from the book she was reading. A passage Morgan was eager to tell Emma made her think of her.

She felt the familiar sadness creep in when Emma was finally forced to hang up and get some work done. It was the same sadness that would wash over her in the early days when Emma was in the campground hiding out. When they would part ways, Morgan would feel as if she were leaving a part of herself behind with Emma.

She looked at Ophelia as she plugged her phone into the charger and Ophelia batted at the cord in a lazy and gentle manner. "I'm a fool, Ophelia. I can't believe I'm back in my feelings like this."

No sooner had the words left her lips than she got a text back from Sara.

Emma

EMMA HUNG UP WITH MORGAN and got into her car. She couldn't stop smiling. Morgan's vulnerability and natural beauty charmed her to no end. She was somewhat jealous of the cat, as through the conversation she watched it curl up in Morgan's lap, and Morgan absentmindedly pet the animal as they talked. Emma remembered laying her head in Morgan's lap, and how Morgan would run her fingers through her hair and trace the lines of her face as they would talk or watch movies together. She missed the small intimacy of it and Morgan's gentle touch.

Then she reflected back on her day, and night with Lizbeth, and the morning, too. She had to figure out what Morgan's place would be in her world. And what she was doing with Lizbeth.

She was warm from the inside as she turned the volume on her radio up as she drove down the street. She knew there was a bookstore between her office and the halfway house. There was just enough time to pull in and stop and purchase the book Morgan talked about and read to her from. The sound of her silky voice as she read the passage to her lingered and left her wanting more. She wanted to read the whole book herself.

Morgan's voracious reading and passion for her favorite books and authors was one of the reasons Emma found it so easy to love her. Morgan was the type of person who loved literature almost more than real people. She would talk about books and characters as if they were, in fact, real people to her. Lizbeth shared that passion as well. Both of these women were remarkably well read and wicked smart.

Emma grabbed a chai latte at the coffee bar inside the bookstore and found the book quickly.

She was through the door five minutes before her cut off, book in arm and latte in hand. The house manager checked her off and she made her way to her room.

Her new roommate was not in the room, so Emma was able to unwind in peace. She set the new book on the corner of her dresser and grabbed the journal, and her pad of sticky notes for annotating her questions.

Excerpt from Morgan's Memoir

MY LIFE WITHIN THE SOCIETY was exactly what I needed. At least in the beginning.

Eli and Sophia lived in the apartment across the hall from mine. There was this incredible sense of community, as negativity is highly discouraged. Obviously, it is not against the rules. But when you have negative thoughts, you are instructed to stop and think about what in your mind is causing them and ask yourself how you can reframe it and identify what the source of your negativity was and address it directly. The community itself was very structured. There was a kind of governing board that oversaw the rules and regulations and structure. They would convene regularly and address issues and grievances. Eli and Sophia obviously sat on the board. I did not want anything to do with it and hoped to avoid it altogether.

It was an assurance, per Eli, to ensure law and order versus full anarchy.

My first full day there, at 7:30 in the morning I made my way down to morning meditation and yoga. Before the session began, Eli introduced me to the other members. There were fifty other units in the complex (not including the units that were used for retreats). Five per floor. Ten were empty, leaving forty occupied, or to be specific, 38 not including mine and Eli and Sophia's. Some were occupied by couples, some were full of families, a small group of us were singles.

There were 28 kids ranging from 5-16 opting for the homeschool option I would be in charge of, and we would begin next week. Eli had already put in the paperwork for the approval of a homeschool program, giving me a week to get supplies and curriculum ready to go for them.

The first meditation almost seemed geared toward me. Like Eli had listened intently to what was plaguing me.

As we sat on the cushions on the floor, sage burning around us, lights low, New Age music softly playing in the background, Eli, seated cross-legged on a cushion in front, facing all of us, Sophia to his side, sitting in the same manner, started with an introduction, "To stay stuck in feelings of guilt and shame we are not serving the higher purposes of our community and most importantly, ourselves. Close your eyes. Inhale deep, hold it at the top and let it all go. Release your shoulders and unclench your jaw as you let it out. We work hard to forgive others for what they do to us but forgiving ourselves is something we never consider. Inhale again, holding it at the top, this time, exhale slowly. What does forgiveness mean to you? How much courage must it take to forgive yourself? Forgiving yourself allows for a new beginning. You are worth a new beginning. Inhale again, slowly. Filling the nostrils, the throat, the chest and into the belly. Slowly release from the belly, the chest, the throat, the nostrils. Letting go of those feelings of guilt and acknowledging you are human and flawed, allowing that you will make mistakes as part of the human experience, forgiving yourself is one of the biggest power plays in life. Inhale, again slowly, from the nostrils, filling the throat, the chest, and your belly. Hold it in. And on your exhale, push out with your breath, all those feelings of angst, self-loathing, guilt. You are worthy of love, new beginnings, and peace. Go forth today with peace of mind and awareness of the good you are capable of and the good you bring to this world. Namaste."

I didn't even realize it, but I was crying silent tears when I opened my eyes. Eli was looking directly at me, his dark eyes were seeming to penetrate through my soul as they always did when he looked at me. I felt vulnerable and naked under his intent gaze.

I looked down and away. I waited for the other members to get up and make their way to the yoga studio and made my way to Eli's side. "Was that for me?"

"It was for all of us, Morgan. We all struggle with feelings of guilt. You feel responsible for Jonathan. There's someone in here who feels guilty because they were a drunk at one time, someone who feels lustful thoughts for someone who is not their spouse, for cheating on an exam. The list goes on. You are not the only one with burdens weighing you down. The very fact you brought yourself here shows how you are working toward wanting to heal."

"I'm sorry, that was a lot of hubris on my part in assuming it was for me specifically."

"Because the human experience is so common, we all essentially experience the same feelings in varying degrees at any given moment. So often we think topics are meant for us or directed to us, but it's just that we all have so much more in common than we think."

Night time since Jonathan died, had been a time of dread for me, especially if I was sober. After my decision to join The Society, that was not the case. I laid down in my bed after the first full day and wished for him to show up, but he never came. It was the first night I realized I could heal and wanted to heal. Though I wanted him to show up, he didn't, and I was okay that he didn't. I could miss him, and long for him, but I could be okay without him.

I settled in quickly after the first day. The routine provided a sense of comfort for me. The twice daily meditations and thinking about Eli's words regarding the human experience made me feel closer to the members who sat with me at each meditation and moved and breathed with me through the daily yoga practices.

I began to gain weight and fill back in. I looked healthier. I felt better. I was smiling and laughing and enjoying the people around me.

The one-year anniversary of Jonathan's death came and went during my first week with The Society. On the anniversary of his death, I lit a white candle in my apartment and prayed for him. I spent the majority of the day in quiet reflection and trying to forgive myself and forgive him.

Feeling settled and more at peace, I took time to go visit my parents after being with The Society for two months. Our cars were in a locked garage and keys were kept at the front desk by Eli and Sophia's assistants (Sola on days and Laura on evenings). I checked out my keys and took the drive after giving my itinerary to Sola.

I was sitting on the dock behind my parents' cabin that extended into the turquoise lake.

My mom took one look at me and hugged me hard. "Morgan, you look like yourself, again. You look so healthy." Her eyes were tearful.

"I'm so sorry for all that I put you through over the last year."

"You were hurting, and it makes me hurt you felt you couldn't come to us," my father said. "You used to come to me, to us, for everything. And you just stopped."

"After getting with Jonathan, I wanted to be more independent. But I realize I just kind of replaced you and your help with relying on him. And then I just couldn't cope, and I was embarrassed that I couldn't cope. Or at least cope in a healthy manner. But I am now. And I am learning I can do this on my own. I found a new job and I sold the condo."

"You sold the condo? Morgan, why? The deal when we bought it was that even if you moved out you would rent it out. You were supposed to keep it to build equity and wealth. We discussed this." My father was frustrated.

"Daddy, Jonathan killed himself in it. I just couldn't. I was beaten within an inch of my life in it. I took the equity and invested it. Just like you talked to me about before. But I couldn't keep it."

"Where are you living now?" my mother asked.

"I have an apartment near Fallbrook. It's a nice community." I was vague for a reason. I wasn't ready to explain to them how I was living as a part of a commune.

"What are you doing for work? Did you find a new district?"

"I'm working as a private tutor, homeschooling kids."

"I thought you were adamantly against homeschooling?" my mother challenged me. Leave it to her to not be capable of just being happy for me.

"I've been through a lot over the last year and I'm working on expanding my views. This is different than traditional homeschooling though. This is a collective of kids who have parents that don't want to put them in traditional school environments. So, they are still getting the social emotional component."

My mother raised an eyebrow at me but didn't push me.

"The pay? Is it competitive to what you were making in public school?" Dad has always been about the bottom line.

"No. It's a lot less, but the stress is less, and the environment is good. And I'm still making enough to cover my monthly expenses and not stress."

"Well, you look good. You look happy. Are you dating again?" my mother asked, leading my father to shoot her a look.

"I'm still not ready to date again. I can't think about being with anyone right now. I'm only just now learning to love myself again."

Which was true. The Society did not lack in people I would find intriguing or attractive, and I could see some of the single people checking me out when I was in the shared spaces with them or as I moved through the hallways. But learning to just be okay on my own and exist in my own skin was a bigger priority to me than jumping into someone's bed. See, progress!

I just couldn't open my heart or mind to anyone yet.

Before I knew it six months passed. I had grown extremely fond of and close to Sophia and Eli. We almost always shared at least one meal a day together and we constantly came and went from each other's apartments. I loved being around Sophia, particularly. Her warmth and beauty never ceased to captivate me.

I was doing better about communicating with my parents since joining The Society, and I visited a handful of times. After my six-month point, my parents decided to come down for a visit and I was anxious about showing them where I lived, but I couldn't put it off forever.

As I waited for my parents in the lobby, I paced back and forth across the space until I saw them walking up to the door. My mother looked skeptical as she walked in and assessed the sign over the reception desk. "The Society?" she asked.

"It's like a community here. Let me show you around." I hugged her and my father and walked them in and led them past reception. "This is the pool area here... And here is the courtyard... Over here is my 'classroom' where I work with the kids-" I was taking them through each area when my father cut me off in the classroom.

"You teach the kids here? In your building? Morgan, what is going on here?"

"I will fill you in when we get up to my apartment."

I took them to the elevator and then down the hall to my door. When we got in I showed them my space and sat them on the couch.

"I know on the surface this sounds crazy, but listen," I began before giving them a very brief summary of The Society.

"Morgan, you are in a cult." My father's tone was dark.

"It's not a cult, Dad. I'm not brainwashed. I just live in a collective community with like-minded people. Positive people. Happy people. No drugs. No insanity. I'm not in a harem with a cult leader. I make my own decisions and I can leave at any time. They are not isolating me, obviously, as you are here. Yes, there are rules and a schedule, and we do meditations and fastings, and I have responsibilities to the others in the community as they have a responsibility to me, but it's not what you think."

"Morgan, honey, if you can leave anytime, come back to Tahoe with us." My mother was begging me. "The trauma from Jonathan and everything else you've been through, you are just not making good decisions for yourself or your life."

"No. I'm here. I enjoy it here. I'm thriving here. I don't know why you can't be happy for me. I'm happy for you up in Tahoe living your dream with your cabin and your campground. I love this apartment. I love this life here. I love my community." It was not a lie. I truly loved everything about The Society and my life.

After the weekend, my parents did not feel any better about my situation when they left. Each day they tried a little harder to get me to come with them.

I refused. They even met Sophia and Eli briefly, which didn't help at all. "I don't like the way Eli looks at you. Like you are some property of this community," Mom said.

"Mom, you just have a sordid perception of this situation, and you are putting your own spin on it. Eli is married to Sophia. They are happily married. He's got zero sights set on me."

After they left I went across the hall to see if Sophia was free. She took me to a coffee house, and we sat outside. "What is wrong?" she asked.

"My parents. They are driving me insane. They sheltered me my whole life. Bailed me out when I was in trouble. I never really did anything on my own until Jonathan came into my life. And when he died, I didn't know how to cope, because they always made choices for me, and I let them. And then I went from relying on them to relying on Jonathan. I needed to go through my own hell, I think. And I did go through hell. And I came out better for it. Now they are concerned about me living in The Society. They're calling it a cult."

Sophia smiled. "You are going to get that. People don't always understand. But you are a grown woman. You can make your own decisions. If people can't be happy for you, maybe it's best if they are not in your life."

"Yes. But I also want my parents to be happy for me. To understand. To be proud of me."

"You can't live to make others happy, Morgan. You have to live for yourself first and foremost. Are you happy?"

"I am. Because of you and Eli. I am. You guys saved me."

She leaned in and hugged me. I let myself surrender to her embrace and it felt good. Her fingers pushed my hair back in a gesture meant to comfort, but the closeness in the gesture shot electricity through me for the first time in forever.

I moved away fast with my pulse racing. I smiled at her bashfully and busied myself with my coffee cup.

We moved on to other topics and eventually made our way back to the complex. I had a difficult time looking at her or accepting her small affectionate gestures the rest of the evening. I recognized there was a good chance with all of the time I was spending with Eli and Sophia that I might have developed a small crush on Sophia. But – she was stunning. And so smart. And kind. And gentle. And very affectionate, which I loved all of it. I *loved* her.

It was the night where restlessness first began to creep in. It had been over a year and a half since Jonathan died, and as long since I had been touched or touched another person. I missed intimacy. I blamed my crush on my lack of contact over the last year and a half and decided I would do my best to ignore those feelings and find a new distraction. Besides, I learned my lesson; three is a crowd in any relationship.

I decided it was time to start dating maybe. Or at least make myself available to do so.

As I walked through the hallways or in the common spaces, I decided to pay attention to the people around me.

There was the single father with the two boys I was working with. Every time I saw him walk with his boys to the classroom area, I noticed how his eyes lingered on me. Most of the women in The Society were dressed for yoga classes almost all of the time. Black leggings that leave little to the imagination and yoga tops. I had regained my figure and muscle tone since joining The Society, so I knew the look he was communicating, and he was handsome enough; but I didn't want to get involved with someone with kids, much less two of them.

There was the woman who worked as a bartender in the Hillcrest area. I noticed her checking me out in yoga class. There was something about her I couldn't quite get into. She was too something. I was not sure what though.

There were plenty of choices, but I found a reason to stay away from all of them. Maybe I wasn't so ready after all.

I was sitting poolside to enjoy the sunshine and a good book outdoors after I finished with my students one afternoon when one of the single men came in. I watched him from behind the dark lenses of my sunglasses, he appraised me as he set his towel and phone on a nearby chair. I watched him as he began to swim laps. He was attractive and, due to the lifestyle we lived in The Society, he sported a nice physique from daily yoga and clean eating.

After he completed his laps, he got up and was toweling himself off. Out of nowhere he decided to speak to me. "How have you liked living here?" He sat in the chair next to mine.

"I'm enjoying it. I feel good about life again being here."

"It was a nice shift in my life, too." He made himself comfortable in the lounge chair and smiled. "You're Morgan, right?"

"Yes. I'm sorry, I don't have your name." I smiled at him. It sounds crazy that I wouldn't know his name after six months of living so close in a small community, but other than my students, their parents and Eli and Sophia, I kept to myself.

"Sean." He smiled back at me. "You are working here with the kids as a teacher, right?"

"Yes. It's been wonderful. So different from public school. Less stress, and the kids are all so wonderful. What do you do?"

"I'm a graphic designer. I work for a marketing firm downtown. I also do the materials for The Society."

We made small talk for a little while before I excused myself and went back to my apartment. I didn't want to give too much away up front. It's not like I wouldn't see him shortly after for evening meditation.

I went upstairs and cleaned up and warmed up a light dinner (leftovers from the dinner Sophia made last night- on top of being beautiful, smart, and kind, the woman could cook). I double checked my appearance before heading back downstairs.

Sean was already seated on a cushion waiting for the practice to begin. He patted the cushion next to him when he saw me, and I gladly took it.

When Sophia and Eli came in, Sophia saw I was sitting with Sean and sent a subtle smile and nod my way. My cheeks flushed with the gesture, and I looked away.

After the meditation as I was standing, Sean took my hand. "Morgan, wait." His thumb caressed over the top of my hand gently.

I stopped and smiled at him as the rest of the members were making their way out of the room and heading to their respective apartments. Eli and Sophia were waiting for me at the front. We had already arranged to meet up and enjoy a glass of wine and talk about a few affairs for the school program.

"I was wondering if we could have dinner sometime?" His hand was soft and warm on mine and the warmth emanated from him through me.

"I… um…" I was suddenly nervous. "That… that would be nice. When?"

"Tomorrow if you are not busy?"

I nodded. "Yes. I can meet you in the lobby. What time?"

"Seven, right after evening meditation?"

"Great. Yeah. I'll see you then. At meditation and yeah."

I turned and almost ran to Eli and Sophia. They escorted me to their apartment, and we sat on their wide balcony.

"So, you and Sean?" Eli asked, smiling.

"I mean, it's just dinner tomorrow."

"It's a good match if it works out." Eli sat across from me.

"Maybe. We'll see." I was suddenly shy. Sophia was bringing the glasses and the bottle of wine out.

I kept the conversation focused on what I needed for the school program and deflected the personal questions which was unlike our usual time together.

As I stood to take myself across the hall, Sophia followed me to the door. Ever since our day at the coffee shop, I couldn't quite think straight when she was around and could barely look at her without wanting to touch her. Even now with the potential distraction of Sean, I found myself wondering what it would be like to kiss her.

"If it's not too late when you get back tomorrow night, come tell me how it goes?" She was standing close to me in the doorway; I could smell her perfume and feel her body heat.

With a forced smile I assured her I would.

The next morning, when I went into morning meditation, Sean again saved a space for me next to him. I sat next to him, and we chatted, keeping it light, while we waited for Eli and Sophia to come in and begin the session. And it was the same for evening meditation.

After which, he escorted me out of the room and through the lobby out to his car. He was a gentleman, opening the doors for me. As I walked through the main doors past him, I could smell him, similar to Jonathan, clean and crisp.

I was nervous leaving the building with him when we checked out with Laura. I had not been on a date since Jonathan. Sean, in a lot of ways, reminded me of him. He was gentle in nature like Jonathan. And so bright and witty like Jonathan once was. And I couldn't shake how similar he smelled. It made me slightly dizzy and unnerved at how similar they were.

As I sat across from him at the restaurant, a dimly lit romantic Italian joint, with a cozy atmosphere, I truly analyzed his features and tried to figure out what it was I was actually feeling. I was shaking slightly. I adjusted my shawl around my shoulders and pulled it a little tighter.

"You're nervous." He was not judging me, so much as observing.

"Yeah. A little." I tried to breathe and relax. "I have not been on a date in a very long time. At least very long for me."

"I know you have not dated since you got to The Society."

"You noticed?" I could feel my cheeks flush.

"It's not a big community. You tend to notice when someone piques your curiosity."

"What about you? Tell me. Have you dated a lot since coming in?"

"I've gone out with a few women. But the ones who were not part of our community, they didn't really understand me or the greater purpose. So, I made the resolution that I would only date within The Society. And then I tried to go out with one or two members, but we didn't really fit. And no one else held my interest until you."

"I've been here for over six months. You just now asked me."

"When you first got here, you were like a scared animal. I was afraid to approach you. You obviously needed some healing. I needed to wait until you were in a better place."

"You were watching me that close?" As odd as it sounded, it touched my heart how he held back and respected my journey and observed it.

"You were pretty when you arrived, but there was a darkness in your eyes. It was beautiful to watch the light return to you." There was earnestness in his eyes and in his voice. "But it leads me to wonder what hurt you so deeply that you succumbed to such darkness?"

"I don't want to darken our evening with it. Can we shelve that for when we know each other better?"

His hand reached across the table, and he laced his fingers through mine. "When you are ready, I am here to listen."

"What brought you to The Society?" I gently removed my hand from his and placed it in my lap. Not meaning it to be a rebuff of his affection. I just wasn't sure what I wanted.

"My ex-girlfriend, actually." He laughed. "We started dating and a few months in, she finally introduced me to the building, and I moved in. Then, she got an opportunity for promotion within her company. The promotion required her to move out of state. She asked if I wanted to go, but I love my job, and I love the community in the building. We talked it over with Eli and

Sophia. She is still a member of The Society. She is actually working with Eli on building a small community in Arizona where she moved. They allowed me to stay in her space when she left. We tried to do long distance, but it just didn't work. I don't hold any ill will toward her. We're still friends. She's an amazing person. She led me to The Society."

Once we got past the initial awkwardness, I was able to relax, and we ultimately enjoyed our time.

Once dinner was finished, we walked around the Gaslamp district and into Ghirardelli for dessert. We made our way back to his car and drove back to the building. We checked back in with Laura, and he dropped his keys with her.

He was in the other wing, so his elevator was across the lobby from mine. In the vacant lobby, standing in front of my elevator, he took both of my hands. "I had a wonderful evening with you, Morgan. You're a remarkable woman."

"I had fun, too." It was not a lie. It was nice to have the companionship.

"I know you are healing. I don't want to rush you or push you. But I want to do this again."

I looked into his eyes. He was safe. I could feel it.

I let myself lean in closer to him.

He came in closer, closing the gap and kissed me softly on my cheek. "I'll see you in the morning."

I looked at my phone and saw it was close to midnight. I chose to not go to Eli and Sophia's but went straight into my apartment and to bed.

Once I got home, I laid in bed and started thinking about Sean, but the similarities to Jonathan gave me anxiety, so I let my thoughts trail off to Sophia. I fell asleep thinking about her.

It was as if I summoned her presence, because she was at my door knocking as I was having my breakfast and coffee. I let her in and offered coffee and some homemade yogurt (the only food I've ever mastered making, and that is because though it's time-consuming, it's rather simple and requires no real effort) and fruit. She accepted and sat on a stool at the bar counter separating the kitchen from the main living area.

"How did it go with Sean?" she asked eagerly.

"It was nice."

"Just nice? You came in late. Laura reported near midnight."

"It's just weird to be dating again."

"But you like him?"

"We are going to go out again, if that's what you are asking." I sat on the stool next to her and sipped my coffee.

"Do you have reservations about him?"

"I have reservations about anyone right now. Romantically, I mean. Mostly myself."

Sophia mixed her yogurt in the bowl. "This is really good, by the way. Do you think you are going to hurt him? Or that he'll hurt you?"

"I literally broke Jonathan. He killed himself because of my betrayal."

"Morgan, we've been through this. It is not your fault. You're not responsible for his choices."

"I know. And I was just starting to get there, but now I'm thrown back into this uncertainty. It's like dating is triggering all my insecurities about what I've been through. All my trauma. It doesn't help that Sean reminds me so much of Jonathan in so many ways. He even smells like him."

Sophia had a dab of yogurt on her lip, and I instinctively reached over and wiped it with my thumb. Her eyes gave a flash of heat as my thumb brushed across her lip.

"I'm so sorry. I didn't mean to get in your space. I didn't even think about it until after I did it."

She took my hand that had just been on her face. "You're fine, Morgan. I just wanted to check on you after last night. I need to go help Eli prepare for morning meditation. See you shortly." And just like that, she was gone out of the door.

I took my time cleaning up the breakfast dishes and coffee mugs, contemplating her visit and my date with Sean.

I went down to morning meditation and took my seat next to Sean. He leaned in and gave me a delicate kiss on my cheek. I smiled and let his hand rest on my knee as we waited to begin.

Sophia and Eli came in and I could feel the weight of Sophia's gaze on me. I looked back at her trying to figure out the meaning of her watching me.

Midway through the day, as I was working with my various kids in the classroom, Eli came in with a vase full of peonies. I forgot I mentioned last night to Sean that they were my favorite.

"Someone made quite an impression on their date last night," Eli grinned as he set them on my desk.

A few of the older children made "wooo" noises as I made my way to where Eli was standing near my desk.

"Thank you for bringing those in."

"Sean is a good man. He is the last person who will hurt you."

"I can see that." I plucked the card out of the pink and white bouquet. 'I hope these bring out that beautiful smile of yours – Sean.' And so they did. I smiled for the first time in a long time. Like really smiled and felt a small taste of happiness.

Eli nodded to me as he walked back out quietly.

For the next several days I met with Sean for meditation. I would catch Sophia watching us and tried not to make anything of it.

Sean and I went for another dinner. He did not press me to move fast or spend too much time. He was content to honor my boundaries. I couldn't cross past a certain line for some reason. Maybe part of me felt like I didn't deserve him. Maybe it was because he was so similar to Jonathan.

He did not really kiss me until our fifth date. It was not the kiss so much as how long it had been since I kissed someone that finally woke my body fully from its hibernation, and though I craved more, something in me panicked and held him at bay. My body, mind, and heart were at war with each other.

On our sixth date, I finally told him what I lived through leading me to The Society. We went to a sunset dinner on the coast and after dinner sat in the cool sand wrapped in a blanket from his trunk, shoes off, and feet deep in the cool, silky sand. The waves crashed blue and white in front of us, coming up almost to where our toes were buried.

As he wrapped the blanket around my shoulders, he caught sight of my locket and touched it gently. "You wear this every day. Is there a story to it?"

I pulled it from his fingers and clutched it. I didn't like it to be in anyone's grasp but my own. "It's part of what led me here. My fiancé, the one who killed himself... It was supposed to be my gift on our wedding day."

He was silent, watching me. Waiting for more to come out.

It was time to tell him the entire story. I cried as I told the tale. It was the first time I sat in my feelings regarding the situation and truly felt all of it. The vulnerability of total exposure felt good. I needed to let it all out.

He wiped the tears from my cheeks and looked at me, quietly.

"If you hate me, think I'm a terrible person, I get it."

"You're not a terrible person. You're not a bad person. You were impulsive and careless, but not bad."

"I'm scared I will fall into old patterns and habits. You're so wonderful, and thoughtful and kind. I don't want to hurt you."

"I will take this as slow as you need. I promise you, you're not going to hurt me." He kissed me, holding me close. "You're worth fighting for. You are a beautiful and free spirit, Morgan. The key to loving you is to not hold you to conventional standards. You didn't intend to hurt Jonathan. You weren't on a mission to destroy him willfully. You can't keep looking at yourself as this monster."

I cocked my head to the side as he wiped the last of my tears. "Thank you."

"For what?"

"For seeing through my bullshit. For seeing me as a person who is worthy."

~ *IX* ~

Love and Other Complications

The Present

Emma

EMMA LOVED SPENDING TIME WITH Lizbeth. But what she appreciated most about her was that she had her own life and did not center her focus solely on time with Emma. If they could squeeze in a Saturday together, or their quick morning coffee time in Emma's quiet office before the chaos of their days began it was time cherished, but not demanded.

Emma was growing to love her alone time in her house. And even the FaceTime calls and short texts with Morgan, though she was finding those to be fewer and further between trying to balance work, life, and Lizbeth also.

Emma was starting to feel a bit guilty that she had not once mentioned Lizbeth to Morgan.

Inspired by Morgan telling her how she went to Jonathan's grave, Emma took herself, alone, to Bailey's gravesite. She called Mary Anne to find out where Bailey's final resting place was. Mary Anne gave her the address and offered to come with her.

Emma was touched by the offer but declined. She needed a moment alone with Bailey and her thoughts and set up a time later in the week to have lunch with Mary Anne.

Mary Anne chose a beautiful stone with a brass insert. When the insert was opened a lovely picture of Bailey looked back out. Emma took the picture of Bailey at a cafe in Rome. Bailey sat with her head in her hands and her strawberry blonde locks were blowing delicately around her face. Her piercing blue eyes stared back at Emma.

This was her first visit to the grave. She had no opportunity until this day. She closed the insert and stepped back to take in the stone.

'Bailey Anne Frankson-Landry

January 16, 1977 – March 12, 2021

Friend, daughter, wife

Only when you drink from the river of silence shall you indeed sing.

And when you have reached the mountain top, then you shall begin to climb.

And when the earth shall claim your limbs, then shall you truly dance.'

EMMA RECOGNIZED THE QUOTE FROM Khalil Gibran. Bailey fell in love with his poetry when she found one of his books amongst Teta's old books Emma had kept on a shelf.

Emma brought a dozen white roses dyed blue, a nod to the very beginning of their friendship and off again/on again romance. There was a bronze vase fixed to the side of the stone. Dried and dead roses sat in it and Emma pulled them out and inserted the blue roses. She walked the dead flowers to the trash bin and made her way back.

Never having been one for spirituality or prayer, she sat herself at the foot of the grave unsure of what to do or say. She tried to 'find God' (whatever that meant) when she first got to the prison but found it hollow and empty.

She took a deep breath and looked up at the sky through the branches of the tree that shaded the spot. "Bailey, I don't know what to say or why I'm really here. I met someone. You know that I'm sure. She's experienced loss, too. She thinks – or she thought – the loss was her fault. I know this, the reason you're here, is my fault. My fault on so many levels. I was a bad wife. I prioritized my own ego and my success over your emotional well-being. I drove you to cheat. I will never, ever understand why on earth you chose to cheat with Rhys Mills. But that is beside the point. It's still my fault. I choked you. I took your life. I hope you know I loved you. I never meant to hurt you. I never meant for this to happen." Emma went quiet. She was not sure what it was she was looking for as a sign. "I met another woman, too. She's easy to be with. Smart. Ambitious. But I don't know. I don't know what I'm supposed to be doing right now. I don't know if I should even be with anyone. It seems odd to be with anyone that isn't you. I'm so very sorry. I will always be sorry."

It was quiet around her. She sat in the stillness and took it in. She was never one to appreciate standing still. It was the particular aspect of her which drove Bailey mad. Emma always stayed busy and was never fully present in any moment. Her mind was constantly busy three steps ahead.

She inhaled deeply and looked around. Mary Anne had the option to bury Bailey next to her father but chose not to. She found a space Bailey would have liked. The tree above was a cherry blossom tree and it was blooming. Soft pink petals were fluttering down as Emma sat there. The spring time birds were singing in the trees and flying overhead.

When she was on the run, she saw Bailey and dreamt of Bailey all the time. Since she had turned herself in, those visions and dreams ceased, but the feeling of closure never came.

"I don't know what I was expecting in coming here. There is a sense of finality in seeing your stone and knowing you're here. I guess I'm looking for a sign of forgiveness or closure so I can move on. Is it selfish of me to ask for that? Given what I did? Do I deserve it? I'm starting to feel normal. I'm starting to feel like I'm living a whole new life. I'm moving on and finding joy again. But I still think of you. You were my first love, and nothing will change that. Nothing will erase you from my memory."

Emma sat still in the peace of the cemetery for what seemed like an eternity until she saw a blue jay land on a nearby branch. His bright blue feathers stood out amongst the pink cherry blossoms.

"That's from you." She was transfixed by it. He called out and flew off.

Emma stood and brushed the petals that had fallen on her off and moved back to the top of the stone and rested her hand there for a moment.

"You are not replaceable. What we had and what was done can never be erased. Not ever. Your presence in my life, your love helped shape me to be who I am. You are the foundation of everything in my life. I loved you with all my heart. In my own selfish way, I loved you. You taught me so many lessons. I love you, always."

Emma wiped her tears and stood for a while longer. She pondered a million times before what might have been if she had not killed Bailey. She knew herself better than to think she would have stayed with her. But Bailey would be alive. Doing what? Who knows? Making art? Maybe still with Rhys? Maybe with someone new? Maybe she would have gone back to work at the museum? Teaching classes. Maybe, just maybe they would have been able to maintain some semblance of a friendship after all was said and done?

No. There's no way. They could never be just friends. Therefore, they would be completely cut off from each other. She herself would have probably fallen back into her old ways of casually seeing many women, not settling for one. Just work and flings. These thoughts played a loop in her head over the last few years.

It had been some time since she allowed herself to consider these thoughts. But the thoughts now, were running along on their own. If she had not killed Bailey, she would have never met Morgan. She would never have run away and gone to California and up to Lake Tahoe. Or maybe, being single, she may have wanted to go. But she doubted it. It would have been unlikely she would have taken that much time off of work. Vacations were something of a demand to be met, given by Bailey and obliged by Emma.

With an exhale, Emma brushed the remaining fallen cherry blossom petals out of her hair. She slowly made her way back to her car. Emma got in and grabbed her phone and pulled up a travel app and looked at the price of plane tickets before making a purchase, and then took herself back home to her office in the upstairs bungalow to finish working on a case.

Morgan
MORGAN HAD DECIDED TO JOIN Sara on her trip to Seattle. She needed a vacation and time with Sara without distraction to assess her feelings overall.

She was beginning to feel like an afterthought to Emma. She was not used to this feeling with having once been the center of Emma's entire world when they were together. As Emma was busy pulling away from her and rebuilding her life, Sara was ever present.

Sara's friend Riley was a remarkable hostess. Her home in Sequim, a small town almost two hours from Seattle (and a ferry ride to boot) was beautiful.

In the mornings, Riley, Sara and herself walked to a small private beach with Riley's dogs watching the waves crash along the shore as they drank coffee.

One evening, Sara turned in earlier with a migraine, leaving Riley and Morgan to talk.

"Sara is really into you." Riley and Morgan were sitting in the backyard in front of a fire.

"I know."

"You aren't really there though are you?"

"Sara told me your wife was killed. How long ago?" Morgan was a master of deflection.

"It's been a few years. Four to be specific."

"Are you dating again?"

"No. Not really. It's hard. Eva was the love of my life." Riley smiled as she reflected back on her wife. "Her student shot her in the parking lot of the school. It threw my whole life out. I didn't just lose her. She had a son we were raising together, and his father hated us. So, I lost him, too. Although, I just got to see him recently for his sixteenth birthday. But that's a whole other story."

"I was engaged a few years ago. To this really wonderful guy. He killed himself because of me. It threw my life into a total tailspin. Since then, I've only ever dated one person, really. And it was a whole mess. I'm just trying to figure out who I am and what I want, really. I don't have any intention of hurting Sara, in case you were wondering. And I think that's my whole reservation along the way. I just want to make sure everyone is safe."

Riley sighed. "You can't control everything. You can't ensure everyone is always going to be okay. You need to just let yourself love and be loved. And if you aren't feeling it, well, you need to let her go."

Morgan nodded in agreement. After staying up for another couple of hours with Riley, she let herself into the bedroom where Sara was sleeping peacefully. She laid down next to her and traced Sara's eyebrow with her finger, before planting a soft kiss on her forehead. She had a lot to think about.

AFTER RETURNING FROM HER TRIP, Aaron came over to Morgan's. He had made a desperate mission of his life to try to teach her to cook. And he was the only one ever patient enough to do so.

Morgan was sitting on the counter of her kitchen with Ophelia in her lap as Aaron was busy 'showing' her how to properly dice an onion.

"You are supposed to be learning, dear."

"Watch one, do one, teach one, learn one. That's what my dad told me. I'm watching this one." Morgan grinned.

"And get your dirty cat off your counter! You are going to get cat hair in the food!"

"Ophelia! Did you hear that? He called you dirty!" Morgan kissed her head and set the cat on the floor.

Morgan sipped her hard seltzer in the can and got down off the counter.

She moved to change the song streaming over the Bluetooth speaker on the bar when the phone rang. It was a FaceTime from Emma.

She looked at Aaron.

"Is it her? Is it Emma? Or is it Sara? Which one is it?"

Morgan mouthed 'Emma' and answered. "Hey! It's after eight your time. Isn't that past your bedtime?"

Emma smiled at her, causing her heart to skip three beats. "Ha-ha. You're funny."

Aaron stopped what he was doing and came around to where Morgan sat down in the chair at the kitchen table. "You are right! She is even hotter in real life," Aaron hissed.

"You have company. I can let you go. We can talk tomorrow," Emma offered.

"No. No. Please no. Ignore him. That's Aaron. My friend."

"Yes. Ignore me. I'm just her kitchen bitch."

Emma laughed. "You still don't cook, do you?"

Morgan blushed. "No. I still don't cook. Aaron has been trying to teach me. So, you are free all night?"

"I'm mostly all caught up, so yeah. I'm yours tonight. Kind of. Seriously. I can call you tomorrow though."

"No, babes. I just ordered a pizza for her to be delivered. I'm heading out. You guys enjoy!" Aaron blew kisses at the phone and made his way out quietly.

"Where are you?"

"I'm in my bed with a glass of wine."

"I wish I was there."

"I wish you were, too. I sent you something in the mail though. Maybe it might entice you to come out here and visit."

"I think if I came out for a visit I would never come back."

"Would that be the worst thing?" Emma's voice was husky and made Morgan's hair stand on end.

Morgan looked away smiling. "I do have a life here." *And kind of a girlfriend, too.*

The smile left Emma's eyes, and Morgan felt a piece of herself soften. She didn't want to hurt Emma. She didn't want to lead her on. But she didn't know what she wanted or how to even move forward as far as this situation was concerned.

Morgan stayed on the phone with her until she could tell Emma could barely stay awake.

The pizza Aaron ordered was delivered and Emma continued to tease her about her not cooking.

Morgan put away the leftover pizza and cleaned up her kitchen. Heavy-heartedly, she picked Ophelia up and made her way to the bedroom.

She put the cat down on the bed and flopped down next to her. "I wish I knew what I was doing."

Ophelia just stared back at her with her wise green eyes, not providing her with any answers.

"I have to ask myself if I'm clinging to something just to avoid moving on. I mean, what we had in the past wasn't even really legitimate, Ophelia. We never really knew each other. I have to ask myself, honestly, if I knew she killed Bailey, would I have even fallen for her to begin with? Am I just caught up because she's fine as hell and good in bed? Stop looking at me all judgmental like that."

Ophelia rolled to her side stretching out and looked away from Morgan.

"Great. You are sick of me, too. I'm sick of me. I need to stop."

Emma

AFTER A WEEKEND OF CONTEMPLATING her life, she was driving from the halfway house to work, Emma felt bad that she had not yet told Morgan about Lizbeth and vice versa. But she felt like things were not serious with Lizbeth, so until it got to that point, she was entitled to just enjoy things as they were.

As far as not telling Lizbeth about Morgan, the waffling and refusal to get on a plane was justifiable to Emma in keeping Morgan as a non-issue.

Once in the sanctuary of her office, Greta had her mail organized the way she liked it on the lower right-hand corner of her desk. Her open files in the upper left. Her schedule and to-do list in the center, next to it her messages, with her *Starbucks* dark roast coffee black and steaming next to it.

She looked up at the painting with the Bryan Stevenson quote. She was not the sum of the worst thing she had ever done. She was starting to believe this. She was going to do something for the community which was beneficial for others more than her bottom line.

Brandon knocked on her door and stood in the doorway. "Lunch today?"

"Sounds good."

Brandon was lingering in the door, as Emma was sorting through her papers. "Savannah wants to know if you want to come over for dinner Friday when you pick up the dog."

"Yeah, that works. I feel like you have more to say than lunch and dinner plans." She set her papers down on the desk and scrutinized Brandon.

"How much do you hate the halfway house?"

"With every fiber of my being."

"What if I told you when you check out on Friday, you are checking out for good?"

"Seriously?"

"Seriously. I got the phone call just now."

Emma exhaled. "Four more days."

"Congratulations." Brandon smiled.

"I'm not sure if it's a congratulatory occasion but thank you."

"Emma, you could have easily just gone and stayed away. You could have disappeared into Mexico and never taken accountability for what was done." Brandon never said "what you did," always "what was done". "You came home. You did your time. You did good while you were in prison. You came out and are making the choice to do something that gives back to those who didn't have the advantages you have. Congratulations is in order."

"Thank you, then."

"How's Lizbeth?" Brandon came in and sat across from Emma.

Emma grinned. She couldn't help but smile when she thought about Lizbeth. She was dynamic. "She's awesome. But we are taking it seriously slow."

"How's Morgan?"

"She's good. We text pretty much all day every day. Talk here and there when we can. But it's all uncertain. We don't know where it's going. There's a lot to navigate. I sent her a gift card for an airline ticket. I don't think she got it yet. If she has, she hasn't said anything."

"What if she turns up and in person you don't have the same chemistry any longer? It's been a few years since you've been face to face."

"I don't think that's the case. We've been FaceTiming and to see her... to see her... all of the feelings I've ever had just rush back. And you should see her when she sees me. It's all still there."

"I don't envy you trying to juggle the two of them." Brandon shook his head. "I mean, you used to juggle a lot of them in college. But at our age... two is a lot."

Emma stuck her tongue out at him. "I can't let Morgan go. Not yet. Not until I know for sure where she fits into my life."

"I think it's pretty clear if she's not jumping on a plane."

Emma shrugged as Brandon got up and walked back to the door. "See you at lunch," she called out to him.

EMMA SAT ON HER SMALL rack in the halfway house, feeling a million times lighter with the knowledge that she was not coming back when she left on Friday. She was contemplating the two women in her life. If Morgan were to show up suddenly, what would that be like? Would she be so willing to cut Lizbeth out? She was starting to grow truly fond of the woman. However, there were no signs of taking matters to another level. Which Emma took as a sign.

She had brought Morgan's journal out of its drawer. She could hear the neighbor's kids playing in their yard.

She felt like even with the duality of her love life, everything was actually right in the world. She was content for the first time in as long as she could remember.

Emma flipped through the pages of the journal and her copious sticky note annotations finding the silver ribbon place holder.

She thought about Morgan during their FaceTime call and how she looked at Emma on the screen, wondering what the root of her holding back truly could be.

Excerpt from Morgan's Memoir

LIVING AMONG THE SOCIETY REALLY was amazing. I loved my life with them. The homeschooling program I started for the kids was, for the most part, easy. The kids were smart and inquisitive, and the parents were not overbearing or demanding, they gave me their implicit trust in educating their children.

The regimented schedule with daily yoga and twice daily meditations, the strict dietary requirements, and occasional fasting, were good for me. I was thriving. The Society was also thriving. All units were taken, and a waiting list was developing. The workshops were constantly sold out, retreats were booked out, and the yoga classes were always booked and became appointment only.

I barely left the building unless I went out with Sean or Sophia. I had no need to. I had all of my bills paid on autopay and never paid attention to my bank account or its balance.

My life revolved around our community. Eli would make a suggestion, and it was done. Sophia would have a request and I was at her service. It's just the way it was.

Sean was an added bonus. He saved my spot next to him for the meditations. He cooked. He did not demand of me. He respected that total vulnerability and intimacy was not something I was ready for. But the time we spent together was easy and effortless.

I was not ready to go to bed with him or anyone. If things got heated and I shut down, Sean would bite his lip and take a deep breath and tell me it was okay, and he understood. This had been going on for over three months. I don't think another man would have been so understanding. He was only so understanding, I think, because of The Society. You think differently when you are there and amongst them. It's less about the self and more about the collective and those you share your energy and space with. There is a practice of restraint, and regimen which allowed him to be okay with not having sex.

I joined Sophia and Eli for a weekly dinner together with me, and Sean began to join in occasionally.

My attraction to Sophia, I hoped would wane as I got closer to Sean, but it was not. I was careful to not let on how I felt and limited our time alone to public outings.

On a lazy Saturday afternoon, Sophia knocked on my door. I had been whiling away the morning lost in a book. I was in sweats and no makeup. I opened the door for her in all of her glamor and makeup. I was convinced she woke up looking like perfection.

"What are you doing today?" she asked, sitting on my sofa.

"Nothing. Not. A. Thing. And I'm loving it." I sat across from her in the chair.

"Come shopping with me. Eli and I have a trip coming up and I need a wardrobe refresh."

I heaved a sigh. "I'm not a shopper. You know my fashion sense."

"I know, but I want to spend the day with someone who is easy to be around and go with the flow. That's you. Besides, I feel like we haven't had much time to hang out in a while." She pouted with her full lips.

I rolled my eyes. "Okay. Okay. When you put it like that. Let me change and put some makeup on though. I can't be seen in public looking like this when you look like... well ..." I gestured at her.

She got up off the couch and followed me into my closet looking around at the garments on hangers. My wardrobe was largely unused due to what I teasingly referred to as a uniform of yoga clothing. I was finding it disconcerting to be in such close quarters with her. I pulled a pair of jeans out of a drawer and found a tank top. She opened the chest I kept my accessories in and started rifling through them. I went into the bathroom to change, and she followed me in, standing in the doorway watching me.

"You are really beautiful, Morgan," she said out of nowhere.

"Thank you." I was not sure what else to say.

She set a few rings and bracelets on the counter. "You're a natural pretty. You don't need makeup and wardrobe. You just need to be happy and you're striking. When we first met you in Mexico, I could see there was beauty in you, but you were deep in it. Understandably so, now that I know your story."

I pulled my jeans up and grabbed the shirt off the counter. I didn't say anything, but I let her watch me, and her gaze was intent, carrying more with it than friendship. I knew the look well. Sean. Sunny. Jonathan. Countless others looked at me the same way at some point. It was the way I looked at her when I didn't think she was watching.

She saw me watching her in the mirror. "I've never been attracted to a woman. I have always been able to appreciate the beauty and attributes of other women, but I never thought about what it would be like to be with another woman. Or want to even consider it."

I was putting on my makeup and continued watching her watch me in the mirror as she stood slightly behind me. I stayed silent, listening to her talk.

"But you're different. There's something about you that makes me think differently. Maybe it's because I've dreamt of you. I still do sometimes."

"You are off-limits for me on so many levels."

"I know. But I owe it to you and to myself to be honest."

I finished my makeup, and she grabbed my necklace from the dish I kept it in when I showered, and draped it over me, standing close when she fastened it, her breath on my neck. I clutched its heavy locket as she lingered behind me. Goosebumps rising over my flesh as it came alive under her breath. "Have you spoken about your feelings to Eli?"

She ignored my question. "I know I am not alone in this feeling though. I have seen you look at me. I have felt you holding back."

"And by having this conversation, we accomplish what?"

"Honesty. With each other. With our hearts."

"Have you been honest with Eli?" I was looking at her eyes in the mirror.

She turned and looked away. "Yes. He knows, we've scratched the surface of it in a discussion a while ago, but nothing as deep as it probably should be. It will come up eventually, I'm sure. At some point we will discuss it."

"Did you really want to go shopping or just come over and talk?"

"Both." She grabbed my hand and slid the bracelets up my arm.

A large part of me wanted to grab her and pull her in to kiss her. It would have been the perfect opportunity. But I didn't. Couldn't. Wouldn't. I wouldn't jeopardize the relationships I built within The Society.

Sophia didn't have to check out with Sola or request her keys. And when I would go out with her, I didn't either. I could come and go with her.

After wandering around the shops, and then lunch, with her acquisitions piled at her feet at the outdoor table she scrutinized me across the table. "What is going on with you and Sean?"

"Surface wise, he's perfect. He's sweet. Kind. Smart. Patient. He's been hanging in for months and I still haven't given it up."

"How long has it been since you have?"

"The last time was when Jonathan caught me with Sunny. So, we are going on two years."

"How do you do it? How do you not cave?"

"I'm not ready. I'm not ready to give that part of me away again. That vulnerability. I want to. I want the physical release. I want to feel the weight of another person against me. On me. But I can't be that bare with anyone right now. The very idea gives me physical panic."

"And Sean is okay with just hanging out and waiting indefinitely?"

"He's persistent. He says I'm worth it." I shrugged.

"Do you love him?"

"I don't know. I don't know what it really means to love someone. I thought I did. But I didn't. I don't."

"I think you loved Jonathan. I think you also loved yourself. I think you loved Sunny. Love looks different with different pairings."

I looked down and away. I had done a lot of healing to a point, but I was not fully able to absolve myself of the weight of what had happened.

I was quiet for a moment, just contemplating what she said, she asked, "Where is Jonathan buried?"

"Not far from here. Why?"

"When is the last time you went to him?"

"Almost two years."

"Let's go." She flagged the waitress down and paid the bill before standing to make her way out.

I stood and followed her. When we got to her car she handed me her phone. "Put in the address."

I typed in the address of the cemetery and didn't say another word while we drove. I watched as she navigated the familiar streets and drew nearer to the cemetery. The campus, Jace's bar, my former condo, my whole history passed by the windows. Strangely enough, I didn't miss it. I didn't long for it. It just was.

Once we arrived at the destination and she navigated through the gates, I guided her along the winding road to where Jonathan lay.

After parking along the narrow road, she followed me to his stone. I stared at his name etched in granite. There were fresh flowers and decorations around the stone. No doubt Tiffany left them there recently.

I sat at the foot of the grave. Well, more like collapsed to my bottom. I put my knees up and leaned onto them.

Sophia kneeled behind me, and I leaned back into her as she held me. "You shouldered this alone, all of this time. You still don't really talk about it. You still blame yourself and carry this weight on your shoulders by yourself."

I could not stop the tears that started.

She draped herself over my back with her arms around me. "He had an illness. You can't be blamed for that. He loved you and you loved him. But he was selfish with his love. You made mistakes. But to punish yourself and deny yourself love indefinitely is cruelty. It is not love. It is not honoring yourself. Jonathan is in another place now. Do you think he is sitting over you, happy you are denying yourself because of what happened?"

There was no answer I could come up with for her. I knew deep down she was right.

"He is here by his own choice. You have tortured yourself and denied yourself for long enough. Morgan, you are beautiful. Smart. Strong. Worthy. This is not your doing. It is not. Let go of him. Let go of your guilt. You didn't put his head in the noose. You didn't ask him to do it. You cared for him. You loved him. You carried him in his dark days."

I was sobbing hard now.

"Breathe in. Come on. Breathe. Inhale. Exhale the guilt. Force it out. Breathe in with me. Take in the love. The happy memories. The wonderfulness you experienced. Hold it in. Now let it go. Exhale the guilt.

The burden. The darkness." She sat with me and coached me through each breath. The sun was starting to set by the time I was calm.

"Thank you," I whispered, fatigued.

"Let's get us home."

As I looked up, Jonathan was sitting across from me. He was not angry. He was just there. Peaceful. He nodded to me. That nod was my release. My forgiveness.

I stood up and looked back down at him. "It's done, Morgan," he said. I looked back at Sophia to see if she could see him. She showed no awareness of him.

We got in the car and drove to a nearby *Starbucks* so I could clean myself up. She was waiting for me outside with a coffee when I came out. "How do you feel?"

"Better, actually."

"You've been holding on for too long."

I took the coffee and got into the car. She was right.

We made it back in time for evening meditation and I took my seat next to Sean who greeted me with a gentle kiss on my forehead.

Peripherally, I could see Sophia look down and away.

After meditation, I slept deep, but not dreamless. I dreamt not of Sean, and not of Jonathan, but of Sophia. Being entangled in her arms and legs and breathing only her breath.

WEEKS LATER, WHILE I WAS beginning to feel like maybe it was time to allow Sean and I to take our relationship past the middle school level of sweetness I kept us locked into, we were having dinner with Eli and Sophia. We were in Sean's apartment. Impeccable and minimalistic, his space was representative of his personality. Uncomplicated and neat, with a subtle beauty in its plainness.

Sophia and I took our wine out to the balcony and looked out over the hills behind the complex. The sky was bright with stars and a sliver of a moon. We had indulged that night. Sean was an amazing cook, and the wine was heady and full-bodied. We were finishing the second bottle. Something we did not do often, leading us to already be slightly buzzed. Eli and Sean came out to join us.

Sean opened the third bottle and refilled my glass, and I was thinking tonight would be the night I would blow the dust off and give in. I looked at him in the moonlight. Prior to Jonathan, this would have been locked in and done by now. Also, prior to Jonathan, we would have broken it off a long time ago.

Sean put his hand on the small of my back as he stood next to me, and I leaned into him.

"You two are quite cozy." Eli smiled.

"He's been good to me. Good for me," I admitted.

"It's been mutual." Sean kissed the top of my head.

Sophia took a sip so big it consumed almost half of her glass. She was far more of a lightweight than me. She laughed. It was an odd laugh. Almost mean sounding, and very against her nature.

I looked at her with my head cocked.

"It's a good thing then." Her tone held a bitter edge.

"Sophia?" I was unsure of her meaning.

"It's a good thing then, that Eli told Sean to get involved with you. To ask you out. Ordered him."

I looked up behind me at Sean. "Is this true?"

"Sophia." Eli's voice carried a warning.

"I didn't know until recently. You see, I like Morgan. Not like as a friend. But I *like* her. Which has been confusing enough for me. And my husband, ever so astute, was catching on. He saw how she looked at me and how I looked at her. So, he went to Sean and told him to distract her. Ask her out. Get involved. That way I would have no choice but to let it go. So yeah. It's true."

"Sophia!" Eli said, sharper this time.

"Eli, you yourself tell us to be honest and true to ourselves and others at all times."

I stepped away from Sean and was looking at him. "Why didn't you tell me? This was all a set up? You were not really interested in me. You were *ordered* to ask me out."

"It was not exactly like that," Eli intervened.

"How was it, Eli? Sean? Do either of you want to tell me what this is? Is this why you have been so okay with letting me take my time? Because you're not truly into me? You're only here because you are acting on orders?"

"Morgan, no. I was inquiring about you. As I was asking around, Eli came to me and encouraged me."

"Bullshit."

Sean flinched, a wounded look on his face.

"Morgan!" Eli reprimanded. "How do you question his integrity? You've been with us long enough to know."

I spun and looked at him. "Why would you do this? Why would you think I'm so low as to go after your wife? My friend? You questioned *my* integrity, did you not?"

Eli looked at the two empty wine bottles and nearly empty glasses. "No. You know what? We are not going to talk about this tonight. We will meet tomorrow in the office after yoga. When we all have clear heads."

"Yeah. Great idea." I was angry. I drank the last in my glass, slammed it on the small table on the balcony and stormed off through the apartment, out the door, and down the hall letting the door slam behind me.

I was midway through the corridor, hot with anger, when I heard the door slam a second time and Sophia shout my name.

She ran down the corridor and grabbed my hand. "Come on," she said, leading me to the stairwell.

We took the stairs down the six flights and out into the lobby. She dragged me out the door into the garden courtyard. The fountains trickled on either end of the courtyard and the white flowers were glowing blue in the moonlight. We were breathless from our near run down the stairs. My chest was aching, and my head was fuzzy. I wanted to collapse into a pile.

She spun me around and her hands were in my hair. "Kiss me," she demanded.

Automatic, I pulled her in, and I kissed her. It was electricity and heat and hunger and everything I had been missing as our lips met and I tasted her tongue against mine.

I could feel her heart beating hard against me and her breath was ragged, and she was trembling. Her eyes burned as she looked at me.

"Sophia?" Eli's voice came cracked from the doorway.

She broke away from me and looked wide-eyed at Eli. Tears rolled down her cheeks.

I pulled my hands away from her and put them up as I backed away.

I disappeared up the stairwell and slowly climbed all six flights of stairs and collapsed on my bed when I got into my apartment. Not having turned on a single light.

I was lost in my thoughts in the darkness when there was a knock on my door. I got up and looked out the peephole and saw Sean. I opened the door and let him in.

He didn't look at me as he came in. He walked past me with his head down and sat on the couch.

I turned the lamp on and sat across from him in my chair.

"Full disclosure, Morgan. I'm going to be fully honest with you and you need to be fully honest with me."

"Okay."

"I was and am genuinely interested in you. You caught my eye and captivated my imagination and my heart from the beginning. I just could tell you did not want to be bothered. You were focused on healing. You were focused on learning how to fit in with us here. Eli did suggest that I try to hook up with you. But it was merely a nudge in the right direction. I have since fallen in love with you. You are this amazing, beautiful person. You are captivating in your wit and grace and you're so beautiful and humble. A woman like you has everything, and you have every right to be full of yourself, but you aren't. I sit back, patient and waiting on you, because in the past, I would jump into bed and into relationships with women, never bothering to know who they truly are. I was into the sex. The feeling good.

Here it is several months in, and we still haven't made it past second base. I *am* okay with it. Why? Because you are worth waiting for. I know you are a woman I can make a life with. You are more than a good time."

My chest ached. I was right where I was with Jonathan all over again. My hand came up over my mouth and I shook my head. I had not really done anything to change had I? Or was this a test to see how much I have learned? It was too much. I stifled a sob.

"Be honest with me, Morgan. Do you have feelings for Sophia?"

I nodded and looked away.

"Does she have feelings for you?"

"She says she does, but who's to say? She's confused."

"I told you before this, you are an unconventional woman. You should not be held to conventional standards. I'm okay with the two of you being together. And not because I have some teenage fantasy of what that could be for me. I'm not asking for that. I am merely saying, if you need to be with her and can still be with me, love me, I'm okay with it."

My hands gripped the arms of the chair, and my knees drew up and I shook my head vehemently.

"Morgan, talk to me."

I was suddenly very sober. The events of the evening crashed in around me and made me very aware of so many things.

"Sean, I adore you. You're a good man. You're an amazing man. You are sexy, smart, wonderful. You are more than I could ever think to ask for. You remind me so much of Jonathan – all the best parts of him without the darkness. But you're also uniquely you. I enjoy spending time with you. But I don't think I'm in love with you. I think that is why I have not been able to cross that line. I kissed Sophia tonight. She followed me out of your apartment, and we went to the courtyard and she asked me to kiss her. I kissed her. And it was everything I could do to keep from dragging her up here and ripping her clothes off."

"That's lust. That's not love."

"It was passion. It was heat. It was something I don't feel when I'm with you. The overwhelming all-consuming feeling that washes over you and makes you lose all sense."

"Morgan, that is not love. It isn't true and real love. It's not any feeling that lasts."

"Says who?"

"Says anyone in a long-term relationship. You admitted your longest relationship was Jonathan. When the passion cooled and real life hit, you ran and cheated on him." His finger went to my locket, and he tapped it, as if to remind me of all of my sins.

"I think you need to go."

"Morgan-"

"Go. Get out. We will talk about all of this with Eli and Sophia in the morning."

After he left, sitting in the dim light of my living room lamp, I opened my bank app for the first time in what seemed like forever.

My accounts all started when I was in high school, with my father as a co-signer. I never in my life considered removing his name from them. It kept life easy when I was in college for him to move money into my accounts, and after I was on my own, I just never wanted to remove him. Now, I regretted that decision. My father had locked all our joint accounts. I had no access. I was not surprised he did that.

I had one other account that was mine solely. That was the one I used for my direct deposits, the one my pay would go directly to, and my bills were auto paid out of. It was the account I gave to Eli for my pay. There was very little in the account. A few hundred dollars. I questioned the accuracy, feeling like there should be more, but too tired to make sense of it. It all came down to this – I had nothing. No means. Nowhere else to go.

~ *X* ~

M o v i n g   O n

The Present

Emma

IT WAS A MONDAY AFTERNOON, the first Monday since Emma had been reinstated to the bar. She had just argued her first motion since her reinstatement and won.

She was seated at her usual table at the deli waiting for Brandon for lunch. She texted a GIF of a champagne bottle popping to Lizbeth.

'Celebrate on Saturday. I have something in mind for you,' Lizbeth replied with a winky face emoji.

Emma blushed and put the phone down as Brandon took his seat across from her.

"Which one are your texting?" Brandon asked, grinning at her.

"Liz." The waitress came and set down Emma's sandwich order and took Brandon's order.

"Do you even talk much to Morgan any longer?" he asked after the waitress left.

"I do... But it's getting old. We talk for hours and FaceTime and whatever. But she has no desire to make a move. I sent her a gift card for a plane ticket, and she hasn't booked anything. She has a million and one excuses. So if it fizzles to nothing, it is what is."

"Are you and Lizbeth getting serious?"

"No... She's newly divorced. We have fun. She's amazing. I mean... like really amazing. It may eventually get there. But right now..." Emma shrugged.

"For what it's worth, Em, forget about Morgan."

"I can't. It's not that simple. The way I left there was no real closure."

"But the relationship wasn't grounded in reality. Do you think she could fit into your life now?"

"I don't know. But if she doesn't want to, there's nothing I can do to make her, and I will have no choice."

"You need to put an expiration date on your offer."

"If Liz wants to get serious, then yeah. The choice will be made."

Greta was there to greet her with a high five when she got back to the office. "Your mail is on your desk. Your intern interviews are waiting for you and Mr. Fitzgerald is in the conference room."

"Thank you, Greta."

Emma sat in her office behind the desk waiting for Brandon to come in and grab her for the interview. Greta put her mail on the right-hand corner of her desk. Her appointment book was open in the center.

Emma pulled her phone out and texted Morgan. 'Hey... Sorry. It's been super busy. I think about you all the time though. I hope you are having a great day. Call later?'

Morgan

MORGAN WAS CONTENT WITH HER routine. Ever since living within The Society, routine was the biggest help in allowing her to make sense of her life.

She woke up, went for a run (if the weather was treacherous or cold inside on the treadmill in the closed in patio space she had converted to a home gym area), and she still practiced yoga daily, showered and dressed, went to the campground to handle business, pick up dinner, come home. Occasionally an outing with Aaron or her parents or Sara. Now she was peppering in time for

Emma via phone calls and texts as they came in and squeezing in dates with Sara.

She was, however, frustrated by the short FaceTimes and quick texts. Emma was all consumed with her work. In all fairness, Emma had warned her she was a bit of a workaholic, but it did not feel good to be set on the back burner. This part of the reality of Emma was something she struggled with. When Emma was on the run, Morgan was Emma's entire life. There were no other distractions or duties. She was a captive audience who built her days around Morgan's availability.

She was feeling restless and wondered whether or not she should call Emma or write her a letter telling her how she was feeling. The quick five minutes here and there were insufficient for her.

As they became more insufficient, she began using Sara as a fill in. She ignored the feelings of wishing Sara was Emma.

She went to visit her therapist and sat across from her. She had not gone regularly since before she met Emma. She increased the visits after Emma left for a time, but still did not feel the need for regular visits.

"I don't know what I want from Emma or what I expect. I don't know what I am doing with her."

"What expectations did you have before she left?"

"That we were going to build this life together."

"What changed?"

"I found out she killed her wife. But then I learned the whole story and realized we started this relationship without any real information about each other."

"And you have been working on it over this last year?"

"Yes. We've been communicating. But now I don't know. I have this push and pull. I want to be with her. I want to talk to her, and I want her to know me. But now the reality of her sentence coming to an end, and she wants me out there to give it a real go together, is frightening to me."

"Why does this scare you? Is it because you have garnered true intimacy with someone?"

~ 226 ~

Morgan bit her lip and looked away, crossing her arms across her body.

"Morgan, historically, you have fled or sabotaged every relationship you allowed true intimacy in. You are afraid of it. Why are you so afraid of this intimacy?"

"I mean, to be fair, I'm doing everything right with Sara. Except telling her about my communication with Emma. She knows everything about me. I know everything about her. I don't know why I can't let Emma go, though. I know it's not completely fair to Sara that I'm holding on to Emma. It's not fair to Emma that I have Sara here, and she doesn't really know about her."

She left her appointment and grabbed her mail on the way home.

As she was walking up to her front door, she sorted through the envelopes.

One envelope stood out above the others. A thick envelope from an airline. She opened her door and tossed the other envelopes on the table and opened the one from the airline.

Inside, she found a gift card. The attached letter read, 'I'm waiting for you. Come see me – Love, Emma.' The amount of the gift card was more than enough to cover the airfare from Reno to the airport nearest Emma, first class.

Morgan smiled. The airfare was not an issue for her. She had more than enough in savings. Her reserve for the visit was wanting Emma to know all of her first before making a decision. And there was the issue of what to do about Sara lingering.

She tossed the gift card and letter on the table and took a picture of it. She sent the picture to Emma with a one-word reply: 'Maybe.'

Morgan pushed her hair out of her face and picked up Ophelia before sinking into the cushions of the couch. She scrolled through her phone on a food delivery app.

Nothing looked appealing.

She opened the airline app and looked at flights. There was one that looked like it could work. But she didn't book it.

She called Aaron instead. "Remember when I told you Emma sent me something?"

"Yes. Did you get it?"

"It's a voucher for an airline ticket."

"Girl, when are we going?"

"We?"

"Yeah. I need to go. I'm your bodyguard. She's a convicted murderess."

"Not funny."

"I'm still going with you. Did you book your ticket?"

"No."

"Why not?"

"If I go, I may not come back. I don't think I can leave her again."

"I wish I felt that way about Kevin. I want him to leave most of the time."

"Shut up. You love him and you know it."

"I do love him. But he's annoying. He's a slob. Hey, I gotta go. Customers just walked through the door. If you book tickets, let me know so I can book, too."

"K. Love you, bye."

Morgan ordered dinner and kept returning to the app, looking at the flight.

While she was cleaning up after dinner, she got a response from Emma, 'Not the response I was hoping for.'

'I love you. Talk soon,' was her reply.

She sat her notebook out in front of her on the bed and Ophelia was batting at the pen in her hand playfully.

She looked at the headline she wrote across the top of the page: 'Reasons I'm afraid of letting Emma go.'

Based on the time, she had given up on hearing from Emma that evening. She removed her makeup and made herself comfortable. Ambient techno music filtered softly from her Bluetooth speaker on the bedside table.

She stared blankly at the paper. Reasons were starting to come to her but to put them on paper made them real. Making them real meant she had to face them.

The music paused and the FaceTime ringtone came across the speaker. Morgan dropped the pen and looked at her phone. It was Emma. Her heart fluttered and she scrambled to turn off the speaker and answer the call.

"Hey. I didn't think you would be calling tonight."

"I love when I get the bare and clean you, no makeup and just natural. But yeah, I know. I've been pretty awful about things." Emma looked remorseful. Charlemagne was laid out across her lap. She shook her head and flashed the smile that never ceased to make Morgan weak in the knees. "I promise, I will be better about it."

"It's okay. I understand."

"No. It's not okay. It's what I did to Bailey. It's how I avoid feelings I don't want to face. It's how I don't need to deal with life any longer."

"What feelings are you trying to avoid?"

A pause and look off to the side. "Not knowing where we stand or what we are doing. What either of us want for each other."

It was Morgan's turn for a pause and a sigh. "The ever-present elephant in our rooms. How much time do I have you for tonight?"

"As much time as you want or need." Morgan watched Emma move Charlemagne and make herself comfortable in the bed, removing her glasses and setting them aside.

Morgan moved the notebook and pen and mimicked the gesture. "What do you want to talk about tonight?"

"I just want to talk about anything. Just spend time the only way we can for now."

Morgan settled in and she felt the peace of mind of having Emma's undivided attention for the next few hours, until a drowsy Emma finally signed off with a phone ready to die.

Though it was three hours earlier in Tahoe, Morgan was drained and exhausted when she hung up.

Sara texted her a few times while she was talking to Emma. She looked at them, 'What's up tonight? Do you want to get together?' with a winky face emoji. '??? Are you there?'

She responded, 'Sorry. I was at therapy and came home and took a nap. I'm feeling a bit under the weather. Brunch tomorrow?'

'I look forward to it. Feel better, beautiful.' A heart emoji after.

The endorphins that came flooding in while talking to Emma dissipated and she looked at her empty notebook paper and pen and ripped the page out. Writing it out wouldn't help her understand it any better. She threw the paper across the room and Ophelia jumped down to play with it.

Emma

AFTER TALKING ALMOST ALL NIGHT to Morgan, she awoke groggy and restless, deciding to work from home this morning, shooting Greta and Brandon a text.

Coffee in hand, Emma went up to her office to look at files and could not focus. She went back down the stairs and sat on the porch in the early morning light. Charlemagne sat himself down near her feet and looked out over the porch over the front yard, too old and lazy to chase anything.

She was unsettled by the fact she was hung up on Morgan, but Morgan who at one point had been so open and vulnerable to her was now holding her at bay.

Emma understood she did hurt Morgan. She took advantage of Morgan by hiding her history and past from her. She was hoping the two of them could work through it. Learn to understand each other and move forward, together.

But Lizbeth was a nice distraction. She thought about her impending day with Liz on Saturday. She had texted Emma last night and told her a dress code for Saturday's day, and that she was planning the whole itinerary for them. Emma loved that Lizbeth had a great sense of adventure.

She found herself wishing she knew what a real life with Morgan would be like though.

Up in the tree overhead, she saw another blue jay sitting amongst the buds.

Emma smiled. She knew she was being slightly ridiculous by taking it as a sign from Bailey.

Emma felt peace inside and a sense of relief. No matter what was to transpire with Morgan, or Lizbeth she was going to be okay. She basked in the feeling of relief and hope. She sat with her feelings in the silence of the early morning. Something she was never known to do. Suddenly her files could wait. They were not going anywhere.

None of the neighbors who lived there when she lived with Teta were still there. They had all passed away or moved. The street slowly began to wake to the day and people began to come and go and children came out to play. She waved and nodded to a few of them as they went by.

It was a pretty spring day. The air was warm, and the sky overhead was clear and blue. She finished her coffee and decided to finally go back inside.

She went back upstairs to the office and opened the window overlooking the spacious backyard. Charlemagne laid himself in a dog bed near the desk and napped while she shuffled papers around on her desk. She made some notes about one case, then stacked the papers back into the folder. She stood, bent and scooped Charlemagne under her arm, and made her way back downstairs.

She wandered into her bedroom and grabbed Morgan's journal.

Excerpt from Morgan's Memoir

AFTER I KICKED SEAN OUT of my apartment, I felt true anger. I was steeped in it for the first time in as long as I could remember. I had not allowed myself to feel anything since before Jonathan died. It actually felt good to be angry. So I allowed myself to sit in it. Feel it. I paced. I broke a vase. I yelled. I was trapped. Broke. Hurt. Angry.

The next morning, I went downstairs for the morning meditation and Sean saved the spot next to him for me. I stood at the front of the room and contemplated if I should take it or be petty and take the seat at the back of the room. His eyes looked up at me pleading.

I walked slowly, still unsure what I was going to do until I did it. I sat next to him. His hand went instinctively, habitually to my knee.

I hissed under my breath, "I am still very, very angry, hurt, and disappointed."

He hissed back, "Likewise. But until we talk it through, recognize, I still have love for you." His response fueled even more anger inside of me. If Jonathan could have still had love for me, maybe he would have been alive. We would have gotten married. Had our baby. But instead, in his hurt and darkness he was dead, and my life was a boiling cesspool. This inconvenient fact made me even angrier.

Through the meditation and yoga, Sophia and Eli expertly played perfection and problem free. Smiling, calm, placid. I was further incensed by their veneer of perfection. It was all bullshit. Everything about this situation was fake.

After meditation and yoga, Sean and I followed Eli and Sophia to the office.

The guise fell and Sophia looked broken, Eli aflame in anger.

I sat on the arm of the couch on one end, Sean on the far end. Eli and Sophia on the love seat across from us. Everyone was looking at me. Sophia, with love and anguish. Eli with distrust, and Sean with disappointment.

I looked down not chancing to meet anyone's gaze, still seething.

"How do we want to proceed with this?" Eli asked. His voice carried the hurt.

"What do you mean? That's between you and Sophia," I answered.

"No. This involves you. Since it involves you, it involves Sean."

"What involves me, does not, in fact, involve Sean. We are dating. Not married."

"Morgan, I would hate that you would throw away your whole relationship with Sean over one small issue."

I sat back petulant.

"Full disclosure now. Sophia came to me in an effort to be fully open and honest with me. She admitted she developed feelings for you. Feelings which she didn't understand. We thought perhaps over time the fascination would taper off. But as time wore on-"

"Eli, why don't you let Sophia speak for herself?" I was annoyed.

Anger flashed in his eyes. Something I never saw before in him. "Let me speak. I was seeing that you, Morgan, were feeling alone and perhaps in a state where you were ready to start dating or exploring a relationship with someone. Sean had been single for some time. I heard he had inquired about you. So yes, I set it up. I gave him the push he needed. And you cannot deny it's been good for you both. It has taught both of you a lot. But for the love of God, Sophia still has feelings.

"I saw you in the courtyard last night. I saw the way you kissed her. I saw how you were with each other. I can't compete with that. I can't." Eli stopped short.

"Where is this going?" Sean asked.

Sophia's cheeks flushed.

"I cannot let my wife go. My wife wants Morgan. She wants to be with Morgan. I want to allow it. But only in the sense we are all together."

"You want a threesome?" I asked. I was no stranger to that dynamic in my past. I had been part of a few, but it was not something I fathomed at this stage in my life.

Sean's jaw dropped.

"I want you to join us, as part of us. As in marry into us," Eli said. "I can't just let you have my wife alone. We entered into this marriage in an agreement that all things are shared, and all things are experienced together. Everything shared."

I felt sick. "And what does Sean have to do with this?" I asked again.

"I want him to be okay with letting you go."

My head was spinning.

Sean's hands went up and he shook his head. I was looking at him for some sort of direction or answer because there wasn't one.

"If the two of you together decide you want to stay together, and this is an arrangement you can't fathom, I understand. If you, alone, Morgan, decide you don't want this arrangement, we understand but we will have more to discuss."

My hand went to my mouth. "Sophia, how do you feel about this?"

She sighed. "Last night, I asked you to kiss me. That kiss was mind-blowing. I felt feelings in your kiss I have never felt before. Your kiss breathed a life into me I never thought existed. But as Eli said, I'm married. I made a vow for a lifetime. I want you, but I am bound to him. This is the compromise."

"Sophia, you've never had a relationship with a woman. You kissed me. Yes, it was exotic and sexy for you, but you don't know what it means. What it's like. You are curious, and I get it. Eli, you are not into me. You don't want to be with me. Sean, for that matter, doesn't want to be with me, either."

"That's not entirely true." Eli came back as Sean retorted, "Don't speak for me."

I stood and moved behind the couch. "What would this, for a lack of better terms, harem look like for you, Eli? What would your expectation be of me, of this relationship?"

"We would keep what we've built. You bring so much to The Society. You bring joy to the children and a sense well-being and peace to their parents because they now have someone they can trust in the care of their children and their education. We can grow your program into an entire venture. Maybe a full-on charter school? You are beautiful, smart, funny, sensitive. There are a lot of attributes that are admirable, and I would be lying if I said I hadn't thought of what it would be like to be with you, or watch you with my wife."

My stomach turned slightly. As I mentioned – Eli was movie star handsome, but now all of those charms slipped away, and I found myself disgusted.

"Morgan, I am a human man. I am not infallible." He was able to sense my disgust, I'm sure it was showing on my face. I've never had a poker face.

"I'm going to leave now. I need time to think." I left everyone where they were in the office and walked out. Nauseous. Angry. Hollow. Afraid. Alone.

I went back to my apartment and sank into the couch and cried. I was angry. I was hurt. I felt dirty. But I was scared to leave The Society. I had grown to love my life within its safe walls. Now it was tainted. Could I sit through Eli's meditations and Sophia's yoga? Could I walk amongst these people and feel the same? Could I fall in love with Sean? Could I fall in love with Eli and Sophia?

Could I go anywhere else? I was broke. I had too much pride to ask my parents to help me. Admit that I needed them. I didn't want that. And I had no access to enough money to go anywhere else. I had surrendered and canceled all of my credit cards. My account was nearly empty. Everything else was on lockdown. I was trapped. Helplessly, hopelessly trapped.

My head was spinning, and I just wanted to go back to my peace and quiet. Actually, that's a lie. I wanted to go get high. In my head I began calculating how long it would take me to get to the border and down into the nearest farmacia.

There was a gentle knock at my door. I wiped the tears and opened it to find Sean standing there, bracing himself on the door frame with his arms. Mournful and heavy his eyes searched mine for some sort of emotion.

I moved aside so he could once again enter. He sat on my couch and looked at me as I sat next to him.

"Morgan," he took my hands in his.

"Sean... I don't know what to say. I don't know what to do."

"Where are you hung up?"

"I don't want to leave here. I love The Society. I love what we stand for here. I love the children I work with. I love this life. I have nothing outside of this. No one. No money. Nowhere to go."

"Do you love me? Do you think you *could* love me?"

"I don't know."

"Do you love Sophia?"

"I don't know."

"I think I love you. I think we can build a future together, Morgan. You and I together. We could build a life and put this drama behind us. Go back to the peace we were living prior to this. Together." His fingers laced through mine. "You stay here, you keep your life here. You don't even have to consider this foolishness with Eli and Sophia."

There came another knock on my door. I took my hands away from Sean and put them over my face and let out a moan before getting up to answer it.

I opened the door to Sophia. I checked the hall for any sign of Eli, but he was not there.

She came in and looked at Sean. "Can you excuse us, please?"

Sean looked away and stood. "Morgan, come find me?"

I nodded at him and watched him leave.

Sophia came to me and put her arms around me. "Morgan, I don't want you to leave. If you choose Sean, Eli will send you both to Arizona. He will come up with a reason to send you there. If you choose no one, he will make it so awful on you, you will have no choice but to leave. I've seen him push others out before. It's ugly. It will be an all-out assault on you. I know you have nowhere else to go. You don't talk to your parents. Your life is here. Here with me. With us."

My back was to the bar, and she was pressing in on me. Her soft, warm body was against me, and I couldn't breathe except for the subtle mint of her breath and perfume. I put my hands on her face and kissed her. The urgency and desperation in her kiss as she responded to me, was all I needed to make my decision.

I couldn't choose Sean. I couldn't spend my life with someone I did not feel passion for, that did not prompt the flame within me. What it truly boiled down to though, was I couldn't bear the thought of leaving The Society, and I had nowhere else to go.

She pulled away from me. "Will you join us? Stay with us?"

I felt sick even saying yes, but the alternatives were worse. I nodded in lieu of actually verbalizing the yes.

She kissed me again, soft and sweet. "You will be happy. I promise. I will make sure you are happy. Come on. Let's go tell Eli."

I was trying to think fast about how this was going to work and how I was going to negotiate this in a way in which I could maintain some semblance of myself. Not that I possessed much self at this point.

I sat back in Eli's office, with Sophia holding my hand tight.

"Morgan, you have no idea how much this pleases me." He smiled.

"How is this going to work?"

"Obviously, this is not a legal arrangement. But, we can get some papers drawn up, and I think it would be good to have some sort of ceremony to make it official at least for us."

"I don't want to... what's the word I'm looking for... Consummate? Consummate anything until this is official then."

"That's fair."

"How will it work? Am I just Sophia's? Am I yours too?"

"We all belong equally to each other."

I felt ill. Physically ill. "So I just move in with you and live among you?"

"You can keep your place. But come and go from ours and us from yours."

"I want a reduction in my rent."

"Fair."

"And if this fails, I want a pay out."

"That can be negotiated."

I felt like a high-priced whore. I was selling myself because I was afraid to leave the confines of the life I had grown to love and the community I was accustomed to living among. I felt desperate and cornered not having any other options.

"Is this a ceremony we invite friends and family to? Members of The Society or just for us? Will others know of our arrangement?"

"It's up to you. How do you want to do this?"

I shook my head. The world was spinning around me, and I had no idea what I was doing or saying. I was on autopilot. Suddenly everything around me was unrecognizable. My life. My self. What I was doing or saying. How did I get here? "I guess, let's at least have it open for The Society. My family will not want any part of this." My answer was a whisper.

Eli approached me and put his hands on my hips and lowered his lips to mine. I responded to the kiss physically, but inside, I just felt dead. "Morgan, this will be beautiful. I think this arrangement will be good for all of us."

~ *XI* ~

The Lies We Tell Ourselves

The Present

Emma

EMMA WAS SITTING IN HER office at home, the window open behind her letting in the breeze. She could not focus after reading about Morgan and the arrangement between her and Eli and Sophia. She was so angry. Not with Morgan but with the obvious emotional manipulation by Eli and Sophia.

She Googled The Society and a series of articles popped up.

She clicked one and the pictures of Eli and Sophia popped up. Morgan was not exaggerating. They were extremely attractive. She exited the article. She would wait for Morgan to tell her in her own words what happened.

She got up from the desk and went downstairs. She looked at her watch, it was still too early to call Morgan.

She went onto her phone and pulled up a site for flower delivery and picked out a bouquet of peonies and lilies and set them up for delivery for today before feeding Charlemagne.

It was a Saturday morning and Lizbeth had gone out of town to visit her parents. She was grateful though for a day to herself.

Emma picked up the small dog after he finished his breakfast and put him in the car. She took the four-hour drive down to visit Abby. It was a beautiful day, and the drive was mostly two-lane highway through the rural Midwest.

She passed through small one light towns, abandoned barns, pastures with livestock. She was excited to be spending the night out with Abby and would have time to consult with her and talk. Abby's advice was always sound.

Abby and her wife, Rowan, had done well, and moved to a small farm after retiring early, and invited Emma to come down and enjoy her first full weekend of freedom with them. She pulled up to the sprawling property and made her way to the door of the large white colonial home. She was surprised to see Simone and her wife, Jess, and their teenage daughter McKenna, were there as well when she knocked on the door.

She was greeted with hugs and love from all of them, which made Emma emotional. She was wiping the tears from her eyes as they ushered her in the doors. She would not have blamed any of them if they turned their backs on her after what she had done.

"Let me show you around." Abby took her arm and Rowan took her bag to one of the guest rooms up the stairs.

Emma wished more than ever Morgan was with her. She wanted Morgan to meet her friends and for her to love them as she did. She knew they would love her, for sure. She felt guilty she was thinking about Morgan.

Then she pictured Lizbeth by her side. She pictured the easy-going energy and bright smile, and soft touch of her hand in hers. She knew Abby would approve of Lizbeth.

Abby showed her the barn housing four beautiful horses, the area where the goats lived, and the chickens. There was a large pond in the back of the property and trails that started on the property and wound their way through the nearby woods for hiking and horseback riding.

Rowan was growing a variety of fruits and vegetables in a plot of land just before the pond.

Abby brought Emma back into the house and showed her where her room would be and the basic layout. "You want a drink?"

"Please."

"Wine? Beer? Cocktail?"

"Whatever is easiest." Emma sat at a stool between Rowan and Simone at the vast kitchen island while Abby uncorked a bottle of wine and poured Emma and herself a glass.

While everyone was filling Emma in on what she had missed, her phone alerted her with a text. She was tempted to not check it at all, but knew it was Morgan.

She smiled at the picture of the flowers she sent in a vase with Ophelia sniffing a large peony bloom.

" Who's got you smiling like that, Aunt Emma?" McKenna asked.

"Emma only smiles like that when there's a love interest," Simone chided.

"Are you still talking to Morgan?" Rowan asked.

"Was that Lizbeth?" Abby chimed in at the same time.

"Morgan? Lizbeth?" Simone asked. Simone had not been great about visiting or writing Emma throughout her incarceration. Not because she was upset, but financially such a drive did not fit into their budget. Simone and Jess did not go on to find financial independence like Abby and Rowan. They were both freelance artists with inconsistent income, and now working within the gig economy to supplement their income. Simone and Jess also refused to watch the documentaries or coverage of the case because they felt it was exploitative to their friend and capitalized on a hurtful tragedy. They also did not want to be watching it and for McKenna to see anything and ask questions about her Aunt Emma that would tarnish how she felt about her.

Emma filled her in on meeting Morgan and how the relationship evolved since. She included the tension and uncertainty of how they wanted to proceed, whether they would just stay friends at a distance or try to rekindle what they started. And then the newest complication with now having Lizbeth in her life. "Morgan and I had no real closure, and we made a lot of mistakes. But I feel like we met for a reason. I feel like the parallels in our stories and the feelings we have carried mean something. But there's something about Liz. I just find myself being more and more wrapped up with her. I'm getting to where I miss her when she's not around."

Abby swirled the wine in her glass and looked thoughtfully at Emma. "I wouldn't put all of your eggs in one basket, Em. You have a lot of life left. I get that Morgan was a support for you during a tough time, but that doesn't mean she's the one. If it was so meant to be, there would be no hesitation. I'm Team Liz."

Emma looked down into her glass. Abby was absolutely right. She knew it. One by one each of the women present seconded Abby with a "Yep, Team Liz," of sorts.

The group spent the entire evening cooking, talking, and getting caught up. Emma was slightly mad at herself for only scheduling one night here. Chastising herself internally for not leaving the day before. It was well into the early morning hours before everyone made their way upstairs and to their respective rooms.

Emma felt slightly guilty for not sending more than a goodnight text to Morgan, but she did not want to leave her cohort. They spent hours talking about memories from the past. Explaining to McKenna how they all met and the crazy things they had done and experienced.

Emma sent, 'I'm sorry. I'm at Abby's getting caught up with everyone. I hope you had a wonderful day. I will call you tomorrow night when I get back home.'

'Okay. Have fun,' was all Morgan responded with.

Emma did not know how to interpret the response.

She shook her head and stuck her phone back on the nightstand.

Morgan

IT WAS MONDAY. SHE KNEW the extent of their conversations would be short until Friday. She had time to think. While she waited for her food delivery, she called Sara.

"What are you doing?" she asked.

"Nothing. Wondering when I would get you to myself again." She could hear Sara was smiling.

"I just ordered Chinese. Come over."

"Bet. I'm on my way."

Throughout the night Morgan tried to keep her thoughts on the woman in her living room and in her bed. But the nagging thought of how she could just as easily be on a plane to Emma kept her distracted.

Sara was tuned-in to the fact Morgan was distracted.

"Where are you?"

"Um. Here."

"No… You are God knows where. What's on your mind?"

"I'm just dealing with a situation with a friend and it's wearing on me. It's nothing. I promise."

"Tell me about it. Maybe I can help."

Morgan smiled a half smile that didn't quite reach her eyes. "I will be fine, I promise."

"When are you going to trust me? When are you going to give me all of you?" Sara was sitting all the way up, the sheet pulled up to her chest.

Morgan sat up and grabbed her sweatshirt pulling it over her head. "Sara, I'm trying. I really am. I just have a lot to deal with. I don't want to drag you into it."

"I want to be dragged into it. I want to be there for you. I want a real relationship with you. I want to look at a life with a future with you in it. But you won't let me." The tears in Sara's eyes were real.

Morgan suddenly felt like shit. She leaned in and kissed Sara. "I'm sorry. I will do better. I will. I promise. I can't talk about this situation right now. I will, soon. When I'm ready. Please respect that I need to sort it out in my head first."

"Morgan, you need to know, I'm in love with you. I love you. I am tired of playing it cool. You need to know how I feel about you."

It was a gut punch to Morgan. "I think I might love you, too."

"You think?" The tear slipped down Sara's smooth cheek.

"Sara…"

Sara got out of the bed and began to dress herself.

"Sara, wait."

"Wait… for what? Maybe? I don't want maybes. I don't want games. I want a future with someone who loves me. Whatever you have going on, you need to figure it out. Maybe call me when that happens. Maybe I will still be around."

Sara left. The door slamming on her way out.

By Friday, Morgan was no clearer about whether or not she would be taking the trip, or whether or not she should call Sara.

Friday evening, Emma texted, 'Do you have time to talk?'

Morgan FaceTimed her.

"Can we talk?"

"I think I know what this is about." Because when it rains it pours. She closed her eyes and saw Sara storming out of her house again.

"Morgan, these last few years we've spent the time getting to know each other on a level I never thought possible to know another person. Add to it what we started without ever knowing when I was there. I need to know... I need to know if we have a future together. If you are in this or not." Emma's voice cracked on the last line.

"You haven't finished reading yet. You don't have all the story yet. When you have all of it, then you can decide if I'm worth such devotion." It was weak, but it was worth the stall.

"Morgan, I don't need to read your journal to know."

"I'm changing the subject. Tell me about your plans this week."

Emma rolled her eyes and shook her head. Morgan could see the frustration and disappointment. Morgan was frustrated with herself, but she had to be true to herself, a fact she was certain of.

The conversation did not flow as it normally would between them. The unsaid expectations and anticipation of "what next" held them both back.

When Emma hung up, Morgan took herself to the lake. She hated herself for holding back, but she knew in her heart she needed to make sure she was absolutely certain which relationship would be best for her, if either of them were really worth it for her.

To give herself over completely again to Emma required absolute certainty. She had been all but destroyed when Emma confessed to her. She had given herself so completely to a person who was for all intents and purposes a stranger. She did not want to hurt herself again, and she did not want to hurt Emma.

She also hoped Emma would try to find the patience to bear with her.

Then there was Sara. Beautiful, loving, and peaceful Sara who was uncomplicated. No strings attached. No drama. A woman who could handle herself. A woman who wanted to be there with Morgan and live an uncomplicated life together. A woman who she unintentionally hurt with her indecision.

She hadn't really learned a thing, had she?

Emma

EMMA WAS IN HER FAVORITE black suit, and Lizbeth was on her arm in a form fitting cocktail dress. They were exiting the theater after a production of *Hamilton*. Liz stopped on the sidewalk outside the theater. "You want to grab a drink?" Her grip on Emma tightened.

"Sure. Of course." Emma changed direction to a martini bar on the opposite corner of the theater.

Once they were seated in the dark booth with a drink in front of them, Lizbeth became uncharacteristically coy.

"Liz, what's up?" Emma asked, concerned.

"How long have we been spending time together?"

Emma stopped to think. "I don't have an exact date pegged. But it's been a while now."

"We've been taking it slow. And I appreciate that. I mean, the ink on my divorce was barely dry... And you were dealing with things, too. And I was looking to just have fun. Have someone to spend time with... I wasn't expecting to catch feelings or anything..."

Emma held her breath. She knew what was coming. "Liz-" she began.

"No. No... Let me finish. I understand if you are not there. And I don't expect you to meet me where I am. But I need to be honest with you and fair to myself. I miss you when I'm not with you. I look forward to our time together. Like stupidly. I count down the hours. I wonder if you think about me the way I think about you. I want to go to the next step. I want this to be more than a fling. More than casual. I want to make this official. But if you don't, I'm willing to keep waiting. For a while anyway."

"Wow." Emma spun her glass on the table watching the olives swirl. "I mean, Liz... I'm torn. Not because you aren't amazing. And not because I don't feel the same way. I just still have a few loose ends." Emma took Lizbeth's hand. "I want to make sure all of the i's are dotted and t's are crossed so that everything is right."

"I understand. I get it. But I want you to know, I'm ready when you are."

Emma leaned over and kissed Lizbeth. "I am ready. Just give me a little more time to finish what's left undone."

She wanted to wait for Morgan, and she initially thought it would be Morgan or no one, but she had not anticipated Lizbeth. Or falling for Lizbeth. She didn't think that anyone would knowingly even want to be involved with her after what she had done.

When Lizbeth left the following afternoon, Emma was restless. She needed to cut ties with Morgan. It was time. She owed it to Lizbeth who wanted her unquestioningly.

She texted Morgan, 'Are you available?' But then deleted it.

Morgan said Emma needed the whole story, so tired or not, she picked up the journal and her sticky notes for questions and continued to read.

Excerpt from Morgan's Memoir

I WAS WEAK. I WAS scared. I didn't want to leave The Society. I didn't want to ever talk about what I had done or been through with anyone else, so this was, in my mind, the best I could do. On top of that, I didn't want to admit to my parents that I screwed up again. I didn't want to be seen as a failure.

While I was here, I never would have to acknowledge my past. Everyone pretty much knew, and they knew it didn't define me as I was in their world. It was never mentioned. It was an inconvenient fact. It was easy for me to ignore my parents and to ignore anything that was not immediately happening around me.

I left the office and took the stairs to Sean's apartment. Each step I took to the sixth floor was heavy and hard. I didn't want to tell him what I had agreed to. I was ashamed of myself and my choices. I liked Sean. I respected him. I considered why, as I climbed the stairs, I couldn't have just fallen in love with him. What was fundamentally wrong in my head, my heart, my soul, that I couldn't just be in love with him and run away with him.

Would being sent to Arizona have been so bad? He would make a great husband. A good lover if the way he kissed me was any indication (which it usually is). A good father. But I knew I wanted more. I wanted to feel love and passion deeply. Not just settle. And then, there was the fact he reminded me so much of Jonathan. It was eerie at times how alike they were. Inside there were always the small reminders – Jonathan liked the same band. Jonathan would have said the same thing. Jonathan would have done whatever the same way. I knew at least with Sophia I would have the passion and desire. I was not exactly sure how I felt about the arrangement as a whole, other than dirty. Here I was doing to Sean what I did to Jonathan. Yet another thing they had in common.

I stood in front of Sean's door for an eternity. I just stared at the door. I was empty and I did not know what I was going to say.

I finally just knocked.

He opened the door and pulled me into him. He took my presence as a sign I chose him. I wanted to throw up. I hated myself for not being stronger. I hated myself for what I was about to do.

I pushed him back and stood with my back against the door. My hand was on the door knob so I could leave quickly if I needed to. That knowledge gave me a sense of security.

"Sean, I'm sorry."

"Morgan…"

"No. Listen. If I choose you… We would have been sent away. Or cast out. I'm not ready to leave. I need this place. I can't leave. I don't want to go to Arizona. I don't want to be forced out. I am not in love with you. I wish I was. I don't know what is wrong with me that I'm not."

"Are you actually in love with Sophia?"

"I don't think so."

"Is it Eli? Are you in love with Eli?"

"No."

"But you are choosing them? You realize you sound crazy, right?"

"I'm choosing me, Sean. I'm choosing me. By choosing them, I'm choosing myself. I need to be here. I can't leave here. I can't face life outside of here. I've built a sense of stability for myself. To leave my routine, to leave my safe place will send me back to the temptation to stay medicated. Last night, that's all I wanted – was to leave and go to Mexico and get a bunch of pills. I can't leave."

"You mean face your demons? While you are in your routine here, you are safe from all of it. You're safe from your parents, the world, your guilt. While you're here you are protected from reality."

"It's keeping me from destroying myself."

"You don't think that by settling into a life as their plaything you won't be destroying some part of yourself? Morgan, I want to help you face those demons. I want to help you. I want to be your strength." I could see he was genuine in wanting to be there for me. He wanted to be mine. He wanted to heal my wounds and be there for me. But I couldn't accept it. I didn't want him. I didn't love him, and I would only destroy him if I stayed with him. I wasn't worthy of his love and devotion.

"I'm leaving now. I'm sorry." I turned to open the door, but he grabbed me and pulled me back.

"Morgan-"

"Let me go. I'm sorry. I tried. I really did. But I can't." I couldn't look him in the eyes, and I was fighting my own tears.

"Morgan," his arms were around me, tight, he bowed his head onto my shoulder. I instinctively wrapped my arms around him. He reminded me of Jonathan so much, especially with this show of vulnerability. Fragile and unguarded, traits you don't see often in men. For a moment I considered running away with him. Maybe if I chose him, made him my priority I could redeem some of what I lost with Jonathan. Maybe this was my second chance, and I was blowing it. "Morgan, what if we just left together? Not even to Arizona? We could stay here in San Diego and make a life together. You could get back to teaching. We could build something together outside of The Society." His breath was warm against my neck, and his voice was soft, pleading.

"I am not ready for life in the real world. I'm not ready for the temptations. I'm not ready to face my demons out there. Sean, let me go. I'm sorry. I'm so sorry." I lost the battle against my tears, and I was crying hard. I couldn't stop the floodgate that opened. His vulnerability reopened every wound created by Jonathan. I was hurting yet another kind, sensitive and beautiful man with my selfishness.

I slipped out of his embrace and made my way out of his apartment without looking back at him.

I went back to my apartment and locked the deadbolt and chain behind me. Eli and Sophia had keys to every unit in the building, and Sophia had a habit of just turning up in mine sporadically. I just wanted to be alone.

I spent the remainder of the day trying to make sense of my decision. I didn't eat. I didn't lesson plan. I didn't do anything but lay in my bed and stare at my ceiling. I counted my breaths and tried to calm the rage and panic swirling around inside of me. Self-doubt. Self-loathing. Vacillating between the two and the urge to flee the newest shit pile I created for myself.

When evening meditation came around, I went downstairs and entered the room. I went to take my usual seat next to Sean, but Sophia grabbed my hand and led me to a spot with her and Eli at the front, facing the crowd of members.

Sean made eye contact with me and looked down, shaking his head. Believe me, you don't really want any of this, I wanted to say it out loud to him. I wanted him to know he was dodging a bullet.

As Eli began his preamble for the evening meditation, he looked back at Sophia and I, and smiled. "Good evening all," he started with his characteristic quietness and calmness, his velvety smooth voice falling over the crowd. This time, the calm, respect, and admiration I normally would be awash in – was gone. I tried to keep the bile from rising and forced a smile. "I am happy to share with you some delightful news. The leadership here within The Society is gaining one more. Morgan Hale will be a third partner and wife in this venture. We will have an official ceremony to celebrate this union soon. In honor of this, I would like to set our intentions tonight to family and what that means."

As he continued I looked out at the faces of the members. Most people seemed strangely happy with this news. Others seemed unfazed. Sean kept his eyes downcast and would not look up in our direction.

I was uncharacteristically unfocused during the meditation. It was the first time since I joined, I was not swept up in Eli's words and tone, being awash in his calm. Sophia, next to me, kept her hand in mine throughout the meditation. I could feel her calm, and her peace. She was absolutely content with this change in dynamic. I wanted her calm. I wanted her peace. I wanted her assurance that I was making the right decision.

After the meditation concluded we were flooded with members congratulating us and hugging us. Sean slipped out quietly and unnoticed. I forced a smile and shook hands and hugged the members. I pretended to be the happy bride-to-be.

I went with Eli and Sophia back to their apartment after the service and sat cross-legged on the couch.

"That went well." Eli was smiling. Sophia sat next to me and wrapped her arm through mine.

"We have a lot to plan." She was looking at me earnestly.

"We have a lot to still figure out," I said. "A third in leadership?"

"I meant it. You are joining us. This is a lifetime commitment, Morgan."

I unwound myself from Sophia and stood up off of the couch.

Eli took my hands. "You've never committed long-term, I can understand to you the prospect is scary. You self-sabotaged your last long-term relationship and you were unable to commit to Sean. I understand all of this, Morgan. But do you understand all of what you are getting with us? You are getting the ability to fully be yourself and express yourself. You are getting the continued safety and security of The Society. You can be truly happy if you allow yourself to step outside of the fear, Morgan, and embrace this. Embrace all that we are offering you."

"I understand all of that."

"Then what is wrong? What can we do to make you comfortable with this?"

"A long engagement or whatever we are calling this. Understand my boundaries. I'm not ready for intimacy yet. I'm not ready to cross that line with anyone yet. I haven't since Jonathan died. I need to ease into this." I was looking at Eli, with my hands still in his, and Sophia moved behind me with her hands on my hips.

"Anything you need, you will have," she whispered into my neck.

Eli interlaced his fingers in mine and kissed the top of my head. "Whatever you need."

It was the first night I stayed in their bed with them. Sophia slept in the middle, flanked by Eli on one end and me on the other. She fell asleep entangled between us, her feet wrapped between Eli's and her arm over my body. Despite my many reservations, my emotional exhaustion allowed me to sleep heavily and dreamlessly.

I slept through Eli waking up and slipping out of the bed. Sophia sensed my waking, her eyes opened, and she stretched with a sly feline smile. "Good morning."

I could not help but feel happy looking at her smile. She was beautiful when she was made up and in public, but she was even more so when she was clean-faced and bare. I pulled her in and kissed the tip of her nose. Her long hair was piled up in a messy bun on the top of her head, some loose strands tickled my face as she hovered over me. "I like you being here," she said.

I let my hands travel down her back and trace the line of her curves. "I can't complain either."

She reached over me and looked at the screen on her phone. "I don't want to get out of this bed yet."

"We have responsibilities. Where's Eli?"

"Making breakfast. It's his turn."

"Well, you are well aware I don't cook. You will not want me on that rotation. I hope it won't be one of your expectations?"

"We will figure it out." She threw a sweatshirt on over her tank top.

I padded out to the dining area behind her. "How do you like your coffee?" Eli asked.

"Strong. With cream."

He brought over a steaming mug and a plate with a poached egg on an English muffin and set them in front of me before planting a kiss on my cheek. "How did you sleep?"

"Surprisingly well," I answered. "Thank you."

I resigned myself to my fate with the two of them, and just relaxed into an easy routine. Meals and bedtime with them. Slipping over to my own apartment to shower and dress alone. Giving and receiving affection to the both of them. Getting my certification to teach yoga, leading meditations occasionally. Teaching the children and conferencing with the parents. Drafting plans and ideas to create a full-on charter school with Eli, where the ideology of The Society would be worked into the curriculum.

Things were not so easy on Sean. The members had seemingly turned their backs on him. Eli was subtle in how this happened. I would overhear conversations between him and other members, calling Sean weak willed, or how he just doesn't seem to fit in with our ideologies any longer.

Soon, other members stopped talking to him and socializing. He was deemed a pariah.

One day, Sean was no longer at morning meditation. He just stopped showing up. I found out later that the board had 'tried him' and Eli had evicted him, and his apartment was cleared. I felt the weight of this decision in my heart, which Eli admonished me for. "Other people's decisions are not yours. They choose how they live. Not you. You bear no responsibility in Sean's choices just as you don't over what Jonathan did."

"He loved it here. He believed in what we were doing here. For him to leave is just heartbreaking."

Word had gotten around about The Society, and outsiders were joining the meditations and workshops Eli and Sophia were hosting. Retreats were booked out far in advance. A waitlist for living within the community was created. It was not long before Sean's unit was occupied by someone else.

We set a ceremony date. It saddened me somewhat, as I did not feel like I could involve my parents in this day. My exchanges with them were brief and I had not been to see them, nor had they come down to see me. They made it clear they were not happy about my life choices. Dad confessed to me that he locked me out of my accounts to keep my finances safe. I felt like sharing with them I was entering into some sort of throuple situation with the very man they pegged to be a cult leader would send them over the edge, so I kept that quiet. I also ceased communication with any of my friends or social network. I couldn't remember the last time I had opened any of my social media accounts, and rarely even left the building. There was no need. We had shoppers and assistants who would fetch anything, and it was just deducted from my pay. I just started putting everything on Eli's account when I ordered things.

Occasionally Sophia and I would go out and go shopping or we would have a date night with the three of us, or a beach day, or short daytrips.

Contracts were being drawn up to include me in the decisions and assets on a clause that would increase with each year I stayed within our 'marriage'. After ten years I would have a full third stake. Each year leading up to it I was awarded 3% upon the completion of the year, effective the date of our ceremony.

My alone time with Sophia was my favorite. She was affectionate, and loving, and loved to touch and be touched. I was never fully alone with Eli for long, but he was sweet and made sure to always give some sign of affection when we were together. But all in all, I felt like he was only obligated to be affectionate with me to please Sophia. For me though, it was never about love. It was business now. A form of survival.

Six weeks prior to our 'wedding', Eli and Sophia and I had gone out to dinner. Sophia and I had been getting increasingly heated when we were alone, and my walls were increasingly crumbling. At the dinner table, Sophia was pushing the limits of her affection in public. I was concerned Eli would be uncomfortable with the spectacle she was making, but he made no mind of it as she kissed me across the table.

I wanted her. There was no denying it further.

After returning from the dinner, I convinced myself I had held out long enough.

I pulled Sophia to the bedroom. Eli followed behind by a few paces.

Kissing her deep, and slow, I knew exactly what I wanted to do and how to do it. My sole purpose was only to please her.

Stripping her down slowly, I let my hands trace every inch, feeling her, touching her, lingering.

Eli sat himself in the armchair in the corner of the room facing the bed. His hands rested on the arms of the chair and his ankle crossed over his knee. His eyes were locked on us.

I released the knot at the back of my dress and let it fall off me. Sophia's gentle hands touched me, but I didn't let her for long. I guided her back onto the bed and took over her body.

I let my hand travel up her leg, graze over between, and up her belly before teasing over her breast. She pulled me in to kiss me and I let her have her way on that.

I used my hand and pushed her back down before allowing it to slowly travel down again and bring her to the point right before climax and stopped. I kissed her again, slowly, feeling her hunger. I took my time with my lips making my way slowly down between her thighs. I took her again almost to the point of climax and backed away.

Her beautiful body was glistening, and she was breathing hard. Her hands kept reaching for me to pull me into her, to take her to completion.

I sat on my knees between her legs and let my hands tease lightly over her as she writhed under me, demanding more. I could feel the weight of Eli's gaze from the corner. I didn't need to turn to look. I could feel his eyes. I could hear him breathe in an undercurrent to the sound of Sophia's whimpers and moans.

I finally went in after keeping her at bay for long enough and let her have her release. She was glorious in the way her body arched and she cried out. I brought her back-to-back, not allowing for respite.

She was wracked and shaking, and I moved to lay beside her. She pulled me in close with her lips against mine, her hands went to make their way down my belly, and I stopped her. "No... Not tonight. Tonight, was about you."

I finally looked at Eli, and he had not moved. I could not read the expression on his face. I could not tell how he truly felt.

He quietly left the room into the bathroom. I could hear the sink running and he was running through his nightly routine. He seemed unmoved and unfazed by what just occurred. Maybe all the restraint and self-discipline he preached was not bullshit after all.

"How are you?" I asked Sophia quietly.

She grinned at me, "I'm more than okay. Are you sure you are?"

"Seeing you this happy is all I want right now."

Eli came back in, ready for bed and moved the blankets down, climbing in next to where Sophia was laying above the duvet.

As he got into the bed, I got out followed by Sophia. We got ready for bed as if nothing had changed, and made our way back in. She slept in her typical fashion wrapped between us.

The next morning there was a slight shift in how Eli responded to us. He was slightly more demanding in his affection. He kissed me deeper, his hands lingered longer when he touched me. At night, he all but pulled Sophia to him, holding her firm.

For the next few weeks, I was consistent in pleasing Sophia in bed, and resolute in not letting her have me in return. Eli sat in the chair and watched us, silent every time.

Sometimes he would immediately lay with us and touch Sophia and kiss her or lay beside me and let his fingers brush over my back, caressing me much like he would a lap cat.

I knew they would make love when I was not around. Sophia told me how they would take advantage of the alone time when I was teaching or occasionally taking time for myself in my apartment, though those times were less and less frequent. I had no idea how he was able to maintain such composure in just sitting back and letting me take his wife time and time again without demands of his own.

I had no desire to be touched. I didn't want it. I was content to keep Sophia happy, and Eli seemed content in his role as silent observer.

~ *XII* ~

What You Thought You Saw In Me

The Present

Emma

HER NON-PROFIT UP AND running, being readmitted to the bar, and Teta's house renovated and furnished, Charlemagne home with her permanently, there was nothing left on her to-do list of post incarceration. She was working, her fines were paid, and probation was easy. Once a month check in, do a drug test and make sure she remains in some form of therapy.

She liked her new therapist. She was slightly older than Emma and had a big sisterly feel to her which made it easy for Emma to open up to.

She questioned Emma's choice to not fully let go of Morgan. "I felt at one point like she may have been it for me. After Bailey, after what I did, she was this lightness in my dark. And she carried me through this whole ordeal. She helped me heal. She saw past what I did and made me feel loved. I couldn't see anyone else doing that for me."

"But yet she won't take the final step of coming to you?"

"She won't. She hasn't. I don't know if she will. I have this incredible woman waiting for me to say 'yes, let's be official.' But I'm holding out waiting for Morgan to choose me. It's just so fucked up. I feel like even though Liz is into me, and we are having a great time together, deep down she will never understand me like Morgan can."

"Do you still feel guilt?"

"Yes and no. But it depends on the day. Some days when it's really quiet in the house, I think about what life would have been like if I hadn't done what I did. Would Bailey and I have made it? Probably not. There was no way I could have forgiven her for what she did. I was destined to be alone. But she would have carried on. I don't think Rhys would have stayed with her though. She probably would have haunted me throughout the rest of my life. She had a way of finding me and seeking me out. Always when I thought she was history. Maybe we would have stayed friends."

Emma left her appointment and went to the office. She had backed off Morgan in the past weeks. She decided that the option was there. Morgan was clear on it. The ball was in her court, and Emma was not going to push it further. She was ever more ready to let it go though. She couldn't stay in the holding pattern forever. It was wholly unfair what she was doing to Lizbeth on top of it all.

She walked in and Greta handed her a stack of papers. "Your one o'clock is here and waiting."

Emma looked at her watch. It was 12:45. She appreciated punctuality in clients. It was an appeal case that Emma was confident she could help the public defender assigned to the case overturn. The case was plagued with prosecutorial errors and bias from the judge.

"Give me five minutes to get situated and you can send her in."

Emma sat through her client meeting, an intern by her side taking notes. Her mind was a million miles away.

She was replaying the questions from her therapist and pondering if she could do what she knew had to be done.

Morgan

AS MORGAN WAS LEAVING HER front door to go for a run, she received a text from Emma. 'We need to talk.' It had been another several weeks of quick calls and short FaceTimes, and she still would not commit to a trip to visit. She knew Emma was running out of patience with her waffling. She was fully aware how she opened this door to the possibility of being together when she sent the initial letter to Emma. And she had been irrational in sending it.

The entire run she thought of the pros and cons of a life with Emma or whether or not she should call Sara. What she would have to give up and what she would gain with either of the women vying for her affection. She also weighed the pros and cons of letting Emma go completely. They were at a comfortable place where if either of them stepped away, it would easily be explained by a long-distance fizzle out. She began to think she was content to be friends and leave it at that. Looking at her history of how her love had been destructive to anyone she gave it to, she felt this might be the best decision.

There were pros and cons for Emma, too. And she considered those as well. Pros for Emma included... Well, okay, she couldn't think of any pros Emma would really have in being with her. But she could think of all the cons.

Running was something she did to clear her mind, but she came back with no more clarity than when she left.

Up the stairs of the porch and through the front door she bounded. Clean the house. Deep clean. Baseboards and bathroom grout and blinds. Shower. Grocery store. Yoga flow. Check the phone periodically – a text here or there from Emma but no phone call. Emma had an entire life – one she was not a part of – a life before they met. A life which included a wife and a history. And friends. And a successful career. She thought maybe when Emma got released she would return to her and live in Lake Tahoe. Run the campground together. Maybe she could set up a law clinic here.

Seeing how busy and successful Emma was, readjusting back into her old life, she knew she would be the one expected to leave. Morgan did not know if she could handle another full uprooting and starting over again. It had taken her a long time to get where she was, and she mostly liked her life.

Sara had recently been talking to her again. And she was making strides. She had told Sara all about Emma. Full disclosure.

Sara was understanding and encouraged Morgan to find closure. Assuring her she cared enough to be there for her.

She had a sleepless night, spent lying awake analyzing her feelings and an irritable morning sitting with her coffee.

It was late afternoon before the anticipated FaceTime call finally came in.

"I'm so sorry, I wanted to call you last night, but I have a trial coming up, and time got away from me while I was going through evidence. My intern is an idiot, and it took me forever to explain to him what he was supposed to be doing."

Morgan smiled and laughed quietly. "I can only imagine how hard it must be to work for you."

Emma pretended to look wounded and laughed with her. "I am demanding. In all fairness."

Both of them were silent. Looking at each other through the screens.

"Are we ever going to talk about what it is we are doing?"

"Emma, I'm scared. You have to know that."

"What exactly are you scared of?" Morgan could hear the frustration in Emma's voice and see it written on her face.

"Everyone I have ever loved has been ultimately destroyed by me."

"I'm tougher than you give me credit for. But honestly, Morgan, my patience is beginning to run thin. If we just want to be friends, that's great. I understand. But I need to know. I'm over here waiting for you, but I can't wait for forever."

Morgan closed her eyes for a minute. "I understand."

"I'm not trying to pressure you. I'm not. I know you have to do things in your own time. But I'm ready to either take the next step with you, or let you go. I would prefer it to be the step where we go to the next level. But we've been dancing around this dynamic. You tell me you love me. But you won't even acknowledge that I've sent you a ticket to come see me so we can figure this out."

"Emma, I'm sorry. I do love you. I *am* in love with you. I want to be with you. But I just don't know if I can."

"I have to go, Morgan. I love you. But right now, I can't." Emma's eyes were glassy.

Morgan nodded silently. "I love you." Her voice was quiet, and the screen went dark.

Morgan threw the phone and let out a growl. She threw herself on the bed and stared at the ceiling. The room went dark, and she didn't move. Ophelia jumped up on the bed and made herself comfortable in the crook of her hip. Still, she didn't move.

Emma

EMMA WAS UNSETTLED BY THE way they left things upon hanging up. But she also did not want to spend the rest of her life playing games. Life was too short for that kind of bullshit.

How hard is it to make a decision? You either want to make it work or you don't.

She picked her phone back up and thought about calling Morgan back but put it back down.

She spent the next few days in trial. She was working with Lizbeth as co-counsel on an appeal. When the verdict came in, as Emma was expecting, a win in their favor, she and Lizbeth met Brandon for drinks.

Lizbeth got up to grab a round. Brandon looked at her across the table. "Emma, seriously, what's going on? This is the best news ever, and you're in a mood."

"It's Morgan. She just doesn't want to commit. Can't commit. I don't know."

"Cut her loose. Be friends. But you don't need to waste any more time. You have a history. She got you through a rough time in your life. But you deserve someone who will and can give you all they have, without question or hesitation."

Emma sighed. "I had high hopes. You're right though. Abby said almost the exact same thing."

"Look at Liz. She's smokin' hot. She and you not only go well together as a couple, you work well together. What the fuck are you doing?"

"I'm a fool. I know."

"Get your shit together, woman. You will regret it if you don't."

Emma rolled her eyes.

"I'm just sayin', Emma. You know better."

One of the many bonuses to Lizbeth was that she was established on her own. And though she relished time with Emma, she enjoyed being solo. Work nights she preferred to go back to her own home, leaving Emma to her own devices.

Emma kissed Lizbeth goodnight in the parking lot of the bar and returned to her house. She let Charlemagne out, gave him his dinner and retreated to the bedroom with Morgan's journal.

Excerpt from Morgan's Memoir

THE DYNAMIC THAT DEVELOPED BETWEEN Eli and Sophia and I was strange. Eli was increasingly an outsider as Sophia and I grew closer. Their rendezvous together alone were decreasing. Eli was increasingly moody in regard to this.

The paperwork was signed and notarized, and everything was moving forward for the ceremony. It was going to be in the courtyard of the building and was going to be attended by all members of The Society. Our ceremony was going to be presided over by one of the senior members of our group.

I wanted to be happy about this. I wanted to feel like I was doing the right thing, but inside I was increasingly saddened by this. I would reflect on who I used to be and who I became, and I was unrecognizable to myself. I was not light-hearted and sociable any longer. I was not the free-spirited butterfly in the wind Jonathan described me as. I was brooding, and somber and reliant on a strict routine to get me through each day. I was disconnected and disjointed.

As the ceremony was drawing ever nearer, Sophia was beginning to pick up on my growing despondency. She suggested we go shopping for dresses for the farce that was to be our 'wedding'.

She was zipping up a dress along my back when she asked me, "You are not happy are you?"

"What makes you think that?"

"Your smile doesn't reach your eyes. You still won't let me touch you – you don't accept my love or Eli's."

"I don't know what to tell you, Sophia. I'm working through it. I'm trying. I love my life. I do. I love being in The Society. When I'm working with the kids, I'm super happy. When I'm teaching yoga, I feel at peace. I love our routine and watching the expansion and growth of what we are building. I want us to work. I want this life. I do. Emotionally, I think I will get there. I need time. I know what I'm doing is right by all of us."

She turned so I could do her zipper. "I just worry you feel like this compromise is greater than the benefit to you."

I finished pulling up the zipper and planted a small kiss in the crook of her neck. "I have nothing left. I have no one left. I haven't spoken to my parents in months. I have no friends left in the world. All I have is The Society, you and Eli."

We walked out of the fitting room and stood on the platform in the three-way mirror together. The dresses were matching and as we stood together, Sophia smiled and took my hand. "I just want you to be happy."

I knew she meant it. She was genuine in her sentiments. And I knew she loved me. She hung on every word I said, and her eyes always drifted to wherever I was in the room. When I would catch her gaze, she would light up and smile.

As the days got closer to the ceremony, I found myself avoiding Eli and Sophia as much as possible. I found more excuses to spend time alone in my apartment, or staying busy working on lessons and grading papers or working on finalizing the plans for opening the charter school. Eli and I had begun going on excursions to preview buildings that were available for lease. We found several that would work, it was all a matter of details in picking one. But I couldn't commit to the one I liked best for our venture. I was gun-shy, just like with everything else in my life. I couldn't commit.

SOPHIA WANTED US TO SPEND the night together before the ceremony so we could get ready together in the morning. We stayed the night in my apartment.

When we woke the morning of the ceremony, Sophia and I skipped the group meditation to reflect together on our impending day. She started the day by asking me to meditate alone with her. She was taking this commitment and this ceremony so seriously. My thoughts were that it was a survival mechanism. I was a hostage to my choices.

As we sat together in quiet contemplation I thought instead of all the reasons I should go forward with this, all the reasons I should leave. But I was too much of a coward and I hated myself for it.

She made us mimosas with our breakfast, and I pretended to be joyous. I did it for her.

One of the members who worked for a spa came up and did our hair while another did our makeup. The chatter was light and I played along, smiling and laughing, and trying to not get drunk on mimosas, though I really wanted to.

Hair and makeup done, and alone again with Sophia, I retreated back into my quiet space in my head as I slipped out of my robe and into my dress.

After she zipped the back of my dress, she undid the clasp of my locket. "I don't think you should wear this any longer."

My breath stopped, and she could read my reaction.

"Morgan, this is a tie to a painful past. One you have put behind you. It's not who you are, and it's not who you are growing into." She put it gently into the chest I kept my accessories in.

"I have something better for you. Something to represent you and I and Eli. It's from the both of us, but he wanted me to give it to you today." She went out of the room, and I could hear her in her bag.

She came back and presented me with the iconic blue Tiffany bag. "This is too much, Sophia."

"Nonsense." She waved her hand at me smiling. "Open it!"

I opened the blue box inside of the bag to find a glittering, diamond encrusted skeleton key on a chain.

She reached over and pulled it out of its box and put it around my neck. "There is a card from Eli, I think," she said as she fastened the clasp.

I looked at the beautiful piece around my neck. It felt weightless and looked foreign when I had been so used to the heavy silver of the locket.

I looked at the card in my hand and opened it, reading Eli's neat script in black ink, 'Our Lovely Morgan – The key to happiness is in you. Not just for you, but for us. Thank you for being ours.' Eli's signature was next to Sophia's flourished writing.

"I didn't realize we were being so traditional. I didn't get either of you a gift. We never discussed it." I was blushing.

"It's okay. You are the gift." She gave me a gentle kiss on my lips and went back to getting ready.

As the ceremony began, Eli walked with Sophia on one arm, and myself on the other, down the aisle to our officiant.

The preamble that came when we arrived made mention of how lucky we were to have all found each other and how love saved us in various ways. I was not wholly paying attention. All I could think about was how badly I wanted to run away.

I thought about Jonathan and how our wedding was supposed to look. What my life would have been had I not thrown it all away. I'm sure we would have bought a house. The condo with a toddler would have been too small. We definitely would have gotten a dog. Jonathan would have published a book by now. I would have been seeking an admin position by then, at least that was my plan. My thoughts spun darker. I would have probably still been cheating on him, if not with Sunny, another woman, because now I am fully aware of who I was. My life would not have been perfect under the surface. I was kidding myself to think I would have been less of a mess than I am at this moment – about to enter into a sham marriage – all to avoid facing my own reality in the real world alone.

The officiant took a white silk scarf and tied it around our three hands, speaking about unbreakable bonds between souls, and gave each of us an opportunity to speak.

Eli went first, "Sophia, if you asked me ten years ago when we first were married, what would our relationship evolve to, I would have never guessed it would have led to this. Building a spiritual empire that seeks to better the world we live in, and finding our Morgan and bringing her into the fold with us. Today, I reaffirm that love for you. Morgan, you have brought so much to our lives. It is my honor and privilege to welcome you into our hearts and our future, with great love."

"Eli, ten years ago you made me the happiest woman ever. We shared a vision together and made it happen. This vision has evolved over time as we have evolved and grown. We've grown stronger. We've grown together. Morgan, I knew the moment we met in Mexico how special you were. I knew when we parted ways you would find your way back to us. Watching how you have overcome your demons and becoming so integral to us, to me, has been so affirming. I love you, and I love what we will continue to grow together to become."

It was my turn to talk, and I froze. My vows to Jonathan were fresh in my mind, though it had been years since I thought of them. The bodice on my dress was constricting my breathing.

After a long pause my words finally came to me. "Eli, Sophia, you have welcomed me not just into The Society, but your lives and your future. You have reminded me of what it means to have a life of purpose and one worth living. You have given me breath and you have given me hope. *Dum spiro spero*. While I breathe, I hope." I was careful not to use the word 'love'. I was not in love. I was in survival mode. But I did have hope. And fear. Mostly fear. But I had hope that I would be okay through this.

Eli purchased a set of three matching bands with diamond inlays and they were placed on our fingers.

The reception was standard for any wedding ceremony. There was dancing, food, cake, champagne. No one present would have realized I was not truly happy for this day. I felt trapped and miserable. The weight on my finger from the ring felt like it was a million pounds.

I wanted to be in love. I wanted to give myself to some*one*, not be brought into an established relationship as a third.

After the reception ended, and we made our way back up to the apartment, my heart was beating fast and hard. I did not know how this dynamic would change now that everything was 'official'.

Before making his way to his corner chair, Eli held me close against him. His hands caressed my face and my back and he kissed me, this time with heat and passion, unlike before.

Sophia turned me around and kissed me next. Eli began to undo the zipper on my dress, letting his hands linger as the fabric fell away. He was taking a liberty he normally did not. He left all the intimacy to Sophia. His hands caressed my body as they moved back up and removed my bra. He was gentle, deliberate in each movement, taking his time. Sophia pulled me closer to her, allowing me to better undo her zippers and hooks.

Eli took his seat in the corner allowing me to take Sophia and please her.

I was taken off guard when, normally, after Sophia climaxed I would hold her and we would all curl up together, Eli slid into the bed behind me. I could feel he was naked, and his desire was pressing up against my back. His arms were wrapped around me, and he whispered, "Morgan, let me love you. Let me please you."

My hands ripped his off me and I scrambled out of the bed. I grabbed his shirt off of the floor and threw it on as I made my way to the door. I bolted across the hall into my own unit and threw myself on the bed.

I couldn't handle the idea of him touching me. I didn't want to give myself to him in such a way. I had given all of myself that I could tolerate to give. I wished they could see it. Understand it. Understand my pain and my fear.

I was crying silently in the dark, lying on my bed.

Minutes later, Sophia opened the door and came stepping in quietly. She laid herself beside me and held me close while I cried. "Morgan, it's okay. It's okay," she whispered, trying to soothe me.

We slept together alone in my bed.

When I woke up, Sophia was already awake, sitting up next to me. "I'm sorry about last night," I said.

"I'm sorry, too. I had no idea Eli was going to do that. We got into it after you left. I was not okay with what happened."

"I can't blame him. I mean, we are all married. I'm for all intents and purposes your wife and his."

"But you've been clear about your boundaries. He should have respected you."

"I need to work on things, too. What time is it?"

"6:45. We have to get ready for meditation and then head to the airport."

We planned a 'honeymoon' for Cabo, at the resort where we all met. Sophia and I made our way across the hall. Eli had made breakfast and coffee and sat at the table looking gloomy.

"I'm sorry." His voice was soft, and he looked at me with true remorse in his eyes.

I would be lying if I said I wasn't touched to see his emotion. I sat down in my chair at the table and took his hand and kissed it. "I'm sorry, too. I promise to try to work on it."

"I promise I will be more patient as well." His eyes met mine and I forced a smile.

I wanted to believe him.

It was surreal to walk into the resort with Eli and Sophia, compared to the first time I had walked into the building.

Physically, I was healthy, and my body was full, and toned and lean, compared to the pale and emaciated mess I was the first time. Sophia and I were in low-cut sun dresses, and Eli in a linen suit. I could see people watching us. A small paranoid part of me was wondering if they knew what our arrangement was, and I tried not to care.

After checking in we wandered around town and Eli stopped in front of a tattoo shop. "Morgan, what was the Latin phrase you said yesterday with your vows?"

"*Dum spiro spero.* While I breathe, I hope."

"We should get it tattooed. All of us." He walked in, dragging Sophia and I behind him.

We sat in chairs facing each other, under the needle. Reggaeton music thumped over the speakers. Sophia and I laid back with our shirts tucked under our bras, getting our ink placed on our ribs, Eli on the underside of his wrist.

We spent the first night after leaving the shop, at the bar in the resort. Sophia and I drank too much. I couldn't tell where Eli was on the drunk spectrum, but she and I passed out. We woke up with Eli between us, wrapped around him.

He did not seem to mind. He was chipper and happy the next day as he left us to go for a round of golf with a friend who lived locally in one of the resort communities.

Sophia and I made our way into downtown after a late breakfast at the country club and a massage and facial at the spa. I walked past the farmacias I used to frequent and looked past them. A part of me wanted to wander in and buy a bottle of Adderall. Just one. Sophia seemed to read my mind. "You don't want that. You don't want to go back."

"Part of me does, a little. I can't lie."

"What about it do you miss?" Her nose wrinkled with distaste as she asked.

"The euphoria. The absolute 'I don't give a fuck' feeling."

"What are you holding on to so tightly?" She stopped in her tracks as we were walking up the hill to the restaurant Eli and his friend were meeting us at for dinner. Spanning out below us, a strand of bars lined the beach.

"What do you mean?" I asked stopping to turn around and face her.

"Think about your yoga training. What do we say about the hips? It's the center of our being, our root chakra. It's also where we store a lot of our traumas. You still struggle with basic hip openers in your yoga practice. That whole part of you is shut off. You won't let me or Eli touch you. The moment we get too close to real intimacy, sexual or otherwise, you shut down. You won't fully give yourself to us, though we've given ourselves to you. You married into us, yet you still hold back. It's all surface. On the surface you belong to us. But you have one foot perpetually out the door. You don't think I want to please you in return? Give back to you what you give to me? That I don't crave to feel you or taste you or satisfy you?"

"Sophia, why are we doing this right now, right here?"

"Because, the fact you still crave that poison, but you won't let someone touch you, is concerning."

"I told you I understand I am not being entirely fair. I told you I'm working on it, it's the best I can do." I could see Eli and his friend seated in the outdoor courtyard of the restaurant. Eli was eyeing us from the table. "Come on. Our husband or whatever is waiting for us."

Sophia rolled her eyes at me and took my hand as we walked in.

"Andre, these are my beautiful wives, Sophia and Morgan. Ladies, this is Andre. He's the man who gave us the initial backing for our building."

Andre shook our hands. "I thought Eli was crazy when he told me he had two wives today. But seeing as how lovely you two are, I can hardly say I blame the man."

Andre was handsome enough. He carried himself like a man with capital to invest. He was significantly older than Eli, with sharp gray eyes and a prominent nose. His hair was silver with shades of dark sprinkled through it, and a lean muscular build despite his age. I noticed he wore no wedding ring. He and Eli mostly dominated the conversation and kept it revolved around finances. The Society initially borrowed the majority of the funds from Andre, and did so well, they paid him back twice as fast as the terms had been negotiated.

Eli was asking for more funding to build a second building since the wait list had grown so long he could essentially fill the building within completion.

Sophia and I just sat like two quiet accessories. We drank margaritas and Mexican coffee as we listened to Eli and Andre. Sophia listened intently and chimed in from time to time. I pretended to listen, but I was stuck on what Sophia said to me on the street before we walked in.

I knew I was frustrating both of them and it was unfair. But I was resentful at them for pushing me, which made me only want to lock in harder.

I did not relent the entire trip. Not when Eli slipped into the shower with me. Not when Sophia tried to take charge and throw me down on the couch in the suite. I was able to skirt around and slip out and away.

We returned from our honeymoon and paperwork was firmed up and plans set in motion for The Society to have a second building up in the Inland Empire area, near the Temecula wine country.

While I was shutting Eli out, and he was increasingly busy with building the second building, Sophia and I were growing closer. We spent the majority of our time together when I was not teaching the children. We created workshops and started a Yoga Teachers' Training Program to run out of the studio. We were building our own sections of The Society and raising them up. Money and members were pouring in in various capacities. I settled on a building and finished a final proposal to open a charter school as Eli suggested.

Eli was growing increasingly frustrated in that not only had he not been granted access to me as a husband, he was losing access to Sophia. More than once in a while she and I would fall asleep together in my apartment.

After rejecting him yet again, he rolled over me, pinning me down underneath him. I could feel him hard and pulsing against my hip. "Morgan, I am your husband. You said vows to me. I want you. I deserve you. You deserve me. You deserve to free yourself from whatever is holding you back. Let me make love to you. Let me feel you." His hand was making its way down my belly. I was frozen in fear, not sure if he was going to truly take me by force at this point.

"Eli, get off of her." Sophia's voice was low. "You're scaring her. You're scaring me."

His head turned and faced Sophia. "Is this how it's going to be? Just the two of you? I'm just here to watch now? Sophia, how long has it been now since you have made love to me?" He was still on me, but his focus was intent on Sophia.

She looked away ashamed.

"I can't deal with either of you right now." He got up and grabbed his robe, tying it on as he slammed his way into the bathroom.

The next day, he was short with Sophia and I, not just in private, but in front of the other members.

When we got back to the apartment for dinner, I cornered him. "Eli, you can't disrespect Sophia and I like that. It's not good for the members to see you act –"

"Morgan, you literally have no footing to stand on in telling me how to treat you or Sophia. When you thaw out, you can give me your two cents."

I turned around and walked out of the apartment. I went back to my haven and looked around.

I did not feel good. I had not felt good in quite some time. Was it worth staying here? Could I make it on my own?

I put the chain and the deadbolt on the door to keep Sophia out as well. I needed to be on my own. I needed peace and I needed space. I had no qualms about sleeping alone and away from the both of them. It was the best night's sleep since I first moved to The Society.

The next day after meditation and after class, Sophia tried to talk to me, and I blew her off. I could see a few of the male members who were close to Eli side eyeing me. I could see other members were talking in whispers as I walked by. There was a perceptible shift in the energy around me.

I went back to my apartment and threw the deadbolt and the chain. I pulled up my bank account for the first time in forever. My account was negative. Not by just a little bit. I pulled up all my bills and saw how past due I was. Everything had been on autopay. I looked at my deposit history. Eli had turned off my payments months ago. Around the time I agreed to be part of their relationship.

I scrambled to my accessories' chest and grabbed my locket and in a drawer a small envelope of cash I kept for emergencies. I had about two thousand I kept in an envelope for emergencies just in case. This was just in case.

I grabbed a hundred out of it and ran down to the lobby. I asked for my car keys and Sola gave me an odd look. I ignored her while I waited for my keys. "Where are you going?" she asked.

I ignored her.

"What time can I tell Eli you will be back?"

I snatched my keys and didn't give an answer.

I got in my car and drove to Jonathan's grave. I don't know why it was my first choice to run to, but it's where I went, after stopping for a bottle of tequila.

I sat on the ground at the foot of his grave and cried. I thought about how long it had been since he took his life and where our life would have been if only I just treated him the way he deserved to be treated.

We would have been married for almost four years. Our baby would have been born and she would have been smart and sensitive like him. Maybe I would be pregnant with our second child now. I was drinking from the bottle as I wallowed on the 'what might have beens'.

I destroyed him, and in the wake of his destruction was my own. I thought I was on a path of healing and recovery, only to replace one addiction with another. The safety, security and rigidity of the schedule and life of The Society replaced my addiction to uppers.

In the process I had given up every aspect of myself. I had given up my friends, my parents, my home, my soul and my sanity.

I sat and I drank. Sophia was blowing up my phone and I ignored her. I had been sharing my location with her, so to avoid her tracking me, I turned off my phone completely.

I sat past the sunset, cold and drunk and alone. I missed evening meditation. I couldn't give a fuck. Self-care looks many different ways, doesn't it?

I finished almost a quarter of the bottle of tequila as I sat in the cemetery, having a one-sided conversation with Jonathan about what could have been, what should have been, and what had become of us.

"There's so many ways this could have worked if you hadn't pussed out on me. We could have been together and been happy. I know we would have worked out. In the most unconventional sense, maybe you could have been more lenient with me. Allowed me to be myself a bit more. If not, I'm sure I would have still kept a girl on the side. If not Sunny, someone else would be there. That's just who I've always been, I guess. But we could have made life work. You know it, too." I took a swig of the tequila and stared hard at the flowers in the vase next to the flat stone. White roses. They had Tiffany written all over it.

I tugged at the diamond key around my neck and fidgeted with the ring on my finger before drinking more. "Fuck my life, Jonathan. We destroyed each other. I pushed you to take your own life. Your death ruined my life. I've never recovered. I don't think I ever will." The tequila burned as it went down my throat. My vision was blurred. I don't know if it was tears or drink.

A squad car pulled up and an officer got out. It was the same officer who had been with me when Jonathan died, and took the suicide note and taken me home, and was in the hospital with me after I was attacked. Jiminez. This guy really does show up when I'm at rock bottom. An armed guardian angel clad in blue polyester and a bulletproof vest.

He sat next to me on the grave. "I haven't seen you in a while."

"I thought I was past all of this. Turns out, I'm not." I held the bottle out for him, offering him some.

He gave a lopsided smile and pushed my hand down, finding the screw top lid and spinning it back in place. "There is no way you can drive. I don't even need to give you a breathalyzer. I can smell you from here."

"I know."

"Do you need a ride home?"

"Do I have to go home?"

"You can't stay here."

I leaned my head on his shoulder. "Here you are to rescue me again."

He laughed quietly. "I try."

"I'm beyond saving, you know that, right?"

"You just have to want it."

"I thought I wanted it. But I don't. I just want to feel better."

"One day you will. Come on. Let's get you home. Make sure you come get your car before too long, though, okay?"

I nodded as he helped me up to my feet.

I let him drive me back to The Society building. I walked across the lobby and was greeted by one of the front desk girls. "Good evening, Mrs. Martin." Being called by a name not my own solidified all that was wrong.

"Hale. My last name is Hale. It was supposed to be Staley. It is *not* Martin."

I ignored her as she stammered out an apology and stumbled into the elevator.

I went to my unit and skipped going to Eli and Sophia's.

I ate a rice cake as I stumbled into the bathroom and undressed.

I stood in the shower under the hot water. I was starting to sober up. I heard my door open and shut and Sophia's form entered the doorway of the bathroom.

"Where were you?"

"Not here."

"I know that. Where did you go?"

"I have no one left but this place. Did you know that?"

"Are you wasted?"

"Wasted? No. Slightly tipsy, maybe."

"Why? Why would you go and do that to yourself? Why didn't you come and talk to me?"

"Because, honestly, I didn't want to. I don't even want to talk to you now. I need you to leave." I turned off the water and grabbed a towel.

Sophia's large eyes looked hurt. She reached her hand out to me and I walked past her without further acknowledgement.

"Morgan!"

"Good night, Sophia. Beautiful, beautiful Sophia. Good night." I slammed the bedroom door.

I laid in the bed and willed for Jonathan to show up. I didn't care if he was grotesque and angry or sweet and handsome. I just wanted for some version of him to tell me what a fuck up I was and how I could best fix it.

Whether or not he was a figment of my imagination, or higher consciousness he was there. He sat on the bed next to me in his funeral suit. His cold hand lay on my back. "Morgan, get the fuck out of here. Leave. Write them a letter, denounce any claim you signed for and leave."

"Where will I go? I have nothing and no one left."

"Your parents will never turn you away."

He stayed with me the entire night. I felt his cold hand on my flesh as I slept.

In the morning, I skipped meditation again. I skipped yoga, too. I scheduled movers and rented a storage unit.

I sat in front of my laptop and drafted a letter to Eli and Sophia. 'Eli, Sophia; I thank you for all that you have done to help me. I have learned so much from the both of you. I appreciate not just what you taught me, but how you loved me. I am so sorry, but I cannot stay. I cannot stay with you. I cannot stay within The Society. For whoever takes my place as the instructional teacher for the children, everything is in place, and the curriculum is set and designed. It should be plug and play. I have to learn to be on my own. I renounce any claim you allotted to me of The Society. Effective immediately. With Love, Morgan.' I printed it, signed it, placed it in an envelope with my wedding band and the Tiffany necklace, and stuck it under the door of Eli and Sophia's apartment.

~ *XIII* ~

Let You Go

The Present

Emma

IT WAS A LAZY SATURDAY. Atypical for Emma and Lizbeth. Emma was in the kitchen cooking breakfast and Lizbeth was sitting on the counter watching Emma move around the small space.

Emma was surprised at how comfortable her presence was. Lizbeth's long braid over her shoulder, and her cozy law school sweats and hoodie. She had her hands wrapped around her coffee mug. It had been a month since she brought up wanting to go to the next step and Emma successfully avoided any further mention of it.

"So…" Lizbeth said slowly from behind her coffee mug.

Emma braced herself. She knew her luck was running out in avoiding the conversation. She placed her quiche into the oven and turned to face Lizbeth.

"Have you cleared up your loose ends?"

Emma averted her eyes.

"Can you tell me what the loose ends might be?"

Emma took Lizbeth's coffee mug from her and stood between her knees. She cupped Lizbeth's face in her hands. "I want to tell you all of it. But I am honestly afraid that it will change everything about us. But I think it's mostly clear." She kissed Lizbeth's nose.

"Don't try to distract me by getting all sweet." She was smiling as she pulled back away from Emma. "I want you to talk to me. Trust me. Trust that I'm genuine about you."

Emma backed away and turned to refill her coffee. "There was kind of someone in the background of my life. It was the girl I was seeing before I... Before I came back and..."

"Emma, I know what happened. I know you were on the run. You went to prison. You don't have to avoid it. You have nothing to be ashamed of. It was a tragic accident, and you paid the price for it."

Emma's eyes misted over as she leaned against the opposing counter facing Lizbeth. She shook her head. "People say that. But it's hard. So, yeah, I was involved with her. Morgan. I hurt her when I hid the truth from her. And then she figured it out. And I left and I turned myself in. While I was in prison, she wrote to me. We began talking regularly. I kind of thought we were going to end up together. But as time has gone on, and you and I have been spending time together, I have put her on the back burner. But I haven't fully committed to cutting her loose. But I think it's time. I can't deny what I feel when I'm around you. I can't deny what we are building together."

"So... When do you plan on letting her know?"

Emma shrugged. "I need to figure out how to have the conversation with her. I've been blowing her off recently. Making excuses to not talk. Maybe she knows. Or suspects. I thought of maybe just not having the talk and letting it go. But she deserves closure."

Lizbeth nodded. And a slow smile crept across her face. "So that's it. We're official?"

Emma chuckled. "Are we in high school? Official? Am I supposed to give you my class ring?"

"Stop. You know. Like we can start meeting the family and friends? Posting about us? Whatever?"

"Yes. Official."

Morgan

MORGAN NOTICED EMMA WAS PULLING away. She couldn't blame her. She was doing what she had become so good at doing over the course of her life. Pushing people away.

She was annoyed with herself, but she also didn't do anything to change the behavior. She noticed Emma was not responding to texts as fast. She noticed the FaceTimes were less frequent. The most noticeable shift was how Emma stopped saying "I love you" or other cute pet names or sweet sentiments.

Emma was not going to beg. She never needed to beg, and she definitely was not going to start now. She extended the offer and the ball sat idle in her court. Morgan was frozen. Even Aaron was annoyed with her. He had told her that unless she was going to go out there and give it a go, she needed to shut up about Emma.

She decided to call her.

When Emma came across the screen, Morgan was taken aback. It was a midweek evening. Normally Emma would be in a cozy sweatshirt up in her office. Instead, Emma was dressed in a nice black cashmere turtleneck sweater and looked like she was going somewhere.

"Hey." Emma smiled.

"Are you busy?"

Emma's blue eyes averted to the side, and she bit her lip. "I just got back from lunch with a client."

"A client? This late for lunch? On a Thursday?"

"She has court on Monday. I was going over a few case points."

Morgan could sense that though it might be true, there was something Emma was holding back. Her gut twisted. "Oh. I feel like we haven't really talked in a while."

"True. It's been a busy few weeks." She watched Emma walk up the stairs to her office and recline back in the office chair. Emma was nonchalant and Morgan could feel the distance.

Morgan paused. She wanted to tell Emma to be patient, but she recognized it was unfair.

"I need to tell you something," Emma said quietly, breaking the silence.

"I think I know what you are going to tell me." Morgan could feel the lump in her throat.

"I... I met someone. I don't know... how to talk about this. I don't really know. But that's where I was today. We met for lunch, and she *is* a client, but there's definitely something there. We've been together for a while now. But it's getting serious."

"I understand. It hurts to hear that. But I understand." Morgan was fighting tears.

"I value you. I value what you've done for me in helping me heal. You are so amazing and wonderful, and you are the person I pictured myself with forever. But I can't keep hanging on a string waiting."

Morgan felt her heart sink and the lump in her throat was unavoidable. "I understand." Her voice cracked.

"Morgan..."

"I know. You deserve to find someone. You deserve to be loved. I wanted to be the one. I did." Tears were spilling over. She hated that she was this upset.

"I wanted it to be you. But I couldn't be kept on hold forever."

"I know."

Emma's sapphire blue eyes looked concerned. "Morgan..."

"I can't talk about this right now." Morgan wiped her tears with her sleeve. "I'm going to let you go."

Emma sighed on the other end. "Okay, Morgan. I'm sorry."

Morgan hung up and powered her phone off. She shuffled it across the comforter to the other side of the bed.

She had no right to be hurt by Emma. This was all on her. She was the one who reopened the communication, with all the possibilities, and then panicked.

Albeit, she rationalized, she never said or promised that the love they would share, or the relationship would be romantic. It had been assumed by both parties because of the history they shared.

Emma loved her. She knew without a doubt. But she was unsure if Emma in a platonic form was enough for her. But now the choice was removed from her.

Emma

EMMA HATED THAT SHE WAS ending the call in such a way. But it was only fair for Morgan to know.

She had thought Morgan would be the one. But wouldn't there be a certainty if that were the case?

She went back down the stairs where Lizbeth was settling into the bedroom. "Was that her?" she asked.

Emma nodded.

"Did you tell her?"

"It's over. I told her."

"Are you sad?"

"She cried. That was hard. But it needed to happen. Seeing her sad, of course, hurts a bit. But I'm happy to be with you. I want you. I choose you, for a reason."

After Lizbeth dozed off, Emma found herself restless. She kept reflecting on Morgan's fat tears sliding down her cheeks. "I'm going to have to let you go." Morgan's words echoed in her ears.

She saw the journal on the corner of her nightstand and slipped out of the bed with it in her hands. She owed it to Morgan to finish reading it and send it back to her. It wasn't her story to keep. But she made a promise to read it all.

Excerpt from Morgan's Memoir

WHEN THE MOVERS ARRIVED, I escorted them past the front desk where a very confused Sola sat. I didn't acknowledge her or give reason for the team of men with dollies that followed me up the elevator.

When Eli caught sight of the movers he was incensed. He pulled me by the arm across the hall as the team of men were packing my belongings in boxes and carting them down the elevator.

"Morgan, you can't be serious?"

"Oh. I am."

"You are just going to leave us? Like nothing?" Sophia was crying.

"You will be fine without me. I can't be here. This is not good for me. I said it all in the letter. I release all liability and whatever. I need to go."

Eli put his hands over his face and sat down. "Where are you going to go?"

"I don't know. Let's start with the fact that you have not paid me since our little arrangement began, so I have no money. My parents locked me out of my own accounts because I was here. Let's continue and explore the fact that now that I look deeper, you've never been paying my whole salary. My accounts are a mess. I'm a mess."

"How can we fix it? Is this about money? Fine. I will give you money. Do you know how this is going to look to the other members?"

I shook my head. "It's not even about the money. It's my fault for being blind to it all. I bought into whatever it is you are selling because I wanted it. I wanted the peace and the joy. But it's all bullshit, Eli. It's about you. Your hubris and your desire to be something greater than what you are.

"But it's not just that. It's more than that. I never wanted to ever use this line, but it's true. It's not you. It is me. I need to work on me. And being here I'm just hiding from doing what I really need to be doing. I am covering my pain and burying it instead of dealing with it. The fact remains, I can't get past my sense of guilt and allow either of you to even touch me or love me tells me I'm still broken. You can't love me through this. I need to love myself first. You can't buy me with your offer of money, either. I'm not doing the work as long as I'm here pretending I'm okay. I'm clean. But I'm not okay."

It was the most adult conversation I ever had. Everyone involved got closure. I thought I was going to be able to walk out of the building with my head held high. I moved to leave and Eli jumped up and grabbed my arm.

"Morgan, you don't just get to walk out on this. On us. I will give you whatever you require. You will stay here." His fingers pressed hard into the flesh of my arm as he pulled me to him.

I tried to pull away and he took his other arm and pulled me to him, steering us up against the wall. He was nose to nose with me. His body blocking mine, his eyes piercing through me.

"You don't get to just come and go, Morgan."

I didn't back down. I looked him in the eye. "Let me go. Now."

He dug in deeper. "You belong to us."

"I don't, Eli. I don't. I don't belong to you. I don't belong here."

"Think about Sophia. The kids. People rely on you. I rely on you. This community. You can't just walk away from us."

"I can. And I am. And if you don't let me go, right the fuck now, I will scream. What will your members think then?"

"Eli... Let her go." Sophia's voice was soft from the opposite side of the room.

"Morgan, think twice. If you walk, you never, ever get to come back."

"I have thought. I'm okay with never coming back."

His hands released me, and the blood circulated back into my fingers. I knew I would bear bruises from his grip.

I walked past Eli, brushing his shoulder with mine. I grazed Sophia's hand reluctantly, hopefully communicating that I was sorry to her.

For as adult as I had tried to be with this conversation, my next stop was not. I drove down to Rosarito, Mexico. I got a room and hit the farmacia. I had been clean for so long. I don't know what prompted me to make this decision.

I think, in retrospect, it was because I was proving I had my autonomy back.

I crushed the pills on the bathroom counter and left them there in a line.

I went and walked on the beach by the resort. The blue of the Pacific stretched out before me. Infinite.

I was suddenly aware how alone I was. I had not talked to my parents in almost a year. I had no friends left, to speak of. I walked away from Eli and Sophia and The Society. I had nothing. I had no one.

I was responsible for me and me alone. I was not responsible for anyone else, and no one could claim responsibility for me or my actions. I walked past sunset and relished the feeling of independence. I was not hiding anything. I was not running from myself.

I walked back to my room and looked at the line of crushed Adderall on the counter. I took the straw and inhaled it in.

I allowed myself to be carried on the feeling of euphoria. I did it not to hide from my feelings of guilt or to avoid Jonathan's ghost. I did it because I wanted it and I could. It was not Jonathan's fault. It was mine and I owned it.

I went down the street to the nightclub with a large devil's head built around the structure and gothic style architecture and I danced. I was celebrating my independence and my accountability.

As my high wore off, I let it versus taking more. I opened the door to the veranda to allow the salt air and the sound of the ocean in, and I spread out in the bed as the sun was rising. I slept deep.

I woke up reflecting on the parable of the Japanese potters. When the pottery breaks, they fill the cracks with gold. The broken pieces and flaws add beauty. I reflected back to a book I read with my students which explained how the broken pieces were where the strongest light came in. Being broken was not the worst thing I could be.

I drank coffee alone on the veranda and walked around the town. I found an outdoor patio to sit on and watch the people as they passed by. I wondered how many of them were just as broken as I was.

I checked my phone and saw a message from Sophia, 'Come home when you are ready, Eli will let you come back. I miss you.'

I blocked her number.

I had not eaten, and I was not hungry. I went back to the room and crushed more Adderall.

I snorted it without hesitation.

I stripped off my clothes and went to get into the shower. Before stepping in, I looked at my reflection in the mirror. Cracks appeared in my flesh in my reflection. Large and deep. Black gaps appeared jagged as if my body were coming apart. Slowly, through the black, gold began to appear until all of the black was gone and filled with luminescent gold and light. I knew what I needed to do.

After my shower, I packed my bags and checked out of the hotel and began to drive north. I went back across the border and then up past San Diego and then LA. I stopped and took more Adderall. I was wearing out. I needed the energy to get to Lake Tahoe.

Eventually the palm trees gave way to evergreens.

I drove into the night-lights blinding and streaking, stars scattered above me. I was transfixed on the lights and stars.

I was on a two-lane road and it was velvet blackness save for the headlights and tail lights and stars.

I didn't see it coming. I didn't know I was following too closely. The red lights growing closer and brighter.

The sound of metal crunching, my head being snapped forward, the slamming of collarbone against seatbelt. The powdery burning from the airbag deploying. But the stars. The stars were so bright. Like glitter against velvet.

There was screaming.

There was a banging against my window. I looked at the person banging.

She was bloody. She was crying. She was desperate.

I undid my seatbelt and opened the door. "Do you see these stars?"

She grabbed my shirt. "Call 911! He's dead! Dead!"

"Who's dead?" I asked. My breath made fog against the cold.

I was strung out and I didn't care that I was cold. I didn't really care about who was dead, either. "Did you see the stars?"

She let go of my shirt and grabbed my phone from my cup holder and dialed 911. I could hear her frantic and yelling at an operator. I didn't care what she was saying.

I walked to her car and looked inside.

The driver was a man. His head caved in from where impact with the steering wheel occurred. Mouth agape. Bloody, broken teeth. Brown eyes unseeing, staring at the incredible stars. His head was open. Blood covering skin. Pink flesh. White poking through. That thick coppery smell of blood.

Flashing red lights. Blue lights. Sirens loud.

The girl was crying and hysterical. She was pulling at the lapel of an officer.

An officer approached me. He was backlit by the headlights of the ambulance, and as he came into view I half expected to see Jiminez and was half disappointed that it wasn't him.

"Do you have ID?" he asked me.

I nodded and walked back to my car. I gave the officer my driver's license and sat back in the seat.

"Ms. Hale, do you want to tell me what happened?"

"The stars. They were so beautiful. And then this. I think I killed him." My stomach churned and my heart became a bass drum in my chest and in my ears as the realization dawned on me. I was responsible for yet another death.

"I'm sorry?"

"I was looking at the stars. I mean, did you see them? Look?" And then the tears – first hot as they leaked out and then cold against the air down my cheeks. "And then... I crashed into him and he's dead."

"Have you been drinking?"

"No." It came out in a choked sob.

"Did you take anything else, perhaps?"

I nodded.

"What might that be?"

"Adderall. A lot of Adderall." A whisper.

An EMT came over to assess whether or not I was injured. He flashed lights in my eyes and asked me questions. The bruises on my arms from where Eli had grabbed me bloomed in purple bands around my biceps. He asked me about those. I told him it was nothing.

Handcuffs were placed on my wrists and I was in the back of the squad car. I just watched the stars as we drove to the station.

I was booked and locked into a cell. I laid on the thin rack of the police station holding cell. I was wired and couldn't sleep, but every time I blinked my eyes, I could see the driver. It wasn't the same as when I would see Jonathan. But I saw him just the same.

I was booked and in the morning, arraigned with a public defender by my side. Apparently, the driver in front of me was drunk and stoned. He stopped because he saw a deer. I crashed into him. His car had been recalled for defunct airbags, but he had never done anything about it. I was being charged with DUI and involuntary manslaughter.

My attorney called my parents for me, and they sprang for my bail. I didn't want them to be called.

But I needed them. I needed to know someone was still on my side.

Dad came and posted bail and I was given my bags that were in the back seat of my car. My car was impounded on the lot, pending use for evidence.

A silent drive from the station to a diner for lunch. There was nothing to say in the car, and nothing to say at the table either. When he left the table to go to the bathroom, I dug around the bottom of my tote bag, where I knew there was a slit in the lining, found two Adderall in the lining and excused myself to the bathroom when Dad came back.

I crushed half of one and inhaled it.

I pushed my food around on the plate and looked out at the teal water of Lake Tahoe glittering in the sun. I didn't speak to my dad, and he didn't speak to me. I could feel the weight of his disappointment. He opened his mouth and inhaled as if he was going to say something, but then stopped himself, several times.

He had to go back to the campground, so he dropped me off at the house and took off before I even got up to the door.

I made my way up the walkway. I was not dressed for the chill of Tahoe, but I was so high I didn't care. I also didn't care that my mother would know immediately I was not right.

I knocked hard on the door and when there was no answer I went searching for the hidden key my mother always kept for me.

I found it in a small fake rock behind a potted plant and let myself in. I walked through the orderly kitchen into the living room with the windows looking out over the lake. I turned on the fireplace and sat on the couch. My mother always kept the house two degrees too cold.

I thought about calling her to see where she was when I could hear movement upstairs.

I picked up a coffee table book about the art of Degas and thumbed through it while I waited for her to come down.

When my mother rounded the corner of the stairs, she screamed. "Morgan! You scared the living daylights out of me. What are you doing here? You look awful."

I stood up and launched into a dramatic retelling of everything that happened since I last saw my parents, keeping it PG-13 and leaving out the intimate details of my sex life, or lack of full sex life. My story came out rapid-fire and rambling.

"Morgan, are you high right now?"

"Why didn't you come with Dad this morning?"

"Answer me."

"You answer me."

"Because I don't think I can handle any more. Are you high?"

"I might be."

"How long are you planning on staying?"

"I don't know. Forever? I mean not here with you forever, but up here. I'm going to the campground to see Dad."

"No. No ma'am. You are not. You are not getting in my car and driving high. And you need to eat. I'm making you pancakes. Your dad texted me that you didn't eat at the diner."

"I'm not hungry."

"Sit down." I don't care how old you are. When your mom uses *that* tone, the authoritative tone which used to precede a grounding or a talking to, you listen. I sat back where I was. My high was wearing off and I was getting sleepy. I hadn't slept in over twenty-four hours.

I sat on the couch, grabbed a blanket and let my mother make me pancakes.

As I ate, she put on a movie we used to watch together when I was younger, and I drifted off to sleep.

I did not wake up until the following morning. I woke up sore and stiff from sleeping on the couch. Dad was already in the kitchen making coffee and scrambled eggs.

"Morgan, you look like shit."

"I feel like shit. Thanks."

He set a cup of coffee in front of me and sat across from me. "I went through your bags last night. I found your stash of pills in the lining of two bags, and I flushed them down the toilet. If you are going to be up here, some things are going to change. I have a history of bailing you out. You've never really dealt with consequences in your life. You've been trying and I will give you that. But you've made some terrible choices. Your mother filled me in last night on what's gone on. I'm disappointed, but it's partially my fault for never teaching you when you were younger. You lived this stunted adolescence and now here you are, 36 and strung out on my couch."

"Dad... Wait... Hold on before-"

"No. Morgan. Just stop." My mom entered the kitchen and sat down at the table with us.

"Morgan," she began, taking my hand across the table. "You haven't dealt with Jonathan. You haven't dealt with anything, and we are not equipped to help you through this. You need real help."

"We talked to your attorney yesterday. We are pitching a plea deal for your case. They can't prove impact from your car caused the fatal injury to the other driver-" Dad continued.

"Do we know his name?" I interrupted again.

Dad sighed. "No. We didn't get that information. But you admitted you were under the influence of a controlled substance when impact was made. Your attorney will talk to you more about this, but we are going to offer probation and in-patient rehab, and they take manslaughter off of the charges."

Mom picked up where he left off, "We are sending you to rehab. We found a program in Reno. It's four months in-patient, followed by six months of out-patient care. It's a nice place. We looked at it online. They have an opening. You will have therapy. You will be dealing with these issues you keep masking with your poor decisions. If you refuse to go, you can't come back here any longer."

I looked at my father and he looked so disappointed and broken. I couldn't tell them no.

I just nodded. He was right. I didn't like who I had become. I still had not dealt with my issues though that was my whole point in leaving The Society. I just wanted to mask my guilt and self-loathing and feel good, without doing the real work.

My attorney called me a few hours later and I met him in his office. He called the prosecutor, and a deal was made. I was scheduled to appear in front of the court and plead guilty to the DUI and then head to rehab. The court date was scheduled.

I dreamed of the man who died every night. It was not like the hauntings from Jonathan. It was just seeing his corpse again and again. Reliving the crash. Hearing the metal.

I did some digging around and found out his name. Braedon. His girlfriend was Hope.

I met with Hope the day before I was set to see the judge.

We were at a local restaurant in downtown South Lake Tahoe. She sat across from me. Her black eyes from the impact were still very apparent under her makeup. She looked young and fragile.

"It's not your fault, if that's why you are here?" She was quiet, sipping a milkshake.

"But it is."

"I don't think it is. So, if you are here for some strange forgiveness-"

"Look, I had no business driving. I was not in my right mind. I can't keep living with no consequences."

"If it will make you feel better, then, yeah. Okay. I forgive you."

I sighed. I didn't know what I expected of her. "I'm just sorry. I understand what you are going through. My fiancé killed himself a few years ago, and I found him. It fucked me up for a long time. I'm still not over it. And I -"

"We were high. Like really high. We smoked pot laced with opium and we had been drinking before that. We got into a big fight and then for some reason – he wanted to take a drive so we could cool off and clear our heads. The deer jumped out. He slammed on his brakes. Then you slammed into us. You sat there in your car for a long time. I sat in mine for a long time. I just stared at him. He was dead. And you just kept sitting there. I could see you in my mirror staring at the sky. I thought you might be dead, too."

"I dream about him. Do you?"

"I can't sleep at night because I see him like I'm still sitting next to him." Her eyes looked like mine once did. Haunted and deep.

"Have you gotten high since that night?"

"No. I never want to be high again. I've been going to NA meetings."

I paused and looked at her. "How old are you?"

"Twenty-four. Braedon was twenty-six. We worked together. That's how we met. We worked at the casino. We were both dealers."

"You have a whole life ahead of you," I barely whispered.

"I do. It took that night for me to realize it. So, I'm getting my shit together and living my life. I'm going back to school. I'm getting my degree. I'm going to be a social worker."

Jonathan's death paralyzed me. Braedon's death pushed her to be a better human. We were not the same. I put cash on the table to cover our bill and stood. Hope stood as well. I didn't know what to say or do next, so I just looked at her.

"Yeah... So... If you need me to say it's all good, it's all good. I'm gonna be alright. I forgive you or whatever."

I extended my hand.

She shook her head and walked out without another word.

The next morning after a sleepless night of seeing Braedon's disfigured face and hearing Hope tell me what she thought I wanted to hear, I stood in front of the judge. He looked down his nose at me as I admitted driving under the influence, and I admitted remorse for my actions. I meant it, I truly felt awful for all that I had done. The judge accepted the plea deal, and my fate was sealed. I was to check into rehab that afternoon. I had probation for one year.

Mom stood in the doorway while I packed, making sure nothing nefarious made its way into my bag. What could have made it in? Dad said he flushed my stash I had hidden in the open linings of my bags. I was crying silent tears of self-pity as I packed. "Mom, I'm sorry. I know I fucked it all up. I'm really, truly sorry. I don't know what's wrong with me."

"Morgan, just go do the work. Heal. We will be here when you get back. It will all be okay, eventually." Normally her pragmatic attitude would have annoyed me, but I needed it right then. I needed her assurance that I just needed to do the hard work and it would be okay. Everything would be okay.

I sat in the back seat of the cab of my father's work truck while he and my mother drove me down the hill and into Reno. He played classic rock and tapped the steering wheel in rhythm to the music like he always did. But there was no chatter between him and my mother. My mother just stared out the window silent and icy. I quietly looked out the window watching the road.

On the outskirts of the town was a sprawling facility. Aside from the massive gates wrapping around the grounds, it looked like a resort. My father drove to a guard shack at the gate and gave my name. The gate opened and he drove in. He gave my name again at the lobby before the doors were unlocked and we were led to a waiting area.

We were promptly called into an office where a psychologist and a nurse awaited.

They introduced themselves to me as the head of my care team. They explained the rules, phone calls, and visitations. I was to surrender my phone, my bag was being searched as we spoke by security, my parents could visit me on Sundays for two hours, my mail would be searched, and there would be drug testing after all visits.

I would have structured days like with The Society, but I would have therapy, group and individual along with homework. My parents sprang for me to have a private room which was extremely generous of them.

I was examined before going in. Urine and blood tests, poked and prodded. My schedule would begin after I was considered to be detoxed. Tonight I could get settled into my room, have dinner and detox.

In the time I was there, I actually was forced to work the steps, do the work, face my issues and my demons and it was scary. My parents, in a family therapy session, made it clear this was it. Get my life together. There would be no more bailouts for any reason.

I wrote to Tiffany and Jo and apologized to them for my part in Jonathan's demise. I wrote to Sophia and Eli and apologized to them as well. Jo and Tiffany both wrote back to me. They apologized for how they treated me at the funeral and for laying the blame of Jonathan's death on me when they knew how broken he had been. It was closure for that chapter, at last. I was not at fault for Jonathan's decision.

Sophia wrote back to me. She asked me to come back to her and Eli. She didn't get it. A part of me missed her, but not enough to embroil myself back into the mix of it. It was a conditional love, and I knew it was not fully healthy.

I wrote to Hope, wishing her well and wishing her luck in the pursuit of her degree, but she never wrote back.

I was able to really look at myself and my decisions and face my fears and my true addictions.

I worked on improving my relationship with my mother and apologized to my father for making him feel like he was responsible for the stupid things I had done.

I read Bryan Stevenson's book while I was there. Reading the pages of the book, I found what I needed to hear all along when I encountered the quote, 'each of us is more than the worst thing we've ever done'. It was my mantra and it helped me get through those really tough days where I felt the demons I was facing were bigger than I could handle.

I am not the worst thing I have ever done. It is a part of my history. It has made me who I am today. And I carry no shame for what I've been through, what I've done or who I am.

After getting out of rehab, I went with my father down to San Diego and we retrieved my things from storage, and I moved into my apartment.

It was time for rebuilding. It was time for accountability. It was time for me to live. On my own.

I wasn't looking for love or for hook-ups or friends. I just wanted to learn how to live. Handle my business. No bailouts and no distractions.

I got my own place. I for all intents and purposes took over the campground. Slowly, my father was relinquishing all the duties to me, seeing as it was my inheritance, after all. He allowed me to call the shots during the off-season to close off sections for renovations. I never would have thought I would find joy in running a campground, but it was peaceful and I could see I was making my dad proud. I didn't miss being a teacher. I didn't miss my life. I was finding new joys in the peace I was cultivating.

Months had gone by when this beautiful stranger came strolling through the campground. Even wearing a mask in the middle of the pandemic I could tell there was something in her eyes and in her voice. She shattered my walls and captivated my imagination from the very beginning.

Emma Landry.

She paid in cash for the most remote site in the campground. She was backed in, surrounded by two large boulders in the very back. The fact she paid cash and wanted to be kept off the books should have been red flags for me. I ignored them. I needed to know her.

I could sense she knew I was interested. It was not manipulation so much as she obviously was in need of something, and she could sense I could fill that need for her.

I tried to play it cool and failed miserably. She threw my world into a tailspin. Nothing in my past mattered any longer. She consumed my every waking moment.

She was a natural flirt and for the first time, I went home at night and wondered what it would be like for her to touch me. I craved a human being's love and affection for the first time in years.

I would seek her out day after day. I wanted to know her in every sense of the word. She never gave up much about who she was, but I felt like I knew her. We danced around our pasts, but I knew her, and she knew me. Or so we thought.

It was after ten days of my seeking her out, or her lingering in the camp store when I was there working before I couldn't handle it any longer. I was hoping she would make the first move, but she wouldn't. She was holding back. I could sense it. She was also the type that never had to make the first move. I could see that.

It was raining and she hadn't come by the store all day. I kept looking at the door every time it opened, hoping it would be her.

When my day was over I thought of just going home, but I couldn't. I walked across the street to where her RV was parked.

I watched her as she cooked dinner. I tried to focus on her conversation. Did I mention how incredibly smart she was? She could talk easily about anything and everything. I never realized, she was never really talking about anything related to her. She kept the subjects revolved around current events and the world and culture and travel. Never about her. Never at any depth anyway. But I didn't care. I didn't notice because I didn't want to. I was captivated by her. The sound of her voice. The way her eyes shone. I could get lost in the blue of her eyes.

She sat next to me on the couch of the RV. There was an electric fireplace blazing behind her as she sat facing me on the couch. Expensive wine in plastic stemless wine glasses. And she was looking at me like she knew why I was there. Getting to know her in the short time, I was able to clue in on her cockiness. She was used to women throwing themselves at her. She never had to make the first move and she wouldn't.

She knew. So, I said it. I told her I was falling for her.

The first time my lips touched hers, there was a light inside of me I had thought would never shine again. Her kiss breathed life back into me in a way Sean, Sophia or Eli couldn't. There was a need and a connection deeper than I expected or ever experienced.

But despite these feelings, I held back my whole story and she held back, too.

Emma Landry.

I knew her name. I knew some of who she was. Pieces. Fragments. Attorney. Smooth talking. Wealth and finer things, evident in the wine she drank and the bespoke clothing she wore. But she was warm and affectionate. Attentive. She was everything I ever wanted and never knew I needed.

I gave myself over to her completely. I let her have me when no one else could get close. Something in her wore me down and allowed me to be loved and adored by her. Her love was all consuming. And I suddenly didn't want her to know all my history. It scared me to have her know all of the details for I didn't want her to pull away. To take away that love or look at me differently. She knew just enough to know I knew hurt and pain. She didn't need to know all of the choices I made and the details of the horrible road I traveled.

After several months of being loved by her, planning a future with her, I was awoken in the night. "Bailey," she cried out. I knew she had been married before. I knew her wife cheated on her, and she left her.

Something in her shifted. She showed up on my doorstep and she was different.

She collapsed on my couch and I did something I didn't want to do. I Googled her. I saw her life before me. I saw her wife. She was beautiful. I saw Bailey's social media feeds and I saw the articles. Bailey was missing and so was Emma. But Emma was on my couch.

I questioned her when she woke up. I needed to know. I needed answers. I questioned her.

I had to know.

Emma killed Bailey.

It was an accident. But I didn't care. Hearing that this woman I had given my love to, and my vulnerability after so long of keeping myself pent-up… I couldn't deal with it. I sent her away.

She went back to her home.

She confessed.

All of a sudden she was all over my television.

She is in prison as I write this. I'm compelled to watch all of the interviews and all of the coverage. I see her whole life laid out for strangers to pick apart. But I knew her. I knew the real her.

I miss her. I still want her. I don't know if we will ever be together again. But I pray for her to return to me someday.

Emma

EMMA CLOSED THE JOURNAL AFTER reading the last line. She looked at the accumulation of all the sticky notes with the questions. It was interesting to read about herself from Morgan's perspective. She wondered if Morgan wrote it all out with the knowledge that she would eventually give it to her to read.

Who am I to question her or her story? She is not mine. I released her. She released me. She pulled all the sticky notes out and tossed them in the trash can.

In the morning she brought the journal to the office and put it on Greta's desk with a note to mail it to Morgan's address. She stuck a small piece of paper inside the journal, poking out of the top, '*Morgan, thank you for sharing your story. I understand you and your hesitance now. I miss what we had, but I am always here for you, whatever that looks like going forward. Love, Emma.*'

She had Lizbeth. She had her career. She had her house and her dog. The choices had been made, and there was a life to be lived.

She let go.

~ *Epilogue* ~

Getting Lost in the Blue

Morgan

IT WAS EARLY AS SHE made her way through the campground in her golf cart. She had not been sleeping well. After getting up at four and being unable to go back to sleep, she went for a five-mile run and then did an intensive yoga flow. But she was still restless.

Two cop cars came zipping past her and into the campground. She followed them in her golf cart. They pulled up to a space where a large, expensive diesel Class A had been parked for the last couple of days. It was a retired couple that Morgan had liked immediately. They had gotten together later in life, and both had invested well. They were 'full-timers' living in their RV and traveling from state to state. Every three weeks they were on their way somewhere else.

She pulled up behind the cop cars and could hear the commotion inside. The woman was yelling about a theft.

One of the officers knocked on the door and the husband came out.

"I'm so sorry for the commotion." He looked worn and haggard, and mostly sad. He saw Morgan and made eye contact with her.

"You wanna tell us what is going on? Your neighbors here in the park called us concerned."

The man sat on the steps of the rig defeated. "My wife has been recently diagnosed with early stages of dementia. She forgets things and it scares her. She thought someone came in and stole her purse. She had been cleaning and organizing and she was in a state, and she put it in the freezer. We just found it." As he finished explaining, his wife made her way to the screen door. Her face was tear streaked.

"Officers, Morgan… I'm so terribly sorry. I don't know…" Her tears began to flow again.

Morgan backed out of the spot to allow the officers to finish up what they had to do in taking statements and reports. She felt terrible for the couple, and it was not really any of her business.

THE NEXT MORNING, SHE WAS greeted again by a police presence in her campground. Again, parked at the same couple's RV.

She walked over on foot. The husband was distraught. He had awoken and his wife was missing. Her phone and all of her belongings were present, but she was not.

Morgan walked back over to open the store and office. Too much drama before nine in the morning. As she was opening the back door of the office, she could peer out to the beach front part of the property, next to the dock where the paddle wheeler comes in from giving tourists tours of the deep blue turquoise waters of Lake Tahoe.

She could see a pile of clothing neatly folded and a rock on top of them to keep them in place. She made her way to the pile and looked down. There was a letter folded under the rock on top of the neatly folded pile of clothing. It had the name 'George' neatly printed on it. She remembered suddenly the distraught husband and his wife was Anne. The husband was George.

She ran across the street and into the mix with the officers and the husband.

"I think I know where Anne is." She had tears that she could no longer control flowing down her cheeks. "There's a note. And her clothes. They are on the beach."

She led the officers and George through the camp store and out the back door of the office to the neat little pile in the sand.

Lake Tahoe is over a thousand feet deep at its deepest point. No one who has ever disappeared into its bluest depths has ever been found.

George needed someone to hold on to, and Morgan became that person. He was gripping her arm as he collapsed into the sand next to the pile, pulling her down by his side.

He took the letter and handed it to Morgan. "Read it. I can't."

Morgan looked at the officers who nodded at her. She opened the paper and read aloud, "'My dearest George,

You were the love of my life. I had given up on love. I had given up on so much. But you gave me life over the last two decades. Thank you for that.

I'm scared now. I don't like what is going on. I don't like these moments where suddenly I don't know you. Where I just don't know.

You gave me life and love. And I don't want to burden you in your last years with dealing with this. With dealing with my fear and a situation where I will continue to deteriorate before your very eyes. I will not do that to you.

I am going to have to let you go. I am going to disappear into the blue. Into the peace. Into the cold. Into forever. Your love saved me, and my love will set you free.

Love,

Anne.'" Morgan was crying as she read the letter to George.

George was staring dumbfounded out at the lake, silent tears streaming from his eyes. He was still clinging to Morgan's arm. She wanted nothing more than to run back into her office. This was too much for her.

She pictured Anne stripping her clothes in the moonlight and walking into the frigid water, diving in and letting herself sink, surrounded by the blue, surrounded by the cold. The freedom and the suffocation simultaneously taking over as she released herself and released her love.

The image played in her head the rest of the day, and through the night. She called Sara. It was time to do the right thing. It was time to release those she loved. Releasing the ones, she loved was the ultimate gift of love.

Emma

I'M GOING TO LET YOU go. Emma replayed the exchange in her head over and over again. They had not spoken outside of a few short text messages in several weeks. Those words were loaded with so much connotation.

Weeks had gone by, and she and Lizbeth were growing more serious. It was still at a point where neither one was talking about moving in. Emma remained cautious and did not push limits or boundaries. Emma just enjoyed the process of getting to spend time with Lizbeth for all of her amazing qualities. Like Emma, she was a workaholic and accomplished and educated. She was, as Emma, self-made coming from a blue-collar upbringing and working hard through scholarships and student loans to build herself up. And Lizbeth liked her space just as Emma liked hers.

One evening, as she was returning from a dinner with Lizbeth, she saw an unfamiliar car in front of her house. As she pulled into the driveway, she saw a figure sitting on the porch. It was dark, and the scant light of the porchlight barely illuminated the figure sitting there on the step.

She got out of the car and went through the house so she could open the front door to see who or what was waiting for her.

She opened the door to find Morgan sitting on the porch steps waiting. "Morgan?"

Morgan stood up and turned around to face Emma.

There were no words as she reached out and laced her fingers through Morgan's and drew her in the door.

The feeling of her body next to Morgan's and the feeling of just breathing her in were a thousand times enough. Emma just held Morgan, resting her forehead against hers, nose to nose, and taking it all in.

"I had given up," Emma whispered.

"You had every right to."

Emma brought her lips to Morgan's and kissed her, the feeling of Morgan's lips on hers made Emma dizzy with emotion. She could not bear the thought of even letting Morgan escape from her embrace.

"When I met you the first time at the campground, I knew, looking in your eyes, my future was with you. Being near you, that is all I have wanted since." Morgan made no move to leave Emma's embrace, her lips barely away from Emma's as she talked. "I had no issue in giving you all of me. Being yours. It was the first time since Jonathan I could give myself over to anyone. That I wanted to give myself to anyone. I thought we could build something together without acknowledging what it was that led us to each other. We had secrets and we had pain. And I feared so much after you left, that we loved each other for the wrong reasons, and we loved the incomplete versions of ourselves.

"I was so scared. I realized after you left that I was repeating my patterns. I thought I had given over all of me, but I had not. Just as you had not. And once I started giving you all of it, I was scared that it would not be the same because you had me, and had known me as a different version of who I am. And I knew a different version – an incomplete version of you.

"And then you met someone. And the possibility of a future without you was not one I wanted. I want you. I want only you. I love you. I love all of you, with all of who I am."

No more secrets. No more questions. No more doubts. No more ghosts. This was the love they had both been waiting for.

Not 'The End', so much as a new beginning.

~ *Afterword* ~

I DO SO LOVE MY playlists when I write. It's what drives the story in my mind. I put in my air pods and walk my neighborhood as the music plays. As I lose myself in the lyrics or a particular lyric, the characters come to life in my head, and they tell me the story.

Here is the playlist that drove this story to completion:

Alice in Chains- It Ain't Like That
Leisure – Be with You
Zhu – Lost it
Hozier – Work Song
MISSIO – I Do What I Want
The Killers, featuring k. d. Lang – Lightning Fields
Shy girl – Twelve
Depeche Mode – In Your Room
Part Human – Touched
St. Vincent – Masseduction
Synergy and Tasha Baxter – Lust
Elle King – Under the Influence
Fiona Apple – Criminal

Poe – Haunted

Tool – Sober

David Byrne – I Should Watch TV

Fink – Looking Too Closely

Cannons – Bad Dream

Love and Rockets – Haunted When the Minutes Drag

Elliot Moss – Slip

Black Violin – A Way Home

Dave Matthews Band – The Space Between

Madonna – Rain

MS MR – Hurricane

Live – I Alone

~ *Other Books by Marisa Billions:* ~

This Too Shall Pass, a mother will do anything to save her son
Like Sapphire Blue

A fourth book is in the works.

Scan the QR Code for the Spotify playlist for *Into the Blue Again*

Follow me on social media for the latest information and new releases.
TikTok: @authormarisabillions
Instagram: @authormarisabillions
Facebook (or Meta? Who knows anymore):
Facebook.com/AuthorMarisaBillions

Authormarisabillions.com

Made in the USA
Middletown, DE
24 December 2022

17426496R00184